THE GATE OF DAYS

THE GATE OF DAYS

THE BOOK OF TIME II

GUILLAUME PRÉVOST

Translated by

WILLIAM RODARMOR

SCHOLASTIC INC.

New York Toronto London Auckland
Sydney Mexico City New Delhi Hong Kong

ISBN-13: 978-0-439-88380-1
ISBN-10: 0-439-88380-6

Text copyright © 2007 by Gallimard Jeunesse.
English-language translation copyright © 2008 by William Rodarmor.
All rights reserved. Published by Scholastic Inc., by arrangement with
Gallimard Jeunesse. SCHOLASTIC, APPLE PAPERBACKS, the
LANTERN LOGO, and associated logos are trademarks and/or registered
trademarks of Scholastic Inc.

Arthur A. Levine Books hardcover edition designed by Phil Falco and
Elizabeth B. Parisi, published by Arthur A. Levine Books,
an imprint of Scholastic Inc., October 2008.

12 11 10 9 8 7 6 5 4 3 2 1   9 10 11 12 13 14/0

Printed in the U.S.A.   40
First Scholastic paperback printing, September 2009

CONTENTS

CHAPTER ONE

Burglary

The inside of the dinosaur's stomach reeked of epoxy and paint. Sam Faulkner crouched all the way in the back of the space, just where the body narrowed to a long fiberglass tail, and he was ready to move — to get out of not just the huge Baryonyx where he'd been hiding all evening, but out of the Sainte-Mary Museum. As soon as the guards completed their rounds, he would slip over to the coin room, take what he needed — Sam preferred to think of it as borrowing — and return to the dinosaur until the museum reopened in the morning. Then he would rescue his father.

He had never *wanted* to spend his nights hiding in a dinosaur's butt, Sam thought wryly. Indeed, if someone had told him two weeks earlier that he was going to steal from the museum — or that he would travel to ancient Egypt or World War I, or that his father was stuck in the fifteenth century as a prisoner of Dracula — he never would have believed them. But once you knew time travel was possible, and that a squat little statue in your basement could send you hurtling into the past, all sorts of possibilities — even necessities — opened up as well.

He tensed at the sound of footsteps in the hall. Two night watchmen switched on the light and walked by, a couple of feet from him, talking.

"The Baryo there isn't finished either. Seems the painter won't come back till he's paid what he's owed."

"There's no more money for it," said the other man. "The curator says the city won't increase the subsidy. We need some new exhibits to bring people in. Did you read in the paper about that Greek thing they auctioned in London? The Navel of the World or some such? An old stone, and it went for ten million dollars in less than ten minutes! Our little museum can't afford that!"

"No kidding! Won't be long before they start firing people to cut costs!"

The guards were still grumbling as they crossed the hall to the far door and went out, leaving Sam alone again. He wolfed down two chocolate-nut bars he'd thought to buy from the vending machine and waited for the next round. The guards passed through again an hour and a quarter later, arguing about the merits of their favorite hockey teams. One was a staunch supporter of the Canadiens; the other swore by the Maple Leafs. Even though Sam felt that no one could match the Senators when they were on a roll, he was careful not to speak up. If the dinosaur suddenly gave its opinion on the Stanley Cup, the two men would surely have heart attacks.

Sam looked at his watch. It was past ten o'clock, and he had about fifty minutes to carry out his plan. In order to operate the stone statue that allowed him to time-travel, he needed a coin with a hole in it, one that could date from any period of history. Once the coin was set onto the sun carved in the center of the stone, the statue would shoot him through time to some period of its own mysterious choosing; there was no way to know where he might end up. But on one of his adventures, Sam had learned he might be able to choose his destination if he had *seven* of these magic coins. And as his father was in the clutches of Vlad Tepes — a bloody tyrant of medieval Romania, the man who had served as a model for Dracula — there wasn't a moment to be lost.

The problem was, Sam had only three coins. His cousin Lily had suggested that he try the Sainte-Mary Museum, which held a number of bequests from Garry Barenboim, the strange old man who once owned the house that contained the stone statue. On a reconnaissance trip earlier that day, Sam learned that Barenboim had left the museum gold knives and forks, eighteenth-century hats, a mammoth tooth, a crystal goblet said to have belonged to the explorer Jacques Cartier, and an Aztec necklace — all things Sam suspected the man had gathered via time travel. He had also left five coins with holes in their centers, coins of just the right size.

And that was how Sam came to be crouching in a dinosaur's rear end at ten o'clock at night.

When he was sure the guards couldn't hear him, he left his hiding place and switched on his cell phone, finding his way by the screen's bluish light. Velociraptor to the right, triceratops to the left: All he had to do was head straight toward the front desk, going as far as the local history hall. The coin case was at the far end of the room.

Shrouded in darkness, the museum was as unnerving as a haunted house, with dozens of threatening shadows that seemed about to bite. *Come on,* Sam told himself, *there's nothing alive in here, just dusty old stuff.*

And yet . . .

When Sam opened the door to the hallway, he thought he heard something like a key clinking against metal. He hid behind a statue of the sea god Neptune holding his pointed trident. Maybe one of the night watchmen had forgotten something. Going back was too risky, so Sam hunkered down, making himself as small as possible, and held his breath. There was a rustling noise on the floor, a flashlight beam in the next room, then nothing. Sam counted to a hundred before standing up. The coast was clear.

Hugging the walls, he reached the local history hall without any problem. There the entire story of Sainte-Mary was told in large dioramas. Costumed mannequins illustrating the town's different historical periods stood between each display. As Sam walked toward a milkmaid emptying her pail, he saw a shadow moving about ten yards away, by the coin room. A dark shape was leaning over a display case and fiddling with something that made a slight squeaking. Sam slapped his cell phone against his thigh to hide the light, but it chose just that moment to ring — or rather to vibrate, because Sam had wisely switched off the guitar riff he used as a ringtone. Except that in the heavy silence of the local history room, it sounded as if one of the wax figures had switched on its electric razor!

The shadow whirled around, the beam from its flashlight catching the milkmaid's plump cheeks. Sam crouched behind her pail as best he could, but it was too late. The burglar — the *other* burglar! — was already rushing at him. The man raised his flashlight to hit Sam, who was just able to dodge the blow by rolling to the foot of a mannequin of Gordon Swift, Sainte-Mary's first and most venerable mayor.

Sam barely had time to stand up before the man was after him again, and a furious scuffle followed: He punched, Sam ducked, he tried to knee Sam, Sam twisted away, Sam kicked out, the man parried the blow easily. All this was done in total silence, so as not to alert the guards. The man was powerful and apparently trained in this kind of hand-to-hand combat. He looked like a professional thief in a skintight black tracksuit, and he had taken the precaution of wearing a hood and gloves to hide his face and hands.

As Sam tried to grab him, he ripped the soft fabric of the burglar's tracksuit. The jerky light of the flashlight revealed a strange tattoo on his shoulder: a kind of U with flared ends and a big circle between them. The man must not have liked having his clothes torn, because he began hitting harder. He even managed to slip his hands around Sam's neck and gave a grunt of triumph as his thumbs started to crush his victim's Adam's apple.

With a sudden hip thrust he'd learned in judo, Sam knocked the man off balance, and the two of them tumbled into the legs of His Excellency Mayor Swift, who promptly toppled backward with a crash of shattered glass. The museum alarm system started to howl and the hallway lights came on. The burglar scrambled to his feet, releasing Sam. Blinded and choking, Sam glimpsed the hooded figure pause briefly at the coin case before racing out the door beside it. Over the howling of the siren, he heard shouts.

"He's headed for the front desk! Hurry!"

The guards raced past the local history room without stopping, and Sam forced himself to stand up. There might be a chance to turn the situation to his advantage. He rushed to the coin collection. The display case housing the Barenboim bequest was wide open, its lock forced, but he swore as he took in the situation. All the coins with holes in them had disappeared, except one that the thief in black must have missed. There were two burglars after the same treasure!

"He's going for the service entrance!" cried a night watchman.

They'll be coming back, Sam told himself. *They're sure to come back.* They would search every nook and cranny of the museum, and the Baryonyx's belly wouldn't be much help to him. He had to leave now. But the only possible way out . . .

Sam glanced down the hall. Empty. He pocketed the remaining coin, crouched down, and ran in the opposite direction from the fugitive, keeping his ears cocked. The alarm had fallen silent, and he could hear muffled voices. When he reached the front desk, he looked in every direction. The service entrance was over by the locker rooms. It opened onto a dark hallway, and he could feel a breeze: the exit!

Outside, the guards were yelling, "Stop, thief! The museum's been robbed!"

As Sam felt his way down the hall, he bumped against a door handle on the right-hand wall and turned it. From the smell, it was a room where garbage cans were stored. He leaped inside, knocking over a broom cart, and yanked the door shut. His heart was pounding and the rest of his body felt as if a train had run over him.

After a few minutes, the guards came back. They hadn't been able to catch the man in black.

"I'll . . . I'll call the police," gasped one, out of breath. "You try to see what he stole."

They walked down the hall without showing any interest in the brooms. Sam slipped silently out of his hiding place and quickly covered the last yards separating him from freedom. Fresh air! He ran down the steps, raced across a grassy rise, and sprinted to the corner without turning around. Taking streets at random, he didn't stop running until he'd put several blocks between himself and the museum.

It was only then that he realized he no longer had his cell phone.

CHAPTER TWO

Bad News

The next morning Sam pushed back his sheets and jumped out of bed — and immediately winced: His body was a mass of pain. Making his way slowly to the mirror, he saw that by luck his face had mostly been spared, except for a large bruise around his right eye. His alarm clock blinked 6:42, and he was tempted to go back to bed and rest.

Under the circumstances, however, he felt his bruises hardly mattered. From experience and calculation, Sam had determined that time passed seven times faster in the past than in the present, so a day here was the equivalent of a week when he was time-traveling. His father had been imprisoned for the last twenty of Sam's days, which meant he had spent almost five months languishing in some vermin-infested cell. Sam could imagine him frighteningly thin, huddled on a pile of sodden straw, licking water oozing down the walls or using his last strength to drive away hordes of hungry rats. How long could he hold out under those conditions?

Sam energetically rubbed his eyes and went to his closet to inspect the box with the few things he hoped might help him reach his father. One was the Book of Time, a handsome old volume with a cracked red cover whose pages, which were all identical, revealed the time-location of the last time traveler to use the stone statue. The book had shown Sam that his father was in medieval Wallachia, a prisoner of the murderous tyrant Vlad Tepes. Next to the book was a small plastic bag containing three examples of coins with holes that made the stone statue operate. One of them was clearly very old, with a writhing black snake embossed on the metal. As his father had left it for him before he disappeared, Sam thought the coin might have come from Vlad Tepes's time. The second was more recent and bore Arabic inscriptions. The third looked like a plastic poker chip with a hole. From under the bag, Sam took a sheet of paper with the text from an old book of spells he'd found during a "field trip" to Bruges, Belgium. The book had belonged to Klugg, an alchemist and all-around despicable human being. Its original text was in Latin, but his cousin Lily — with whom he was getting along better and better — had been good enough to translate it for him:

HE WHO GATHERS THE SEVEN TOKENS WILL BE THE MASTER OF THE SUN. IF HE CAN MAKE THE SIX RAYS SHINE, ITS HEART WILL BE THE KEY TO TIME. HE WILL THEN KNOW THE IMMORTAL HEAT.

The words didn't mean much at first glance, but for Sam the text was full of promise. His biggest problem was his inability to control his leaps through time. The jumps could be fifty years ago or five thousand — anything was possible. How could he ever reach his father under those conditions?

The Latin suggested that in order to get the key to time — and thereby choose the era you wanted to travel to — you had to get seven coins and arrange them properly on the stone statue, with the coin in the center of the carved sun indicating where you wanted to go, and the others placed in the six slits or rays that radiated out from it. Counting the coin Sam had picked up at the museum, he now had four.

The final item in the box was a bound book of photographs that Lily had borrowed from the Sainte-Mary Library. It was about Bran, one of many castles Vlad Tepes had frequented, and an illustration in it had caught her eye. It showed graffiti crudely scratched onto one of the dungeon walls: HELP ME SAM. The book's author had admitted to being perplexed. The photograph's caption read: "This graffiti was uncovered during the restoration of the Bran dungeon. According to some analyses, it is several centuries old. The fact that it is written in English adds to the mystery: Had Vlad Tepes captured one of the King of England's subjects during a military campaign? And who was this Sam the message was addressed to? Whatever the case, it provides further proof that it was not good to be a prisoner of the Prince of Wallachia."

When he thought about it, though, the graffiti actually made Sam feel hopeful. For some unknown reason, Vlad Tepes had decided not to execute his father immediately. Instead, he had sent him to cool his heels in one of his cells, which gave Sam some chance of finding Allan Faulkner alive. Moreover, if he had written those few words, it was because he saw Sam as the only person in the world able to get him out of there. He trusted his son, with a faith so exclusive and poignant that it put a huge responsibility on a fourteen-year-old's shoulders.

In a way, their roles had suddenly reversed: It was up to the son to look after the father. And despite the infinite sweep of time that separated them, Sam renewed his promise to Allan every morning: He would save him, whatever the cost.

Sam carefully returned his treasures to the back of his closet, then pulled on a shirt and some pants and went down to breakfast, moving slowly because of his bruises. He expected everyone to still be asleep, but Lily was already in the kitchen, hunched over a bowl of cereal.

"Lily, you're awake!"

"Since five a.m.," she whispered as she chewed. "I had a nightmare." She caught sight of his face. "Sammy, what happened?"

Sam grimaced. "I went to the museum last night to get the coins — only someone else got there first."

"You did? What? Who?"

"Let me get some breakfast," he said, pouring himself a big bowl of cornflakes. "What was your nightmare about?"

"Stupid stuff . . . You know Nelson, Jennifer's brother? I dreamed we were next to the swimming pool at their place, and he started to melt, like ice cream! First his feet got all soft, then his hands, and then his head started to drip. Jennifer was running around looking for ice cubes and yelling for her mom, but he kept on melting. In the end, all that was left was a little blue puddle, the color of his swimsuit. Stupid, isn't it?"

Sam took a spoon and stirred the cool milk, watching as a white sea swamped the golden flakes.

"Maybe not," he answered teasingly. "Maybe you want him to melt for you!"

11

Lily looked appalled. "Thanks a lot! Nelson is a total idiot! He can't say a sentence longer than four words, and his bedroom is covered with gun posters. Can you see me in love with a guy who decorates his room with guns? Besides, he's ugly."

Sam smiled slightly. He'd been very careful not to broach the delicate question of romance with his twelve-year-old cousin; he knew she'd let him have it. Besides, when it came to matters of the heart, his own record was pretty pathetic. The proof: For three long years he hadn't found the courage to go knock on the door of Alicia Todds, the only girl he'd ever loved. And when he'd finally seen her two days earlier, she'd been on the arm of a tall, arrogant blond boy. Smooth move, Sam!

"But if you were at the museum," Lily continued, "I guess you had something to do with this?"

She held out the *Sainte-Mary Tribune*. The headline on the front page proclaimed: "Strange Burglary at S-M Museum."

Sam took the paper and read it as he ate his cornflakes. The article didn't tell him anything that he didn't already know, and to his great relief it didn't mention his cell phone. Maybe it had fallen in a dark corner during the fight, and no one had picked it up. "The question of a motive remains open," concluded the reporter. "The thief or thieves went to a lot of trouble, but in the end all they took were a few coins of no great value."

"No great value for a *Tribune* reporter, maybe," he grumbled.

"Okay, Sammy, can I have your version now?" Lily said.

But before Sam could answer, they heard footsteps in the hall. "Meet me at the bookstore at eleven," he whispered just before Lily's mother, Evelyn, burst through the kitchen door, wearing a blindingly electric purple bathrobe.

"What did I tell you, Lily?" she screamed. "Am I talking Chinese or something? You're forbidden to be with your cousin till I say otherwise! He stole your phone three days ago, he wanders around God knows where with God knows who, and he won't give us the slightest explanation of any of it! Do you want to do the same?"

"I'm not doing anything!" protested Lily. "I'm eating my breakfast!"

"So why the whispers? What's he trying to put over on you now? You heard Rudolf's warning, didn't you? Sam is on a slippery slope, and for all we know, he's doing drugs! I'm warning you, Lily, if I have to be after you all the time, I'll send you to Camp Deadlake so fast it'll make your head spin!"

Aunt Evelyn seemed to be obsessed with lockups and discipline. Sam knew Deadlake was a summer camp famed for the strictness of its counselors — the female equivalent of the boot camp Evelyn had threatened him with recently. Now she turned and looked at him for the first time. "What happened to *you*?" she shrieked. "Did you get in a fight?"

"Evelyn, for heaven's sake! What are you talking about?"

Alerted by the shouting, Grandpa had hurried downstairs. His hair was sticking up every which way, and in his hurry, he'd buttoned his pajamas wrong — at sixes and sevens, as Grandma might say.

"What do you mean, what am I talking about?" said Evelyn, even louder. "Look at Sam! He has a black eye — probably because some drug deal went wrong!"

"Sammy, what happened?" Grandpa asked with real concern. "How did you get that shiner? Weren't you going to spend the night at Harold's?"

Sam had indeed told his grandparents that he was going to spend the night at his friend Harold's, even going so far as to have Harold agree to lie for him. He was sorry to drag Harold into it, but there was nothing else to be done.

"We went to the skateboarding park to do some aerials, and I went up for this really difficult jump. And then" — Sam tried to look embarrassed — "I guess I landed on my face. After that, I decided I wanted to come home to my own bed."

"I don't believe it," Aunt Evelyn declared.

Grandpa turned back to her with an exasperated expression. "And why not?"

"They were whispering when I came in. This damned boy is trying to suck Lily into more of his dirty tricks! He does nothing but plot behind my back!"

"Calm down, Evelyn," Grandpa ordered. "They're just children!"

"That's right, go on defending them! Just like Allan! You and Mom, you've always defended Allan! The poor little darling, right? He could do whatever he felt like! Come home at all hours, collect disgusting things, get bad grades — it didn't matter! But me . . ."

She heaved a sigh of rage.

"Anyway, you see what indulging all his whims has led to: He's vanished into thin air and left *you* to take care of his son! What you and Mom don't seem to understand is that Sam is going down exactly the same road, and you just close your eyes to it!"

Evelyn stormed out of the kitchen in a blur of purple sleeves, bumping past Grandpa as she headed for the hallway. Sam normally felt a pretty limited affection for this irritable aunt, who seemed angry at the entire world except for Rudolf, her boyfriend of the moment. But this time she had really gone too far. If he had the power, he would cheerfully send her and her ludicrous bathrobe to the Bran Castle dungeons to take his father's place. After all, maybe Dracula liked purple.

CHAPTER THREE

Seven Coins

Sam repressed a grimace as he pulled the bookstore curtains shut. Every time he lifted his arm, it felt as if a malevolent spirit were sinking an axe into his back. Luckily, his grandparents had believed his story about the skate park and had even offered to provide ice packs or heating pads for his bruises. But Sam had turned them down. Everything was fine now, he had said; everything was fine.

As soon as he was able to get free, he ran over to his father's antiquarian bookstore on Barenboim Street, more determined than ever to pursue his investigation. He especially wanted to discover the connection between last night's burglar, his mysterious tattoo, and the old coin he had overlooked. Sam took it from his pocket now. It was almost worn smooth, but you could make out a U with flared ends on either side of the central hole.

Overall, it looked a lot like the tattoo on the man in black's shoulder. A coincidence? Of course not.

Sam had searched the Internet to find something matching the symbol, but hadn't gotten a satisfactory answer because he wasn't able to frame the question clearly. But the mark resembled a hieroglyph, so Sam suspected that ancient Egypt was the place to look. As it happened, Faulkner's Antique Books was pretty well stocked in that area, so Sam planned to do a little browsing in the store, which he'd never bothered with before. As an extra advantage, he would be close to the stone statue for whatever might happen next.

Once hidden from prying eyes by the curtains, Sam carefully examined the sections that the bookstore devoted to history. Three shelves were given over to Egypt, each with several thick dictionaries and art and history books. After some browsing, he found what he was looking for in a nineteenth-century *Encyclopedia of the Pharaohs*. The strange U with a circle appeared in a chapter called "The Egyptian Pantheon." It was actually a pair of horns with a solar disk between them, and was an attribute of several gods and goddesses, among them Isis and Hathor, who wore a headdress resembling the symbol. The book didn't give many more details, but it confirmed Sam's hunch: ancient Egypt, the gods, the sun — all of these fit with the stone statue!

As he put down the encyclopedia, Sam noticed a small volume with a black dust jacket that must have been shelved incorrectly. It was a novel by an author he knew well, and for good reason: William Faulkner, one of the greatest American writers of the previous century. Allan practically worshipped Faulkner and was sorry not to have a family connection with the man he called "one of the seven wonders of world literature." The book's title was appropriate: *Intruder in the Dust*. But how did this novel come to be in the history section?

Sam opened the book at random and got a surprise. The dust jacket didn't contain the Faulkner novel, but a small black notebook whose first pages had been torn out — at least fifty of them, to judge by the stubs still attached to the binding. His curiosity piqued, Sam inspected it more carefully. There were blank pages, more blank pages, and then a phone number. Sam thought for a moment and then went to the phone.

A pleasant voice answered his call: "First Canadian Bank of Sainte-Mary."

"Oh — oh, yes," Sam recovered, trying to make himself sound as adult as possible. "My name is Allan Faulkner, and I'm calling in regards to my account?"

"Oh, yes, Mr. Faulkner," the woman said. "What is your code word?"

"Elisa," Sam said, and spelled it out. It was his mother's first name, and a complete guess, but he heard keys clicking on the other end of the line.

"Well, you know, sir, that you have a significant mortgage payment due to us on your house."

"A mortgage payment?" said Sam blankly.

"Yes, Mr. Faulkner. The monthly repayment of your loan?" she said coldly. "Your payments are *five months* overdue. You have one more month. If you can't pay us the full amount then, we'll be forced to foreclose."

Sam sat stunned. From what he'd heard, foreclosure meant the bank would take over the house — and he couldn't let them have the stone statue!

"How much does my — how much do I owe?" he asked.

The woman named a sum that Sam was sure was far beyond anything in his father's bank account.

"I'll — I'll take care of that as soon as possible," he gasped and hung up the phone.

Sam would need to talk to his grandparents. Though he knew his father had been borrowing money from them for some time, they must have no idea of the extent of Allan's troubles — and he had no idea how they would cover this. But they had a whole month, and there wasn't anything he could do about it right now.

Sam pushed the matter firmly from his mind and went back to the little black notebook. There was nothing more written in it until the very last page, where Sam found a few words scribbled by his father, like a memo or a shopping list:

MERIWESERRE = 0
CALIPH AL-HAKIM, 1010
$1,000,000!
XERXES, 484 B.C.
LET THE BEGINNING SHOW THE WAY
V. = 0
IZMIT, AROUND 1400?
ISFAHAN, 1386

And at the very bottom, underlined twice:

BRAN

19

Bran, Vlad Tepes's castle! Where his father had gone! And quite deliberately, since he had taken the trouble to write his destination in the notebook!

Feverish with excitement, Sam read and reread the few lines, struggling to guess their hidden meaning. His father loved puzzles — everything from trivia quizzes to Rubik's Cubes to Sudoku — and it was possible he had left this as a coded message for Sam, but it was equally possible the list was just the jottings from some obscure piece of research. Dates, exotic names, figures . . . Sam racked his brain but couldn't come up with anything.

"Good grief, Dad," he cried in exasperation, "couldn't you have been a little clearer for once?"

"Talking to yourself?" asked a familiar voice behind him.

Sam jumped. "Lily! What are you doing here?"

"We had a date, didn't we? It's eleven o'clock, in case you haven't noticed."

"Eleven o'clock, right! I was thinking and . . . Are you sure nobody followed you?"

"I came in through the garden window, like you e-mailed me. Does this have to do with what happened at the museum?"

They sat down on one of the sofas that were supposed to make the Faulkner bookstore's clients — when by some miracle there were any — feel at home, and Sam described his adventures of the last eighteen hours in detail. His cousin listened carefully, nodding when he finished.

"Do you know who it could have been?" she asked.

"I'm not sure, but I have an idea."

"An idea?"

"Well, you remember what we found out about that archeology trip to Egypt twenty years ago, when my father found a stone statue in Setni's tomb? There was another intern the same age as him who was also involved in the excavation. And from what I understand, just like my dad, this intern would sometimes disappear for a couple of days."

"So what?"

"I'm convinced that the guy and my father discovered the stone statue together and they both used it."

"That was twenty years ago."

"Yes, except that when my father disappeared three weeks ago, someone left a weird message on the bookstore answering machine. It was a strange metallic voice, like it was disguised. It said something like 'Allan, can you hear me? Stop being a jerk, Allan, pick up!' Then when nobody answered, 'All right, I've warned you.' It was definitely threatening."

"What do you make of it?"

"This guy was looking for Dad, and I'll bet he wasn't trying to sell him life insurance. He seemed to know him pretty well."

"So you think it was this mystery intern from Egypt, and he's coming back now?" Lily sounded skeptical.

"It's just a guess, but I don't have any better ideas. The guy knows the whole story from the beginning, and he's already used the statue. Don't you think he could've gotten the book-store address and tried to reach my father? Or heard about Barenboim and paid a visit to the Sainte-Mary Museum?" Sam paused. "Or worse, he could've spied on me."

"Spied on you?"

"I've been coming here every day for almost two weeks. It would be easy to see me and follow me!"

"Is that why you closed the curtains? And suggested I come in through the garden?"

"Just to be on the safe side."

"But if somebody's watching the bookstore, why meet here?"

Sam smiled grimly. "Because I've decided to make another trip, of course."

"You're kidding!"

"Do I look like I'm kidding? I have to go, Lily, and I need your help."

"But I thought that without the seven coins you didn't have any chance of finding your father! And you only have four, don't you?"

"Yeah, four counting the one from the museum. But think about the guy who used to live here, Barenboim. When he died, he left half a dozen coins to the city. And then there was the high priest Setni — I met his son Ahmosis in Egypt, remember?" Lily nodded. "When the archeologists searched around his sarcophagus at Thebes, they found coins made two or three thousand years after the tomb was sealed. How could medieval coins show up in an ancient tomb? Setni must have gotten those coins from different periods in time! And if I go traveling again, I'll be able to get some too."

"Wait a minute!" said Lily. "You told me you needed a coin to come back. Suppose you can't find one when you're there? Think about it! How would you get back? Isn't that what almost happened in Bruges?"

"This time I'll take care of that. I'll put a spare coin in the statue's cavity — the part that lets you transport objects. That way, no matter what happens, I'll always have a coin with me and be able to come back. That is, if you keep the Book of Time safe and you concentrate a little, of course."

Lily nodded slowly. During Sam's previous adventures, they had discovered that Lily could bring Sam back to the present if she happened to be thinking about him at the moment he touched the stone statue. She reached for the Book of Time in her cousin's backpack and opened it at random. Each page displayed the same engraving of the walls and steeples of the city of Bruges in 1430 — the time to which Sam had ventured last. "But if you use your emergency coin there, you'll lose it, won't you?"

"Yes, but if I just keep sitting around here, my father will die sooner or later. I need those seven coins, no matter what."

"All right," Lily said. "Go get your things and we'll meet in the basement."

Sam went upstairs to change. When he joined his cousin a few minutes later, he was wearing a shapeless cream-colored linen shirt and pants. It wasn't a very fashionable outfit, but unlike modern fabrics, the ancient material let Sam travel through time without losing his clothes.

Lily had already entered the secret basement storeroom that Allan Faulkner had created to hide the stone statue. She was perched on a yellow stool next to the cot, the only cheerful bit of color in the gloomy room, which was lit by an old-fashioned night-light.

"If Alicia Todds sees you in your new pajamas," she said, laughing, "she'll never look at you again!"

"Go ahead, laugh! Here, I'm leaving you these two coins." He handed her the plastic chip and the coin with the black snake. "When I'm gone, you'll find a third one next to the statue. Put all three in a safe place with the book and the notebook until I come back."

"Don't worry, I'm starting to get used to this," Lily said reassuringly. "But you've got to promise to be careful, okay? Avoid battlefields and crazy alchemists, especially. It won't do your father any good to have you stuck in the past."

"Cross my heart and hope to die," said Sam firmly. "First Viking I see, I'll run as fast as I can."

He was overdoing the self-confidence a bit, but there was no point in worrying his cousin.

"Well, when it's time to go . . ." he said to buck himself up.

He walked over to the statue, which was in the darkest part of the room. He could just barely make it out in the dim light, a vaguely oval stone about twenty inches high, completely ordinary-looking. As he knelt beside it, Sam felt a complicated mix of apprehension and eagerness, with the second overcoming the first. He also noticed that the two coins in his palm were getting warmer, as if heated by some invisible current. The process was beginning.

He decided to put the museum coin in the transport cavity and the one with Arabic writing in the center of the sun. It snapped into place perfectly, with a faint click: The stone must have some sort of powerful magnet built into it. A dull humming rose from the center of the statue, and the basement floor vibrated slightly. Sam turned toward Lily, but his eyes were already veiled with a kind of fog, and he could make out only her shape. He put his hand on top of the stone, and a wave of fire shot up his arm into his whole body.

CHAPTER FOUR

The Delphi Shepherd

Hunched over the short grass, Sam had the painful feeling that he'd been turned into a human torch, then shot through space at the speed of light. Yet his fingers, hands, and shirt-sleeves showed no burn marks. "You will know the immortal heat," the Bruges alchemist's old book of spells had said. It might have added: "And your guts will be turned inside out." Sam could feel his breakfast cereal fighting his stomach, determined to escape. By taking a few deep breaths, he was just able to repress his nausea.

"Aha! You're back!"

The voice came from behind him, and Sam turned around as quickly as his uncomfortable position allowed.

"Aw, I guess it isn't you!" said the voice with a touch of disappointment.

Ten yards away, a young man of about twenty was watching him curiously. He had dark, curly hair, and was wearing a patched old tunic tied with a string around his waist. He held a knobbed staff in his right hand, and apparently went around barefoot.

"Are you his son?" the young man asked, squinting as if he were straining to remember something.

Sam didn't react immediately. His first instinct was to look around for the stone statue. It stood nearby, fortunately, with the museum coin glinting brightly in its cavity. Sam took the coin and slowly stood up, feeling dizzy. He had landed in a dry, mountainous place, with thickets and scrawny trees growing between the rocks. The sea lay below in the distance. But which sea?

"Hey, won't you talk to me?"

The young man sounded annoyed, but Sam needed a few more seconds to gather his wits. He could hear bleating very close at hand, just on the other side of the hill. Was this guy a shepherd?

"I'm sorry, I . . ." Sam began. He paused before continuing, surprised by the unusually warm, melodious *os* and *oi* sounds of the words that sprang naturally from his mouth. Instant language ability was another inexplicable facet of the powerful magic worked by the stone statue. "I . . . I'm a bit lost."

The shepherd shot him a suspicious glance. "Your father told you to come, didn't he?"

My father, Sam repeated to himself. Could this be Vlad Tepes's era? Despite his slight remaining dizziness, he took a few steps toward the young man.

"My father? Do you — do you know my father?"

"You bet I know him! He did the same thing you did the other day."

The shepherd was pointing at the stone statue, which was half covered with weeds.

"You can tell me where he is, then?"

"If he told you to come, you must know that, don't you?"

"Er, yeah, of course," Sam agreed cautiously. "That is, more or less . . . What I don't know is *exactly* where he is."

The young man folded his arms on his chest and looked stubborn. "If you don't know that, it means he didn't tell you. If he didn't tell you, then you're not his son. If you're not his son . . ." He hesitated a moment before continuing: "Give me two ram's heads and I'll talk with you."

"Two ram's heads?" said Sam in astonishment. "I don't have two ram's heads!"

"He gave me two ram's heads, he did! If you don't give them to me, it's because you're nasty. If you're nasty, it's because you're not nice. If you're not nice, I won't talk with you."

Sam realized that the young man, despite being older than he was, still thought and spoke like a young child. The shepherd suddenly turned and ran off, singing as he went. "Yes, yes, he came! He sure did come! He had something to do, oh yes, something to do! He gave me two ram's heads!"

In spite of his stiff legs, Sam was forced to run after him. "Hey, wait! I have to find my father! It's really important!"

But the shepherd raced nimbly among the stones, and Sam, who wasn't used to walking barefoot, watched as he quickly disappeared into the bushes. When Sam reached the top of the hill, he saw a steep valley where some thirty goats were grazing. They looked up as they saw their shepherd racing toward them, still repeating his singsong: "I made pretty earrings from the pretty ram's heads. He's the one who gave them to me because he had something he had to do!"

Sam slowed to a walk and shouted: "Hey! I have to talk to you!"

The dog guarding the herd spotted Sam and rushed toward him, barking. A big ferocious animal with tawny fur, it stopped dead a yard from Sam and growled while its master cheered him on: "Aha! Argos will take care of the nasty man who doesn't want to give his ram's heads! Good dog, Argos, good dog!"

But contrary to what Sam feared, the animal didn't attack him. Instead, it slowly stretched out its muzzle and sniffed his calf. And when Sam extended his hand in greeting, the dog gave it a little lick.

At that, the shepherd's behavior changed completely. "Aha! Good dog, good for you! If Argos and you are friends, it means you aren't nasty. You may not be your father's son, but you're not nasty either. Good dog, Argos!"

Sam was able to walk calmly down the slope with the dog at his side, wagging its tail. It was all hard to believe. The air was warm and the sky a deep blue. The goats resumed their grazing. It could have been a stroll in the country on any beautiful spring day, except that Sam didn't know what part of the world he was in, and certainly not what time period.

When Sam caught up with the herd of goats, the young man spread his arms and then shook Sam's hand enthusiastically, as if they were meeting after an absence of many years.

"My name is Metaxos, and I wasn't sure you were coming as a friend. But Argos knew, didn't he? Follow me. I'll give you milk and honey and we'll share the hut, all right? Maybe you've come to look for something, right? And maybe after that . . ."

His eyes were shining, and Sam's heart sank. Metaxos reminded him of a bum he'd run into several times on Barenboim Street. Depending on his mood, he either insulted passersby or tried to kiss them. The town welfare service took him away one day, and he hadn't been seen since.

"I'm looking for my father," said Sam. "Do you know where he is?"

"Your father?" said the shepherd with a big smile. "What if he wasn't your father? Because if it was your father, he'd tell you where he was!"

"Vlad Tepes," continued Sam. "Does that name mean anything to you?"

"Vladtepes? That's a funny name, by the ram's horn! Not a name from around here, anyway. What's your name? I gave you my name, you have to give me yours."

"Er, Sam."

His answer seemed to fill the shepherd with joy. "Aha! Sam! Sam of the stone! Samos, yes, of course, Samos! Are you hungry, Samos? Come to the hut, I tell you. I'll give you milk and honey!"

Without giving Sam time to think, he whistled between his fingers to call his goats and began to drive them toward the bottom of the valley, while shouting incomprehensibly: "*Oldiloi!* Hey, *Oldiloi! Oldiloi!*"

Argos followed the herd, barking, and the whole menagerie raced down the hill at breakneck speed. The shepherd, the goats, the dog — they were all crazy!

Sam was soon left behind and had to hustle not to lose sight of the group, bruising his feet on the rough ground. After twenty minutes of an exhausting cross-country hike, he reached the edge of an olive grove. A rough wooden hut stood nearby. The goats had scattered among the trees and Metaxos was lighting a fire. There was no other house in sight.

"Where were you, Samos?" shouted Metaxos. "I thought you went back into your stone!"

"It's just that . . ." Sam gasped, "you're a little fast for me."

"Aha, of course! I'm the best shepherd in Delphi. Down there, they say, 'Metaxos runs like the wind!'"

Delphi, thought Sam. The name reminded him of something, but what? *I'll pay more attention in history class next year,* he promised himself.

The young shepherd wiped his soot-blackened hands and looked his guest over. "By the way, did you bring anything?"

"Did I bring anything?"

Metaxos shook his head, looking disappointed. "You don't really know enough to be his son! Why did you come here, if you didn't bring anything?"

"To find him! I'm looking for my father, I told you!"

"But he was dressed like you and at least three times older than you, for sure! I don't have a father, did you know that?"

"I'm really sorry, I —"

But the shepherd, his face somber, went on with his thought. "I don't have a mother either. No, no mother."

"I — I lost my mother too," admitted Sam, who was starting to wonder if he would ever get the information he needed.

"You lost your mother? How?"

"Well . . ." It was hard to explain that she'd been in a car crash three years earlier, and had died of her injuries after the car rolled down the embankment a couple of times — especially since Sam suspected he'd landed in a time when the wheel might not have been invented yet! So an automobile . . .

"She fell," he said. "From the top of a hill. A hill like that one."

"By Apollo!" exclaimed the young man in horror. "Hills are for picking flowers and herding animals, not for dying! You must be very sad, Samos. It's not the same for me. I don't know who to weep for because I never knew my parents. I was left on the steps of the great temple on the twelfth day of the month of Bysios. The priests took me in."

Priests, temple, Apollo . . . Sam was somewhere in antiquity. He was sorry he'd never learned to tell the Greek gods from the Roman ones.

"But it seems I'm not to live in the city," said Metaxos. "The priests made that clear to me. I'm like my animals. All I need is sky and grass, and my dog with me. But I'm a good shepherd, I am! The best in Delphi! And I always save my prettiest goats for the temple!"

Sam felt a wave of pity rising in him. Metaxos wasn't crazy; he was just terribly lonely.

"I have to find my father," Sam whispered quietly.

The shepherd suddenly seemed to understand. "Of course you have to find your father, Samos. You already lost your mother, so . . . Come on, come into the hut."

He took a burning stick from the fire and lit a small clay lamp near the door. They entered the modest dwelling, which was built of branches plastered with a rough mix of clay and straw. There were just two rooms. One had a stone fireplace in the center. The shepherd explained that he used the other room to pen animals that were sick or were about to have babies. If Aunt Evelyn had dropped in, she surely would have whipped out her air freshener: The place smelled like the monkey house at the Sainte-Mary Zoo.

Metaxos shone his light on a pile of things at the very back that at first glance looked like garbage — shells, bits of twisted metal, scraps of cloth — but that he seemed to prize.

"This is where I store my treasures! Look!" He bent over and pulled out some sharp fragments of a hard green substance. "You see, Samos! Your father left these here! Yes, your father!"

Sam held them up to the flame. Plastic, apparently. Pieces of green plastic. "Were there many of them?"

"Oh, more than I have fingers on my hands. It was afterward, when he came back here, that he crushed everything with his foot. And this strange pottery of his, it was everywhere. But I saw him do it, yes I did! I even saw what I wasn't supposed to see!"

"What did you see, Metaxos? You can tell me, can't you?"

The shepherd's face darkened. "No, no, I have to keep quiet. I promised. Silent as the grave, or else . . ." He glanced outside, fearful of being observed. Then he pointed at the pieces of plastic again. "But I can show you that, can't I, Samos? That's not the same, is it?"

"This is the thing my father brought with him in the stone, is that right?"

"Yes, yes! You must be his son, to know that! He came with that thing, all green!"

"Was there anything else?"

Metaxos hesitated. Then, while still watching the olive trees outside, he reached into the pile of bric-a-brac, pulled out a small metal rod, and handed it reverently to Sam.

"I heard the noise, you know. Oh yes, with my two ears! A noise that could only have come from the gods!"

Sam rolled the object in his hand. It was a drill bit, probably from a cordless drill, which wouldn't need to be plugged in once it was charged. What in the world had his father wanted to do with a drill?

"He gave you two ram's heads so you wouldn't say anything, right?"

Metaxos put his hand on his mouth as if he weren't allowed to answer.

Sam continued, "And it was the green thing that he brought that made so much noise? Did you get anything else from my father?"

The shepherd glanced furtively at the other side of the room. On a battered wooden chest — it looked salvaged from a shipwreck — stood a kind of doll dressed in gray cloth. Sam took the lamp and walked over. It turned out to be a clay statuette about six inches tall, a roughly female shape along the lines of a well-endowed lady wrestler, with a crudely sketched face.

"I made it myself," declared Metaxos proudly.

"It's very pretty. Is it a woman?"

"Oh yes, but it's more than a woman. It's my own mother!"

"Your mother? I thought your parents abandoned you."

"This is my new mother, the one who protects me. I mean my mother in Delphi. Sometimes I try to go see her, but I'm really not allowed to. Argos looks after the animals when I'm not here."

What he said was becoming more and more jumbled, as if the mention of his "mother in Delphi" upset him.

"What is she called?"

"She isn't called . . . well, not by her name. She's . . . she's the oracle, you understand?"

"The oracle?"

"Don't you know the oracle, Samos? The Oracle of Delphi? Your father, he knew about her."

"Oh yes, of course, the oracle," Sam recovered, without having the slightest idea what he was talking about. "I'm just a little surprised. The oracle, that's really somebody."

"That's for sure! But it's true that she's very fond of me. And your father made this tunic," he added, stroking the little statue. "He did a good job, didn't he?"

Allan must have done it to make friends with the shepherd — in addition to giving him two ram's heads that he had found God knows where. Because honestly, who travels through time carrying the heads of sheep?

"You can hold her if you like," added Metaxos. "She'll be good to you too."

Sam delicately took the small curvaceous figurine. Her dress was cut from a rough linen much like what he himself was wearing — further proof that his father had been there. As he turned the doll over, he noticed lines and dots on the cloth. "Did my father draw these?"

"Oh, yes. He's very good with his hands. Want me to show you?"

He untied the string that held the tunic on the statue and handed the cloth to Sam. Unfolded, the dress was a rectangle the size of a sheet of paper, with holes for the head and arms. A series of little squares was drawn on it in charcoal, with dots and letters that Sam couldn't decipher.

"Do you know what this means?"

"No. I don't know how to read. The priests tried to teach me once, but . . ."

The squares appeared to be houses lined up one after the other, with arrows and notes in some foreign writing. *It must be a map*, thought Sam, *with street names for landmarks*. He was about to ask if a neighborhood like the one pictured existed in Delphi when Argos began to bark loudly. Metaxos rushed to the door. A group of men armed with staffs was climbing the path to the hut.

"Hey, Metaxos, are you there? Don't be afraid, my boy. We mean you no harm. We just have some questions to ask you."

"It's the good priest," whispered the young man. "He's come looking for me! He thinks that . . . he thinks that . . ."

He wasn't able to finish, and his whole body was trembling.

"What does he think?" tried Sam.

But the shepherd only retreated deeper into his hut as the group approached.

"Ho, Metaxos! We know you're there! Your goats and your dog are here. Don't be childish!"

Sam decided he had better intervene. "He's here. He isn't hiding!" he called.

A half-dozen men were crossing the olive grove. They were all bearded and swarthy and wore the same kind of tunic as Metaxos, except that their tunics were clean. The oldest one, whose white hair fell to his shoulders, was probably the "good priest." He walked up to the door and looked at Sam. "Who are you?"

"I'm a friend of Metaxos. He's coming."

"I've never seen you around here. What is your name?"

"It's Samos," said the shepherd, suddenly appearing. "Yes, a friend of one of my friends. Samos of Samos!"

"Samos of Samos?" repeated the old man. "Your parents didn't have much imagination! But I want to talk to Metaxos. Come here, my boy."

He seemed annoyed by something, whereas the others looked stern. The priest put his hand on the shoulder of the shepherd, who lowered his eyes. "Metaxos, did you go down into the city three days ago?"

The young man stared at his bare feet, rocking slightly back and forth.

"Metaxos, it's very important for me to know. Did you go to town three days ago?"

The silence seemed to go on forever. All that could be heard was the buzzing of insects, the goats bleating a little distance away, and the quiet panting of Argos, who was lying under a tree.

"I think you were right, Lydias," said the old man with a sigh. "He must have been in Delphi that day."

"Of course I was right," exclaimed a short brown-haired man, waving his staff. "I saw him with my own eyes. He was prowling near the Treasury of the Athenians and —"

Metaxos suddenly bent down, slipped sideways, and tried to get away. But they all grabbed him at once, and he was soon collared and pinned to the ground.

"I didn't do anything, good priest!" he shouted as two men pulled him up, holding him tightly. "I'm a nice shepherd."

"See that?" shouted Lydias. "He tried to escape! That's certainly proof!"

"Metaxos," continued the priest in a patient voice. "Metaxos, listen to me and stop sniffling. Did you steal the Navel of the World from the Treasury of the Athenians? Yes or no? Tell me the truth, Metaxos. It's your only chance!"

His eyes full of tears, the shepherd looked at him. "I didn't do anything, good priest! I swear I didn't do anything!"

The priest shrugged in annoyance. "The archon will surely want to question them. It's too bad, but we have to take them to prison!"

CHAPTER FIVE

The Stranger

When Sam emerged from the valley and saw the city, it took his breath away. Delphi was a white pearl surrounded by stone, a majestic eagle's nest in the heart of the mountains. Houses with tile roofs clustered around gleaming structures whose angular facades shone in the sun. The scene was all the more striking because the town seemed lost in a world of cliffs and precipices. There were no villages or farms nearby, just jagged rock and empty sky.

Delphi may have been isolated, but it was hardly deserted. A dense crowd thronged its streets, and the yellow path snaking below it was jammed with carts and pilgrims.

After three-quarters of an hour of silent walking, Sam and Metaxos were escorted into a building guarded by soldiers with tall metal lances. They shoved the two prisoners into a windowless room in the back, with no furnishings beyond a few straw mats tossed on the ground.

"I'm going to get the archon," the priest said. "In the meantime, think carefully about what you are going to tell him."

He closed the door, and the two youths were plunged into darkness. Metaxos huddled in a corner, sniffling, and Sam stretched out on one of the mats. He was now positive that he was in Greece. Athens, Apollo, tunics, temples, columns — it all fit. But in what century? That was a mystery. From a conversation Sam overheard at the gates of the city between a soldier and a priest, he deduced that Delphi must be some kind of holy place where the Greeks came to consult the Pythia, or oracle, who gave his — or rather her — opinion on various questions. Like in *The Matrix*, except this was the original!

But far more important to Sam was that fact that his father had come to Delphi. Better yet, *he had come to Delphi just three days earlier.* Three Greek days didn't mean much in the big picture, of course; his father could have made the trip several months ago in his original time. Just the same, Sam had missed him by a hairsbreadth today. He imagined for a moment what such a meeting might look like. Once the first moments of astonishment and emotion had passed, they would find a quiet spot — in front of Metaxos's hut, say — and tell each other about their adventures. Allan would explain what had brought him to Delphi with a drill, and Sam would warn his father of the dangers awaiting him in Bran Castle. Together they would return quietly to Sainte-Mary — back to square one, and back to normal life!

Of course things hadn't turned out that way. Still, Allan's visit to Delphi gave Sam a new perspective on events. What if he really did meet his father during his time travels? It wouldn't be who his father was now, of course — it might be the college-aged Allan, when he was studying in Egypt, or the Allan of just a few months ago, when he was first beginning to use the stone statue again. Still, whenever it was that they ran into each other, all Sam had to do was warn him not to go to Wallachia in the future — and then there'd be no need to chase after the seven coins, or to go risking his life with Dracula!

But there was some bad news too, and it was called the Navel of the World. Sam didn't know exactly what that was, but he remembered the Sainte-Mary Museum guard's comment: "Did you read about that Greek thing they auctioned in London? The Navel of the World or some such. Ten million dollars in less than ten minutes!"

So the Navel of the World had recently been stolen in Delphi and even more recently — a few thousand years later, actually — sold in England. Between those two events, his father had come here with a drill. His father, whom Metaxos had surprised committing an act so reprehensible that he didn't dare talk about it. His father, who would lose the house, the bookstore, and the stone statue unless he could make an impossible mortgage payment. His father, who had become a thief — unless there was some other explanation.

"Samos!" whispered Metaxos. "Are you still here?"

"Of course I'm here," answered Sam, annoyed.

"Samos, I'm afraid. They're going to kill me."

"Don't be silly. They just want to know where the Navel of the World is. Can you tell me what it looks like?"

"You know less about it than your father," Metaxos remarked. "At least he —"

40

"All right, all right," Sam interrupted. "I know less about it than my father — I get it! Just be nice and tell me what it is."

"It's the stone that shows the center of everything, Samos! When Zeus wanted to know where the center of the world was, he sent two eagles flying from opposite ends of the earth. The two eagles met above Delphi. They dropped the stone. That's how we know Delphi is the navel of the world."

"And this stone — where is it exactly?"

"The original is in Apollo's Temple. But the Athenians carved their own stone and covered it with gold. They were going to offer it to the god at the great feast. They stored it in their Treasury in the meantime. That's where your father . . ."

He started sniffling again, and Sam instinctively reached in his pocket for a handkerchief. He found only the museum coin and the statuette's cloth dress.

"Can you tell me what happened three days ago, Metaxos? Did my father tell you something? Like what he planned to do with the Navel of the World?"

"No, no!" the shepherd protested. "If I talk, I'll never go to the hills again, never! I'll never see my goats again, or my dog! I won't talk about your father, ever!"

Just then, the door flew open. "Are you two finished moaning? Come along. The archon is here."

The soldier led them to an oval room with a domed ceiling. A fat man with a chubby face sat at a marble table, his arm shuttling rhythmically between his mouth and a bowl full of grapes. The white-haired priest was pacing behind him, looking angry.

41

"Ah," said the priest, as he saw them approach. "So, Metaxos, have you been thinking? If you are the thief, you better tell us right away, my boy, so we can get the object back as soon as possible."

The shepherd fell to his knees imploringly. "It wasn't me, good priest! By Apollo and Hermes, it wasn't me!"

"So who was it, then?" snapped the old man. "Several people saw you prowling around the Treasuries that day, and you left town at nightfall clutching something in your arms. Can you tell me what you were carrying so carefully?"

"Don't . . . no," babbled Metaxos. "I . . . I . . ." He could no longer say anything intelligible.

"Do you realize what we've done for you all these years?" exploded the priest. "Who took you in when you were just a squalling baby on the temple steps? Who raised and fed you, and gave you your goats? Is this how you thank us, by robbing our best ally's Treasury?"

He grasped Metaxos under the armpit and forced him to his feet. "Do you know what will happen if we don't find the Navel of the World, Metaxos? In three months the Athenians will take their things and abandon the city. The Thebans, Boetians, and Corinthians will go next, and then all the others! Delphi will be deserted, the oracle silenced, and you'll be pasturing your goats among ruins!"

Metaxos looked terrified. "Good priest, good priest . . . don't kill me! I didn't do anything!"

"Who is this boy with him?" asked the archon, without pausing in swallowing his grapes.

"A friend of Metaxos," answered the priest. "Samos of Samos, I believe. They were both at the hut when we caught them."

"Does he know anything?"

"Metaxos claims he only arrived this morning."

"Is that true, Samos of Samos?" asked the archon without looking up.

"It's true," Sam said in a voice that he wished sounded more confident.

"And you don't know anything?"

Sam summoned all the courage he could muster. He was about to try something risky, but there was nothing else to do if he wanted to get out of this quickly.

"I think Metaxos found out something and he's very frightened," he said all at once.

"No, Samos!" the shepherd protested. "Keep quiet or I'll never go back to my hills!"

Sam ignored him and instead took the statuette's dress from his pocket and held it out. "Metaxos picked this up when he came to Delphi."

The archon deigned to look at him for the first time. "What is it?"

"A kind of map, I think."

At a nod, one of the guards stepped forward and brought the piece of cloth to the marble table. The archon looked at it every which way while making a sucking noise, as if he had something stuck between his teeth, and finally spat out a seed.

"It's a map of the city, all right," he said. "Crudely drawn, with names: 'theater,' 'temple,' 'Treasury of the Athenians.' That last one is marked with a cross. You say Metaxos picked this up on the Delphi road?"

Sam nodded.

"What if he had drawn it himself, instead of finding it?"

The priest, who had approached, shook his head. "Impossible. We were never able to teach Metaxos to read, much less write. Moreover, the shape of the letters looks like the way Greek is written in distant cities, not here."

"Cities more distant than the island of Samos?" asked the archon, glancing suspiciously at Sam.

"Much more distant, yes."

"So the thief would be a stranger, is that right?"

"It would seem so. Besides, Metaxos would hardly need a map to find his way to the Treasury of the Athenians. He spent his entire childhood in that neighborhood!"

"That's true," admitted the archon. "In that case . . . Tell me, Samos of Samos, do you have any idea what could have so frightened your friend?"

Sam cleared his throat as discreetly as possible. He had to come up with a convincing lie while making sure Metaxos didn't contradict him — no easy task. He stared hard at the shepherd, trying to send brain waves: *Trust me! Just repeat everything I say!*

"From what Metaxos told me," Sam began, improvising wildly, "he saw the map, got suspicious, and went to the Treasury of the Athenians. But when he got there, someone attacked him and threatened to kill him if he talked."

"Someone? Did you see someone at the Treasury of the Athenians, Metaxos?"

The shepherd opened blank, staring eyes as if his brain were momentarily disconnected: *I'm sorry, the number you are calling is temporarily out of service. Please try again later.*

The archon leaped to his feet and raised his fist to Metaxos. "Did you see the thief? Can you describe him? Speak!"

"It was a man," shouted Sam, to keep the archon from striking Metaxos. "About fifty years old, with short gray hair, a square jaw, and blue eyes."

The description had simply popped into his head. It was different enough from his father's appearance that it wouldn't cause Allan too much trouble if he ever came back here. Sam quickly went on: "Metaxos wasn't able to tell me more because everything happened too fast. The man had a knife and almost stabbed him, I think."

"Is this true?" asked the archon, his fist mere inches from the shepherd's face. "Was that the stranger you saw?"

It took a few moments before Metaxos's gaze showed a flicker of life. Then he nodded slowly. "Yes, that's . . . that's what I saw."

"Why did you refuse to talk? We've lost valuable time!"

"I — I was afraid. The stranger's knife, yes."

Sam heaved a sigh of relief. Apollo and his fellow gods had apparently taken his side.

"When did this happen, exactly?"

"After . . . after consulting the oracle," murmured the shepherd, as if under the effect of a powerful drug.

The archon stepped back, and the priest smiled slightly.

"That seems to fit. The lock at the rear of the building was broken at about that time, at the changing of the guard. It didn't take the thief more than a few moments to enter the Treasury and seize the Navel of the World."

"We still don't know how he was able to break the bolt, though," remarked the archon, reaching for another cluster of grapes. "Besides, nothing proves that Metaxos wasn't the thief's *accomplice* — and the Athenians won't be satisfied with his good looks or his simpleton manners. If they aren't given proof of his innocence, they will demand that he be punished."

Metaxos began to moan softly, like a dog unfairly reprimanded by its master.

"There may be a way to provide that proof," the priest suggested. "A proof that the Athenians themselves couldn't argue with."

"I'm listening."

"If this boy is truly guiltless, the oracle will declare him innocent," said the priest. "Otherwise . . ."

CHAPTER SIX

The Oracle

Actually reaching the oracle turned out to be no mean feat. At the foot of the temple, a dense crowd jammed a walkway lined with trophies: six-foot-high vases and shields, inscribed white pillars, a gilded statue of a lion, a bronze palm tree with a glittering owl perched in its fronds, and so on. You would have thought the people were extras for a scene in *Ulysses Against Hercules*.

The area was so crowded that the arrival of Sam and Metaxos, surrounded by the archon, the priest, and two guards, didn't go unnoticed.

"No shoving!" shouted one man.

"In Apollo's name," complained his neighbor, "you can't cut in line ahead of us!"

"We've been standing here for two hours," agreed the first man. "Wait your turn or —"

"It's the archon," interrupted a woman behind them. "Be quiet!"

They climbed the sacred path, making their way as best they could among the grumbling faithful. The organizers of the temple had clearly forgotten to arrange for VIP access. As they reached the first steps of the temple, the priest spoke into Sam's ear: "The two men holding their helmets over there are Athenians. They are here to keep an eye on us, so watch what you say or Metaxos could pay the price. Here — when you enter, give this as an offering."

He put two roughly circular bronze coins in Sam's hand. They didn't have holes, but Sam couldn't help but be startled: Each bore the head of a ram with long, curving horns. Two ram's heads! That was what his father gave Metaxos to buy his silence: two coins of the local money.

"I must go speak to them," said the archon, who went to confer with the representatives of Athens. Meanwhile, over to the left, two temple attendants were splashing water on a goat and watching its reaction. Sam had heard the priest at the city gate explain this to the soldier as well: If the animal shook itself vigorously, it was a favorable sign, and the visitors could be admitted. As Sam's group was waved forward, one of the attendants recognized the priest and hurried over to him.

"Master, it's you! If we had only known! Come this way, we will —"

"No, Selemnos, it is important that we proceed by the proper stages. We are being watched," he added, glancing at the Athenians.

The attendant followed his gaze and seemed to understand. "Well, in that case, please be good enough to make your offering."

Maybe it was seeing the goat, but Metaxos's good humor

gradually returned. He started to hum as he threw the two coins that the priest had given him onto a cloth.

"I gave my two ram's horns too! They aren't as beautiful as my beautiful earrings, but I'm going to see the oracle!"

From a mental-health standpoint, things weren't looking so good.

They stepped under the portico, a soaring, sculpted marble canopy supported by massive columns, then entered the temple proper. The archon soon joined them, followed by the Athenians.

"We have reached an agreement. None of the four of us must approach the boys while the oracle renders her judgment. We will stand ten paces behind them and keep totally silent. Each will listen to the answer and submit to the verdict. If the words' meaning is not clear, we will ask the usual interpreters for their opinion."

"Who should speak directly to Apollo?" asked the priest.

"Our Athenian friends want it to be Metaxos himself. He was the first to be accused, so he must confront the god."

"And the other one?"

"Samos of Samos? Our friends have trouble believing his version of the facts. They wonder about his connection with the stranger. It is essential that he also be present."

"And what guarantee do we have that they will not be bothered afterward?"

The younger Athenian, whose sharp eyes had been scrutinizing Sam, came forward, his helmet clanking.

"The representatives of the most glorious of Greek cities have given their word. If the two suspects have not stolen the

Navel of the World, they will be free to go. This Athens has decided!"

The two boys were asked to step deeper into the temple, where a smell of burned wood and aromatic herbs reigned. A servant had them sit on a wooden bench in front of a white curtain, as if to watch a puppet show.

"She's going to come," Metaxos whispered, suddenly very excited. "She's going to come!"

"Do you know what you're supposed to do?" Sam asked.

"Of course! With the oracle, I'm never afraid!"

Sam would have liked to share Metaxos's enthusiasm. He knew he was innocent, but he was afraid the Pythia would suddenly declare his father to be the real thief — in which case, the best way to recover the stolen goods would be to imprison his son.

There was a rustling behind the curtain, and the servant nodded gently. "Apollo is prepared to listen to you, young men."

"Is that right?" the shepherd exclaimed. "Is the oracle there? Back there?"

"Metax?" hissed a low voice on the other side of the sheet.

The curtain parted slightly, and Sam saw a middle-aged woman in a gray robe looking at them in surprise. She had stepped down from a three-legged metal stool and was standing next to a wide crack in the ground — perhaps a scar from an ancient earthquake. Her part of the sanctuary was lit by torches, and in the shadows you could make out a tree, a twisted, bullet-shaped stone — the original Navel of the World? — and various other objects. When she saw the archon and the priest a few yards away, she snapped the curtain shut. It clearly wasn't usual for the oracle to show herself to her visitors. But the servant acted as if nothing was amiss and tiptoed out.

Metaxos stood up. "Oracle! Oracle of Delphi! Breath of the god Apollo! Did Metaxos steal the Athenians' golden stone?"

He sat down and winked at Sam.

At first nothing happened except for a slight clicking of teeth, as if the Pythia was chewing on something. Then a strange swallowing sound was heard, and she seemed to spit on the ground — *like the archon*, Sam thought. *Everybody spits here!* After a short silence, a hoarse voice rose that would be hard to imagine coming from a woman's throat.

"Apollo, the god most beloved of the gods, has heard your request, Metaxos. Here is his answer: Does the lamb steal the grass it eats from the mountain? Does the bird steal the water it drinks from the fish? Metaxos has never taken anything except the air he breathes and the milk he drinks from his animals' teats. It is Apollo's pleasure to give them to him."

The oracle then fell silent. A second passed, then ten seconds . . . Sam wasn't sure he grasped the message's hidden meaning, but overall, things were looking pretty favorable. In fact, the good priest was the first to express his pleasure.

"So much the better!" he exclaimed. "We now have proof that —"

From behind the curtain, the Pythia cut him off. "Apollo's breath has not expired! There is something else that men must know!"

Sam shrank on his bench: His father was surely about to be accused!

"Apollo, son of Zeus, has many times crossed the sky in his golden chariot," the hoarse voice continued. "He follows the

51

course of the sun and sets the rhythm of the day. He knows the value of time and of the passing hours. Men of Delphi, let the shepherd's friend depart. Let him depart now. May he return through the gate of days that led him here. But he must hurry: One of his people is trying to close it. Apollo has spoken."

Sam had no time to think about the warning, because the more suspicious of the Athenians was on him in three quick steps.

"Whoever you really are, Samos of Samos, it would seem the gods have decided in your favor. But don't celebrate too soon. We will catch the stranger one of these days, and when that time comes, believe me: He won't steal anything ever again."

An hour later, Metaxos and his dog were chasing each other among the olive trees, delighted to be together again. The shepherd put his hands on his forehead to make them into horns — like the Minotaur? — and head down, charged his dog, who was barking joyously.

"Don't you want to play with us, Samos?"

"Not now. I'm thinking."

Sam was leaning against a wall in the hut's shadow, trying to make sense of the Pythia's warning. Apparently the Greek gods — or at least those who traveled with the sun and knew about the passing of time — shared some idea of the high priest Setni's magic. Egyptian gods and Greek gods, all wrestling with the same eternal question . . .

"One of my people," Sam repeated to himself. Someone from his own time, probably, who was trying to close the gate of days. Was it to prevent him from traveling? To keep his father from returning? And how did you close the "gate of days," anyway?

"Come out and play, Samos!"

"Thanks, no. I have to leave."

Sam had been turning the coin in his pocket over and over. What if he spent an extra night here? The Treasury of the Athenians was so close; wasn't it likely that it held at least a few coins with holes in them? His father had done half the job by breaking the lock with his drill. If Sam was careful . . .

Argos suddenly bolted inside the hut, followed by his master, who tripped and fell to the ground, laughing. "Metaxos is going to eat you up, you hound from Hades!"

There was also that comment by the Athenian representative: "We will catch the stranger one of these days, and when that time comes, he won't steal anything ever again." Did that mean his father had stolen other things from this time besides the Navel of the World? And that he could be expected to return soon? Who knows — maybe if Sam stationed himself by the stone for a while, he would see him reappear!

"Here, Samos, this bread is for you."

A sweaty Metaxos emerged from his poor shelter, holding a nearly whole round loaf under his arm. He gave Sam a slice a handbreadth wide.

"This is the Navel of the World," he added with a sly look.

"I'm sorry?"

"This is what I was hiding the other night when the guards saw me leaving the city. A nice loaf of bread my Delphi mother gave me; a nice loaf she baked for me! But you mustn't ever tell anyone that the oracle takes care of Metaxos, all right? It would shame her, since I'm just a shepherd. That's why I had to keep quiet."

Sam was astonished. "The Athenians could have had you put to death," he said. "You risked your life so you wouldn't betray your Delphi mother?"

"I was right, since Samos came," he answered candidly. "The gods rewarded me well. For that matter —" Metaxos put his other hand in his pocket. "You deserve a reward too. You can give these back to your father."

He held something out: Dangling from wires were two coins with holes in them. *Two coins with holes!*

"These are the pretty earrings your father made with the ram's horns. He gave them to me before the stone swallowed him."

Sam laid them cautiously in his palm. Two coins, the right size and with nice holes in them, mounted as pendants and bearing the ram of Delphi. His father must have stolen them from the Treasury of the Athenians.

"I'll give one back to you, anyway," Sam blurted, trying to master his emotion. "You can pick it up next to the stone after I'm gone."

"That way I'll have a souvenir of both of you!"

"Yes, and I'll have a souvenir of you."

All that remained was for Sam to leave for good. Metaxos let him understand that he didn't want to accompany him to the stone statue, and that he would retrieve the precious coin later. Indeed, the shepherd seemed almost relieved to see him go, as if the threat of being torn from his hills and sucked into nothingness would disappear with Samos of Samos. He barely waved good-bye, just turned his back to go tend his animals. Was that a way of making the farewells easier?

Sam climbed back up the hill toward the meadow where he had arrived only that morning — an eternity ago! In the distance, the sun was setting on the glowing sea, and he saw a black dot racing above the waves. Was it Apollo's chariot, crossing the sky at the end of the day? After all, nothing was impossible.

CHAPTER SEVEN

A Rabid Rabbit

Sam lay on the basement's cement floor for a moment, catching his breath. Aside from nausea, one of the most uncomfortable effects of his trips was the echo effect he experienced on his return, where every sound and movement around him was repeated with a slight delay. This déjà vu effect had been invaluable when he faced big Monk during the Sainte-Mary judo tournament the previous week, because it let him anticipate his opponent's moves and eventually win the championship. But it was very unsettling, and Sam spent several minutes waiting for it to wear off.

He then left the secret storeroom, taking care to pull the tapestry that hid the entrance back in place. The bookstore was empty, and he was able to change his clothes — nothing like a good pair of jeans! — before wolfing down a chocolate bar that he had thought to stash in one of the kitchen cabinets. He then climbed out the ground-floor window and crossed Mrs. Bombardier's and the Fosters' backyards. The Fosters' dog, who was usually pretty friendly, bared its teeth at him; maybe it caught a whiff of its distant Greek forebear.

After making sure Barenboim Street was empty, Sam hopped the fence and took the bus to his grandmother's, praying that Aunt Evelyn wouldn't be home. Alas, Apollo must have withdrawn his blessing en route. Sam had barely gotten off at the bus stop when a brand-new Porsche 4×4 drove up onto the sidewalk, heading straight toward him, and stopped in a squeal of tires a foot away. Evelyn's boyfriend Rudolf — that's what she called him, "my boyfriend," even though at fifty he was long past being a boy — jumped out.

"Well, well, if it isn't Samuel! Mind telling me where you're coming from?"

"Is that any of your business?" Sam said coldly.

The passenger-side window came purring down, and a familiar voice rode a gust of air-conditioning out of the car.

"Of course it's his business, you rude thing!" screeched Aunt Evelyn. "Someone has to be concerned about how you spend your days! If your father hadn't disappeared and forced your grandparents to —"

"That's all right, darling," said Rudolf. "I'll deal with him."

He strode toward Sam as if he were about to give him the beating of the millennium. Ever since Allan Faulkner had disappeared, Rudolf had shown an unfortunate tendency to view himself as the head of the family, and to see in Sam a particularly intractable future delinquent. He had first suggested the boot camp in the United States for Sam not long before.

"You didn't have lunch with Grandma, did you? She left to play bridge just now and was wondering where you'd gone to."

"I let her know," replied Sam. "I was at Harold's all afternoon."

"Harold, eh? He's very convenient, Harold is." Rudolf's glittering blue eyes looked anything but friendly. "Tell me, what did you do to your aunt this morning?"

"This morning?"

"Yes, when you were trying to involve Lily in your dirty little tricks. You got Grandpa upset at Evelyn."

"What?" shouted Sam. "She's the one who got hysterical! We were just eating our cereal when —"

Rudolf drew back his hand and seemed about to hit him. "Don't *ever* speak about your aunt that way!"

Sam was about to defend himself when he noticed Lily waving wildly at him from the back of the car. He didn't understand what his cousin was trying to tell him, but he figured that a fight with Rudolf would only cause her extra problems. So he stepped back and lowered his eyes.

"That's better," Rudolf snapped, mistaking his reaction for submission. "Don't you know your aunt has weak nerves? She's very sensitive to being called hysterical. And your father hasn't always behaved well toward her. In fact, it's partly *his* fault that she's in the state she is. So if you're planning to go the same route, you'll have to deal with me."

Sam shrugged and held his tongue.

"We're going to spend the night at a hotel near the water park. When we get back, I don't want your grandparents telling me you've gotten into trouble again. All right?"

Sam nodded slowly. He was only half listening to Rudolf rant because he was trying to understand the charades Lily was acting out in the backseat. First she drew something in the air: a rectangle . . . a rectangle that you unfold . . . a book . . . the Book of Time, for sure! Okay, what next? She slipped her right arm under her left one, then put both hands above her ears and began to wiggle them while shaking her head . . . A rabbit? What did a rabbit have to do with anything? She also opened her mouth in a funny way, as if she were trying to bite. . . . A crazed rabbit that hopped out of the Book of Time? It didn't make any sense!

But Evelyn was raising her window and Sam couldn't see anything more through the tinted glass. Rudolf walked back to the car, pointing his finger at him. "Don't you give your aunt a hard time, boy, ever again!"

He slammed the door and roared off, probably pleased by his show of strength. Rudolf really was a self-satisfied idiot.

When Sam got to his grandmother's, he first checked to make sure he was home alone, then attacked the refrigerator. He stacked a tray with a big glass of orange juice, two slices of cold pizza reheated in the microwave, the remains of a pasta salad, a piece of cheese so artificial that the milk it was made of probably came from a plastic cow, two chocolate yogurts, and a nice red apple that he polished with his napkin. He carried all this to the table and devoured it at a speed close to the world snacking record.

His hunger satisfied, Sam went up to his room, pulled on a clean T-shirt, and rummaged in his closet for the hidden box. He found the collection of photographs of Bran Castle and the sheet with the alchemist's Latin text, but not the Book of Time or the coins. Lily hadn't put them back, apparently. Was that what she was trying to tell him in the car?

He hurried to her bedroom next door, a place he didn't often have occasion to enter. Before discovering the stone statue, Sam and Lily had avoided each other as much as possible, each viewing the other as a living monument of purest stupidity. Their time-travel adventures had brought them much closer, but hadn't given Sam time to visit his cousin's domain.

A very strange place, a girl's bedroom — all mauve and pink, from the bedspread to the curtains, and including the pillows, lamp, bandanna on the chair back, book bag, and dance slippers. Orlando Bloom ruled the appropriately lavender walls: Orlando Bloom as an elf, Orlando Bloom as a pirate, Orlando Bloom as a Trojan warrior, Orlando Bloom sitting with his legs crossed, Orlando Bloom standing with his arms crossed, Orlando Bloom lying down with his fingers crossed. He was clearly a full-time demigod.

All right, wondered Sam, *where could she have put them?*

He opened closets, looked under the bed, and parted the curtains: nothing. He moved books, pulled out the bookcase, and felt behind the chest of drawers: nothing. Zan, Lily's favorite stuffed animal, lay on one of the stereo speakers and seemed to be mocking Sam's efforts. He was a floppy dog with short gray fur, a pointed snout, and long, dangling ears. *Ears!* His cousin wasn't pretending to be a rabid rabbit, but her pet pooch! *Arf!*

Sam grabbed Zan and shook him, but the dog was too small to contain a book. He then inspected the speaker Zan had been on, tipping it back and forth. Sure enough, something moved inside. He gently removed the black screen covering the loudspeaker and — bingo! — out slid the Book of Time and his father's black notebook. The three coins with holes were neatly taped inside the speaker case. Sam carefully replaced the screen. His cousin might have dubious taste in colors, but when it came to hiding places, she couldn't be beat!

Sam waited until he was back in his room to open the big red book. The same title appeared on every page: "Delphi, the Sanctuary of Apollo." Two black-and-white engravings showed the ruined city from above and the Temple of Apollo with its few remaining upright columns. The text recounted a legend in which Apollo had to defeat a terrible serpent before establishing his temple and his cult. There was also a reference to the Navel of the World, or *omphalos*, the famous stone that the two eagles dropped to mark the center of the earth.

The omphalos . . .

Sam sat down at his computer and launched an Internet search. He wasn't so much interested in the history of the omphalos as in what had happened to it recently. He found a few photographs of the stone — it was indeed bullet shaped, the way it had looked behind the temple curtain, with braided ropes carved on its sides — and some articles that confirmed his hunch. The original of the Navel of the World was on display at the Delphi Museum, but a number of copies of it existed. One long-missing gold copy had recently turned up and been auctioned in London for the equivalent of $10,125,000. The seller was Arkeos, a private company that specialized in high-end antiquities. It reportedly received the piece from an anonymous collector whose name it had agreed not to reveal; the buyer was a major Japanese bank.

Sam clicked on the arkeos.com link and swore under his breath when he saw the company's home page appear. Arkeos's logo was a pair of tapering horns enclosing a solar disk — the same strange U as the one tattooed on the burglar's shoulder!

How could that be? Unless . . . Sam dreaded what he was starting to suspect. Had his father stolen the Navel of the World in order to sell it to Arkeos? Was he perhaps in league with the thief at the museum? If the thief had been an archeology intern with Allan in Egypt, they might have been friends — but then he probably wouldn't call and threaten Allan, nor would he beat up Allan's son! Of course, according to Sam's theory, the other intern also knew how to time-travel, so he could have stolen the omphalos himself. But where would he have found a stone statue? As far as Sam knew, the Barenboim house sheltered the only one in Sainte-Mary — in North America, as a matter of fact. And Metaxos had been so certain that his visitor with the ram's heads was Sam's father.

"What kind of a mess did you get yourself in now, Dad?"

But Allan didn't answer him, any more than he had that morning.

Sam opened the black notebook and scanned the odd list again.

MERIWESERRE = O
CALIPH AL-HAKIM, 1010
$1,000,000!
XERXES, 484 B.C.
LET THE BEGINNING SHOW THE WAY
V. = O
IZMIT, AROUND 1400?
ISFAHAN, 1386

It still didn't make much sense, but thanks to the Web, Sam learned a little more about each of these things. Meriweserre, whose name was spelled several different ways, was an Egyptian pharaoh of the fifteenth dynasty. Al-Hakim was a Middle Eastern ruler around 1010. Xerxes was a Persian emperor who fought the Greeks. Izmit and Isfahan were cities, one in Turkey and the other in Iran. Had his father gone to all those places and all those times? Or was he planning to go there? And what was the connection with Bran Castle?

As for the rest of the message, only the money amount made sense. Was Allan supposed to receive a million dollars as a commission on the Navel of the World sale? Or was it the value of some other archeological treasure he planned to steal? A million dollars would certainly pay off the mortgage, allowing him to continue time-traveling — and to continue stealing antiquities.

Sam decided to store all the information he'd gathered in his computer. As he copied a picture of the omphalos into his images folder, he came across the family photo album he'd scanned a few years earlier. He usually avoided looking at it, because the past was still too painful. But today, after everything he'd learned — including the mounting evidence that his father was a thief — Sam wanted to look back at that wonderful time when he had both his parents and no harm could ever reach him.

Feeling heartsick, he stared at the screen. The slide show ran through their big Bel View house; Allan feeding him a baby bottle; his mother laughing at the county fair; a Christmas tree surrounded by presents; his first bicycle; a group shot, again with his mother, who was hugging him tight. . . . It felt both wonderful and unbearable.

The next photo showed him building a snowman with Alicia. The picture must have been taken right after the Todds moved in next door, since he and Alicia looked about nine years old. From then on, Alicia's sweet face, blond hair, and big blue eyes appeared along with Sam more and more often. For two years they had been inseparable: same school; same friends; same books, whose chapters they read aloud to each other; same movies, whose favorite scenes they would endlessly reenact; same hysterical giggles when their parents came upstairs to make sure they were asleep.

Then Elisa Faulkner had died, and a black shroud fell over everything. Sam had felt he was tumbling into a bottomless pit, a well of sadness and bitterness that he couldn't escape without severing the sorrow that still connected him to his mother. He hadn't wanted to see anybody, not even Alicia. In the space of a few weeks he'd broken everything off.

Three years passed that way. The Faulkners moved out of Bel View, Sam changed schools, and even though he thought about Alicia all the time, he'd never had the courage to see her again. Until three days ago, in fact, at the judo tournament, when she'd appeared on Jerry Paxton's arm. The tall boy's presence and the festive mood in the gym made Sam feel awkward, and he hadn't been able to tell Alicia what was really in his heart: that his love for her hadn't changed, and that just by looking at him, she could tell it never would. There were a lot of things Alicia needed to hear, including the apologies Sam owed her, which he had left too long unsaid. And this time, waiting another three years was out of the question.

Sam looked at his watch. It was four-thirty. Maybe Alicia would agree to see him.

CHAPTER EIGHT

Alicia Todds

Sam hadn't been back to the Bel View neighborhood in ages, and when he saw the first white colonial-style houses with their big lawns, he felt almost dizzy. Everything was the same, yet everything was so different! The maple trees that lined the avenue, the colorful bushes and flower beds, the blue mailboxes by the paved walkways, the sidewalk where he first learned to skateboard — well, where his knees and elbows first learned — the lamppost he had swung around so many times . . . Except that he wasn't ten years old anymore, the bus hadn't just dropped him off after school, and his mother wasn't waiting with a grapefruit-orange juice cocktail ("It's full of vitamins, Sammy!") and his favorite cookies. Today he was a stranger: a stranger to his childhood, a stranger to his neighborhood, a stranger to what he might have become if everything hadn't changed.

Sam stopped to let his heart slow to a normal rhythm. His house — his old house — was the third from the corner, the one with the green window trim. Alicia's was next door. Number 18, where he was standing, belonged to Miss Maggie

Pye, who had occasionally babysat for him when he was little. As it happened, she was standing over her rosebushes, garden clippers in hand.

"Miss Pye?" he called over the fence.

She turned, probably surprised not to recognize the voice. "What can I do for you?"

"It's me, Sam. Sam Faulkner."

"Sam Faulkner?" she said, adjusting her glasses. "Good heavens, it's Sammy Faulkner!" But she didn't make a move to come greet him. "I wouldn't have recognized you! What are you doing around here? You must have moved away three or four years ago, eh?"

"Yes, three years ago," said Sam. He felt a bit disappointed by the chilly welcome, but after all, what had he expected? That the neighbors would rush into the street, setting off fireworks and yelling, "Hallelujah! Sam's back!"?

"It was a real tragedy," said Miss Pye with a sigh. "Still, you grow up, you get over it. At your age you have other things on your mind, don't you?"

She stood there smiling tensely, her free hand resting on her flashy jeweled necklace. Miss Pye was so fond of jewelry that Allan had dubbed her "Miss Magpie" — irresistibly drawn to anything that gleamed, clinked, or sparkled. Sam wondered if she thought he wanted to steal her precious necklace.

"Well, see you next time, Miss Pye."

"Okay, see you then."

She turned back to her roses as if nothing had happened. Sam felt especially let down because in the old days they had all liked each other. When he had his appendix out, for example, Miss Pye had dropped by the hospital to say hello and even brought him a box of candies. True, she had devoured them while he watched, but then, she never could resist treats wrapped in shiny paper!

And then later that day, his mother had set out for the hospital in her car, and crashed down the embankment.

Swallowing his sudden sadness, Sam briskly walked up the path to the Toddses' house and pressed the doorbell. A few moments later, the door opened.

"What can I do for you?"

It was Helena Todds, Alicia's mother. She was almost as beautiful as her daughter, with the same golden hair, but her features weren't quite as defined. She was also shorter than Sam remembered.

"Are you looking for something?" she asked in a friendly way.

"I — I'm Sam Faulkner," he stammered.

Helena Todds's eyes widened. "Sam Faulkner! Of course! Sam!" She gave him a big hug and kissed him firmly on both cheeks. Sam could feel something melting in his chest. "You're all grown up now! You're handsome too, just like your father! And almost as tall, aren't you? Let me guess: You're on vacation from school, so you decided to drop by."

"That's right. I — I had a question I wanted to ask you."

Helena Todds seemed amused by his embarrassment. "Did you come to see Alicia? She's out now, but she should be home soon. I gather you ran into each other at the judo tournament."

Alicia had mentioned him to her mother! *Alicia had mentioned him to her mother!* His mood brightened immediately. "I was really happy to see her," he admitted.

"And you won too! I'm so pleased you're doing well after all these years! But come in, come in!"

Sam followed her through the hallway into the living room, which was furnished in the same nautical theme he remembered: antique charts on the pale wood walls, a big mahogany bookcase, and navigation instruments scattered here and there. Sam sat down on the big leather sofa next to a low table, where his parents had so often sat when they came over for a drink.

"What about your father? How is he?" asked Helena.

"He's . . . he's traveling."

"Oh, good. On business, right? Is the bookstore doing well?"

"Er, yes. At least it's starting to."

"I think Allan has a good reputation among collectors, and that's something! You know, we worried a lot about you," she added more quietly. "I mean after your mother's death. Allan just shut himself up. He didn't want to go out anymore or talk or see us. . . . I think we should have insisted that he not be alone. Forced him, even! I felt guilty about that afterward, if only for your sake. It isn't good for an eleven-year-old boy to find himself all alone at home after . . . Anyway, I feel I didn't really do what I should have. I hope you don't resent me for it."

Sam was speechless. From his point of view, *he* was the one who had walled himself up in his sorrow — like his father — and kept anybody from distracting him from it, even Alicia.

"Don't worry, Mrs. Todds," he finally answered. "Everything's fine now."

"Including that black eye you're sporting?"

Sam had forgotten about it. "Oh, that's just from the tournament."

"Well, that's better," she continued in a more cheerful tone. "What was the question you wanted to ask?"

A question? Sam wondered. Oh yes, his supposed reason for coming over!

"Well, it's strange, actually," he said, thinking fast. "There was a show about Flemish painters on TV the other day, and I watched it because art is one of my favorite subjects at school. Anyway, I don't know if you're going believe this, but they showed a painting that you'd swear was of Alicia."

Helena spread her hands, not understanding. "It must be a coincidence!"

"That's what I thought at first, but later in the broadcast they said the young woman had been painted by her father, Hans Baltus, and that she married a man named Van Todds."

"Van Todds! That's funny, because I think Mark's great-grandfather was called Van Todds! He lost the Van while crossing the Atlantic. But he did come from there, from Belgium. And if I remember right, there were some painters in the family. What did the painting look like?"

Sam thought back to the day when Alicia's ancestor Yser had posed in Baltus's studio in Bruges, with its smell of oil and camphor. Sam had merely finished the portrait by painting the young woman's hands, but he felt quite proud of the result.

"It was . . . It was very good. The model wore a beautiful black velvet dress with a hat, and —".

The ring of the front doorbell cut him off.

"That must be Alicia; she always rings. Come on, we'll surprise her."

They hurried to the door, which opened to reveal Alicia on the stoop. But she wasn't alone: Jerry Paxton had his arm around her shoulder. Sam, whose heart had earlier melted, now felt it suddenly freeze. Alicia looked at him in surprise and Jerry scowled.

"What are you doing here, Faulkner? You get lost or something?"

Helena spoke up. "It seems to me I can invite whoever I like to my house, Jerry."

Paxton made a vague gesture of apology. He said good-bye to Mrs. Todds, kissed her daughter on the cheek, and walked away, grumbling to himself.

"Thanks a lot!" Alicia said to her mother once she was inside. "Now Jerry's going to sulk for the next two days!"

"If he doesn't like you having your friends over, you better get him used to it right away," replied her mother. "Anyway, now that you're both here, I'll leave you alone. I have some errands to run for your brother, Alicia. He's going to Grandma's tomorrow and I have to buy him some shirts. Sam, I'm really happy you dropped by. If you ever need anything, you let me know," she said with a serious look. "And come back whenever you like!"

She kissed him warmly while Alicia ran up the stairs. It was only at the top that the lovely girl deigned to turn around and look down at Sam.

"What are you waiting for? Aren't you coming up?"

Alicia's room was nothing like Lily's: no pink anywhere, no Orlando Bloom as an elf, no menagerie of stuffed animals. Instead, there were dozens of black-and-white photographs on the walls: landscapes, street scenes both crowded and empty, farm machinery, animals, close-ups of fruit, self-portraits, schoolmates, and an enlarged picture of Jerry above the bed.

"You do photography?" asked Sam.

"For a while now, yeah."

After an awkward silence she went on. "Do you remember when we ordered pizzas for Mr. Roger across the street?" she continued. "I took pictures of the deliveryman and the way poor Mr. Roger looked with fourteen pizzas he hadn't wanted. I guess it started with that."

Sam remembered the episode very well, including the fact that when Alicia's pictures were discovered, they earned her a memorable punishment.

"Well, they're really nice — congratulations!"

He wanted to praise the pictures enthusiastically, express his admiration with the right words, and all he could come up with was "They're really nice — congratulations!"? Pathetic.

He settled uneasily on the edge of the bed as Alicia slipped a White Stripes CD into the player. She sat down in a small red armchair and looked out the window at the garden while Jack White faced the Seven Nation Army, guitar in hand.

At the third verse, Alicia finally spoke. "What exactly do you want, Sam?"

"What do I want?"

"Last week you came over to talk to me at the gym. Today you show up here at the house. You haven't spoken to me in three years and now suddenly you're all over the place. So I'm asking: What do you want?"

There was no reason for this meeting to be easy, of course. But where to start?

"I'm really sorry," he began. "I don't have any excuse — I mean, I don't have any *good* excuse. All those years, I felt like if I allowed myself even a minute of happiness, it was like I was betraying my mother. I had to suffer, you know? At least a tiny piece of what she suffered. I got that in my head and —"

"What about me?" she asked angrily. "What was I supposed to do during that time?"

"I'm really sorry, Alicia. I couldn't help it."

"You know what I thought? That maybe you held me responsible for your mom's death. You were at my house for a sleepover the night you got appendicitis, remember? If I hadn't insisted you stay that evening, maybe you wouldn't have gotten sick. You wouldn't have gone to the hospital, your mom wouldn't have had to take her car to go there, and . . ."

She was clearly trying to keep a lid on her feelings, which seemed as sharp as ever three years later.

". . . she wouldn't have had the accident," she concluded.

"That's crazy!" protested Sam. "Totally crazy! I would never think something like that! You had nothing to do with it! If it was anybody's fault, it was mine! I shouldn't have gotten sick! I should've hung on, been stronger, that's all!"

He stopped, surprised by what he was saying. Was there a part of him that actually felt responsible for his mother's death?

Alicia was studying him from her armchair, less coldly now. To Sam, she looked even more beautiful.

"You see what happens when you keep it all inside, Sam? I was hurt, you know; I was really hurt. I loved you, and I'm not ashamed to say so. The way a little girl loves her Prince Charming. And you were my Prince Charming. Then all of a sudden, *pfft!* As if I didn't exist anymore. I was gone, scratched off the map. I'm sure it was horrible for you, but it wasn't much fun for me either."

Silence fell between them as Jack White sang with conviction, "I don't know what to do with myself." Sam didn't know what to do with himself either.

"Listen, Sam, don't be angry, but I'm not ready to see you again. Not now, anyway. Besides, there's Jerry. He's jealous, as I'm sure you noticed. Maybe later . . ."

She gave him a thin, pained smile, and Sam suddenly realized what a terrible waste those lost years represented for the two of them.

CHAPTER NINE

Pursued by a Bear

The next morning, as Sam climbed through the Faulkner Bookstore's back window, he was still filled with Alicia's face and words; his heart felt almost bruised by their reunion. When he crossed the hall, it took him a moment to process what he saw in the main reading room — and then he stopped dead. The place looked as if a hurricane had hit it. The curtains were thrown open, halogen lamps knocked over, and sofas turned upside down. A mountain of books lay strewn on the floor. Sam ran to the front door, which was ajar, and saw that the lock had been smashed. A burglary! Someone had broken in! It could have been anyone looking for money or valuables — Barenboim Street wasn't in the best of neighborhoods — but when it came to motive, there was only one likely suspect: the Arkeos man from the museum. But in that case . . . Sam felt a stab of fear rise from his stomach and shoot up his throat. The stone statue! What if the man was looking for the stone statue?

In a panic, he raced down to the basement, rushed across the room, lifted the heavy unicorn tapestry, and burst into the secret storeroom. He grabbed the night-light and switched it on. Whew! The stone was still there, perfectly intact. Apparently nobody had been in the secret room. But then what could the burglar have been searching for?

Sam went back upstairs, feeling puzzled. Everything had been turned upside down and carefully searched: drawers yanked open, cushions uncovered, and carpets lifted. One of the tear-gas canisters his father had bought to protect the store had rolled under a radiator. But what seemed to have interested the intruder most were the books. All the shelves were empty. Several books had their covers ripped off; some were stacked, others scattered, and most had wound up in a pile in the middle of the reading room. It was impossible to tell if any works had been stolen, and if so, how many.

Sam dropped into the only armchair still upright and stared at the disaster. What was the Arkeos man after? Information about Allan? The Book of Time? The black notebook? At that thought, Sam congratulated himself for having put both back in their hiding place, fiercely guarded by the vicious Zan. There, at least, they were safe.

The question now was what to do about all this. He'd come to the bookstore that morning planning to go into Time again to continue his quest for two more coins. If he called Grandma now, she would notify the police, which would mean he wouldn't have access to the stone statue until much later. But if Sam didn't do anything, the store would remain unlocked and unguarded, and the Arkeos man could come back again at his leisure.

He spent a moment weighing the pros and cons. Two measly little coins! That meant just a few round trips in Time, which wouldn't take more than a few hours in the present. Besides, it wasn't likely that the Arkeos man would dare to show up at the bookstore in broad daylight. If Sam was lucky, he might be able to get all seven coins by that evening. Then he could take care of the things he had to do: tell Grandma, call the police, and so on.

Once Sam made his decision, he wedged a chair against the front door and changed into his stylish "time traveler" outfit from the Chez Faulkner fashion house. Then he went down to the basement and knelt beside the stone statue. He put two coins in the cavity — the museum coin and the Delphi coin — and placed the third, the one with Arabic writing, in the center of the sun. He waited for a few moments for the faint humming to begin. But just as he put his hand on the rough, rounded top, he heard steps in the basement.

"Sam?" someone called.

He tried to lift his fingers off the stone, but a magnetic force seemed to hold them fast.

"Sammy? It's me, Lily."

Those last words were accompanied by the sound of the tapestry being lifted and the door opening.

"Sam, wait! No! The police are coming. They —"

Sam's arm was starting to burn more and more. He braced himself, straining with all his might not to be carried away, but molten fire was flowing irresistibly up his veins.

"No! You have to . . ."

He felt Lily's cool hand on his burning shoulder, but it wasn't enough. He was already being sucked into space.

Sam landed heavily, with something even heavier pressing against his back. Resisting the urge to throw up, he struggled to free himself from the burden. Then he realized that the thing in question was a body huddled against him, and it was weeping and gagging.

"Illil?" The syllables sounded garbled and unintelligible in his mouth. His cousin rolled onto her side, moaning, then turned away and vomited. In the darkness Sam could see her only as a light shape crouched on the cold, damp soil. What was Lily doing there? By what miracle had she followed him? He looked around for the stone. It was less than a yard away, topped with a skull and scraps of animal skins. A little farther on, he could see a tiny flame rising from a crude dish. Sam suspected what had happened and had a bad feeling about it.

"Ahhhrrg!"

Lily staggered to her feet. She was wearing the same kind of nightgown that Sam wore on his very first time-travel trip, to the island of Iona.

"Ilil! Ata?" he asked. That wasn't exactly what he meant to say, but it was all that came out.

She turned to him in tears. "Ammy! Ata na?" Her face was twisted by pain and overwhelming panic.

"Ilil, mon na!" said Sam, trying to calm her.

It was difficult to talk, as this language didn't seem to have all the words he wanted to say, resulting in a series of guttural grunts. And of course Lily had never experienced the strangeness of the automatic translator before. . . . He took her in his arms and hugged her tight.

"Ammy!" she wailed. "Ammy!"

When she had calmed down a little, she tugged at his sleeve and pointed forcefully at the stone statue. But Sam had no intention of leaving right away, regardless of the seriousness of their new situation. Each jump through time cost him a coin, and leaving without picking up a few extras was out of the question. Besides, if Lily was no longer in the present to help him get back, how would they make the trip home? It was best to think things over before they took any steps.

Sam pulled his cousin gently but firmly toward the crude lamp. Flickering in the slight draft, the flame made shadows on the rocky wall.

"Ngol?" asked Lily.

"Ngol," Sam agreed. It was the only word that came up to express the idea of a cave. Even so, it didn't mean "cave" exactly, but rather "shelter from the winds where we are together" — more or less.

It was then that the cave suddenly seemed to come to life before their eyes. A kind of bull or bison outlined in black floated on the stone, heaving in the shifting light; then a big horse with dots on its body, and another, smaller bison facing them. In all, there were a half-dozen animals painted on the rock wall!

"Langda!" exclaimed Sam, which apparently meant "spirit of creatures that dance on the rock."

He was both fascinated and frightened. The stone had clearly taken them on a gigantic leap into the past. Were they in prehistoric times? Their primitive language seemed to confirm it. Despite his anxiety, Sam felt strangely elated. They'd studied prehistoric art in school, and he had often daydreamed over reproductions of these very same fifteen- or twenty-thousand-year-old paintings. He carefully picked up the grease lamp and held it next to the wall. A herd of deer burst out of nowhere, as if fleeing a predator's attack. Sam and Lily had the first masterpieces of human history under their very eyes!

"Na!" said Lily, pointing at something.

Sam came closer. A nearly perfect red circle had been painted between one pair of antlers, as if the sun were rising behind the deer. Was this a rough draft of the strange U that had inspired Arkeos? *Of course not!* Sam told himself firmly. It could only be a coincidence; it was a vague resemblance at best.

He set down the dish and took Lily's hand to lead her toward what appeared to be the exit: a sloping passageway that rose about twenty yards to another large, dimly lit room.

"Mingo, Ammy, mingo!"

She was right. After making their way around various obstacles — rockfalls and stalagmites — they reached the cave entrance. It was on the edge of a rocky cliff above a river. The air was cool, the weather overcast, and the surroundings looked both wild and familiar: big trees, rushing water, stone outcroppings, and in the distance, grassy mountains. For a moment, Sam almost expected to see the long neck of a brontosaurus or the toothy jaws of a Baryonyx appear between the trees. But of course (with apologies to *The Flintstones*), tens of millions of years separated dinosaurs and prehistoric people — which was just as well!

The only path went upward, so Sam and Lily climbed the hill, stopping often to check for movement and sound: birdsong, a distant growling, a rabbit hopping through the bushes.

That's when they saw it, its powerful brown head rising above some boulders barely a hundred yards away. Nose in the wind, it was sniffing for scents — sniffing *their* scent.

"Igba! Igba!" screamed Lily.

There was no gap in the vocabulary here. It was a bear, a huge bear!

"Ngol!" Sam ordered.

They ran back the way they'd come as fast as they could, bruising their feet on the rough ground. Behind them, the bear growled so loudly that the birds fell silent or flew away. Then it took off after them with surprising agility, its growls filling the air like thunder.

"Nita, Ilil, nita!" Sam urged.

By the time they reached the cave, the bear was only twenty yards behind them. Luckily, its weight caused a rockfall and it lost its balance.

"Grrroarr!" roared the bear.

Lily and Sam rushed into the cave, still hand in hand. Sam dragged her toward what he guessed was the passage leading to the stone statue, hoping the bear would be too bulky to follow them. Bursting into the dimly lit space, he picked up the lamp and searched for a place to hide. The cave's ceiling was rough and its walls laced with cracks, but none were big enough to take shelter in. They could have tried to use the stone statue, but Sam knew from experience that it could take a full minute before it worked — much too long. And what if Lily got accidentally left behind, maybe forever? The bear roared in the distance, its growls multiplied by the echoes in the cave.

"Ammy!" Lily was pointing up at something. Flowing water had carved a kind of natural chimney at the back of the chamber. Sam ran over to it. The vertical crack was about a foot and a half wide. If he gave Lily a leg up, she could probably climb into it. And then by using his arms . . .

"Ilil! Nita!"

She put her foot on the step he made with his locked fingers. She put her other foot on his shoulder, and Sam had to lean against the rock to remain upright under her weight.

The bear was no longer growling, but in its place they could hear an ominous snuffling: It was tracking them. A rubbing noise on the rock revealed it had found the passageway and was getting close.

"Nita, Ilil!" whispered Sam, grimacing.

The burden on his shoulders lifted at the very moment that the bear burst in. It was gigantic, at least ten feet tall, with nightmare claws and evil little eyes that glittered in the darkness. It reared up on its hind legs with a growl of triumph, clawing at the wall. "Nita, Ammy," Lily whispered to him.

But Sam felt paralyzed by fear. Confident that its prey couldn't escape, the bear came a few yards closer, shambling along like a big, harmless teddy bear — except it wasn't coming for a playdate. In desperation, Sam waved his ridiculous lamp, but the bear seemed unimpressed by the tiny flame. The pathetic flicker cast a light on the stone statue adorned with the bones and animal skins; and for some inexplicable reason, the sight enraged the bear.

"*Grrouammmarrrr!*" it roared.

The bear threw its full weight at the stone, pounding it with huge paws until the rock shook. *Blam! Blam!* Chips flew into the air as the bear attacked the stone. *It was going to destroy the stone statue!*

Sam finally snapped out of his daze.

"Nounka igba," he screamed with desperate rage, trying to get its attention. "Nounka, nounka!"

The animal suddenly seemed to remember him, though that didn't improve its vicious mood. It bounded smoothly over to Sam and gave him one last look before pulling back for the blow that would rip his head off.

"Nangada igba gonka!" yelled a powerful voice behind it.

The animal spun around, and Sam had the time to glimpse a hairy man armed with a spear, who was about to heave it at the bear. Then the rocky ceiling seemed to collapse on his head and everything went black.

"Igba na katam," someone said.

Sam opened his eyes. It was almost night. He was lying on the ground with an animal skin pulled up to his chin. A bright fire was burning at the entrance to a nearby cave, with figures gathered around it. The fashion here definitely ran to hair growing out of every possible place: foreheads, ears, legs, arms . . . Chewbacca and family!

"Igba noom noom!" said the one who was speaking to the group.

The others agreed with little clicks of their tongues, and as Sam's head cleared, he made an effort to understand what they were saying. The internal translation was wordy but effective.

"I was collecting stones-with-colors to give blood and fur to the animals-that-dance-on-the rock," said the speaker. "Then the big-male-standing-up growled and growled — *igba noom noom*. It came from the cave-where-animal-spirits-hide, up the hill," he added, displaying a gift for suspense.

Under the animal skin, Sam could feel that his arms and legs were tied. He was a prisoner. Very slowly he raised himself on one elbow to see if he could find his cousin. There were about fifteen people around the fire, men and women, but none resembled Lily — or ever would, even after a head-to-toe waxing. What had happened to her? Had she also been caught or had she managed to escape? Did she think he was dead? Assuming the stone statue was still standing, had she used it to go home?

"I took the stick-that-stabs," continued the speaker, "and went to see if the magic of the drawings had breathed life into the creatures-who-dance. The great igba was there, in the Cave of Spirits. He was hitting the Mother-stone with all his strength!"

Hearing of the Mother-stone's misfortune produced angry tongue clicks. As Sam's eyes gradually adapted to the darkness, he was able to make out the bear's skin, stretched over a frame of branches a few yards away. The animal had been cut into quarters. Pieces of meat were hanging under the shelter of the cave. So that's where the stench was coming from!

"Igba had torn the skins from the Mother-stone. Igba wanted the Mother-stone to be cold, so the drawing magic would not work!"

The clan seemed to agree with this interpretation and showed its discontent by waving its fists at igba, who was in no shape to respond.

"The stick-that-stabs went deep into igba's stomach. He growled and growled — *igba noom noom*. Then the big-male-standing-up fell backward, and I saw the little-white-fur-man."

At once, all eyes turned to Sam, who barely had time to close his eyes and pretend to be asleep.

"Bring him, Sharp-teeth," ordered the speaker.

A moment later Sam felt himself being lifted and his bonds untied. He pretended to have trouble awakening, and the tongue clicks turned quizzical. Sharp-teeth carried him effortlessly over to the clan group and sat him down near the fire. The others came closer to touch him. Stinking of grease, they inspected him every which way, fiddling with his hair, pinching his skin — they were surprised at how smooth it was — parting his lips to feel his tongue, and spreading his toes, amazed that he could walk on such small feet. All this was done with exclamations of surprise and occasionally disgust. It was as scary as *The Night of the Living Dead*, and Sam had to struggle not to shudder at the stroking or the smell.

After a few moments, the speaker ended the introductions and spoke to him. "Where do you come from, little-white-fur-man?"

Sam chose to keep quiet. He was afraid that if he couldn't give a believable explanation, he might irritate these guys, all of whom were a full head taller and at least a hundred pounds heavier than he was.

"He can't talk," concluded a woman. Her extraordinarily hairy mass reminded Sam of Mrs. Pinson, his music teacher, after a major blow-dry failure.

"He can't run either," added her neighbor, pointing to Sam's feet.

"He could never hunt a long-nose with such skinny arms," said a bearded man with a scarred cheek.

84

"He isn't like us," added prehistory's version of Mrs. Pinson. "Is he a two-legged screamer that has lost its fur?"

"Two-legged screamers have long tails," the speaker objected, "and they don't often come close to the shelters-from-the-wind. The little-white-fur-man was in the Cave of Spirits when igba fell on him."

So that was it, thought Sam. He'd been knocked out by the weight of the falling bear!

An old man who hadn't spoken until then stood up and leaned on a crudely carved staff.

"The clan must be careful," he croaked. "Remember the words of He-who-comes-from-far! All those not of the clan who approach the Mother-stone must be killed! All of them!" He took two steps toward Sam and waved his staff under his nose. "They must be killed or the hunt will be bad, the streams will dry up, and the clan will have nothing to eat! That is what He-who-comes-from-far said. That is what the clan must do!"

Sam couldn't decide which was the most frightening: the old man's ruined, scarred eye socket, the stench of his breath, or the decoration on top of his stick — a black bone shaped like a pair of horns with a round shell stuck between them. It was exactly like the strange U on the picture of the deer in the cave — the Arkeos symbol!

The speaker objected, saying, "Come, Death-eye, I was only a child when He-who-comes-from-far visited our clan. He never came back, and many of our fathers said he was dangerous."

"Yes, he was dangerous, but he had power," yelled the old man. "He could kill Sharp-teeth with a single glance, and the entire clan along with him! That is why we must obey him and kill all those who approach the Mother-stone. Or else he will return and kill us!"

Just as Sam started thinking it might be time for him to say something, a high-pitched scream rang out: "ANIANIIIII!" The livelier ones seized their spears, but Death-eye grabbed Sam by the neck to keep him from moving.

"IGBA ANIANIIIII!"

"There, above the cave!" said the prehistoric Pinson, pointing.

"The child-of-the-bear!" screamed the voice. "Release the child-of-the-bear!"

A horned demon had suddenly appeared a few yards above the flames, standing on top of the mouth of the cave, one foot extended into empty space. It had a bleached bear skull for a head, scraps of fur for its skin, and blood running down its arms. The orange glow from the fire combined with the pale moonlight to give the hideous creature an unearthly aura. The brave hunter aimed his spear, but the speaker stopped him as the demon screamed again: "Lightning and fire on the clan if you don't give up the child-of-the-bear!"

The frightened members of the tribe backed away, a few of them covering their ears or eyes. Even the hunter no longer seemed quite so eager to confront the horrible sight. Sam, however, welcomed the intrusion. Decked out in the skull and animal skins that covered the Mother-stone, Lily had come to rescue him!

"Let him go, Death-eye!" the speaker ordered.

The man did so regretfully, and Sam raced up to the cave mouth.

Lily went on threatening the frightened group huddled at her feet. "Lightning and fire on whoever dares disturb the spirit of the big-male-standing-up!" she intoned.

The warning must have hit home, because she and Sam took off running without anyone making a move to follow.

"Hurry!" urged Lily, pointing Sam up the hill.

Without turning around they ran to the spirit cave several hundred yards away and into its murky depths. It was only when they reached the stone statue that his cousin took off the furs and skull and carefully placed them next to the lamp. Her red-spattered gown looked as if it had been dipped in the bear's blood. She took one of the two coins from the cavity and thrust it at him.

"Quick, Sammy!"

Though reluctant to use up one of his five coins, Sam realized they didn't have any choice. As he slapped the ram's head on the sun, he observed the great claw marks and fragments left by the bear. The animal had clearly tried to destroy the stone statue, but why?

When Sam judged the humming was strong enough, he gripped his cousin by the waist and held her as tightly as he could. Only then did he put his hand on the stone's rounded top.

CHAPTER TEN

Slaves!

With a loud thump, the two of them rolled against something hard. Lily remained hunched over with nausea for a moment while Sam tried to orient himself. They were in a dark, low-ceilinged room with wooden machinery of some sort on the left and a rectangular porthole set in the wall. Sam stood up and put his eye to the scratched, blurry glass. The next room contained a huge vat of water and a waterwheel, which wasn't turning at the moment. In their room, some mallets and tongs lay on the ground a little distance away, along with an oil lamp of a model distinctly more evolved than the one in the spirit cave. The stone statue stood against the opposite wall, but covered with such a thick layer of saltpeter that the carved sun was barely visible. Dampness oozed down the walls, and everything felt wet.

Sam retrieved the museum coin from the stone's cavity and bent over his cousin.

"Are you okay, Lily?"

"The skull," she muttered, wiping her mouth.

"It's over. We did it!"

"Did what?"

"We escaped."

"Have you taken up Latin, Sammy?"

"What?"

"You're speaking Latin — and so am I."

"Oh!"

"Terrific, this instant translation thing," she added with a weak smile. "If only I had it with my teacher . . ."

She fell silent and listened. Muffled voices could be heard from the underground area stretching off into the darkness, voices that seemed to be coming closer.

"There's something I have to tell you, Sam. It's about our present."

"I'm listening."

"The police are looking for you."

"The police?"

"Yes, because of the burglary at the Sainte-Mary Museum. They found your cell phone in the room where the theft happened."

His cell! He'd completely forgotten about it!

"They checked the numbers and showed up at Grandma's around noon. You'd already left, and they said they were going to Barenboim Street to find you. Mom and I had just come back from the water park and I rushed over to warn you. But when I tried to catch you —" She looked around at the ancient machinery.

"When they find out the bookstore has been robbed too, there's going to be fireworks," Sam said.

"So that's why all those books were on the floor!"

"It was probably the Arkeos man — the guy with the tattoo," Sam explained. "I think he's looking for something, the black notebook, maybe, or the Book of Time. On the Internet I found this company called Arkeos that sells antiquities —"

"Shhh!" hissed Lily. "They're coming!"

The conversation from the underground was becoming clearer.

"It's the oldest part of the complex, Corvus. We really ought to think about closing it. The leaks are getting worse and —"

"What are you talking about?" thundered a second voice. "It's the middle of summer, and we're swamped with customers! I need all of our facilities at full power! I want you to fix it, and fast!"

"They're nearly here," whispered Lily. "What should we do?"

Sam had her stand up and brush herself off. A yellowish glow appeared in the underground hallway, getting ever brighter.

"I'm not going to let some little leak keep me from opening, Julius. And I don't pay you to tell me that you can't set things right. What do I . . ."

The two men entered the machinery room. Seeing Sam and Lily, they stopped dead.

"What are you doing here?" screamed the one who was holding the lamp, a chubby bald man wearing a toga.

"We got lost —" Sam began.

"Since when do slaves have the right to wander around underground? And where's your uniform?"

"Er . . . I forgot it," Sam said.

90

"What you mean, you forgot it?" He raised the stick in his right hand and gave Sam a sharp crack on the legs. "The baths are about to open and you aren't at your stations? What are your names?"

Lily was quicker than her cousin. "Samus and Lilia," she answered.

"That doesn't ring a bell," said the bald man, waving his stick. "Did Petrus buy you for the end of the season?"

"Yes, it was Petrus," she said coolly.

"Well, I hope you didn't cost me too much, you filthy little lazybones. One really can't find a slave worthy of the name anymore! All right, Julius, I'll give you half an hour to get the waterwheel working again. As for you two —" He gave Sam another blow with the stick. "Go to your work, and hop to it!"

Still spewing abuse, Corvus marched them through the underground passage to a stone stairway leading to the open air.

"My God," whispered Lily as they emerged.

They were in a huge rectangular quad bordered by columned galleries and stone buildings. Trimmed green grass grew in the open central area. In the distance, a mountain with a few planted fields on its lower slopes loomed above the rooftops. The sun wasn't high yet, but it was already pleasantly warm. Servants in simple tunics bustled about, their arms loaded with towels, fruit, and amphoras. Corvus directed Sam and Lily to a room on the right.

"Hustle over to the laundry to change, then go to your stations right away. Petrus should be here any minute. Until then, I'll have my eye on you, believe me!"

He waved the stick over his head for emphasis, and they had no choice but to obey.

"What you think we should do?" asked Lily quietly as they walked toward the laundry.

"We've absolutely got to find some coins," answered Sam, also quietly. "The stone statue works, so that means there's at least one coin somewhere nearby. Where do you think we are?"

"At a Roman bath. They're like public swimming pools, and they were all over the Roman Empire. People would go there to get clean and do business."

A cheerful-looking matron greeted them with a broad smile. "So, children, are you new here?"

"Yes, ma'am," said Sam. "Petrus just bought us."

"So much the better, we're shorthanded these days. You'll be needing something clean to wear, I suppose?"

She took two tunics from the piles lining the walls and held them out to the children.

"These should fit you all right. But you'd better hurry, we'll be opening soon. Were you told what you were supposed to do?"

"Not yet."

"Ah! And of course that lazy slug Petrus isn't here yet!" To Lily, she said, "Go to the women's changing room at the end of the palaestra and ask for Alvina." To Sam: "As for you, the men's locker room is right next door. Old Trimalchion will fill you in."

They came out wearing their new uniforms, wondering what their next move should be.

"Suppose we left right away?" suggested Lily.

"No, we *have* to get more coins! Besides, the guy fixing the waterwheel must still be down there with the stone. Let's wait until he —"

Just then, a sharp crack echoed off the portico's marble panels. "By Jupiter!" screamed Corvus, rapping on the ground. "Are you still dillydallying around here? *Get to work!*"

If Sam had been asked what he planned to be when he grew up — two thousand years earlier, in this case — he would have answered unhesitatingly, "Anything except a slave in the Roman baths!" At first glance, it looked like a job that anybody could do, but it turned out to be exhausting in practice. Trimalchion, an old black slave with two missing fingers, explained the basics of the work, and Sam was quite literally tossed into the bathwater.

He was first assigned to the locker room, where the many clients came to change. He took their clothes, put them in lockers, and gave back towels in exchange — an easy job. But when Corvus passed by, he decided that a strapping young fellow like Sam should be employed doing something more energetic. So Corvus sent him to the caldarium, or hot room, a kind of early sauna. Sam's job was to keep the very hot pool of water clean by scrubbing it with a rough mop. As he scoured the basin, Sam realized that the mosaic on the bottom showed a beautiful white lyre held by a half-naked couple. There was nothing astonishing about that, *except that the instrument was shaped like two horns containing a circle!* Here was the Arkeos symbol at the bottom of a pool in the Roman Empire!

Shaken by his discovery, Sam put down his mop and went to question Trimalchion.

"Excuse me, but do you know who designed the mosaic in the pool?"

"You mean the man and the woman with the lyre? It was redone a few years ago by a local man named Octavius. Why? Is there a broken tile?"

"No, I just think it's beautiful. Are there any others like it in the baths?"

Trimalchion thought for a moment. "Mosaics like that, no. It must be the only one. Now that I think of it, I think the idea actually came from one of Octavius's workers — a peculiar fellow who just disappeared one day without collecting his pay. But the design was already laid out and the master of the baths seemed to like it, so . . . That kind of lyre is supposed to bring happiness and prosperity — not that I'd know anything about that!" Then he added quietly: "You better get back to work. Here comes Corvus."

Realizing that Sam had abandoned his post, Corvus first threatened him with his stick, then as punishment gave him a job that Sam couldn't have imagined in his worst nightmares. For half an hour he walked around the palaestra carrying a pot, and men relieved themselves into it between wrestling or bowling matches. Sam then had to dump the urine into a large vat off to one side, where laundry workers used its contents to wash clothes. Washing clothes in urine — frankly, it was enough to make you puke.

Sam had become a traveling toilet.

After a while the temptation to explore became too strong, and he sneaked off to the stairway that led underground. The wooden wheel was turning again and squeaking like an old door, drawing water up from the vat and filling a tank that in turn supplied the baths. The fact that the wheel was turning must mean that the worker responsible for fixing it had finished his job.

But when Sam reached the bottom of the staircase, he made a painful discovery: A locked and rusty gate barred the way underground. He couldn't get to the stone statue!

"You again!" screamed Corvus when he saw Sam emerge. "What are you doing, snooping around down there?"

This time, he hit Sam twice across the back and sent him directly to the furnace room on the lower level, reputedly the worst place in the baths. There Sam met two gigantic black slaves, their skin gleaming with sweat, who were heaving logs onto big fires. Above the fires, huge cauldrons filled with boiling water produced the steam that heated the caldarium, carried there by a system of ducts. The furnace room itself was as hot as seven devils.

"Work him until he drops!" Corvus instructed the two slaves. "This boy needs to learn who his master is!"

The two men stepped aside for a moment to let Sam pick up his first log, but as soon as Corvus's back was turned, they took it out of his hands.

"The old crow doesn't know what he's thinking anymore," sighed one, mopping his brow. "You won't last long in this inferno. Go sit over there instead."

Delighted by his good luck, Sam was about to sit on a twisted stool when the ground suddenly began to shake underfoot. Without quite knowing how it happened, he found himself sprawled on his back.

The two slaves burst out laughing. "Hah! You didn't expect that, did you, boy? Sometimes the earth gets angry around here. You have to know how to stay on your feet!"

But at the very next moment, an even stronger tremor sent them crashing into each other. White dust poured down from the ceiling and several burning logs rolled out of the fire. Water sloshed furiously against the edges of the huge vat.

"Well, that was something!" said the taller of the two as he straightened up. "That time, it really moved!"

"If it happens again, maybe we better put the furnace out to avoid a fire," remarked the other one. "When this kind of thing starts . . ."

They checked for damage to the furnace, then went up to get their orders from Corvus. Sam followed. At the bathers' level, people seemed alarmed. Towels wrapped around their waists, they were pouring out of the buildings to see what was happening. Statues had toppled over and a few tiles had fallen from the roofs, but the matter of greatest concern was a very deep, dull rumbling. A few dozen customers had gathered in the middle of the palaestra to point at something in the distance: a wisp of black smoke rising from the top of the mountain.

Sam was startled when a cool hand slipped into his. It was Lily, whom he hadn't heard coming.

"Sam! I've been looking for you for the last quarter of an hour, and I've got bad news. Do you know the name of that mountain?

"No."

"It's Vesuvius, the volcano! We're in Pompeii, Sammy — Pompeii!"

CHAPTER ELEVEN

August 4, 79 A.D., Ten A.M.

"It's on fire!" a woman screamed. "The mountain's on fire!" Bathers and slaves gathered around her, looking frightened.

Corvus tried to reassure them. "No, no, that's just a big dark cloud on the mountaintop. Come back to the baths, Citizen Flavia, there's nothing to fear."

"Nothing to fear?" asked a man who had been playing ball in the palaestra. "This tile nearly knocked me out!" He brandished the tile as if Corvus himself had thrown it.

"We know there have been tremors these last few days, Marius, but they're not dangerous. Our establishment is well designed and —"

"What about the earthquake seventeen years ago?" snapped another man. "Wasn't that dangerous? Half the city was destroyed, and the Stabian Baths were badly damaged, as I recall."

At those words, large beads of sweat appeared on Corvus's bald head.

"That was different," he said, sounding embarrassed. "We've reinforced the walls since then, and strengthened the pools."

He switched to a falsely playful tone. "Come, my friends. A cup of our best wine to the first people who go back to the caldarium — on the house!" To the slaves, he snapped: "And you, get back to work and take care of our guests!"

A murmur of uncertainty went through the customers. The sun was getting hot and the sky was a limpid blue; it looked like the start of a beautiful day. There was that unusual smoke, of course, but how could a catastrophe ever happen in such fine weather?

Then Lily ran to the center of the group. "If you don't leave town right away," she said firmly, "you're all going to die!"

Fast as a striking snake, Corvus gave her a resounding slap. It sent Lily tumbling to the feet of the woman called Flavia. "You filthy little liar!" he screamed. "I promise, you're going to —"

But the threat was quickly drowned out by an enormous explosion: *GGRRRBBBRRRAAAOUMMMM!* With unimaginable power, the top of Mount Vesuvius blew off, shooting gigantic chunks of rock into the air. There was a moment of astonishment as they watched extraordinary whistling fireballs cut across the sky and land in the distance.

"The mountain is spilling its guts!"

"The girl's right, we're all going to die!"

"Wait, friends! Vesuvius is far away! Enjoy the spectacle," Corvus urged them. "You can return to the baths afterward."

But most of the visitors were in no mood for relaxation.

"Open the locker rooms, Corvus! We want our clothes!"

"Yes, our clothes!" chorused several voices.

"In that case . . ." he said with resignation. Corvus gave the key ring to old Trimalchion, whom most of the bathers followed to retrieve their things.

One of the slaves who had been stoking the furnace spoke up. "Corvus, if the earth continues to rage, you should let us go to our families."

"What?" shouted the master of the baths, his scalp turning purple. "Since when do slaves decide what they should or shouldn't do?"

"If we stay here, we will all die!" Lily repeated. "Pompeii will be buried in ash!"

"As for you," screamed Corvus, "if you say another word, I'll knock your head off with this stick. Ashes? That's nonsense! Vesuvius is not a fire mountain, everyone knows that! I want all you slaves back to your jobs immediately. Nobody leaves the establishment before nightfall!"

The furnace stoker spoke up again, louder this time. "Corvus, this girl may be right. The ground is shaking and the mountain is on fire. You have to let us leave! Remember what happened to my daughter!"

Corvus's stick hissed through the air and hit the stoker's cheek with a terrible crack. It opened a crimson cut that began to bleed.

"Xenon, Flactus, Trilcien!" Corvus called. "Take Diomedes and lock him up in the warm room, the one with the deadbolt. There are ten sestertia in it for you! And while you're at it, take care of this bird of ill omen!" He caught Lily by the elbow and shoved her into the arms of a huge man with thinning red hair. Sam ran to intervene but was soon seized in turn, as the promise of sestertia energized the other servants.

"Lock the boy up too! That one's done nothing but get on my nerves all morning!"

"It's hailing!" said the laundress in wonder. "Imagine, hail out of a clear blue sky!"

As Sam struggled to free himself from the powerful hands of the tall, thin man restraining him, he felt something bounce off his neck.

"That isn't hail, those are stones!" someone called.

Stones were falling in volleys — some large, some small, but most about the size of an egg. They were rough, irregular, and gray, but curiously quite light.

"Look, it's the mountain! It's spewing stones!"

Indeed, a dark plume had formed over Vesuvius that grew thicker as it drifted toward the city.

"Xenon, lock those three up," ordered Corvus. "And you others, start picking up the stones. I want the palaestra to be clean as a whistle when this is over."

Diomedes, Sam, and Lily were hustled to the women's baths and thrown into the tepidarium, the warm room. The stones pelting the roof made a deafening racket, but the sound didn't keep Diomedes from yelling as he threw himself against the door: "Corvus, damn you! I have to find my wife and daughter! They need me! If anything happens to them . . ."

Lily took Sam aside. "Those stones falling from the sky are pumice, Sam! We saw a documentary about it at school — it's a sign that the eruption has really started. In a few hours, the town will be completely buried in ash!"

"A few hours — are you sure?"

"Maybe less, I don't know. What I do know is that a lot of people died in Pompeii — men, women, children, everyone.

This burning cloud came out of the mountain, and they were all mummified by the ash. People were found centuries later in the exact position they were in at the moment they died!"

"You have any other good news?"

"We have to get out of here, Sammy, and fast!"

Sam quickly scanned the interior of the warm room. It had some high windows, but he couldn't reach them, even standing on Diomedes's shoulders. Nor was there much else of use: amphoras of oil, scrapers for bathers' skin, two discarded towels, a poker to stir the fire, and a few oil lamps burning by the pool. Colored frescoes illustrating the pleasures of the baths decorated the walls, but there was no emergency exit to be seen.

"A plague on that Corvus," raged Diomedes, turning toward them. "May his teeth fall out into his mouth and choke him! My daughter is too weak to walk, and my wife will never be able to carry her. And it's all his fault!"

"Did he hurt your daughter?" asked Lily.

"He made her go up on a balcony to hang flowers, and she fell. She was much too young for the job! Since then, her legs won't hold her anymore. And if what you say is true, if the mountain is spitting fire . . ." He took Lily's hands in his and squatted down to her level. "You're almost the same age as my daughter, yet you seem so sure of yourself! Do you really think we're going to die?"

"Well, there's always hope, isn't there?" Lily murmured, gently freeing herself. "But Vesuvius seems to have come to life, and —"

A brutal tremor rocked the walls then, and the floor heaved. The three prisoners staggered for a moment as the building groaned. A frightening creaking could be heard outside, as if the structure next door had fallen.

"What was that?" asked Lily.

"It came from the south corner," said Diomedes. "I hope the big water tower didn't collapse."

"Is there a way to get out of here?" Sam asked insistently.

"Besides this door, no. Unless . . ." The furnace stoker stepped back a few feet and pointed at the floor. "Look, the tiles cracked. With a little bit of luck . . . Bring me that poker, quick!"

Sam ran to get the iron rod near the fire. "You have an idea?"

"If we're able to widen this crack . . ."

He broke a few more tiles, then began enlarging the crack with the point of the poker. Outside, the shower of pumice stones fell heavier than ever. The light was fading, as if night were coming on.

"Grab the scrapers," said Diomedes, "and help me!"

Sam and Lily went to work with a will, scratching at the grainy cement that formed the room's foundation.

"Are you planning to dig a tunnel out?" asked Sam after a quarter hour of silent effort.

"You're close! The tepidarium and caldarium are raised above ground level. They rest on little columns, and hot air from the furnace circulates between them. That's how the rooms are kept at the right temperature. If we can get into the space between those columns . . . There! We've reached the brick layer. We're almost through!"

He made them stand back, gave a couple of mighty whacks with the poker, and broke through the final layer. Warm steam that smelled of dirt rose through the opening and made them cough.

"Isn't it dangerous down there?"

"The fire in the furnace is out. You two won't be in much danger."

"We two?"

"Yes, you. You're thin, and you should be able to squeeze through. I'm too big, and I'd get stuck. Come on, the hole isn't nearly big enough. Let's get to work!"

It took them another ten minutes to widen the crack enough for Sam and Lily to have a chance of squeezing into it.

"I'll give you a lamp," said Diomedes. "Get down there now! Hurry!"

"What about you, Diomedes?" Lily protested. "What's going to happen to you?"

"Don't worry about me. They're sure to let me out sooner or later." He tried to smile, but Lily and Sam weren't fooled. Corvus had no intention of freeing him.

"Get going!" he encouraged them. "If you follow the wall on the left toward the door, you'll reach a cleaning hatch. It has a wooden cover over it — a good kick should do the trick. And if . . . if you happen to meet my wife and my daughter, tell them I love them."

"I'm . . . I'm sure they love you too," stammered Sam, touched by his sacrifice.

After a final good-bye, Sam stretched out next to the hole, slid his arms, head, and chest into it, and almost immediately felt hard earth under his fingernails. If he kept his head low, he could just move ahead on his elbows and knees.

"Samus, the lamp!" Diomedes handed the oil lamp down

into the hole. Sam nearly knocked it over when he reached for it.

"Your turn, girl! Don't be afraid, it won't take long. Just follow the left-hand wall!"

Sam squeezed down as best he could to make room for Lily. They ignored the shards of brick and cement tearing at their skin as they slowly inched forward.

"You okay?" whispered Sam.

"Yeah, except for the heat and the dark," said Lily.

"It's like a snail race inside a radiator!"

After a laborious progression, they finally spotted the little cleaning hatch. Sam turned his body around — bruising both his shoulder and his hip in the process — so his feet rested against the hatch cover. Hunching down even farther to get momentum, he kicked at it with his heels. Something on the other side yielded and the hatch swung open with a bang.

"Good job, Sam!"

He let his cousin have the honor of getting out first, then she helped him up.

"Whew! Feels a lot better here!"

"Where are we?"

"I don't know," said Sam, lifting his lamp. "But this hallway must lead somewhere."

They stumbled on a door to a narrow staircase that led outside.

"Look at that stuff falling! It's incredible!"

A veritable rain of gray stones was falling on the baths, making a dense layer some four to six inches thick on the ground. The dark plume from Vesuvius now covered the city, so it looked like the middle of winter. Rumbling and occasional flashes of glowing orange light came from the volcano. The sound of shouts reached Sam and Lily from the distance, including Corvus's dulcet tones: "Faster! Lazy bunch of . . ."

"The trick is not to be spotted," muttered Sam. "Hide your face if you can!"

At the top of the stairs they stepped out into the palaestra near the portico. There wasn't much chance of Corvus noticing them; he was busy at the other end of the field, yelling at his men to clean the outdoor swimming pool. In the half-light, it wouldn't be hard to get to the stone statue. And maybe even . . .

"Wait, this way!" said Sam as he grabbed Lily and dragged her back toward the women's baths.

"What are you —"

"Diomedes!"

They crossed the empty vestibule and ran toward the tepi-darium, whose door now rang with the slave's pounding.

"Let me out! *Let me out!*"

"Diomedes, we're here!"

"Samus, you did it!"

Sam shoved at the door with all his might, but it barely budged: The hinges and bolt were too strong. He took three steps back and launched himself against it even harder, but the only resulting crack came from his shoulder.

"Sammy, stop!"

Lily was pointing at something on the opposite wall: a key hanging from a large nail. Here was the history of the world, summed up in the blink of an eye: Men use their muscles, women use their brains!

Sam grabbed the key and turned it in the lock. Soon they were all hugging each other.

"Thank you, children, thank you! As soon as I get my wife and my daughter, I'll take you to safety!"

"That's impossible. We have to get something over by the old waterwheel. We'll join you later."

"The old waterwheel? I wouldn't go there if I were you. That's the weakest part of the complex, and with all these tremors . . ."

"We know what we have to do," said Lily. "Go on, and don't bother about us. Your wife and your daughter must be very worried."

Diomedes seemed about to object, but chose instead to hug them one last time. "Thank you again. And good luck!"

They parted under the portico, and Sam handed Lily one of the towels he had picked up in the tepidarium. "Put this on your head, it'll protect you from the stones."

They hugged the walls, praying that some huge block of pumice wouldn't come crashing down and flatten them. The palaestra now looked like a pebble beach. Over by the pool, Corvus was still barking at his servants, but their ranks had thinned considerably. The air smelled unpleasantly of something like natural gas or chemicals, and Lily began to cough.

"Sulfur," she spat. "We have to hurry!"

"It isn't very far now!"

But an unpleasant surprise awaited them. The building in whose cellar they'd appeared that morning was now half collapsed, with the great wooden wheel partly buried, sunk in bricks and debris. Water had flooded everything, including the stairway leading underground. The place looked as if a paddle wheel steamboat had smashed into the north wing of the baths.

"The water tank must have burst," Sam groaned.

He got as close as he could to the rubble, a soupy mass of debris and pumice. The stone statue was somewhere down below all that, ten or twelve feet under water.

"We don't have any choice," he said. "I'm going down."

He walked over to a beam that was still upright, held on to the buckets of the wheel, and slowly let himself sink.

"Be careful," said Lily. "It doesn't look very sturdy."

Taking a deep breath, Sam lowered himself into the cold, dark water until he reached the debris covering the bottom. He groped his way toward where he thought the stone should be, but soon ran into a tangle of planks. He was able to move only a couple aside before he had to go back up for air. It took several round-trips before Sam was able to reach the stone statue itself, and when he touched it, his heart sank: The top of the stone was broken off and jagged, probably shattered by a falling beam.

"Well?" asked Lily when he surfaced again.

She had taken shelter behind what was left of the overhang, and was using one hand to filter the increasingly noxious vapors. The rain of pumice stones had eased, but the smoke plume now displayed worrisome purple streaks.

"The stone's damaged, Lily. The whole top is gone."

"The whole top? The sun too?"

"No, the sun's intact, except maybe for a ray or two."

"Do you think it'll still work?"

"It *has* to work! Hurry!"

As his cousin joined him in the water, Sam took the museum coin from the corner of his pocket. Would the stone really work underwater, especially with part of it gone? Sam didn't have the slightest idea, but he didn't intend to end up mummified in Pompeii, a morbid attraction for twenty-first-century tourists.

"Hold my hand and don't let go. It's not very deep. You just have to take a big breath. Ready?"

Lily filled her lungs and nodded. Sam put the coin in his mouth. Together they dove and reached the bottom without difficulty. But once they had gone under the wheel, the water began to bubble furiously, and the planks that Sam had shoved aside began to tumble onto them. The earth was shaking again, and now their retreat was cut off!

In the dark, with the water churning all around, Lily started to panic. Sam had to grab her as he fumbled along the wall for the stone statue. When his fingers found its jagged top, he located the sun and clapped the coin onto it. Lily was now struggling to get free — a small, frightened animal desperate for light and air. But that wasn't an option anymore.

Sam tightened his grip on her and put his hand on the rough stone surface. He was beginning to run out of breath too, especially because Lily was kicking him in the stomach, but he had to hold on. After what seemed like forever — yellow butterflies were starting to dance in front of his eyes — something under his hand finally began to stir. Was it the stone or a last, deadly tremor?

CHAPTER TWELVE

Bulldozer

The whole world was shaking and full of incredible noise: *Ka-blam! Ka-blam!* Sam staggered to his feet, spitting out the dust that filled his mouth. Instead of water, he and Lily were submerged in a cloud of flying dirt that was only slightly easier to breathe.

"Lily?"

Sam's eyes stung, and he was having trouble keeping them open. It was almost completely dark, anyway.

"Lily?"

Ka-blam! Ka-blam! Were they still in Pompeii? Had they fallen into an air pocket somewhere while ashes blanketed the city above them?

"Here, Sammy," answered a faint, choked voice. "I'm over here."

"You're speaking English, Lily. Maybe —"

Ka-blam! Ka-blam!

"Are we in our basement?" Lily asked as she groped her way over to him. "What's going on?"

"I don't know, everything's shaking. Let's try and get out of here."

They heard something like the roar of an engine, and a section of ceiling came crashing down a few yards away.

"Excava —" Lily began.

Light streamed down through the opening, revealing iron steps leading upward on their left. The stairs ended a few feet from the ground. Sam lifted his cousin so she could climb out before the rest of the ceiling collapsed. *Rrrrmmm! Ka-blam! Ka-blam!*

Once upstairs, they hurried through a darkened room and emerged blinking in the open air. Around them were sections of ruined wall, a dangling broken window frame, smashed tiles, and —

"Look out!"

A mass of gleaming blue metal hurtled toward them. *Rrrrmmmm! Ka-blam! Ka-blam!* They threw themselves to one side as the blue monster jerked to a stop a yard away. It was a Caterpillar tractor with a huge metal blade in front.

"Good God almighty!" A man in a cap with a cigarette wedged in the corner of his mouth leaped down from the cab. "Good lord, kids! Where the heck do you think you are? This is a construction site! I could've crushed you!"

A couple of workers ran over to see what was happening.

"What's up, Ron?" shouted one. "Did you hit something?"

"It's these two kids, Jed. They just popped up in front of me. It was a near thing, I swear!"

Lily straightened up, brushed off her filthy, bloodstained tunic, and fixed her hair, as if she'd just stepped out of the bathroom. The man called Jed looked at the intruders with annoyance.

"This place is off-limits!" he shouted. "Didn't you see the signs? You're gonna get fined for this!"

Sam looked around. They were in an empty lot surrounded by fences and barbed wire. Old-fashioned earth-moving machines stood amid demolished houses and huge mounds of rubble. Beyond them rose dilapidated gray buildings, not the familiar hills of Sainte-Mary. They obviously weren't back on Barenboim Street! Yet there was a stone statue in the basement of the house, and these construction workers were about to destroy it.

"This belongs to us," said Sam angrily. "You don't have the right to tear it down!"

"We have every right, kid," answered Jed. "City permits and everything. If you lived here and your parents had to get out, that's not my fault. This is the Depression! So fork over the five-dollar fine or I'm handing you to the cops."

Five dollars, thought Sam, *but what kind of dollars? Canadian dollars, American dollars, Australian dollars?*

The bulldozer operator spoke up. "Don't be too hard on 'em, Jed. They're just kids. And you see what kind of shape they're in?"

"Listen, Ron, if hoboes start campin' in the work site, *we'll* be the ones that get fired, believe you me. That what you want?"

"Yeah, but we've got kids, right? What if it was them coming out of that hole?"

Jed shrugged. He didn't seem like a bad guy, just a foreman anxious to finish a job on time and avoid trouble. "Okay,

Ron, but get them the heck out of here. We've wasted enough time."

"You can't tear down that house!" protested Sam. "It's very valuable! There's something unique inside and . . ."

Ron grabbed Sam by the arm and yanked him close. "You listen to what we just told you, or you'll be hauled in for vagrancy on top of the fine. Your house is busted, can't ya see? Go try your luck somewheres else. You got your whole life ahead of you!"

Sam tried to resist, but the workmen were now in a hurry. They collared the children, frog-marched them to the exit, and sent them on their way. Jed kicked Sam in the rear for good measure.

"And if I catch you hangin' around here, I'm callin' the cops!"

Sam and Lily pretended to leave, but then they circled back to the fence, trying to find a way over it. Through a crack between two boards, they watched the bulldozer finish knocking down the remaining walls of the house, burying the stone under tons of debris.

"How are we ever going to get home?" asked Lily.

"I don't know," said Sam, a lump in his throat. "There must be some way." He swallowed. "It's not like we have any coins left anyway."

That realization made him feel worse than ever. Not only had he brought Lily with him into Time and nearly gotten her killed in three different eras, he now had no means of getting her home. They sat down on the ground, their backs against the fence, and he put his arm around his cousin. When he did, he realized that she was trembling despite the warm weather.

"Aren't you feeling well, Lily?" He rubbed her back and tickled her to cheer her up, but all he got was a weak smile.

"I'm scared, Sam."

He couldn't show her his own fear. "We'll pull through, Lily. We've always pulled through, haven't we? Look at the cave — the skull-and-furs trick was pure genius! And you were wonderful in Pompeii too, holding out underwater. You're a great time traveler and we're a terrific team, so we can't get discouraged now, okay? We'll find a way to get back home, I promise. First we've got to find some decent clothes. Then we'll wait for night and come back here, in case some piece of the statue survived. All right?"

Lily mumbled a vague yes, and Sam helped his cousin to her feet and looked around. On the left, there were one-story houses with neat grass pathways running between them; to the right, a row of shacks knocked together from scraps of wood and tin, with a dirt road on either side. There were other neighborhoods visible beyond that, and even a few skyscrapers in the distance. The city was very spread out and looked modern and unfinished at the same time. It wasn't a present-day city, but it wasn't the Wild West either. "The Depression," Jed had said, and that meant they were some time in the 1930s. Sam made up his mind when he saw laundry hanging on clotheslines behind the shanties on the right.

"What would you say to a nice new outfit, cousin? My treat."

They took the path farthest from the shacks, praying that people would be too busy to notice them. They saw three black children playing with a cat in one of the yards, but luckily they had their backs turned. About a hundred yards farther they came to what they were after: a large family's wash, with an array of mended shirts and shorts dangling from the clotheslines.

"I know what you're thinking," Sam whispered to Lily. "It isn't really a store, and we aren't going to pay for the clothes. But we don't have a choice!"

He jumped the low wooden fence and in two steps reached a shabby pair of blue canvas pants — an early version of blue jeans. Sam was usually pretty particular about his jeans; they had to be frayed to just the right degree, wide enough for comfort, and preferably with a low waist, so his underwear showed. But he didn't have a fashion show on his calendar that day, so he plucked off the clothespins and took the pants. He also grabbed a T-shirt that would suit his cousin, provided she liked her shirts very brown and very old. Then he noticed a shirt in his own size and stealthily moved to the end of the clothesline. But the white sheets and pillowcases lined up in front of him suddenly started to move.

"Who's that messing with my laundry?" A corner of a sheet lifted to reveal the face of an old black woman, who looked appalled. "Land sakes, you're robbing me, boy! Matthew! Come to the yard, quick! A little white boy is stealing your shirt!"

Sam leaped back and jumped over the fence without even realizing he'd done so.

"Matthew!" the woman called again. Sam grabbed his cousin by the arm and they took off running. "Matthew, your shirt's running away! You don't expect me to chase after it at my age, do you?"

"Thieves!" shouted another voice. "Thieves at Mama Lucy's!"

Several neighbors appeared at the window, and suddenly the yards were full of people. Two men rushed into the road to block their way, and children ran to catch up with them from behind.

"Thieves! They're robbing Mama Lucy!"

"All right, all right!" said Sam, stopping in his tracks. "We made a mistake. We're giving everything back!"

He waved the clothes as a sign of surrender, but that didn't keep a dozen people from surrounding him, yelling.

"They're the thieves from Mama Lucy's!"

"Let's call the police!"

"Nah, we'll take care of this ourselves! No mercy for thieves!"

"Besides, they ain't from around here!"

A sharp slap came from somewhere off to Sam's right, and his ear stung.

"Yeah! No need for police!"

Someone else punched Sam in the shoulder, and he turned to face his attacker. But then he saw the old woman from the clothesline, trotting toward the group and waving her arms.

"Have you gone crazy?" she yelled. "Leave them alone!"

"They're the ones, Mama Lucy. They stole your stuff!"

"Yeah, we'll show them!"

"You let that child go this instant, Bartholomew Jones," she said. "If your poor mother could see you now!"

The man who had grabbed Sam's wrist let it go and hung his head.

"Is this what they teach you in church on Sunday, boy?" she thundered. "Not to have compassion for the poorest among us?"

"They's in our neighborhood," protested Bartholomew. "If we ain't respected on our own ground . . ."

"Bartholomew Jones, you are some kind of fool! Remind me to box your ears next time I meet you! Have you seen their clothes? You really think they come from some fancy neighborhood for the pleasure of struttin' your rags?"

The man shrugged sheepishly.

"You two come along now," she told Sam and Lily. "I'll see what I can do for you."

The crowd parted, and Mama Lucy led the children to her house with the authority of a victorious general. Once there, she slammed her door in the face of any gawkers.

"You have to forgive them," she said. "Despair and misery makes them nasty! Everyone's out of work, especially here in the colored neighborhood. The kids are hungry, the parents don't know what to do. Lordy! But I don't need to tell you that, do I? You're so pale and skinny, little girl. . . ."

In fact, Lily's face looked waxen, and she had dark circles under her eyes.

"You want something to eat? Sit down, Mama Lucy must have some molasses cookies somewhere. And I'll fix you a nice cup of tea with sugar. That'll make you feel better. Matthew, are you there, big boy? You want some tea?"

Sam and Lily sat down on the faded armchairs, shaken by the turn of events and deeply ashamed at planning to steal from such a good woman. They were in a modest room filled with knickknacks, with a single window and a kerosene lamp that gave a cheerless light. The far wall was corrugated iron, partly covered by rows of old photos. There was also a treadle sewing machine, baskets overflowing with scraps of clothes, doilies on the furniture, a collection of colored bottles, and a half-open newspaper lying on a chair. Sam snatched it up and feverishly turned to the front page. "Presidential Election: Who Will the Democrats Pick?" Right above the headline was the paper's name and the date: *The Chicago Defender*, Thursday, June 30, 1932.

"Lily, we're in the United States," he whispered, "in Chicago in 1932. And look: The presidential elections are coming up!"

He handed her the newspaper, and Lily's eyes widened. "Chicago! In that case . . ."

"You kids interested in politics?"

A tall, slim young man had entered the room, elegant in a white uniform with gold buttons that seemed out of place in such humble surroundings. "Are you the ones everybody seems to be after? The dangerous criminals?"

"No, not criminals. It was a misunderstanding," said Sam defensively. "We lost our suitcases after a trip, and —"

At that point Mama Lucy came in, carrying a tray with steaming cups and a plate of cookies.

"Ah, you've met my Matthew! Handsome, isn't he? He's the pride of my old age! You off to work already, big boy? You don't want a little tea?"

Matthew took the newspaper from Lily. "I have to go to 91st Street," he said.

"Not more of that illegal betting, I hope? You know you could end up in the hoosegow for that."

"If I win, Mama Lucy, it sure helps make ends meet."

She shook her head. "What are you betting on this time?"

"The elections, of course! The candidate the Democrats will choose for the presidential election! It's in all the papers!"

"And how much do you hope to win on that?"

"For a fifty-dollar bet, as much as a thousand dollars! *If* I guess right."

"Roosevelt," muttered Lily wearily.

"Beg your pardon?"

"The Democrats will choose Roosevelt. His vice president will be John Garner."

Sam stared at her, bug-eyed. Roosevelt, all right; he'd heard of him. But that she should also know the American *vice* presidents . . .

"Roosevelt and Garner? I thought those two didn't get along!"

"Don't listen to her," Sam broke in with a forced chuckle. "My sister is a little out of it. Some days, she just says anything at all."

"Roosevelt and Garner," Matthew repeated thoughtfully. "Hmm . . . Well, why not?" He took his white cap from the coatrack and blew Mama Lucy a kiss as he went out the door. "See you tomorrow! I'll try not to get home too late."

The old lady looked after him adoringly. "What a boy! If you knew what shape he was in when I took him in! And now look at him!"

"You . . . you took him in?" said Sam, catching himself. He still couldn't believe the business about Roosevelt or his cousin's amazing store of historical trivia.

"Of course! Him and so many others! A dozen kids must have passed through my house. I've been a widow for twenty years, so what can I say? I don't have anything better to do than give 'em a little love and comfort. Plus loads of laundry!" She laughed at the thought. "Now there, I have done a few loads of laundry! In fact, you should have come and *asked* me for clothes instead of helping yourself. Mama Lucy always has something for kids like you. You don't have any family anymore, I suppose?"

Lily answered first. "Not exactly. We have some relatives here in Chicago. Have you ever heard of the Faulkner grocery store?"

This time, Sam nearly choked on his cookie. The Faulkner grocery store! Chicago — of course! He started calculating at top speed. Before his grandparents had moved to Sainte-Mary to be near Allan, Grandpa had owned a grocery store in Chicago. He was nearly eighty now, so he would have been too young to be working in 1932. On the other hand, Grandpa's father had bought the store in 1919, right after World War I, if Sam remembered correctly. *In other words, there must have been Faulkners in Chicago in 1932!*

"The Faulkner grocery store, honey child? There must be at least two thousand grocery stores in the city. I don't know them all!"

"Do you know how we could get the address?"

"Are you sure they'll help you? Because you can stay here for a couple of days, you know. I'm used to it. And you look so peaked! Matthew isn't here very often, and —"

"I'd rather see them right away," Lily said.

The old lady hesitated. "Promise me you'll drink your tea and eat your cookie, at least? And put on something besides that nightgown thing."

"With pleasure, Mama Lucy."

119

"Well, that's settled! I have a nephew not far from here who just got himself a telephone. He's sure to have a directory. Any business worth its salt will be in the phone book, isn't that right?"

For the first time since their arrival in Chicago, a little color crept into Lily's face.

CHAPTER THIRTEEN

Gangsters, Firecrackers, and Kidney Beans

Locating the Faulkner grocery store turned out to be no walk in the park: Mama Lucy's nephew had a phone, all right, but no phone book to go with it. Still, he agreed to send one of his daughters to the post office, and she came back with the address. The Faulkner store was located on Irving Park Road, right where it crossed Cicero Avenue.

While they waited for the girl, Mama Lucy had plenty of time to tell Sam and Lily the history of the neighborhood, from the arrival in Chicago of the thousands of black families fleeing racism in the South, to the crowding in the shanty-towns and the start of the worst economic crisis anyone had ever seen. As she talked, she rummaged in one of her baskets to put together decent outfits for them. Lily got a lace-trimmed blue dress that was a little short but practically new. For Sam she found a worn pair of knickerbocker pants, a yellow shirt, and an orange vest. The clash of colors was so jarring that Sam was tempted to put on sunglasses.

Mama Lucy also gave them sandals, and as a bonus, a little stuffed zebra that once belonged to one of her foster children.

"This way you'll think of me from time to time," she said, handing it to Lily. "His name is Zeb, and he's eased many a heartbreak."

Lily thanked her and hugged it tight. She wasn't looking very well, and seemed to have somehow shrunk in the course of the afternoon. Mama Lucy's molasses cookies had brought a little pink to her cheeks, but she soon lapsed into an exhausted silence. As they were leaving, the old lady again suggested that they at least spend the night, but Lily jumped up, claiming she felt much better.

Sam didn't know quite what to think. He was concerned for his cousin, as she certainly didn't seem in great shape. On the other hand, he was in a hurry to get to the Faulkner grocery store. Given their situation, who would be more likely to help them than family? If worse came to worst and their great-grandparents turned them away, they could always come back to Mama Lucy's.

With the address and a rough map in hand, Sam and Lily set out early in the evening. They detoured by the construction site, where they saw the crew still working on the ruins of the house, with no chance for them to get inside. Then they headed south along the main avenues.

As they left the vacant lots and poorer neighborhoods behind, Chicago began to look like a real city, with signs, lights, tall buildings, and constant streams of pedestrians. Antique cars *put-putted* down the streets, looking comical with their square shapes and rear-mounted spare tires, making loud *ahooga!*s when they honked at intersections.

"Now those are real cars!" exclaimed Sam. "A lot cooler than Rudolf's four-by-four, don't you think?"

"Don't talk to me about Rudolf," said Lily breathlessly. "I can't even imagine what state my mom's in! She probably gulped her whole bottle of tranquilizers down at once. But I wish she were with us," she added, sounding homesick.

It was at this point that they got lost. Disoriented by the strange noises and the mass of identical buildings, they took the wrong street, then walked around in circles until a young woman standing in a soup-kitchen line gave them directions. She nodded toward Cicero Avenue while her children tugged at her sleeves, crying for bread. Mama Lucy hadn't been lying when she described the desperate shape the country was in.

Once they were back on the right track, Sam and Lily headed straight for Irving Park. As the shadows lengthened, they admired the thousands of little lights that began to dot the city, like so many stars fallen onto Chicago's skyscrapers. Sam craned his neck this way and that, trying to recognize a church or a monument, but he'd only been five or six years old on his single visit to the former Faulkner grocery store — a pilgrimage to the United States that Grandpa had organized — and he remembered almost nothing.

"There!" whispered Lily, pointing to a triangular block of houses at the junction of three streets. "It looks just like the photo in the album."

Indeed, a store with plate-glass windows stood at the corner, with a sign written in handsome lettering:

Fine Groceries
James A. Faulkner

"James Adam Faulkner," said Sam, his voice quavering. "Grandpa's father!"

"What do we do now, Sam? We can't just show up and say, 'Hi, we're your great-grandchildren. Do you happen to know how to send us back to our own time?'"

Sam considered it. This part of Irving Park was pretty quiet, unlike what it would become later: "The busiest intersection in Chicago!" Grandpa claimed. There were just two streetlights, their meager light brightened occasionally by the headlights of passing cars. The tobacconist across the street had already closed, and the grocery store's steel shutter was lowered halfway. From the sound of voices, however, there were still people inside, and a few lights shone within.

"We better go in before the store closes," suggested Lily.

"Do you remember that stuff about the basement window?" asked Sam.

"The basement window?"

"Yeah, when Grandpa told us about being a kid. When he came home too late, he would slip in through the basement instead of the front door to avoid his father."

"So what?"

"He said the bars over the window were loose, so . . ."

"Are you saying we should break into our great-grandfather's store?"

"If we just walk in like this, what are we going to tell him? We can get into the basement through the window. That'll give us someplace to hang out while we figure out what to do next. Besides, if we spy on them for a little while, it might give us some ideas."

Secretly Sam was hoping they would find a stone statue in the basement. He knew it was unlikely, and that his father had been the first Faulkner time traveler, but there was no reason why a taste for adventure shouldn't pass from one generation to the next!

Lily didn't have the energy to argue with him, so the basement window it was. They strolled up the block until they spotted the window, which was at ground level. Somebody crossed the street just as Sam was leaning over to touch the bars, and they quickly huddled against the wall, but the passerby disappeared onto a nearby porch. There were also two cars and a truck parked down the street, but they were empty. Sam crouched down again and shook the bars. They gave a little bit, but only a little. He stood up and pulled, and to his surprise, the whole frame lifted free of the wall, inch by inch. Sam removed it from the window opening and carefully set it on the ground. He climbed in first, then helped his cousin join him before pulling the window back into place. The basement room smelled pleasantly of coffee and spices, but it was so dark that they couldn't see a thing.

"Don't budge, Lily," he whispered.

He cautiously made his way among the barrels and the sacks. Suddenly his foot caught on a crate full of bottles, causing a deafening crash. Sam froze. The noise was loud enough to be heard all over Chicago, not to say New York!

A few seconds passed. They heard footsteps on the sidewalk. Someone was walking toward the basement window! The steps slowed when they reached the window, and in the faint light Sam could make out a pair of polished shoes with white tips. Then the shoes moved away.

"Sammy, are you sure that —"

"*Shhh!*"

Sam groped his way toward the thin ray of light showing under the door, put his hand on the handle, and twisted it, holding his breath. The well-oiled knob turned easily, and he cracked the door open. A little light now reached the back of the basement, and they could hear voices upstairs.

". . . the cops? Why not the army, while you're at it? Don't you know what's what, Faulkner? We're the ones who pay off the cops!"

The tone was sarcastic, almost sadistic. Sam couldn't see beyond the bottom few steps, but he knew right away that they'd come at a bad time.

"Lookit what happened ta Wilson," said another voice, sounding hoarse from years of cigarettes and alcohol. "You know Wilson, the newspaper seller on Milwaukee Avenue, doncha? Whaddya think happens ta him? A fire! Everything goes up in smoke — *pfft!* You shoulda seen him, luggin' buckets a' water, yelpin' about freedom of the press! But freedom's got a price, don't it, Faulkner?"

"You won't get a red cent out of me," said a third voice feverishly.

Sam had no trouble identifying that one. It had Grandpa's tone and a warmth that reminded him of his own father, but a different timbre. Wasn't this the period when Al Capone and his gang terrorized the city — shaking down business owners, among other things? Sam had seen enough movies to know what was going on: James Faulkner was in trouble with the Chicago mob.

"Faulkner, Faulkner — be reasonable. It's just insurance, ya see. It's important ta have insurance! The world's a dangerous place, ya know? Anythin' can happen!"

Crash! Something, maybe a glass jar, shattered on the floor upstairs.

"Sorry, Faulkner. I'm so clumsy!"

This was followed immediately by the sound of a slap.

"Oops! Beg your pardon, Faulkner. I didn't mean ta do that!"

Lily crept up behind Sam. "We can't let them get away with this," she whispered urgently. "We have to call the police."

"The police?" Sam whispered back. "I'm not sure they would help us." He looked around for some sort of weapon, an axe handle or a stick. It would be pathetic, but just in case . . .

"What's twenty dollars a month, Faulkner?" the sadistic voice continued. "To have a store with real good insurance? Especially when you got a nice little family to take care of? You gotta think about their future!"

"You have no right to — *ow!*" Someone had thrown a punch.

Sam walked over to the shelves. One of the crates was labeled "Fireworks."

"Today is June thirtieth," he said quietly. "Independence Day in the United States is July fourth." He carefully lifted the lid, revealing supplies for the celebration: rockets of various sizes and bags of firecrackers. "We need some matches! Quick!"

As they rummaged around, an uneven battle broke out upstairs.

"Here!" said Lily.

She was shaking a paper bag whose contents made the unmistakable sound of matches rattling in their boxes.

"Go stand in a corner," urged Sam. "I'm going to try and make those slimeballs leave."

He grabbed two strips of firecrackers and went back out the basement window. The street wasn't empty — in fact, several cars were driving along it — but Sam didn't care; they might even help his plan. He walked around to the store, lit the first fuse, then yelled as loud as he could: "This is the police! Surrender! You're surrounded!"

It sounded more like a cartoon caption than a police raid, but so what? Sam ran back as the firecrackers began to pop: *Bang-bang-bang-bang!*

"Come out with your hands up!" he shouted.

Then he lit the second strip of firecrackers and heaved it as far as he could down the street. The cars driving up the street slammed on their brakes and honked their horns: *Ahooga! Bang! Bang! Ahooga! Bang!* It was a lively Fourth of July concert — a few days early!

Sam dove back into the basement and hid.

"Son of a gun!" shouted the man with the raspy voice. "What gives?"

"Out the back way!" ordered the sadist. "We ain't done with you yet, Faulkner!"

Sam and Lily heard running in the hallway overhead, going toward the back of the store.

"C'mon, step on it!"

A bolt slammed, and the footsteps were now pounding down the sidewalk outside. Sam counted to five, then headed up the stairs. The gangsters had taken off, and the glass door leading to a courtyard behind the buildings was ajar. He closed and latched it. Shouts and swearing came from the street, and Sam and Lily went to look out the window. Somebody fired a shot — a real one this time — and a car roared away.

Sam walked back into the store with Lily on his heels. The room had been turned upside down, with drawers opened, windows smashed, and damp flour and shards of glass everywhere. But there was no sign of James Faulkner. What had they done with him?

"Aaah . . ."

The moan came from behind the counter, and they hurried over to it. Kneeling on the floor, his nose bloodied, was their great-grandfather, rubbing the back of his neck as he gradually gathered his wits.

"Who . . . who are you?" he asked, trying to stand.

"We were passing by the store," Sam improvised. "There seemed to be some fighting inside, and we thought they might be robbers. We threw some firecrackers to scare them."

"Firecrackers?" James Faulkner grimaced as he felt his badly swollen upper lip. "You scared them with firecrackers? That's a hoot! How did you get in?"

"By the front door," said Lily. "In fact, it might be a good idea to lower the shutters. It would be safer."

"No. My . . . my wife is at the movies. She'll be back soon." Then, as he surveyed the extent of the damage: "Those dirty rats! They smashed everything! I'm going to call the mayor! And the newspapers too! People have to know what's going on in this city! And the police! They can't act as if I don't exist, can they? *Owww . . .*"

He staggered and had to be content with sitting down on a stool near the cash register. To Sam and Lily, encountering James Faulkner was almost beyond belief. Sam had seen a black-and-white photograph of him a couple of times, when he'd tried to please Grandma by pretending to be interested in the family photo albums. The picture showed the grocer with his apron, standing a little stiffly in front of his store. He was of medium height, with a handlebar mustache — a total stranger. There were also a couple of stories told about him, which Sam only half remembered. One was about a dog that escaped from the trenches in World War I; the other had something to do with his not being at his best at his wedding, with a bottle in one hand and whipped cream smeared on his jacket. And here was James Faulkner himself in person!

"We can help you straighten up if you like," Sam offered.

"Thanks. If Ketty sees this mess, she'll go out of her mind with worry. There are mops in the closet in the back. I'll give you a few coins for your trouble!"

Sam and Lily exchanged a glance, but made no comment. Instead, they got busy with mop and broom — Sam seemed destined to do housework in every era! — while James Faulkner dabbed water on his face and swathed himself in bandages.

Lily was gasping from her exertions when someone rapped on the metal shutter a quarter of an hour later.

"Daddy, it's us! We're back from the movies!"

James Faulkner worked the shutter mechanism to pull it up, and a little boy jumped into his arms, laughing.

"It was so funny, Daddy! You should've come! Charlie beat them all up!"

Sam felt his heart tighten: This was Grandpa — *their* grandpa! — when he was still a little boy!

"What happened to your nose, Daddy?"

The emotion was too much for Lily. She took a step backward, sighed like a leaky balloon, and collapsed in a dead faint on a sack of kidney beans.

CHAPTER FOURTEEN

105 Degrees

The fever lasted two days and nights. Lily's cheeks and forehead were sweaty, her teeth chattered, and she could hardly move. Responding to the family's urgent call, a doctor examined her carefully, muttered a few perplexed *"Hmms,"* and eventually admitted that he was stumped. There seemed to be nothing wrong with Lily's throat, lungs, or lymph nodes, and no inflammation was visible. It was a medical mystery — except that Lily was burning up!

"It's out of my hands," said the doctor with a fatalistic shrug.

By the middle of the second night, it didn't look as if Lily was going to live. Despite damp towels and cold compresses, her temperature rose to 105 degrees, which seemed more than her small body could stand. Sam wondered whether the inexplicable fever was a result of time-traveling. Maybe Lily couldn't endure it, being away from her original time for too long. Was her body rebelling against the wrenching leaps through the ages? If that was the case, then no cure existed. And if Lily died . . .

Sam preferred not to think about that. He had dragged her into this whole business, and she had supported him from the very beginning, far beyond anything he could have hoped for. She'd scoured the library for information about Dracula, translated the excerpt from the Bruges alchemist's book of spells, and been catapulted through time while trying to warn Sam about the police. And then there was the masterful way she had saved him from Death-eye and his clan. What would Sam have accomplished without her? If he were to lose Lily now, after losing his father and mother too . . .

Best not to think about it.

Luckily, their Faulkner great-grandparents turned out to be wonderful, especially Ketty. When she learned of the attack on her husband and the role Sam and Lily had played in his rescue, she immediately offered to take them in. She was the one who insisted on calling the doctor; then she installed Lily and Sam in the guest room, and didn't let two hours pass without bringing the patient a glass of orange juice, a treat, a picture book, or at least some words of comfort. Ketty looked severe and subdued in the album photos, but in person she was as nurturing as a mother hen, loving and attentive. Besides, she cooked hamburger steak with fried onions better than anyone!

James was harder to fathom. After the episode with the mob, he bought a black Browning pistol and two boxes of bullets and stored them under the cash register. From time to time, when the grocery store was empty, he would pull the gun out and aim at a bottle of oil or a jar of stewed fruit. Despite his wife's urging, he decided not to go to the mayor's office or the police, saying this would only attract reprisals.

Sam suspected he was just waiting for the gangsters to come back so he could take justice into his own hands.

He also had some peculiar habits. When Ketty was minding the store, James would sometimes head down to the basement without a word. Sam was intrigued — was there a connection with the stone statue? — and on the second afternoon he followed him. Surprise: His great-grandfather was sneaking out through the basement window! He was the one who had rigged the frame! When James came back half an hour later, he smelled faintly of liquor. Sam kept quiet about it, of course, but he wondered: Was this why Ketty always looked so melancholy in the family photos?

And then there was Grandpa — or as they called him, Donovan. Sam still couldn't get used to the idea. Nothing in life prepares you for playing tag with your grandfather when he's six and a half! Donovan was a sweet, helpful boy who spent most of his time playing in the courtyard with his wooden train, building level crossings and tunnels out of left-over crates, cans, and empty bottles.

"*Choo-choo!* All aboard! All aboard! Train leaving the Chicago station! Sam, you wanna be the conductor?"

Torn between incredulity and tenderness, Sam looked at his diminutive grandfather. He would have loved to take Donovan onto his lap and whisper a few scraps of his history in his ear. But he knew very well that any carelessness in the past was likely to change the future, and Grandpa's future was — Sam himself! So he kept quiet, content to watch the train as it raced between the cans.

"*Choo-choo!* Look out for the tunnel!"

Donovan was also very interested in Lily. He wasn't allowed to enter her room — she might be contagious — but he picked her flowers morning and night and made drawings for her.

"You'll give this one to Lily, won't you?" he said, holding out a sheet with a big multicolored sun. "Is she going to get better? Will we play trains together?"

The first signs of improvement appeared on the third day, when the fever began to break. Lily was able to sit propped up with pillows to eat some bread and jam and drink a glass of milk. But she was still very pale, and every sentence she spoke seemed to exhaust her meager strength.

"I'll . . . I'll pull through, Sammy. Don't look like that! You have to go see about the stone statue at the construction site."

The construction site . . . Sam had put off going there, partly because he didn't want to leave his cousin, partly for fear of what he would find. But it was indeed high time. So early that afternoon he screwed up his courage, left Lily in Ketty's competent hands, and headed up Cicero Avenue toward the black neighborhood. First he swung by Mama Lucy's to thank her for her generosity and tell her about Lily. But the old lady wasn't there — the house was closed — so he had no reason to postpone his visit to the site.

Alas, the situation was even worse than he imagined. In the space of two days, workmen had poured a flat cement slab exactly where the house once stood — probably a parking lot for the tenants of the future building. Sam spent a long time with his face pressed to the fence, praying for a miracle: that the earth would open up, say, and the stone statue would shoot out of the ground like a rocket and gently land next to him. But the only things flying around were the clouds of dust raised by the steam shovels and the orders the foremen shouted to their workers.

Figuring he had nothing to lose, Sam went to the entrance to look around, but was quickly sent packing by one of the cement workers: "Hey, you! The Yellow Kid! You got no business around here, so scram!"

He was about to head for home when he noticed a shiny black van parked a little way down the road between two earth-moving machines. The van bore a large white sign on its side: "The Collector's Paradise, Antiques, East 63rd Street & Cottage Grove Ave., Chicago." Below this was the store logo: a pair of Egyptian horns encircling a solar disk.

"Unbelievable!" he muttered.

He walked around the van. The back was closed, and he couldn't see much of anything through the driver's window. He tried the door handle, but the vehicle was locked.

"Hey, Yellow Kid!" somebody shouted behind him. "What're you up to now? Didn't I tell you to clear out?" It was the cement worker from the site.

"You mean this isn't my car?" exclaimed Sam. "Oh, *right!* That's why the key doesn't fit."

"I'll fit my fist to your nose, you see if I don't!"

Now the man was striding toward him: The two of them clearly didn't share the same sense of humor. Sam decided against a second joke and opted for a sprint instead, running to a busy street where he was able to lose his pursuer.

As he caught his breath, Sam thought about the sudden profusion of strange Us: the Sainte-Mary burglar, the

Mother-stone cave, the Pompeii pool, and now an antique shop in Chicago. Was the store a forerunner of Arkeos? Perhaps the answer was waiting for him at the intersection of 63rd Street and Cottage Grove Avenue.

After asking for directions, Sam took the trolley, paying with some of the change James Faulkner had given him. Thirty minutes and two transfers later, he got off in front of the Tivoli Theatre in a street full of businesses and restaurants, with double-parked cars and people crossing every which way. The Collector's Paradise was on the ground floor of a big hotel; the shop window was crammed with knickknacks, clocks, gold watches, and Greek and Roman statuettes identified by little tags. The company logo was painted across the window. Less stylized than Arkeos's, it had little flourishes at the ends of the horns and some discreet shading on the sun. Sam pushed open the door, which set off a rather sinister ringing of bells.

The store was a strange jumble of objects set down here and there, on the floor and on shelves, in no discernible order. An older woman with an oddly round face and sharp eyes stood peering at him from behind a counter. To Sam, she looked just like an owl.

"What can I do for you?" she asked stiffly, no doubt figuring that a boy dressed with so little care — or taste — wasn't likely to add much to her bottom line.

"I'm looking for a present for my father."

"A present for your father?" she repeated. "You're sure you're in the right place? There's a Salvation Army thrift store right next door. Isn't that what you're looking for?"

Go ahead and call my father a hobo, you old biddy.

"Actually, he collects coins," said Sam smoothly.

"Collects coins? Is that so?" she said. "Don't you think he ought to use some of them to buy you a decent shirt?"

Don't get angry, Sam reminded himself. Instead, he tried to remember some of the terms he learned on the money changers' benches in Bruges. "He especially likes Venetian ducats, florins, and Strasbourg gros."

"Strasbourg gros, eh?" said the antique seller, sounding half convinced. "Well, I suppose so . . . I'll show you what I have."

Without taking her eyes off him, she went over to a glass-fronted cabinet displaying medals and ceramics. The woman pulled out a drawer with several rows of ancient coins in more or less good shape, but unfortunately, none of them had holes. Even if Sam managed to find another stone statue, how could he and Lily get home without the coins they needed? He made a show of examining a few of the coins before putting them back on the red velvet.

"These aren't exactly the kind of coins my father collects," he declared. "But you have a very attractive logo on the window. Can you tell me what it stands for?"

"An attractive *what*?" asked the woman, rolling her owl eyes.

"The symbol under the store's name. It's a kind of headpiece that Egyptian gods wore, isn't it?"

If Sam hoped to impress her with his knowledge, he failed miserably. "If you know the answer, what's the point of asking the question?"

"I would've liked to know why you chose that symbol instead of something else," he insisted. "That's all."

"I wasn't the one who chose it," she snapped irritably. "Besides, what business is it of yours?"

The woman slammed the coin drawer shut and retreated behind her counter, brushing past a stand bearing a crystal goblet that reminded Sam of something.

"So, boy, have you made up your mind?" she continued. "Is there something here you'd like? Yes or no?"

Sam tried not to get flustered. If the antique seller hadn't chosen the logo herself, that must mean somebody else owned the business.

"Was the design chosen by the person who's at the construction site? I saw your store's van parked next to it."

The woman didn't answer right away. Instead, her eyes widened further and a nervous tic tugged at the corner of her mouth — or her beak. She looked almost frightened.

"A construction site? What construction site?" she asked uncertainly.

Sam was feeling his way now. What kind of information did he hope to get? Was the antique seller aware of the stone statue's existence? And would she be prepared to tell him about it?

"The construction site in the colored neighborhood," he said. "It's strange that somebody from your store would be interested in old houses getting torn down. I mean, there probably aren't a lot of archeological finds there."

"I don't understand a thing you're talking about!"

Sam decided to go for broke. "The guy with the van wouldn't have that symbol tattooed on his shoulder, by any chance?"

This last suggestion had a radical effect on the woman. She abruptly ducked under her counter, and for a moment Sam thought she had fainted. But she popped back up immediately, an antique musket in her hands.

"You dirty little louse!" she snapped, pointing the flared muzzle at him. "Where did you come from? And what are you up to, sneaking around the construction site?"

Sam quickly stepped to one side, putting himself behind the stand with the crystal goblet. He hoped the antique seller would think twice before blowing everything to bits.

"I was just out for a walk," he said. "I wasn't doing anything wrong."

"So who sent you, then?" she screamed. "I'm warning you, I'll shoot! You won't be the first little thief shot while trying to rob an honest business. You tell me who told you about the work site and the tattoo, or else!"

But her threats were suddenly drowned out by the tinkling music of the bells: a customer. The antique seller quickly hid her weapon under the counter, and Sam bolted for the door, nearly bowling over a distinguished-looking well-dressed man with a monocle. Ignoring the man's protests, he raced outside and sprinted up the next street.

He hadn't learned much about the strange U, but he had gotten something much more valuable: an idea for getting back to the present! Because he now remembered what the vase on the stand reminded him of: the crystal goblet belonging to the explorer Jacques Cartier, the one Garry Barenboim had willed to the Sainte-Mary Museum! Barenboim, Sainte-Mary! Sainte-Mary, Barenboim! Why hadn't he thought of that before?

CHAPTER FIFTEEN

All Aboard

The huge hall of the Chicago train station, which was hung with red, white, and blue pennants, echoed with the lively notes of a jazz band and the hurried steps of travelers.

"Are you really sure you want to leave now?" Ketty Faulkner asked.

"I feel fine," Lily reassured her. "I'm not tired at all anymore."

It was true that Lily's recovery had been as inexplicable as her illness. When Sam got back to the grocery store after his escapade at the Collector's Paradise, he found his cousin sitting on the edge of her bed, about to tackle a stack of pancakes with syrup and a big glass of apple juice. The next night passed without fever, and though Lily still looked a bit pale, she was standing very straight under the track information panels and making an admirable effort to appear healthy.

"So much the better!" exclaimed James Faulkner. "Do you have your tickets and your train schedule? The train leaves in fifteen minutes!"

Sam nodded, holding up the papers in question. "I don't know how we can ever thank you, Mr. and Mrs. Faulkner. Your putting us up, the money you lent us . . ."

"I still think you should wait a day or two," said Ketty. "If Lily's fever comes back during the trip . . ."

"Our family has been expecting us for four days," said Lily. "They must be really worried."

Which in fact wasn't far from the truth.

With perfect timing, Donovan appeared just then to change the course of the conversation.

"Mommy, look! The new Pacific 231! I've never seen such a big train! And it smokes! It smokes a *lot*!"

"Sam and Lily are leaving, darling. It's time to say good-bye to them."

"So you're going away for real?" asked the little boy.

Lily nodded and bent down to him. From her pocket she took the little stuffed zebra Mama Lucy had given her a few days earlier. "Here, Donovan, this is a present for you. His name is Zeb, and he's healed many a heartbreak." She smiled a little to hear herself repeating Mama Lucy's words. "If you ever feel sad, hug him tight and think about us, and you'll feel better." She kissed him very gently on both cheeks and stood up, on the verge of tears.

"Let's go!" said James. "It would be too bad if you missed your train."

The farewells continued on the platform as Ketty gave the children a final flurry of advice, as well as a bundle of food wrapped in a gingham cloth. After a last good-bye, they climbed into car number seven and sat down on the first available bench. Lily buried her face in her handkerchief to hide her feelings.

"All aboard!" cried the conductor as he rang his bell. "All aboard!"

With a powerful jet of steam and a deafening clanking of rods and pistons, the train got under way, gradually picked up speed, and clattered through the center of the city like a molten metal snake. Sam and Lily were quiet as the last buildings disappeared behind them and the train headed across open countryside.

"Do you think we can do it?" Lily asked at last.

Sam unfolded the sheet on which he had written the stages of their trip. "It looks okay on paper. This train will take us to Toronto, then we change to the local for Sainte-Mary. We'll be there tomorrow at the latest."

"That wasn't what I meant, Sam."

She was looking at him with her bright eyes, in which he could see both anxious concern and steely determination.

"You mean, do you think we can find the stone statue?"

She nodded, as if the question was obvious.

"I think so," he said. "We know Barenboim was using it at the start of the twentieth century, because the coins displayed at the museum and those rumors about all his strange visitors prove it. And the stone was still in the basement a hundred years later, so there's no reason to think it moved in the meantime."

"What about the coins? How are we going to manage that?"

Sam looked at the ceiling. "We still have to figure that one out. Barenboim left his collection to the city, so I'm hoping we'll be able to get hold of it."

"Doesn't it seem odd that we haven't picked up a single coin so far? You told me once that to make the stone statue work, there had to be a coin near the statue at the place you were going. That's what happened on your previous trips, right? But we haven't seen a single one!"

Sam had been wrestling with that very conundrum since his lively discussion with the lady antique seller, and had finally come up with a theory.

"I've been thinking hard about that, Lily. There weren't any coins in the cave or the Pompeii baths, or here in Chicago, but the Arkeos logo was there each time, remember? It was on the cave wall, at the bottom of the pool, and on the Collector's Paradise van."

"So what does that tell us?"

"I think the Arkeos man put those symbols there to be sure he could travel directly to certain periods. That way, instead of landing wherever the stone chooses to send him, he has a bunch of stopping places in Time — places where he left his mark. How that works, I have no idea. But I can't think of any other explanation for the way the horns and the solar disk keep showing up."

"It would certainly explain the antique store," admitted Lily. "He wouldn't have set it up if he wasn't sure he could always return to Chicago in 1932."

"I bet he supplies the old lady at the store with his finds and then invests his profits somewhere else. Maybe he even used that money to start Arkeos."

"But if the symbol always takes a time traveler to certain periods, why didn't you ever see it before?"

Sam was quiet for a minute as he mulled this over. "Here's what I think. For the system to work, the Egyptian sign has to be present at both the departure and the arrival place, sort of like a wire stretched between the times. It's like the coins, see? You need one to take off and one to land. And I think that explains the tattoo on the guy's shoulder. He had the symbol that lets him time-travel put onto his body so he could always get back to those specific times. And that would explain why the antique seller got so upset when I mentioned the tattoo. It's the key to the whole setup!"

"Like a built-in ticket to the right places," said Lily approvingly. "I understand. But what about us?" She touched his arm. "You haven't gone and gotten a tattoo, as far as I know. So why have we been finding this sign all along our route?"

"That's where it gets complicated," said Sam, leaning forward. "I've thought it over, and I have a hunch I was tricked at the museum."

"How do you mean, tricked?"

"Well, after we fought and the alarm went off, the Arkeos man rushed to the display case. I thought he wanted to steal coins and he just forgot one — the really worn one with the symbol. But afterward, when I thought about it again . . ." Sam paused to scratch his forehead, then continued: "I think he put the coin there on purpose for me to find it!"

"*What?*"

"Listen to me. First of all, I really don't remember seeing this design on any of the museum's coins that afternoon. That's weird, don't you think? I know you have to look really close to make out the horns, but I don't remember anything like it. And then that coin, the one with the Arkeos design, went with us on all of our trips, right? First in the hole in the statue, then on the sun. So is it an accident that we came across the same symbol three different times? I don't think so. This coin hasn't just gone with us through Time. I think it *guided* us to specific destinations!"

"But why would the Arkeos man want you to use it?"

"I don't know, but since he time-travels too, maybe it's a way to keep an eye on me. With that coin, at least he knows where I go."

They leaned back against the bench, weighing the implications of Sam's thinking, assuming it was correct. The train car was half full, mainly with families and couples. A little girl was running in the aisle, and a group of soldiers laughed loudly at the other end of the compartment. Small American flags hung from the ceiling, and the overall mood was cheerful. The conductor came in, followed by a very elegant young woman, then a man wearing a bowler hat.

"Just like I told you, folks. There aren't so many people in number seven."

While the conductor checked tickets, the man in the bowler went to sit near the soldiers. The young woman headed for the bench facing Sam and Lily.

"Do you mind?" she asked.

Sam helped put her suitcase on the baggage rack. She thanked him with a charming smile, then pulled a pocket mirror from her purse to fix her hair. With her straight white dress, dark glasses, and immaculate elbow-length gloves, she looked like a movie star. Sam didn't realize he was gaping until

146

Lily jabbed him sharply with her elbow, and he decided it might be appropriate to take a little nap.

After an hour's doze — during which Sam's thoughts drifted to a blond girl with big blue eyes — the very real smell of cold cuts pulled him from his reverie. The train was crossing hilly countryside, and Lily had spread the contents of Ketty's cloth on her lap: roast beef, sausages, salami, pickles, buns, cookies, and chocolates.

Sam made himself an extra-large sandwich with all the goodies he could pile up and began to chomp on it, avoiding the woman passenger's eye — he had his dignity, after all. It was then he noticed that the man in the bowler was up to something. From time to time, the man would turn around in his seat to steal a glance at the actress. Sam couldn't see his face, just the movement of his hat, but there was something unnerving about his spying.

"Do you want a drink?" asked Lily.

Sam took a few swallows of lemonade from the bottle, wondering what the stranger could be after. He was about to whisper to his cousin when the train roared into a tunnel. The car was plunged into darkness, and Sam felt something brush by his left side. When the light returned, the man in the bowler had disappeared. Or no, actually — he had changed seats and was now sitting right behind them, not six feet from the young woman!

Sam let his napkin fall into the aisle and leaned over to pick it up. The stranger was wearing a long, dark overcoat, its collar turned up to hide his face. He also had a strange bump at his waist — a gun? But when Sam saw the man's shoes, his stomach suddenly knotted. They were black patent leather with white tips, exactly like those he had seen outside the grocery on the night the mobsters shook down his great-grandfather. *The man in the hat wasn't after the actress: He was after them!*

"Youhavetogotothebathroom," he blurted into his cousin's ear.

"What?"

"You have to go to the bathroom right away," he repeated more clearly.

Lily looked at him with pity. "Have you lost your mind?"

Sam took their itinerary and wrote on the back: "Don't argue. The man with the hat behind us has followed us. I think he has a gun. Go to the toilet in number nine. I'll meet you."

It took Lily a moment to react. Then she stood up and casually walked to the end of the car. Sam counted to twenty to give her a head start, then, after a last smile at the actress, gathered their provisions and headed down the aisle. He opened the connecting door and found himself in the passageway that joined the two cars together. The noise was deafening, and he could see the tracks racing by under the joints in the platform — this was no time to fall through the cracks! He entered car number eight and started to run, ignoring people's stares. He did the same thing in the next car and stopped just before being smacked in the face by a black door marked "Ladies."

"Will you please tell me what you're up to?" asked Lily, popping out of the bathroom like a jack-in-the-box.

"The guy in the bowler," said Sam, gasping for breath. "He has black shoes with white tips."

"That's great! What color are his socks?"

"This isn't a joke! He was the lookout in the street the other evening when the two guys attacked Mr. Faulkner!"

"You mean he's a gangster?"

Sam grimaced. "That bump under his coat sure isn't a book of poetry!"

"But why would he follow us all this way on the train?"

"No idea! They must have been watching the grocery store. Maybe they're out for revenge."

Sam slid the vestibule door partly open to check his hunch. The stranger in the bowler had entered at the other end and was walking up the aisle, carefully studying each passenger.

"Here he comes! Let's go!"

They rushed into car nine and ran right into the conductor.

"Hey, kids, this isn't the Indy 500! Where are you running to like that?"

"My sister has diarrhea. Do you mind?"

Giving them a reproachful look, the conductor stepped aside.

"Thanks a lot," complained Lily once they were in the next passageway between cars. "That was in really great taste. Ever heard of TMI?"

"Did you want a fifteen-minute lecture? Hey, what's this?"

The next car was very different from the others. It had the quiet atmosphere of a restaurant, and about fifteen travelers were having lunch. Two waiters in white uniforms carried silver trays among the crisp white tablecloths, which hung down to the thick carpet. There were vases of fresh flowers, landscapes with lakes painted on the wall panels, and comfortable red velvet seats.

"Watch it!"

Sam caught his cousin and propelled her into the bathroom just as the conductor walked up to him.

"I don't want you hanging out in the aisles, all right?"

Wearing his most angelic expression, Sam agreed. The conductor grumbled his way forward to car eleven, and Lily was able to come out.

"Now we're stuck," muttered Sam. "The conductor in front of us, a mobster behind us! We have to . . ."

Another tunnel. The light suddenly vanished and the roar of the train made the floor shake.

"Quick!"

Sam forced his cousin to her knees and shoved her under the first empty dining car table.

"Will you quit pushing me around?"

"Quiet!" he ordered, scrunching down next to her. "He'll be here any second!"

The train emerged into the light, and Sam lifted a corner of the tablecloth to see a pair of shiny white-tipped shoes coming their way.

"Waiter!" called a hoarse, almost sandy voice.

"Would you like to have lunch, sir?" asked the waiter.

"No, I'm looking for two children, a boy and a girl. Have you seen them?"

"I'm very busy with my tables, sir."

"They were running as if the police were chasing them. You couldn't have missed them."

His tone was urgent, practically threatening. Besides the shoes, all the children could see were the bottoms of some blue canvas pants and a worn gabardine coat.

"Unfortunately, sir, when I'm working . . ."

"I understand." There was a noise like the crackle of dollar bills. "Maybe this will help."

The waiter seemed to hesitate. "Actually, now that you mention it — that's right, a boy and a girl."

Lily dug her nails into Sam's arm.

"They ran out the other end, toward the sleepers," said the waiter. "They were running fast, all right."

"Very good. If they come back, please let me know. I'm in car seven."

The polished shoes vanished from Sam's field of vision, and after a few seconds the tablecloth snapped up, uncovering them.

"Come out of there!" A brown hand reached down to them. "Stealing clothes, hiding under tables — don't you two *ever* do anything normal?"

"Matthew!" Lily cried.

The uniform, the voice . . . of course! The waiter was none other than Mama Lucy's adopted son!

Matthew shook his head. "I was watching you from the kitchen. You kids seem to attract nothing but trouble!"

"That guy belongs to a gang that attacked my grandfather's grocery store," Sam explained quietly. "They didn't get what they wanted, so they decided to come after us."

Matthew didn't seem particularly convinced. "Well, that's as may be. But if that guy is really after you, I know a place you'll be safe."

A customer at one of the far tables was getting impatient. "Waiter, please!"

"Right away, ma'am . . . Okay, I have to hurry or my boss will get mad."

He quickly led them to the other side of the car, to a compartment stacked high with sheets, tablecloths, and napkins.

"I'm in charge of linens for the sleeping and dining cars, so no one will bother you in here. There's not much room, but . . . Here, I'll give you my key. If you get too hot, just open the window."

Several hours passed before Matthew appeared again. Lily and Sam used the time to make themselves a cozy nest among the bags of linens and finish the lunch they'd started. They also came up with a couple of theories about the man with the bowler hat's real intentions, without being fully satisfied with any of them. Was he someone sent by the mob? An accomplice of the Arkeos man? The Arkeos man himself?

Finally, as night was falling, they heard a soft knock at the door.

"Open up. It's me, Matthew."

He stepped inside carrying a bundle of dirty linen.

"Your guy is a tough customer; he doesn't give up easily. He went up and down the train several times this afternoon. He even checked the toilets. Didn't put him in an especially good mood either."

"What if we told the conductor?" suggested Lily.

"Mason? He's as yellow as they come. Don't count on him for help. Are you going to Toronto?" Sam nodded. "I'll help you get off onto the tracks. No one will see a thing."

"Mama Lucy is right to be proud of you," Lily told him. "You really take after her!"

He laughed. "Don't let appearances fool you, missy. I'm helping you mainly for your politics! I don't know who tipped you off, but the Democrats chose Roosevelt and Garner for the presidential elections, just like you predicted! And I picked up a thousand dollars along the way. So if you have any other ideas along those lines . . ."

"That was just luck," said Lily. "I read an article in the newspaper."

"What paper was that? I want to subscribe!"

At his charges' looks of embarrassment, Matthew burst out laughing again. "You really are a strange pair! But I like that! Hand me that bag over there. I have to take clean sheets to the sleeping cars. When we arrive, don't budge until I come get you."

Matthew kept his word. Once the train pulled into Toronto early the next morning, he helped them off the train onto the tracks, out of sight of the other travelers. Then he said good-bye and went back to his job. He had to greet the new passengers for the trip home.

At nine o'clock in the morning, after carefully studying their surroundings, Sam and Lily finally boarded the first train headed for Sainte-Mary. There was nothing the man in the bowler could do to them now.

CHAPTER SIXTEEN

Old Acquaintances

For the first time since he started "traveling," Sam had really become aware of what the passage of Time meant. It was one thing to pay a quick visit to a time and place you knew nothing about, but quite another to meet your six-year-old grandfather or to arrive at a familiar place a century earlier. If Sam and Lily hadn't seen a big wooden sign reading "Welcome to Sainte-Mary" as they left the train station, they might have had serious doubts about where they were.

"What happened to the mayor's office?" asked Lily in amazement. "Don't they need a mayor? And what about the park?"

Sainte-Mary wasn't a city anymore; it was a large village at best. There were so few streets and buildings, it looked like a case of *Honey, I Shrunk the Town!* Only three cars — with boxy lines, rear-mounted spare tires, and the occasional *ahooga!* — were trundling along the main street, from which all modern structures had disappeared. In their place rose two-story buildings with shops on the ground floor and living quarters above. On the sidewalks — just dirt embankments, actually — vendors sold fruit and vegetables out of carts. Street lighting came from a pair of stubby wrought-iron gas lamps, a far cry from the majestic avenue of lights that would brighten twenty-first-century nights.

"Look, the DVD rental place is a men's clothing store!"

"The skating rink! It's a cow pasture!"

"And the big hotel is a public bathroom!"

The changes went on and on. Sainte-Mary looked like a rural backwater, and its crowds wore clothes that were definitely more "country" than in Chicago. But the mood in town was far from glum. People were talking loudly and calling to each other from one end of the row of stores to the other. A few citizens already seemed well lubricated with alcohol.

"At one in the afternoon, for heaven's sakes!" said Lily.

They discovered the reason for this excitement behind what would someday be the area's biggest shopping center: a muddy field where a noisy crowd was applauding a plowing contest. Two workhorses were going head to head, each dragging a clawed device that dug deep furrows in the ground. The supporters of the teams cheerfully shouted insults back and forth.

"You can see why Fontana's fields yield half as much as ours do!"

"If you want those Sainte-Mary nags to pull, you got to feed them!"

Lily asked, "So this is a kind of county fair, right?"

"Something like that," answered Sam above the hubbub. "But there's probably something else happening too. Have you ever heard of the mêlées?"

"Mêlées?"

"From what I understand, there were these big competitions between Fontana and Sainte-Mary for years. They usually ended in gigantic fights, which is why they're called mêlées. I think they usually happened at this time of year, around the first of July."

"On Canada Day?"

"Yeah. But then some people got really hurt, and the fights were banned after World War II. That's sort of how the Sainte-Mary/Fontana judo tournament got started — it's a lot more peaceful."

"So if everyone's here, this is probably the perfect time to look around the town, right?"

They briefly considered going to their school, which was quite close. But what would they find there? A potato field? A pigpen? Instead, they left the Fontana and Sainte-Mary fans' alcoholic huzzahs behind and walked over to Barenboim Street. To their surprise, they enjoyed the relaxed feeling of crossing a downtown free of the oppressive crush of traffic. Children played with jacks or hoops in the street, people stopped to greet one another, more animals could be seen — birds, especially — and the flowers smelled sweet. It might be interesting to live in a Sainte-Mary without a broadband connection and an MP3 player.

Barenboim Street felt more cheerful too. The houses were the same ones Sam and Lily knew, but their paint was a lot fresher and their gardens better tended. Also, the street had a mood of carefree simplicity Sam would never have imagined.

There was one exception to all this, however: the house they were heading for.

When they opened the gate, it creaked on its hinges. Weeds had overgrown the walkway, and the stoop was nearly hidden under piles of junk and scrap metal. A couple of windows were broken, the siding was peeling off, and a weather vane listed sadly on the roof.

"Is this a haunted house set or what?" Lily whispered.

They reached the front door, which swung slightly in the breeze. Gone were the scent of flowers and the chirping of birds, replaced here by the stench of stale beer and clogged toilets.

Sam entered the house first. The main room, where his father would set up his bookshelves seventy-five years later, was littered with wood scraps, broken bottles, and cigarette butts. Someone had apparently started a fire under a window once, and the flames had scorched the wall and blackened the ceiling.

"It looks awful," said Lily, glancing around the room, "but we'd have more problems if someone was living here, right?"

Sam nodded as they headed toward the basement. But just then a teenage boy with a cigarette dangling from his mouth stepped out of the darkened stairway leading upstairs.

"You were right, Bradley, we've got company," he said.

Four or five other teenage boys stood behind him. The speaker blew smoke in Sam and Lily's faces.

"Monk," he said. "Go see if anybody else is coming."

Sam felt a jolt of electricity shoot up his spine. How could big Monk, who had nearly flattened him at the judo tournament, be here in 1932? But it was a lanky boy with downcast eyes who got to his feet and went to check the front door.

When he returned, he announced somewhat wearily: "I don't see anyone out there, Paxton."

Paxton? Was Paxton in on this too?

"Perfect," said the first boy. "We'll be able to talk quietly. Upstairs, everyone!"

At a sign from him, the others surrounded Sam and Lily and crowded them toward the steps.

"What do you think you're doing?" Sam began. "We aren't going anyplace with you!"

Paxton stepped to within a few inches of Sam and jabbed his finger at him. He was smaller than his descendant — Alicia's Jerry Paxton — and had a long scratch across his forehead and a badly chipped tooth on the side of his mouth. Sam suspected they weren't going to be great pals.

"You're on my turf here and you do what I say. Get it?"

Lily shot him a glance begging him not to resist, and Sam allowed himself to be led upstairs. The rooms had been turned into a crash pad. There were mattresses on the floor, a pile of empty bottles, and garbage everywhere. *This is my house,* Sam raged silently, though he knew the thought was absurd. *You might treat it a little better!*

Paxton dropped into a battered armchair while his lieutenants flanked the two intruders. "So you're from Fontana, eh?"

"No, we're not," Sam answered.

"Well, you're not from Sainte-Mary, anyway."

That's exactly where we're from, you jerk — but there was no good way to explain. Aloud, he said, "We just came from Chicago."

"From Chicago?" A glint flashed in Jerry Paxton's grandfather's eyes. Or was it his great-grandfather or great-uncle?

Whatever the case, acting like a jerk was clearly genetic with these people.

"To me, Chicago is worse than Fontana," he said. "I wanna kill all those smart alecks from Chicago. Isn't that right, you guys?" The rest of the gang laughed raucously. "Besides, we need somebody to train on."

"Train for what?" Lily asked.

"Girls shut up!" Paxton yelled. "Especially when they're young enough to hide in their mothers' skirts! We're gonna win that mêlée this year if it kills us. Or we kill them." He grinned. "Shirts off, guys!"

As in a well-rehearsed ballet, the five punks slipped their suspenders from their shoulders and took off their shirts in unison.

"You too," Paxton told Sam.

"What about the girl?" asked Monk. "It'd be better if she didn't watch."

Paxton seemed to hesitate for a moment. "You're gettin' sentimental, Monk, ever since your old man died. But okay, lock her up. I'll deal with her later."

There was nothing very encouraging in this show of generosity. Skinny Monk grabbed Lily by the arm and dragged her out to the hallway. Meanwhile, his bare-chested buddies started circling Sam, fists clenched. He was going to be the punching bag for this afternoon's boxing practice!

To gain time, he slowly unbuttoned his shirt, while glancing right and left. The windows didn't have any panes, so he could jump down into the yard if he had to. But even if he didn't break something, Lily would still be stuck upstairs. As for facing these animals . . .

"Start by hitting him in the stomach and ribs," ordered Paxton, playing his role as coach to the hilt. "For his face, wait for my signal. Go!"

The order was hardly given before his adversaries all attacked at once. Sam felt as if the ceiling had crashed down on his head. This had nothing to do with boxing! He tried to stay upright for a moment, protecting himself as best he could, but soon found himself on the floor, buried under their number.

"That is enough!" shouted a hoarse voice. "I will not say it twice!"

The furor instantly subsided, and everyone turned to look at the door. Standing on the threshold was a small man with copper-colored skin, wearing a bowler hat and polished shoes with white tips. He looked to be about sixty and seemed very calm. Though Sam had never seen his face before, he had no trouble recognizing him. This wasn't a mobster or even the Arkeos man, as he had speculated on the train. It was the venerable Setni, high priest of the Egyptian god Amon, in whose tomb the first stone statue had been found. And here he was in Sainte-Mary, in the flesh!

Paxton sniggered. "Two for the price of one! We'll be in great shape for the mêlée!"

Without warning, he leaped from his chair and rushed at the small man, leading with his right foot. To Paxton's considerable surprise, Setni dodged him easily, then drew a very flexible stick from under his gabardine coat and whipped the air with it.

"I mean you no harm, you crazed young cur. Leave now, and nothing will happen to you."

"We'll see if I'm leaving," barked Paxton, throwing a terrific punch at him. But once again, Setni stepped aside as if he'd anticipated his attacker's move. *The déjà vu effect*, thought Sam, the same thing he'd experienced against the twenty-first-century Monk during their judo match. Paxton found himself off balance with his arm extended and caught a stinging crack on the chin from Setni's stick.

"This time you're dead!" he roared, purple with rage. But Paxton's next attack was no more successful than the others, and he smashed into a wall. He raised his hands to his nose, which was spurting blood.

"Get 'im, you guys!" he yelled.

His companions finally reacted and rushed the high priest. An incredible phenomenon then happened: For the space of a minute, it was as if Time slowed down. Monk and his friends seemed gripped by a strange lethargy, moving with extreme difficulty while Setni struck with his stick at astonishing speed. Even Sam felt seized by some invisible, paralyzing force; he had trouble moving or even blinking. Then with the snap of a released rubber band, Time abruptly began to flow again. The high priest stepped back. Most of his opponents were on the ground, rubbing their necks or hips, dumbfounded by what had just happened to them.

"He's a magician!" moaned a terrified Bradley. "Let's get out of here!"

The gang tumbled down the stairs, scooping up their leader on the way. Leaning on his stick and panting, Setni watched them go. He was drenched in sweat and looked haggard.

"Are you all right, sir?" Sam asked cautiously.

"Yes . . . I am fine. It is just . . . exhausting," he gasped. "I know I should not do it, but sometimes . . ."

He gradually caught his breath and Sam kept away from him, for fear of breaking some sort of spell. At last the high priest straightened up and looked him over from head to foot. "What about the girl?" he asked.

"She isn't far. I can get her."

Setni nodded and the two walked into the next room — Sam's future bedroom, in fact. It held yet more of the paltry treasures accumulated by the Sainte-Mary punks: a spare tire — one drawback of mounting them on top of the trunk! — some farm tools, a case of beer, scales with weights, and so on. Against the far wall stood a wobbly, battered wardrobe. It was apparently possessed by a ghost who was banging on the door, yelling, "Let me out!"

Sam turned the key in the lock and his cousin burst out, all teeth and claws.

"Easy, Lily! It's me!"

At the sight of the small bald man with the weathered face and the bowler, she froze. "You're —"

"I'm afraid there was a misunderstanding yesterday, miss. I had no intention of harming you in the train."

"You followed us from Chicago! Sam saw you in front of the grocery store that night with the gangsters!"

"I followed you from Chicago, that's right."

Sam spoke up. "Lily, this gentleman is Setni, the high priest."

A breath of disbelief hovered in the air. It was as if Sam had recited a very ancient and very secret incantation and summoned a genie or a ghost. The person standing before them was nearly three thousand years old! He came from a world where people built pyramids, worshipped the sun, launched golden boats on the Nile, and mummified their dead. He was the one person who might be at the origin of everything, the one who had traveled through Time further than anyone — and today he had come here to help them.

"Setni?" Lily repeated.

"It's an honor," said Sam, bowing deeply.

"Straighten up, young man," said the high priest kindly. "So, you know my name?"

"I met your son Ahmosis in Thebes."

"Ahmosis! Thebes!" the old man exclaimed. "So I was right. You have indeed been using the Thoth stone. And that is why you emerged from the demolished house."

Lily was surprised all over again. "You mean you were at the construction site too?"

"Of course! Otherwise how could I have found my way to your store? I came to the great city of Chicago to find out why that stone was going to be destroyed. For several months, something unusual has been disturbing the paths of Time, and it is my duty to discover what it is. And then I suddenly see you emerge from the ruins, with the workers all wondering where you could have popped up from."

Something unusual, thought Sam. *What if that unusual thing was me?*

"I guessed that you had pierced Thoth's secrets, and I decided to learn more about you," Setni continued. "To see if you were the cause of these perturbations, for example. You are the first children I have encountered on the paths of Time!"

"So we led you to the grocery store that evening? You didn't have any connection with the gangsters inside?"

"Of course not! I even had to, er, encourage them to leave."

"You chased them away?" exclaimed Sam and Lily together.

"No, *you* chased them away; I merely helped convince them to depart. They fired a shot in the air to frighten me, but I have some experience with combat, as these young louts discovered. In any case, that additional agitation piqued my curiosity. So I watched you for a few days and decided yesterday to approach you in the train car. I did not expect you would give me the slip!"

"How did you find us after that?"

"There are very few Thoth stones in this era and on this continent. Besides, I have often come to Sainte-Mary."

"Barenboim?" wondered Sam.

"You know Garry Barenboim!" the old man cried with delight. "You really are very surprising!"

"We've only heard about him," Lily explained, "but we know that this house belongs to him."

"And so does the stone statue," said Setni.

Sam pointed downstairs. "Speaking of the stone, I'd like to make sure it's still there."

They silently walked down to the basement. It was very dark, and they had to kick out the boards nailed across the little window to get some light and air. What they saw was appalling. It was likely that nobody had cleaned the basement since Barenboim's death some fifteen years earlier. It had a thick layer of dust, a tangle of spiderwebs, mold on the walls, at least two dead rats, and a mound of decaying garbage, some of it related to the lack of sanitary facilities they had already observed upstairs.

"This is disgusting!" said Lily, gagging.

"It is not much compared to the world's misery," answered Setni enigmatically.

They started to clear the back of the basement, where a jumble of rusty machinery prevented them from reaching its darkest corners.

"Well, is it here or isn't it?" asked Lily impatiently.

Sam frantically tossed loom parts and empty thread bobbins out of the way, his energy fueled by anxiety. Finally he shoved a pile of metal spindles aside and uncovered the stone.

"It's beautiful," Sam murmured. He stroked the statue, seeking the familiar vibration. But he felt only a distant trembling, imperceptible to the uninitiated. Something was missing. He looked up at Setni. "The problem is, we don't have a coin anymore."

The high priest's expression remained unreadable. Then he said, "Am I to understand that you have been traveling the paths of Time at random, with a single disk of Re?"

"A disk of Re?" asked Sam, feeling ill at ease. "Well, we started with three of them, but we had really bad luck and had to leave very quickly each time. Either we were in danger, or the stone was threatened. Anyway, we left our three . . . our three disks of Re behind."

The old man looked at him sternly. "Traveling that way is very imprudent, my young friends. There are many things you seem not to know, and . . ." He rubbed his bald head. "Before going any further, I think we had better talk."

CHAPTER SEVENTEEN

Revelations

They gathered in the room with the mattresses, after clearing away the empty bottles and creating a more or less clean space around the armchair. Setni took off his long gabardine and made himself comfortable, sitting cross-legged in the chair. Under the coat he wore a linen tunic and a woven belt with a long leather pouch. He occasionally glanced out the window to make sure no one was coming up the walk, though he remarked once that Paxton's gang wouldn't be back anytime soon. "They are like all cowards," he said. "Strong against the weak and weak against the strong."

For a full hour, Sam and Lily told Setni how they had discovered the stone and described the adventures they'd had up until landing in Chicago. The high priest didn't interrupt, merely nodding when the two described this or that obstacle they'd had to overcome. When their account was finished, Setni gazed into the distance, apparently lost in thought. Then he turned to Lily.

"Come here, my girl." The old man carefully examined the

whites of her eyes. "How many days did you say the fever lasted?"

"Three days."

"You caught Time sickness, no doubt about it. When it happened to me, I spent a week flat on my back, unable to move. Some people die of it, others never catch it. But you are now cured. You just need some rest."

He then questioned Sam about what exactly had happened when the bear attacked the stone in the cave and during the Pompeii earthquake. He also wanted to know more about the Arkeos man and the symbol, though he listened to the answers without any reaction. Finally he folded his hands under his chin and smiled gravely. "Do you know the story of Imhotep and King Djoser, children?"

Sam and Lily shook their heads.

"It happened a long, long time ago, more than eighty generations before my birth. Djoser was a wise pharaoh who had conquered many lands. He was the richest and most powerful of the world's rulers. A word from him was enough to send armies without number to attack an enemy or teams of workers to build the most magnificent palaces. Yet Djoser was unhappy. He had a daughter, Neferur, whom he loved more than anything and who suffered from an incurable illness. Each day when she awoke, her bedding was soaked through, and she was weaker and thinner than the night before, unable to speak or feed herself. Imhotep, who was the king's physician as well as his architect, tried all of the potions known in the Upper and Lower Nile. He sent men to countries near and far in the hope that someone somewhere had heard of a similar illness and knew how to treat it. But in vain.

"One evening, when Neferur was near death, Imhotep asked Djoser's permission to speak in his name to the god Thoth, who is both the most skilled of the healing gods and the juggler of hours and seasons. After the king's physician spent a night in prayer, Thoth finally agreed to help him, on the condition that Imhotep build a monument in his honor, the likes of which had never been seen in Egypt before. Imhotep swore that he would.

"'The pharaoh's daughter has but one more day to live,' the ibis-headed god told Imhotep, 'and there is no remedy in this country that can cure her. If you want to save her, you will have to travel the paths of Time in search of an appropriate medicine.'

"Imhotep agreed, and Thoth designed a stone carved with a sun that would allow him to travel to seven different eras with the help of seven disks of Re, the sun god.

"'You will have but a single day to spend visiting each of these worlds,' said Thoth, 'and each of those days will be as the seventh part of a day here. Once that day is over, if you have not returned or if you have failed, the princess will die and you will die with her. I will follow your progress on this scroll.'

"He showed Imhotep a papyrus, the scroll of Thoth, that displayed a series of hieroglyphs, always the same ones. Finally the god taught Imhotep how to carve stone statues so he could pursue his quest wherever he was. And thus, before sunrise, Imhotep set out on the paths of Time."

Setni paused, opened his leather pouch, and pulled out a sheaf of fine, rolled-up papyri. "I think the scroll of Thoth looked something like this."

The sheets were dark yellow, faded and aged, with black handwritten signs repeated in groups of thirty or forty.

"We have something like that back home," Sam said. "A Book of Time with a red cover and identical pages."

"Do you know where that book is right now?"

"In Lily's bedroom, I guess," he said. She nodded.

Setni made no comment, but didn't seem pleased by the answer.

"What about the rest?" asked Lily.

"I beg your pardon?"

"Imhotep! Where did he go in Time?"

"Oh, the rest of that story! I do not know it."

"What do you mean?" insisted Lily. "You promised us the story of Djoser, and you're stopping halfway through!"

The old man's eyes had a sly gleam. "I did not say that. The fact is, I cannot tell you the story of Imhotep's seven voyages because his account of them disappeared during the invasion by the Hyksos, barbarians from the East. We think his journal was taken out of Egypt, along with many other things. Only a small chest containing a dozen tablets was spared and hidden in the Temple of Amon."

"Where you found them," suggested Sam.

"Yes, a year after I became the high priest. The tablets were especially interesting because they explained exactly where to find the Thoth stone and how to use it."

But Lily wasn't letting Setni off the hook. "What about Neferur?"

"Neferur? Imhotep was able to bring her the medicine she needed — antibiotics from your era, I believe. And as promised, Djoser had him erect a monument unlike any seen before:

169

a stone pyramid, the first pyramid in Egypt! Djoser is entombed there, but it was originally dedicated to the god Thoth — something people have forgotten today. As for Neferur, she lived a long and happy life without knowing anything of her physician's exploits."

"Imhotep made seven voyages," Sam said after a few moments. "How many have you made?"

"Many, many more. How old do you think I am?"

"Sixty or sixty-five," Lily guessed.

"I am forty-seven. What you see in my face are the marks of the distress and suffering of the thousands of lives I have encountered. The world is cruel, whatever century one considers it from."

"Then why have you continued to travel?"

"Because I have no choice. As the guardian of the Thoth stones, I must watch over them and make sure no one uses them for evil purposes. I have even drawn up a map with the location of each one according to its period. It is coming along nicely. Here, take a look."

From his bag he took another scroll, which he unrolled with a hint of pride. The outlines of oceans and continents were approximately marked — probably the way Setni imagined them — and there were dozens of black and red notations. One could make out mountains in dark green; the courses of great rivers in blue, with the Nile being the most recognizable; and dots with names that might be cities or notations on the time period involved. Finally, there were a few tiny pinholes. The overall layout was beautiful but quite hard to read. According to Setni's representation, the Earth was a multicolored archipelago with vague borders.

Parts of it had apparently been explored, but most remained undiscovered.

"How many stone statues are on your map?"

"I have counted about fifty."

"About fifty!" cried Lily. "But the legend speaks of Imhotep's seven voyages. Seven voyages, seven stones, right?"

"That is also what I thought at first. But do not forget that the god Thoth, in his great wisdom, taught the architect-physician how to carve his own stones in order to help him in his research. So seven is the number of original stones. Imhotep's knowledge must have later passed on to other travelers, who in turn have seeded the wide world with stones. I know from experience that someone who travels the paths of Time feels the urge to carve the sun of Re at least once. If he chooses the place with care, and especially if his intentions are pure, the spell can work and the stone comes alive. But he who scorns Thoth's magic and carves a stone solely to become richer or more powerful never gets more than a useless piece of rock."

"Is there anything on your map that relates to Bran Castle?" asked Sam.

To answer, Setni didn't even need to consult his scroll. "I do not claim that the map is complete, unfortunately, or that it ever will be. But if you really want to find your father, there are some things you must learn, in particular about the disks of Re. The way you are using them now is too uncertain. With just one disk, your destination is in the hands of fate. You could wander the paths of Time for centuries without ever reaching Bran Castle!"

"That's exactly why I need those seven coins!" answered Sam forcefully.

"But the seven coins have a major drawback. They will indeed transport you to the desired period, but they remain behind in the one you left. So while you reach the place you want, you deprive yourself of any way to return!"

"But I managed to get back," Sam pointed out. "Several times."

"Only thanks to your cousin, my boy. Despite your ignorance of the workings of Time, you have had incredible luck. Very few humans can bring time travelers back to their point of departure. It is a power possessed by only a few women and is said to be transmitted from mother to daughter. As for developing the skill, one must be a very experienced magician. This girl was born with it."

Sam suddenly found himself looking at his cousin in a new light. It wasn't enough for just anyone in the present to be thinking about you. That someone had to have a gift — a special priceless gift — and Lily had it! She *was* a truly exceptional girl.

But Lily behaved exactly as if they were talking about someone else, keeping her eyes on Setni as she pursued her line of thought. "If you started drawing a map of the stones, that must mean there's a way to travel with certainty, right?"

Setni again reached into his leather sack and took out a kind of wooden button. He unscrewed it, and it came apart in two halves.

"This capsule was given to me by the widow of a Chinese emperor, who was about to die herself. She told me that by slipping a disk into it, the stone would take me where I wanted to go. But a capsule like this can only be used once, and I never dared try it."

"So you have a more reliable way to travel?" Lily pressed him.

The high priest stood and went to the window to look at the street.

"As I said, the legend of Djoser does not tell the whole story. To allow Imhotep to make his voyage, Thoth gave him a third gift in addition to the stone statue and the disks of Re: a jewel that the god had forged with his own hands. It was a finely worked bracelet that he called 'the golden circle.' Almost no written descriptions of it have survived. Imhotep could slip six of the seven coins onto the bracelet before fitting them into the six rays of the sun. That way, when he applied the seventh coin to the sun, he not only reached his desired destination, but all the coins made the voyage with him — even the coin in the sun. Thanks to the golden circle, Imhotep could move as he pleased among the seven times made available to him by the seven coins. It was his key to the paths of Time!"

"And that's why the coins have holes in them!" said Lily excitedly. "So they could be threaded on the golden circle!"

Driven by a sudden impulse, Sam stood and approached the high priest. "Where is it?"

Setni patted him on the shoulder. "The golden circle? To my knowledge, a copy of the original was created somewhere in the Orient, probably on the basis of Imhotep's lost account. As to who has it today . . ."

"What about the original?" asked Sam in an unusually sharp tone of voice.

"It is in my possession," answered Setni calmly. "But I will not give it to you, as you can well understand; nor will I show it to you, because it might turn your head. Its influence is unpredictable, let us say. Some have gone mad at the idea of possessing it."

Sam felt a wave of irrepressible anger rising in him. He must have this golden circle! He needed it to save his father — right away! And if this old man refused to give it to him . . .

Almost in spite of himself, he took a step closer to Setni, but the high priest stopped him with a gesture.

"I can sense your anger, my boy, but think of the treatment I gave Paxton and his gang earlier. You are not yet a match for me."

Setni's firm voice and serene expression made Sam's aggressiveness evaporate immediately. "I'm sorry," he said, feeling abashed. "I don't know what came over me. I couldn't help myself."

"The fascination exercised by the golden circle can corrupt the best-intentioned minds, my boy. Consider your anger a warning, and try to remember it in the future."

"But what's the point of explaining these things to us if it won't help us bring Sam's dad back?" asked Lily.

"In the kind of quest that you are on, my young friends, the truth is far preferable to a lie. It will allow you to make right and necessary choices when the time comes. That time will surely come, and much sooner than you may wish. Too many things are happening around you and the stone. The bear that attacked it in the cave, the earthquake that submerged and split it, those machines that buried it on the work site — do you to think that was all coincidence? A simple twist of fate? Normally, people barely notice Thoth stones, and as for animals . . ."

Setni again unrolled the map and pointed out some of the pinpricks on the papyrus to them. "For my part, a number of signs have warned me that danger was threatening the paths of Time. Look: These points correspond to places where stones have disappeared these last months. Here is the city of Vesuvius, and here is the bear clan's cave."

He pointed to two fairly widely spaced little holes on a colorful and vaguely star-shaped patch that might be Europe. "As I said, it was when visiting another of those places, in Chicago, that I made your acquaintance." He pointed to a landmass shaped like an elongated figure eight that must have been North and South America. "Having heard your story, here is what I think: I am almost sure that the Oracle of Delphi is right, and someone is trying to close the doors of Time. Someone has decided to destroy the stones to prevent you from going home."

A deathly silence followed. Sam and Lily sat petrified, as if an invisible darkness had suddenly shrouded the room.

"Des-destroy the stones?" Sam finally stammered. "You mean it's intentional? But how can someone act at a distance to keep us from coming home?"

"You have not taken proper care of your Book of Time, that is all. The book not only serves as a log of the travelers' voyages, it is directly linked to the stones. If you are traveling through Time — to 1932, for example — and some person who wishes you ill rips a page from your book, the stone through which you arrived will be destroyed. Unless you can find another stone, you would be condemned to live out your lives far from your own time."

"But the Book of Time is hidden in my bedroom," protested Lily.

"You can be sure it is no longer there, miss."

"But why come after us?" Sam asked. "We haven't done anything!"

The priest shrugged. "You may have unwittingly stirred up things beyond your understanding. Take this Arkeos man. The solar horns stand for Re's daughter Hathor, the two-faced goddess who can punish people severely or shower them with gifts. Depending on which path one takes, great good or great suffering can result. The man's ability to use this sign shows a high level of knowledge, and if he has profaned your Book of Time, as I suspect he has, it is not hard to know which path he has chosen."

"Does that mean Sam was right about the tattoo? That the Arkeos sign lets you travel to specific places?"

"Only to some extent," cautioned the high priest. "The sign of Hathor will take you to a place where you have already drawn it, but it does not let you choose a specific place among all those that exist. In other words, you may need ten attempts to reach one particular place. And the more signs there are, the greater the uncertainty."

Sam said, "What really scares me is that if the Arkeos man stole our book, that means he broke into our house. And that means Grandma and Grandpa are in danger. We have to go home as fast as we can!"

"I will not abandon you," Setni promised. "Even if your book is damaged, I have certain resources that I can draw on. You can start by taking the Chinese capsule. It will be more useful to you than to me." He handed the curious wooden button to Sam. "I will explain the rest downstairs," he added.

He headed for the stairs, with Lily at his heels.

"There's still one thing that bothers me," she said. "Can the Thoth stone send us to a period where we already are? What I mean is, is there any chance I'll run into myself at age seven or thirty-five?"

"That is very unlikely, my girl. A body is an assemblage of flesh, bone, and fluids, but a soul is completely unique. Two identical souls cannot be in the same place at the same time. If that were to happen, the soul would inevitably consume itself, unless the traveler were in a hypnotic trance or a magic sleep, perhaps. But otherwise . . ."

"That's good!" said Lily. "I'd hate to see myself twenty years older!"

They stepped into the basement, and Setni again rummaged in his sack.

"This should do the trick. As I told you earlier, an experienced magician can use his own book to send a traveler back to his or her starting place. I doubt that two travelers will be much more difficult than one." He handed Sam a coin.

Sam took the disk of Re in his fingers. It was an ordinary coin, with plant designs twining around the hole in the center, but it gave off a characteristic warmth.

"You are saving our lives, high priest."

"That is also my role, as a servant of Amon. And speaking of which . . ." He stared at Sam, and for just a moment, Sam had the feeling that an invisible hand was touching his brain. It was frankly unpleasant.

"I am getting older," the high priest said gently as he dropped his gaze. "Time is irreversibly wearing me down. I can feel it. And I am not immortal, as you know from visiting my tomb in Thebes."

Sam would have liked to reassure Setni about his age, to tell him that he still had many years to live, but the priest raised two fingers to prevent him.

"Shhh, my boy! I do not desire to know anything about my death, either what precedes or what follows it. That is one of the conditions of fulfilling my task honestly. But whatever happens, the Thoth stones will need a new guardian someday. Someone with enough strength to resist the temptations the traveler faces, enough heart to distinguish good from evil, and enough judgment to keep the course of Time from being changed. This last point is especially crucial. A series of infinite catastrophes could follow if someone decided to change the unfolding of the world — someone like your Arkeos man, for example, who uses the sign of Hathor for his own profit. That is why there must always be someone to guard the stones. And I am convinced that you, Samuel Faulkner, would be worthy of fulfilling that function."

"Me?" Sam blinked. "But I just want to save my father and go home! That's it!"

"Of course, of course," said Setni. "It is too soon, much too soon! But think about it, and when the time comes . . . Well, make what you feel is the right decision."

The high priest took a step toward them. "It is now time for you to leave, my children. You are still far from the end of your road, and many other paths await you!"

He held them briefly in his arms, then led them to the stone. As Sam knelt to put the coin in the center of the sun, he couldn't help asking one last question, the one that had been on the tip of his tongue. "Will we see each other again someday?"

Setni's expression was unfathomable. "Probably not in the way you imagine, young man."

CHAPTER EIGHTEEN

A Matter of Trust

Sam slumped onto his side and remained prostrate for a moment, unable to move. He felt overcome by a great weariness, as if his body had reached the limits of exhaustion. But the fatigue didn't feel so much physical as psychological. The meeting with his great-grandparents and the high priest Setni, his cousin's illness, and the fear of never getting back to the present had all affected him more deeply than he liked to admit. And the main thing, saving his father, still lay ahead.

Even though he already knew where he was, Sam was pleasantly surprised when he opened his eyes: no more mold on the walls, no rusty machinery, no dead rats in the corners! The feeble glow from the night-light felt like a wonderful source of life, and the ordinary yellow stool struck him as being in perfect taste. He was home!

"Lily, are you okay?" he whispered.

His cousin lay huddled against the stone in a fetal position.

"I can hear you fine, Sam," she said in a thick voice. "No need to repeat everything!"

"I'm not repeating anything, Lily, that's just the echo effect. It happens when you come back to the present. It'll pass, don't worry."

She got to her feet with difficulty and gave him a questioning look. "Are we back for real, Sammy?"

"Yes! This is the basement — our basement!"

Lily put her face in her hands and started to cry. Sam gently wrapped his arms around his cousin to comfort her. Then, when he figured that the effects of the trip had somewhat dissipated, he led her out of the storeroom.

Upstairs, things had been straightened up a little. The armchairs were upright again and some of the books had been reshelved. Leaving his cousin at the threshold, Sam went to the front door, where he saw that a brand-new lock had been installed.

"The grandparents were here," he guessed. "They probably came with the police when they were looking for me. They took care of the basics, anyway. Do you feel up to facing them, Lily?"

"Are you kidding? I can't wait to see them!"

They left the bookstore via the backyard and took a bus home, wondering what fate awaited them. By the clock, their little prehistoric/Roman/North American escapade had lasted an entire twenty-four-hour day in the present, so everyone was likely to be furious at their disappearance. Sam didn't know which he should fear most: the cops investigating the museum burglary or the demonic duo of Evelyn and Rudolf. If those two got their hands on him, they would cheerfully cut him to ribbons and ship the pieces to a juvenile detention center. With the police, at least, regulations forbade that kind of treatment.

Grandpa and Grandma's garage was empty and locked.

"Do you think the Arkeos man could have come after them?" Lily whispered anxiously as she took out her keys.

"I dunno . . ."

They went inside, called for their grandparents without result, then raced upstairs. Someone had certainly been in Sam's room. Clothes were strewn on the bed, the night table drawer stood open, a book bag had been emptied onto Spider-Man's head — the foot-high model of the web-slinger was a gift from his father — and . . .

"My computer!" Sam shouted.

His desk was an indescribable mess — more indescribable than usual, that is — and the CPU of his computer was gone!

"Sam!" yelped Lily from the next room.

Sam rushed to her bedroom. The setting was pink and purple, but the chaos there was similar.

"The loudspeaker!" she moaned. "Setni was right!"

The speaker cover lay on the floor, and neither the Book of Time nor the small black notebook remained inside. The three coins with holes were still taped to the top of the speaker case, however, and Sam put them carefully in his pocket. On a hunch, he went back to his bedroom and saw that his closet had also been visited: The cardboard box where he stored everything related to the stone statue was empty.

"He came, Sam! He came here!"

Just then, the familiar roar of Grandpa's car rose up to them from the driveway, sounding like something between a chain saw and a trumpeting elephant. Sam and Lily rushed outside to greet their grandparents, who gaped at them as if they were ghosts.

"Lily! Sammy!" cried Grandma. "Oh my God!" They ran to her arms, and she burst into tears. "My babies! My little babies!"

Grandpa, on the other hand, was a lot less demonstrative. Wearing his grimmest expression, he gestured for them to go inside. When the door had closed behind them, he exploded.

"Son of a gun, Samuel! Are we going to have to lock you up or what? You just don't ever *think*, do you? Do you know how young your cousin is? What did you get her mixed up with this time? Do you realize that the police searched the house — under my own roof, right in front of my neighbors?"

In seventy-five years, little Donovan Faulkner had lost a lot of his carefree ways. He still made train noises, but now they sounded more like a runaway locomotive.

"Why the police?" Sam asked innocently.

"Because of the museum burglary, smarty-pants! You went there with Harold the other day, didn't you? Well, they found your cell phone in one of the rooms right after the theft!"

"And for that they searched our rooms?"

"Drugs, that's what they were looking for! And then you drag your cousin into it! I'm going to wind up thinking Rudolf is right!"

"Did they take anything?" Sam continued, keeping his cool.

"You want to know if they found your stash, is that it? Don't you have any shame at all?"

"Take it easy, Donovan, it's bad for your blood pressure," Grandma said. Then she turned to Sam. "Yes, they took some papers and your computer. They talked about breaking up a gang of drug dealers. . . . They're wrong, aren't they, Sammy?" she said imploringly.

"Of course they're wrong!"

"So will the young gentleman kindly explain what his telephone was doing in the museum?" asked Grandpa.

Sam looked at his grandparents one after the other. There was no way to back out now. The police were after him, and Aunt Evelyn would happily see him flogged through the streets in chains. But if he was going to save his father, he had to be completely free. Sam needed allies, and who better to protect him than his grandparents?

"Are you prepared to listen to me for at least fifteen minutes without yelling?" he said.

They sat down around the table in the living room, and Sam told them everything — or almost everything. He skipped the most sensitive episodes: the Vikings on Iona, for example, and the Bruges alchemist and his knife, and the bear in the cave. He was also careful not to mention his suspicions about his father's thefts, including the mortgage problem, the Navel of the World, and the Arkeos company. When he reached the final stage of the voyage, the Chicago visit, Sam could feel his grandfather stiffen.

He had no sooner finished than Grandpa pounded his fist on his thigh and shouted, "This is just unbelievable! A bunch of fairy tales! Time travel — is that the best you could come up with? If you think the police are going to fall for even a thousandth part of that nonsense, you've got another think coming!"

"I was there, Grandpa!" said Lily. "Chicago, the Faulkner grocery store — everything Sam says is absolutely true!"

"You've got to be kidding! He was poking around in the attic the other day. He must've come across some old photo albums, and that's the whole story! These are hallucinations, and it sounds to me like they come from taking drugs!"

"Don't tell us you never played with trains in the yard behind the store!" Sam protested.

"All the kids played with trains in those days — in a yard if they had one!"

"You must remember us, then. Lily spent three days up in the guest bedroom! You even came to the train station with us on the last day. There was a Pacific 231, and —"

"The train stations were full of Pacific 231s!"

"Well, what about Zeb?" asked Lily, putting her hand on her grandfather's arm. "Remember Zeb, the little stuffed zebra?"

Grandpa hesitated for a moment.

"Zeb," he repeated in a faraway voice. "Zeb . . . Yes . . . He was black and white, with zigzag stripes. I remember I used to put him on my bed and . . . How do you know about that?"

"Because we were there," Sam assured him.

"So is this . . . is this some sort of dream?" Grandpa was at a loss. "I'm going to wake up, for sure! Nobody can travel through time, right? Least of all you. No, it's impossible." He continued to mutter to himself.

He was quiet for a long time, and they took care not to break the silence. Then he suddenly looked at them differently, as if some veil across his memory had been pulled away. "Sam and Lily, that's right! I'd forgotten their names. I was so little! But the girl was sick. That's right, it's coming back to me. And the boy . . ."

He rubbed his eyes, wiping away the tears that filled them. "You're . . . you're right. There was that business with the two kids at the grocery store. They were bigger than me, and I remember the boy very well, with his knickerbockers and his yellow and orange clothes. I can't remember their faces, though. This is crazy . . . I apologize, Sammy. I never should have doubted you — you or your cousin."

He took both of their hands and kissed them hard.

"You stubborn old mule," said Grandma, who was as moved as he was. "If you'd only trust your heart a little more than your head!"

"To be honest, that year wasn't an easy one," he said by way of explanation. "So many things happened after that!"

"What sorts of things, Grandpa?"

"My father . . . I don't like talking about it, and it took everybody a long time to get over it. But that summer, I mean the summer of 1932, he killed a man."

Lily jumped. "What?"

Grandpa bowed his head. "A gangster threatened him one night when he was closing the store. This dirtbag said to give him money or he and his pals would come after Mom and me. Dad had a gun, and . . ."

His voice fell to a whisper and died away.

"The Browning pistol," guessed Sam. "And the mob!"

"That's right. The investigation didn't turn up anything. But looking back now, with what you've told me, I think I know what must have happened. The gangsters had already threatened him once, he bought a pistol just in case, and when they came back . . ."

Grandma walked over, put her arm around her husband, and finished the story. "His lawyer argued it was self-defense, and James Faulkner was acquitted," she said. "But the poor man was broken, and so was Ketty, of course. Her husband already had a weakness for the bottle, and after that . . ."

Grandpa forced a smile. "When I think that you saw the two of them just before that terrible business . . . At least they seemed happy then, didn't they?"

For her grandfather's benefit, Lily gave a detailed account of their stay at the Faulkner grocery store, stressing Ketty's big heart and James's gruff kindness. This seemed to delight him, and he began to get some of his good humor back.

"I like that a lot better!" he said happily. "And if they helped you seventy-five years ago, it would be pretty sad if your grandmother and I didn't do the same today! Not that I think it's going to be easy. Remember, the police are still looking for Sam, and Evelyn is on the warpath. What do you plan to do?"

"Do you know where Mom is now?" asked Lily, sounding worried.

"Rudolf took her to the doctor to renew her prescription for tranquilizers," said Grandma, sighing. "When she found out that you'd disappeared, she had hysterics. She hasn't been very well these last days, but if we break it to her gently, without rushing her, I think she'll understand. I'll take care of everything."

"No way!" said Sam. "Letting anyone else know about the stone statue is impossible, and especially not Aunt Evelyn! Dad's life depends on it! I have a coin from the right time period and the Chinese capsule to get me there. I absolutely have to try to bring him back without anybody else getting involved."

"You mean to go to that Dracula person?" asked his grandmother, dismayed. "In that medieval castle, with knights everywhere ready to kill you? Sammy, you can't be serious!"

"I can take care of myself, Grandma. Otherwise I wouldn't have made it this far! But I'll tell you what: Before I go, I promise I'll learn everything I can about Vlad Tepes. That way, all the odds will be in my favor. It'll just be a matter of a quick round-trip."

"What if you're taken prisoner there?"

Unexpectedly, Grandpa came to his grandson's rescue. "Martha, do you think Sam could live as a man and look himself in the face if he abandoned his father? I reproached myself for years for not being able to help mine. Besides, Allan sent his call for help to Sammy, didn't he? That shows he trusts him more than anybody else. What more proof you need? If I were younger . . ."

But Grandma wasn't giving up that easily. "What about the police? And Evelyn? What are we going to tell them?"

Lily raised her hand, like at school. "I've got an idea," she said. All eyes turned to her. "I ran away."

"What?"

"Yeah, I ran away. The main problem is that my mom and the police think our disappearances are connected, right? And that somehow it's all Sammy's fault. We just have to separate the two. So we'll say I ran away."

"Mind telling us a little more about that?" asked Grandpa warily.

"Let's say I was really in love with Jennifer's brother Nelson, and I decided to run away to visit him at summer camp. On the way there, I realized what I was doing was stupid, so I turned around and came home. Nothing to do with my dumb cousin!" She grinned at Sam.

"Running away — you?" asked Grandma, astonished.

"I'm twelve years old, it's the right age for that sort of thing," she said firmly. "Besides, it'll be fun to do a little acting."

"And what about Sam in all this?"

"Sam goes into hiding long enough to do his research and get his father. When he brings Uncle Allan home, these disappearances won't seem very important."

"But where can he hide?" asked Grandpa. "Evelyn will be back here soon, and the police could show up at the bookstore any time, especially after the break-in the other evening."

Sam raised his hand in turn.

"Um, I think I have an idea too."

CHAPTER NINETEEN

Vacation Homework

Was this really a good idea? Sam studied the bedroom walls, which were covered with posters for the Blond Satans, an obscure hard-rock group leaning to Goth metal. Its members favored provocative outfits — leather jackets with lace ruffles — and outrageous eye makeup, but had the cherubic faces of kids just out of high school. Sam dropped his book bag on the bedspread, which was decorated with a large skull, and tried to look pleased.

"Cheerful, isn't it?" sighed Helena Todds. "Rick is fascinated by all this morbid stuff. I don't know where it comes from!"

"He'll get over it," Sam assured her. "I've had lots of friends like him."

"I'm glad to hear that — it means this won't seem too weird to you! Anyway, Rick is at his grandmother's for three weeks, so you're welcome to use the room."

Sam silently wished Grandmother Todds good luck, condemned as she was to spend part of her summer listening to the Blond Satans.

"I'll let you settle in," she continued. "Alicia probably won't be back until late this afternoon, but if you need anything, I'll be downstairs. We eat dinner around eight."

Sam thanked Mrs. Todds again and even gave her a hug. As soon as she learned that Sam's father had been missing for two weeks and his relationship with his aunt was getting stormy, Helena had welcomed him with open arms. Sam guessed that she still felt guilty about neglecting him after his mother's death and was eager to make it up to him. What Alicia would think about his arrival, however, remained to be seen.

Sam cleared away the clutter on Rick's desk — funny how irritating another person's mess can be — and set down the stack of books he had checked out of the library: a history of Romania, local maps, a biography of Dracula, and so on. His plan was simple: to lie low for a couple of days, avoiding everybody who was after him, and study up on Vlad Tepes. Didn't people say that to defeat your enemy, you must know him first? The clearer the picture he had of Vlad, and the more he knew about Vlad's habits and his life at the castle, the easier it would be for him to rescue his father.

When Sam had pushed the stack of Gothic magazines and bumper stickers aside ("Eternity Is Gothic," "Doom Metal Is Above Music"), he took out a pen and paper. It was time to get to work.

He quickly discovered that it was difficult to describe Vlad Tepes in a few words, other than the fact that he wasn't the sort of guy you'd invite for a fun weekend. Vlad's father, the *voivode* — or duke — of the Romanian province of Wallachia, was the victim of an unhappy geographical situation: His country lay right where the Christian and Muslim worlds met, at the junction of trade routes linking Europe to Asia. As a result, he spent most of his life waging war before being assassinated by the Hungarians. In the Middle Ages, it was a common practice to force a defeated enemy to leave his sons with the victor, and little Vlad spent his childhood bouncing between Wallachia, Transylvania, and the Turkish sultan's court, where he spent four years as a hostage.

It was a troubled and somewhat sad childhood, but he recovered to seize the throne of Wallachia in a daring coup in 1456, when he was about twenty-eight. The same causes produce the same results, however, and Vlad quickly realized that he was the filet mignon sandwiched between the Turks and the Hungarians. Everybody drooled over Wallachia, and Vlad soon found himself waging war in turn, determined not to be swallowed whole by his ravenous neighbors.

At that point, things started to get weird. To make himself completely inedible, as it were, Vlad imposed a reign of terror on his subjects, mercilessly executing anybody — man, woman, or child — whom he felt might possibly be a threat to him, no matter how remote. Chronicles of the time included bloody accounts of the voivode of Wallachia chopping up relatives, monks, advisers, soldiers, Turks, Hungarians, city dwellers, country dwellers, and every other kind of dweller. Worse, he reveled in torturing people, in ways each more horrible than the next: thieves boiled alive in huge pots, rebels tossed onto enormous bonfires, prisoners given crawfish to eat that had fed on their relatives' brains, and a thousand other such delights.

But Vlad's point of pride, so to speak, was unquestionably

the stake, which earned him the name "Tepes," or "Impaler." He apparently liked nothing better than to see forests of stakes — as many as several thousand, according to some records — on which he'd had his enemies skewered, without distinction of age or sex. Even if these descriptions were some-what exaggerated, Allan had clearly picked one of the cruelest jailers in history.

Someone knocked on the door, and Alicia entered without waiting for an answer. She was wearing a tennis outfit and looked wonderful, her skin already tan from the June sun and her blond hair pulled back in a neat ponytail, but she was frowning. She glared at Sam, then went to sit on her brother's bed with her knees drawn up under her chin and a sulky expression on her face.

Sam turned to her and stammered, "I'm — I'm sorry, Alicia, I should have asked what you thought about it first. But when I came here two days ago, I had no intention of mov-ing in with you, I swear. It's just that things are pretty bad at home and —"

She gestured to him to be quiet and not pay any attention to her. His cheeks suddenly burning, Sam felt at a loss. He knew he'd acted pretty high-handedly in imposing his pres-ence on her, but at the same time, he couldn't help but think her gorgeous, more beautiful than beautiful, the ethereal Queen of the Elves lost in a dark cavern. And he, the unat-tractive, miserable human insect, felt thrilled to be there despite the shame he was feeling. Completely pathetic!

Since Alicia remained stubbornly silent, he tried to go back to work. But the words danced on the page, and he felt incapa-ble of reading a single whole sentence. His heart was beating so hard he had to hold his chest to keep it from bursting out. But none of this mattered, because he was so close to her — not six feet away.

Finally, after what felt like half an hour, Alicia decided to speak. "Mom says that your dad has disappeared. Is that true?" Her tone wasn't exactly friendly.

"Yes. We haven't had any word for two weeks. But I promise I'll only be here for a couple of days, just long enough to —"

"That's not what I'm angry about," she interrupted. "Jerry and I had a fight."

"Oh . . . I'm sorry."

"It's not enough to always be sorry, Sam! We had the fight because of you! Jerry told me he was going to call Monk, and the two of them were going to beat you up if you tried to see me again."

Paxton and Monk — like great-grandfathers, like great-grandsons!

"They've had it in for me ever since I beat them in the judo tournament," said Sam cautiously.

"This has nothing to do with judo!" Alicia snapped. "It has to do with me! I had to tell Jerry *again* that there was nothing between us, and I got really angry."

"That was the right thing to do. If he doesn't trust you, he doesn't deserve you."

"I'm not sure he deserves me, but if he runs into you somewhere —"

"I'm not afraid of Jerry, Alicia," said Sam forcefully. "Not on the judo mats and not off them. But if he ever hurt you, he'd have to deal with me."

The words just spilled out without his even thinking, and they happened to be true. Alicia must have appreciated them, because she seemed to relax a little.

She hopped off the bed and came over to look at the books on the desk. "Are you doing schoolwork? Aren't you on vacation?"

"Yeah, but I made a deal with my history teacher. My grades weren't so great this year, so I have to write an extra paper on the Middle Ages. He picked Vlad Tepes — Dracula, that is."

"Dracula? Your history teacher is kind of weird, don't you think?"

Helena Todds called from downstairs just then, saving Sam from having to answer. "Soup's on, kids!"

They spent most of the evening together, listening to music and talking a little. Alicia was still defensive, and she didn't miss a chance to boast of Jerry's boundless good qualities — aside from his obsessive jealousy, of course. But overall, Sam hadn't felt so happy since . . . since when, actually?

The next morning, while Alicia was still asleep, Sam returned to his overview of Dracula's adventures. Like most bloody tyrants, Vlad Tepes came to a bad end. After a cruel six-year reign, he was dethroned by the sultan of Turkey and thrown into prison. But that apparently didn't stop him from indulging in his taste for torture, catching mice and impaling them on little sticks — definitely a creepy guy. A long period of exile and many intrigues followed. Then just when Vlad was about to reconquer Wallachia, one of his own men attacked him from behind and cut off his head. Strangely enough, his former subjects didn't turn out in droves to mourn his passing.

Except that the story didn't end there. Long after his death, Vlad Tepes's dark legend became embroidered with ever more frightening episodes until it merged with the character of the most feared creature in local folklore: the vampire. Vlad was now being called Dracula, which roughly translates as "Son of the Devil," but also referred to his father's membership in the prestigious Order of the Dragon, as *draco* means dragon in Latin. At the end of the nineteenth century, Bram Stoker used these various elements to create the fictional character Dracula, who would take on mythic dimensions and eclipse the actual story of the voivode of Wallachia.

Sam closed the biography and took out one of the coins with holes that his father had left with their neighbor Max before disappearing. A black snake coiled around the hole, which was obviously no accident: snake = dragon = Dracula. Allan had chosen this means to help his son find him, in case things turned out badly. And thanks to this coin and the Chinese empress's magic capsule, Sam would soon be at Bran Castle.

If nothing went wrong, for once.

Around ten a.m., he got a call on the cell phone that Grandma had temporarily lent him. It was Lily, with the good news that Evelyn and Rudolf had come home and were so happy to see her they had bought her story about her running away without batting an eyelash. Evelyn had even been more affectionate than ever, promising to spend more time with her daughter. They had barely mentioned Sam, except to again deplore his lack of manners and moral fiber, the result of the disastrous example set by his father. The same old song and dance, in other words. Lily concluded by announcing that

Grandpa wanted to stop by the Toddses' with a present as soon as he could. What was the present? She didn't know.

Back at his desk, Sam studied the maps of Bran Castle. He was surprised to learn that it wasn't actually in Wallachia but in Transylvania, a little farther north. From what Sam had read so far, nothing proved that Vlad had actually lived at Bran Castle, but his life was so full of unknowns that anything was possible. Nowadays, the castle was billing itself as Dracula's home and had made its reputation among tourists who were fascinated with the character. But it presented Sam with one serious obstacle: The fortress had undergone major architectural changes since Vlad's time, and Sam didn't have the original plans. Entire sections of the structure could have collapsed and been rebuilt, enlarged, or razed. How would he be able to find his way around the castle under those conditions? He had to find a reliable way to orient himself if he wanted to be sure to reach the dungeon.

"Sam! Look what Rick sent me!" In a delicious gust of flowers and cinnamon, Hurricane Alicia burst into the room, waving her cell phone. Sam leaned over the small color screen and saw a badly framed photo of a painting he knew well: the portrait of Yser, painted in Bruges in 1430!

"Apparently you told Mom about it and she asked Grammy to go look in the attic."

"Yeah, I saw a TV program about somebody called Baltus. The painting struck me and —"

"Mom thinks it might be one of our ancestors. Do you think she looks like me?"

Sam angled the phone to reduce the glare. "Yeah, quite a bit."

"Cool, isn't it, having an ancestor who looks like you?"

"I'm sure she was really nice," ventured Sam, who knew exactly what he was talking about.

"When you think this painting was sitting up in an old trunk for fifty years, and that without you . . ."

As Sam studied the image, Alicia noticed the sheet of paper where he had copied the contents of the small black notebook. "What's this?"

"Oh, that? It's another exercise the history teacher gave me. A kind of historical puzzle."

"A puzzle, eh?" She began reading the elements aloud: "Meriweserre equals O . . . Xerxes, 484 B.C. . . . Izmit, around 1400? . . . Your history teacher isn't just strange, he's totally nuts!"

She leaned over and looked Sam full in the face, her blue eyes locked with his. "What are you hiding from me, Sammy?"

He struggled not to look away. "Nothing, Alicia! I'm not hiding anything, I swear."

Her face was barely eight inches from his, and she was so beautiful he could hardly stand it.

"You forget I know you, Sam. After all these years, I can still tell when you're lying. What's going on? Your dad vanishes one day, you move in here because you're not getting along with anybody, you lock yourself away for hours working on Dracula and some crazy puzzle, and then you see a painting on TV that just happens to be in my grandmother's attic!"

"It's a copy," he stammered. "It must be a copy. Artists often used to copy each other."

Alicia nodded slowly, then stroked his cheek affection-ately. "Too bad," she murmured. "You don't really trust me either."

She picked up her cell phone and took a step toward the door. "I'm going over to Melissa's this afternoon. We're plan-ning a camping trip."

Sam struggled to get his pounding heart under control. "Will you be gone long?"

"The day after tomorrow. Want to come along?"

An invitation . . . Sam's brain started to boil. Under any other circumstances, he would have loved to go camping with Alicia — he wouldn't have liked anything better in the world! But the day after tomorrow meant two days, and two days here meant two more whole weeks in jail for his father. He just couldn't do it.

"I'm sorry, Alicia," he said dully. "I already have plans."

"Okay, Mr. I'm Sorry. Have fun with your homework!"

She turned on her heel and went out, leaving Sam feeling shattered. *You total idiot!* he raged. Sam Faulkner, the village idiot! Why hadn't he taken the opportunity to talk to her, to admit everything? Maybe she would have understood. Maybe she could even have forgiven him. Maybe they could have . . . *Maybe, maybe, maybe!*

After Alicia left, Sam found himself eating lunch alone, as the Toddses were at work. Then he went back to Rick's room and switched on the computer. This time he planned to use the Internet to do research on Bran Castle. After many false starts — the Net had legions of Dracula nuts, enough to fill several asylums — he began to find information about Transylvania. And link by link, he located a Vlad Tepes discussion group that was about something more than blood-soup recipes and glow-in-the-dark vampire teeth. From an Australian Web surfer he got the URL of a role-playing site that sounded intriguing: Its home page was straight out of Dungeons & Dragons, but the site also had detailed maps of the various castles the voivode had occupied. In that way, Sam found a game called Strigoi Night for which the game master — a Romanian student who knew English — had drawn on his university's archives to re-create the original plans of Bran Castle. Better yet, the young historian claimed there had once existed an underground passage designed to evacuate the castle in case of emergency. This passageway apparently came out in a mill below the fortress and had been sealed up in the eighteenth century because of rockfalls. Sam feverishly wrote all this information down, feeling that he was getting closer to his goal. Vlad Tepes had better watch out!

The afternoon was almost over when Grandpa rang the front doorbell. He looked both relieved and preoccupied, a feat that involved every single wrinkle in his face and made him look like a withered old apple. He was holding a big plastic bag, which he clumsily tried to hide behind his leg.

"It's been a long time since I was here last," he said, sitting down on the living room sofa. "The Toddses are wonderful people, aren't they?"

"They've been really nice to me."

"So much the better. Your grandmother sends her love, Sammy, and so does your cousin."

"Any problems with Evelyn?"

"No. As Lily probably told you, her plan worked perfectly. Evelyn was so happy, she got Rudolf to speak to the police chief and have them give back the things they seized. I left most of it at home, but I thought you'd like to see this." He pulled the Book of Time out of his plastic bag.

"My God!" cried Sam. "What happened to it?"

The big volume's red cover was more battered than usual, scarred with scuff marks and scratches. It was also faded here and there, as if it had been left out in the sun and the weather.

"You'd almost think it had aged in two days," said Sam in astonishment.

"That's not all," added Grandpa. "Lily says that some pages have been torn out."

Nervously Sam opened the book. It was true: A number of pages were missing. Some had been carefully cut, others simply ripped out. The greater part remained, however, and they showed engravings of the town of Sainte-Mary in 1932. Each page bore the same title: "Sainte-Mary Country Fairs."

"Setni was right!" cried Sam. "The Arkeos man did try to keep us from coming back! But what about the police? How do they explain its condition?"

"It's pretty strange," answered Grandpa. "They claim that all the evidence was stored under lock and key and no one had access to it. Anyway, we can deal with the police later. Have you been making any progress?"

"Yes. I got hold of a plan of Bran Castle. That should save me some time."

"That's great. It sounds like you're on the right track. By the way, there's something I want to talk about that I didn't want to bring up in front of your grandmother. Exactly what was your father planning to do there in Wallachia?"

Sam had carefully avoided this topic before, but now he looked his grandfather full in the face. "I think Dad was partly supplying the bookstore with books from the past — and he may have stolen other things as well." Reluctantly he explained the situation with the mortgage and the Navel of the World.

Grandpa scratched his chin. "I was afraid it was something like that. Your father was very worried about money, unfortunately. We helped him out now and again, but he'd become so distant! And that mortgage . . ." He shook his head heavily. "I'm not sure how we'll manage that. Anyway, thank you for your honesty. Not a word to Grandma, of course. You know how proud she is of Allan."

"Don't worry, I'll keep quiet."

"That's good. One more thing: I brought you this."

From his bag, Grandpa took a package tied with string. With trembling fingers, he untied the knot and unwrapped a chamois cloth. It contained a black pistol.

"It's my father's Browning," he explained. "He was found not guilty at the trial, so they gave it back to him afterward. I've never been able to get rid of it. Maybe I was waiting for a moment like this one. Who knows? I've taken care of it, and it's in perfect working order. It's very easy to use. Look here."

He gave a quick demonstration — cylinder, hammer, trigger — that Sam watched somewhat anxiously.

"There are seven bullets left," said Grandpa. "Might be useful, where you're going."

With some trepidation, Sam took the Browning and hefted it, as if to get better acquainted. Should he take the gun to

Bran Castle? he wondered. It was a tremendous responsibility, and a scary one, especially since he'd never used a gun before. But he and his father were facing a man who skewered people for fun. The pistol frightened Sam, but Vlad Tepes frightened him even more.

CHAPTER TWENTY

Bran Castle

Sam had barely set the Chinese capsule on the carved sun when heat vaporized every drop of his blood, as if ten billion needles had exploded under his skin. Then the boiling vapor condensed, and scalding plasma started flowing through his veins. The trip through time had never been so painful.

He lay dazed for nearly a minute, too weak to vomit or even cough. When he came to completely, blood was dribbling from the corner of his mouth, and he had to spit several times to get rid of the bitter taste. *Thanks a lot, Chinese empress!* Maybe Setni would be good enough to check his gadgets' side effects next time.

Sam got to his feet with enormous difficulty, to find himself standing beside a river flowing through a dense forest. The sun barely pierced the gray clouds, and thick foliage blocked its weak rays. The forest understory looked dark and hostile, like the Ent forest in *The Lord of the Rings*. But the tall outline of Bran Castle could be seen rising above the river a mile or so away — success!

Sam retrieved the Browning from the stone's cavity and checked the bullets. It was reassuring to have it with him, though he didn't plan to use it unless it was absolutely necessary. But as he stuck it in his pocket, the huge risk he had taken by not bringing another coin began to dawn on him. He had assumed the wooden capsule and the black snake coin would travel with him through time, so he chose the immediate security of the gun over the escape promised by an extra coin. But the stone statue was empty — half hidden by reeds, holding neither the coin nor the capsule. *He had no way to get home!*

Well, that was too bad, he decided; he would deal with the problem later. First he had to take care of Allan. The best thing to do would be to follow the stream, try not to be spotted, and find the mill. Mills must be close to water, right? After that he could only pray that the Romanian student who drew the castle plans was an ace historian.

After his earlier flameout, the cool breeze felt good on Sam's face as he walked along the riverbank. The grassy path occasionally became so narrow that he was forced to detour through the forest of tall dark pines with scaly bark. The strangest thing was that there wasn't a sound to be heard, not even birdsong. The forest was mute, as if on its guard.

The closer he got, the more formidable the castle looked. It was perched on a rocky promontory, and its two towers, one round and the other square, seemed to challenge the sky. Compared to the way Bran Castle appeared in Sam's time, this medieval version appeared simpler and more massive, with fewer windows and buildings, and less whimsy in the arrangement of the roofs. It was surrounded by a strong wall and looked more like an impregnable fortress than a country resort. By squinting, Sam was able to make out a couple of helmeted soldiers standing watch on the parapet. He gripped the Browning, not fully certain of his invincibility.

The stream led him to a clearing choked by tall grass and dominated by the charred ruins of a stone mill. The water-wheel had been taken apart and its planks scavenged, and the rest of the building wasn't in much better shape. Half of the structure had collapsed, and chunks of blackened beams jutted from the ruins like rotten teeth. The fire must have happened a long time ago, because yellowish lichen had spread over a freestanding section of wall. If the underground passage really did begin there, he would have some excavating to do!

Sam stepped under what remained of the mill's roof and checked to make sure the floor wasn't going to cave in. The place was a tangle of stone blocks, branches, weeds, and spiderwebs. The upper floor was gone, and a staircase ended in midair. Behind it, Sam could see a room with arrow-slit windows. This part of the ruin was less chaotic, and some stones had even been stacked on the left. A crack in the floor indicated the presence of a trapdoor. Its surface had been swept clean at some point, and a rusty bolt lay nearby. Someone had gone this way.

Sam looked around for something to lift the trapdoor and noticed a twisted metal bar under an arrow slit. As he picked it up, he saw two letters scratched into the wall: *A.F.* Allan Faulkner — his father had left him a clue! He was on the right trail!

Sam grabbed the makeshift lever and strained to raise the trapdoor, his legs shaking. After two unsuccessful attempts, it finally fell open. The hole below it looked bottomless and as dark as a well. Feeling around, Sam touched the top rung of a ladder about a foot and a half down, so a caving challenge was definitely part of the day's program. Sam wondered if he should close the trapdoor behind himself after he climbed down, but decided against it: Best to leave the way open in case he had to beat a hasty retreat.

He descended a dozen rungs before reaching bottom about fifteen feet down, where the tunnel began. It smelled of moisture and mold, and he couldn't see a thing. He took a deep breath and cautiously started walking, touching the walls as he went. A couple of times his fingers brushed something furry that ran away squeaking, and Sam had to talk himself into not running away as well, in the opposite direction. The passageway finally ended in a wall, and he groped around for a moment before he found a fairly high step on his right. A staircase . . .

The steps were uneven and slippery, so he climbed up on all fours. To keep his focus, he started counting the steps to himself: one, two, three . . . As he reached a hundred and sixty-five, his knee bumped an object that would have clattered noisily down the steps if he hadn't grabbed it. It felt like a fat metal fountain pen with a swivel cap — not medieval material, that was for sure. Could his father have dropped it when he tried to enter Vlad Tepes's lair five or six months earlier? If so, that would mean that this secret stairway wasn't used very much, which was all to the good.

Sam resumed his climb, stopping more and more often to catch his breath. He lost count around the three hundredth step, so he tried to think about pleasant things, such as the first evening he and his father would spend together back in Sainte-Mary. Would they go out for pizza? Bowling? A movie? Or maybe just have a quiet meal at home, a couple of sandwiches in front of the TV? An ordinary slice of life in an ordinary family, that was what Sam wanted!

The top of the stairway was blocked by a low door reinforced with heavy iron straps. Sam ran his fingers over it, but didn't find a handle, lock, or hinges. He shoved it with all his might, but it didn't budge. It was as if it were part of the rock. If only he had a little light! *Come on,* he told himself, *take a deep breath and don't panic.* Resuming his inspection, he found a kind of groove at the edge of the panel. The door didn't swing open front to back, it slid from right to left! And when he pushed sideways he felt it move slightly, even though it seemed to weigh tons.

Inch by inch, Sam managed to open a space wide enough to slip through. Unfortunately, there was another obstacle right behind the door, a heavy wardrobe or large cabinet. He could see faint light on either side of it, and hear a man singing in the distance:

> *Through the fair greenwood high and low,*
> *Scabbard and tabard, dagger and bow.*

By bracing his leg against the wall and pushing with his shoulder, Sam was able to slowly shove the cabinet aside.

> *Through the fair greenwood high and low,*
> *Stalking the boar, stalking the doe.*

Sam was in luck. The man's lusty singing covered the squeaking the cabinet made as he wrestled it out of the way. He squeezed through the space, stretched his leg down, and felt his foot touch the floor. Whew! He'd made it!

He peered around. The stairway ended in an arched room hewn out of the rock: an armory, with halberds, maces, shields, crossbows and their bolts, and small cannons and cannonballs, all carefully hung on the walls or stored on the shelves of cabinets like the one that blocked the underground passage. Sam shoved the cabinet back in place, but left the heavy sliding door open — again to save time in case of a quick exit. The room next to the armory had benches and tables with helmets on them, and a fireplace. The singing came from a soldier who was roasting a haunch of meat. Melting fat sizzled in the flames as he swung into the next verse:

> *Shadows are length'ning, the moon starts to glow,*
> *Through the fair greenwood high and low.*

The singing chef seemed to be alone and completely absorbed in the pleasure of his anticipated feast. But Sam would have to pass right by him to exit the kitchen. The man had his back to Sam and wasn't paying any attention to what might be happening behind him — always a mistake.

Sam fetched a club from the armory — one that looked like a baseball bat with a spike at the end. Silently he crept up behind Wallachia's great singing hopeful.

> *Home to the castle, the cottage below,*
> *Through the fair greenwood high and low.*

Weaving her magic, my winsome Margot,
Through the fair greenwood high and —

The club crashed down on the man's neck with a thud.

"Hello!" said Sam.

The cook collapsed, and Sam grabbed him to keep him from falling into the fireplace. Faithful to the conventions of every infiltration game worthy of the name, Sam dragged him into a dark corner of the armory. Considering the state Margot's boyfriend was now in, it would be a long time before he got home.

Glancing through the guardroom door, Sam saw a spiral staircase connecting the basement and the upper floors, no doubt in the round tower. If he remembered the map correctly, the dungeon was located below the central courtyard, on the east side. The most discreet route was always the safest, so Sam decided it would be best to try going through the basement. He slipped downstairs, where the halls were lit by torches spaced at regular intervals. To his surprise, he didn't see anybody in the basement either. He could just barely hear the sound of marching steps in the distance. Were all the soldiers on vacation?

He began to investigate various hallways, hoping to find the dungeons. At one intersection, Sam thought he had reached his goal, but the barred grillwork he encountered protected only a few rows of barrels. After a few additional detours, he discovered a staircase that descended to the depths of the castle, and this one led to his destination.

He peeked out from behind the staircase wall to get a sense of the layout. The prison consisted of a fairly wide, low-ceilinged hallway with half a dozen cells off it, each with a heavy studded door. A soldier sat on a bench next to a table in the center of the hall, carving a piece of wood with an enormous knife. A pitcher of beer stood within easy reach, and the man was whistling a cheerful tune. Amazing — everyone seemed to be candidates for *Wallachian Idol*!

Unfortunately, the guard was facing the stairs, so once Sam stepped into the light, he would have no chance of remaining unseen. Well, he would need to get the keys from the guard anyway. He took the Browning out of his pocket, summoning his courage to use it if necessary. As he did, he felt the object he had picked up in the underground passage earlier. It was a tear gas cartridge, like the ones his father had bought to protect the bookstore! So it had indeed been Allan who'd used the tunnel from the mill. Had he planned to neutralize Dracula by squirting him with tear gas? Why not use a little garlic spray instead?

Struggling to master his fear, Sam stepped forward, gun in hand.

"I've come to free Allan Faulkner," he blurted.

This sounded like dialogue from a cheesy movie, but the soldier looked up in surprise. He had a reddish three-day beard and a flattened nose with a huge gray wart. "What —"

"Allan Faulkner," Sam repeated. "Where is he?"

The guard recovered. "By my mother-in-law's horns! Who do you think you are, you whiffet? Do you plan to flog me with your little stick?"

If he'd had the time, Sam would have raised at least two objections: He was not a "whiffet," whatever that meant, and his "little stick" represented five hundred years of technological progress. But he was in a hurry, so he shot the pitcher instead.

It exploded in a thousand pieces, and the echo of the gunshot filled the hallway. The terrified soldier leaped back and dropped his knife. "It's . . . it's black magic!"

"That's right," confirmed Sam. "And if you don't do what I say, I swear I'll do the same thing to your foot. Free Allan Faulkner now!"

"Allafaukner?" asked the guard. "I don't know who you're talking about!"

Had his father given them a false name? "He came five or six months ago. Fairly tall, dark hair, blue eyes."

"Oh, the madman! But if I release a prisoner, they'll kill me!"

"Would you rather die right now? What cell is he in?"

The man shot a worried glance toward one of the cell doors. Sam raised his gun slightly.

"All right, all right, I'll open up. But point that strange cannon somewhere else. I don't want it blowing up in my face!"

The guard took the key ring from his belt and unlocked the door. "You can go in," he said, stepping aside.

"You first," said Sam.

CHAPTER TWENTY-ONE

Conversation in a Cell

The soldier with the wart bent down to enter the cell. Sam followed, nudging the Browning's barrel into the man's ribs. The stench was pestilential and the cell's floor was strewn with straw, as if they were keeping wild animals instead of human beings. In the near darkness, all Sam could make out was a thin, huddled shape.

"Dad?"

The figure turned slowly to him, and Sam's heart sank. The man was so thin that his cheekbones seemed about to come through the skin. His nearly closed eyes were vacant, and his hair and beard were so long, he looked like the survivor of a shipwreck. But it was definitely his father.

"Dad?" Sam repeated.

"Sa-Sam?" came a quavering voice.

Sam felt something suddenly snap inside. Big hot tears began to run down his cheeks, and he made no effort to stop them. He cried silently, with joy and sadness, at finding Allan after all this time, after all the ordeals and terrors, at finding him in this pitiable state, but still alive — alive in spite of everything. He cried for his father, for Alicia, and for his grandparents who were so far away he wondered if he would ever see them again. He cried for his mother too, and for the pride she must be feeling as she sat in some little corner of heaven and looked down at him. He had succeeded.

But Sam's relaxing his vigilance for that moment proved fatal. Seeing his sudden vulnerability, the guard jabbed him with his elbow. The pistol went flying through the air, the soldier slammed his muscular body into Sam's chest, and they fell onto the straw. Sam rolled into a ball so as not to be crushed.

"You're going to suffer, whiffet," thundered the guard.

But the yell of rage died in his throat as an unknown figure leaped out of the darkness. Another prisoner! He looped his chained hands around the guard's neck and jerked them back. The soldier reared like an angry stallion, but his attacker held firm. A mix of rattles and gurgles followed, then a long sigh, then nothing.

"What a piece of garbage!" said the unknown prisoner. Then, to Sam: "The keys, quick, before he wakes up. They're hanging on a hook under the table."

Sam first retrieved his Browning, then went to get the keys. Back in the cell, leaving his rescuer to deal with his chains, he carefully put his arms around his father. Allan appeared to have lost half his body weight, and hugging him was like hugging a shriveled old man.

"Dad, it's me, Sam."

"Sam-Sam-Sam-Sam," Allan said in a singsong, his eyes vacant.

Sam saw a bucket with a dipper in the corner. "Here, drink this." He poured some of the water on his father's parched lips.

Allan's body was covered with oozing red sores, and the filthy scraps of a threadbare tunic barely covered his protruding ribs. He was no more than a bag of bones in rags.

"Save me, Sam . . . save me."

"I'm here, Dad. Can you hear me? I've come to save you! We're going home!"

"Sam-Sam-Sam."

The other prisoner knelt beside them to unlock Allan's chains. He was about twenty years old, with a narrow face and a determined expression. He seemed to have suffered much less from captivity than his cellmate.

"You're wasting your time, boy. He's been like this for days. I think he's lost his mind." He stuck out his hand. "My name's Dragomir."

Sam shook it gladly. "Have you been here long?" he asked as he rubbed his father's ankles, which showed the scars of the leg irons. Allan continued to chant "Sam" above his head.

"Three weeks, maybe four. You lose track of time fast in jail. I was carrying pepper and saffron from the Black Sea when my caravan was attacked. The master of Bran is demanding a ransom before he'll return me to my family."

"The master of Bran. Do you mean the voivode of Wallachia?"

Dragomir bared his teeth in what was probably meant to be a smile. "Yes, the Impaler. But you're well informed. I was given to understand that it was quite secret."

"What was secret?"

"The fact that the Impaler bought part of Bran Castle. He's very attached to this place but absolutely doesn't want anyone to know about it."

Sam, who was watching his father, didn't quite follow. "Oh?"

"The Impaler could have taken it by force if he'd wanted to, of course! But a war costs men, and he would have revealed that he coveted the castle. Instead he bought the right of residency to the square tower, so he can come and go as he pleases and nobody is the wiser."

This seemed like odd behavior for a warrior duke. "What's so special about Bran Castle that makes the voivode interested in it?"

The young man avoided the question with a shrug. "If you really want to know, go ask him."

"You mean he's here?"

"As far as I know, he is in Wallachia right now, fighting Sultan Mehmed. The lord of Bran is fighting his own war against one of his vassals."

Sam heaved a huge sigh of relief. So that's why the castle's corridors seemed so deserted! "But if the voivode wants to keep all this confidential, how do you know so much about it?"

Dragomir showed his teeth again. "The notary who drafted the contract between Lord Bran and the voivode was imprisoned here for a few months — to ensure his silence, of course. He died of a fever a few days ago."

So there were no witnesses, and there was no evidence of Vlad. That's why historians found it so hard to prove the connection between Dracula and Bran Castle!

Dragomir jumped to his feet. "We should get out of here. There's not much chance the other guards heard us, but they do make rounds."

Sam put his arm under his father's shoulder to help him to his feet. "All right, Dad, we're going now."

Supported by his son, Allan took a first halting step out of the cell, then a second. When he reached the guard's table, he had to shield his eyes against the candlelight with his hand.

"Where . . . where are we?" he stammered.

"In the Bran Castle dungeon," Sam answered. "But that's all over. We're going home now."

"We're going home," Allan said thoughtfully. "Yes, we're going home!" Then, slowly: "Sam? Sam, is that you?" He stroked Sam's cheek with his fingers, staring at him with feverish eyes. "Sam Faulkner! Allan Faulkner's son!"

"Not so loud, Dad. Someone will hear us!"

But his father didn't care. Mad with joy, he hugged Sam in his thin arms and proclaimed, "He came! My son came! Allan and Elisa Faulkner's son!"

As anxious as he was to get out of there, Sam embraced him in turn. How long had it been since his father had hugged him like this?

"Sam Faulkner!" Allan chanted, at the height of exultation. "Sam-Sam-Sam!"

But Dragomir quickly brought them back to reality. "We can't stay here any longer, it's too dangerous!"

Sam gently freed himself and helped his father to the staircase. Allan was so weak that it took a major effort to get him up the steps.

"Right here," Allan muttered once they were at the top. "Right here, I know."

"What's right here?" asked Sam.

"Vlad Tepes, of course," said Allan, whose mind seemed to be wandering. "He's the one who has it — right here!"

"What does he have?"

"He stole it in Izmit," his father continued. "When he was young. I remember now!"

Dragomir turned around, a finger to his lips.

"We have to be quiet, Dad," whispered Sam. "There are soldiers around, and if they catch us we'll never go home."

Allan stopped dead and glared at him. "I don't want to go home," he said in a determined voice. "I'm not going anywhere!"

"What are you talking about?" cried Sam in exasperation. "Don't you get it? If we stay here, we'll die!"

"I'd rather die than leave without it, do you hear? I'd rather die!"

Sam tried to pull him along, but his father resisted, bracing his legs with newfound determination and vigor. "Meriweserre's bracelet," he muttered urgently, as if that would change Sam's mind. "Meriweserre's bracelet! It's in the highest room of the square tower! We can take it easily!"

"We're not taking anything," said Sam angrily. "I don't care about that stuff! Come on!"

He pulled harder, but Allan let himself fall to the ground and started yelling: "Guards! Guards! I'm escaping!"

Dragomir jumped down and clapped his hand over Allan's mouth. "If you don't shut up right away, old man, I'll make you swallow your tongue!"

"Mmm-ards! Mmm-scaping!" Allan mumbled.

"Tell him to calm down or there's going to be trouble," Dragomir threatened.

Sam was suddenly at a loss. To find his father he had run from Vikings, crossed war zones, faced a bear, fought gangsters, and survived a volcanic eruption, and now Allan himself was preventing his own rescue! He was making such a racket, the soldiers were sure to raise the alarm — either that, or Dragomir would eventually strangle him. What could he do?

"All right, all right!" he said with a sigh. "Dad, listen. If you promise to wait for me by the hidden stairs, I'll go get your bracelet. Do you understand?"

"What hidden stairs?" asked Dragomir, his eyes suddenly alight.

"We came in through a tunnel that ends in a mill outside the castle. There's a passageway in the armory that leads to it." He turned to his father. "You remember that passageway, don't you, Dad? And the big dark staircase?"

With Dragomir's hand still over his mouth, his father nodded.

"Do you swear not to scream?" Sam insisted. "And to stay in the armory till I get there?"

Another nod.

"Let him go, Dragomir. He'll be quiet."

The young man obeyed grudgingly, and they set Allan back on his feet, letting him lean against the wall. They were ready to intervene if he seemed about to yell, but he appeared to be more in control of himself.

"Can you tell me exactly where the bracelet is, Dad?"

"In the highest room, Sam. In the square tower."

"What does it look like?"

"It's Meriweserre's bracelet, the pharaoh of the Hyksos! There's no mistaking it!"

The Hyksos, thought Sam. Setni had also mentioned them — barbarians from the East who had once invaded Egypt. But so what?

"There's just the problem of the cage," Allan added, as if it were a mere detail.

"The cage? What cage?"

"It's valuable, you know. They put it in the cage so it wouldn't be stolen! You just have to open it by . . ." He scratched his head anxiously while staring at the tips of his toes.

"By doing what, Dad?" Sam encouraged him.

"Well, there's a big combination lock on the cage. That's right. And then . . ." He gave his son a look of immense despair. "It's what they've done to my mind, Sam! I can't remember anything anymore! I should've explained things for you better. I feel bad about that. But we can go together, can't we? I need that bracelet, you understand? Otherwise I'd rather die here!"

He was getting agitated again, and Sam feared that Dragomir would step in. He absolutely had to get Allan to the secret stairway. After that . . .

"I told you I'd bring it back, Dad. You trust me, don't you? I got you out of the dungeon, I can make it to the tower."

"Yes, son, of course I trust you! Otherwise you wouldn't be here, would you?" With great gentleness, he leaned awkwardly toward Sam and kissed his cheek. "I've always trusted you, Sam."

"When you're done smooching here," Dragomir interrupted, "I'd really like to take that hidden passageway. And preferably without an army at my heels!"

CHAPTER TWENTY-TWO

Meriweserre's Bracelet

They separated at the first level of the round tower. Dragomir promised he would escort Allan to the armory and stay with him as long as there was no danger.

"But if any soldiers show up," he warned, "I'm not going to wait around. Sorry!"

For his part, Sam took a different hallway, which Dragomir said led directly beneath the square tower. At one point Sam had to duck behind an enormous column bearing the Bran coat of arms to avoid a pair of sentinels coming his way. The two men were joking about a feast planned for that evening to celebrate the return of the lord and his men. Bran was definitely a castle for laid-back good cheer.

Once in the square tower, Sam waited a full minute, listening to the sounds that came to him from the staircase. There were a few creaks, the whistle of wind blowing through an arrow slit, and some distant barking, but that was all. He had decided he would climb to the top room and look at the bracelet and what was around it so he could describe it to his father. Then he would head back down, saying that he hadn't been able to steal it. This would make his father happy and also convince him of his good faith. Besides, any place that had one such treasure could well hold others; he might find a coin with a hole to help them get home.

The tower was indeed deserted, as Dragomir had indicated, and no Bran soldiers were even standing by the doors. Through a crude glass window at the second landing, Sam saw a kind of living room with red curtains on the wall and dark wood chests. As he climbed three more stories, the steps gradually narrowed. At one point, they were little more than toeholds, and the stairway walls pressed in so tightly he could feel the coolness of the rock through his linen shirt. After ten more steps, Sam came to a heavy door bound with iron bands and flanked by two wicked-looking lances with jagged blades. The door's circular handle was in the shape of an undulating snake biting its own tail. Sam hesitated to turn it. After all, if an object as precious as Meriweserre's bracelet was really here, the door would surely be locked. But when he pushed down on the snake, the heavy door swung open.

From the threshold, Sam saw a square chamber that was open on all sides. Wide windows overlooked valley and forest, providing an extraordinary panorama of a sea of tall dark pine trees, some gray rock, the colored roofs of some nearby farm buildings, and the sky, close enough to touch. Under each window stood a black bench, supported by legs carved to resemble those of various animals. The seats were covered in vermilion cloth embroidered with images of armored knights battling lions or griffins. Slender ivory columns stood between the windows, decorated with an astonishing number of tiny grimacing faces. Were they meant to represent Vlad Tepes's victims?

This strange little room was otherwise empty except for a central pedestal that supported a wrought-iron cage. As Sam walked over to examine it, he noticed a portcullis mounted directly above the door. Apparently the chamber was usually protected by the grille; it seemed odd that no one had thought to lower it.

The cage was a cube about twenty inches square, with bars shaped like big, waving flames welded together. Inside was a striking miniature model of the entire high tower chamber, eighteen inches on each side, with the same gray wooden window casements, tiny ivory columns, and finger-length black benches with red cushions. A gold bracelet lay in the center on a silver stand . . . Meriweserre's bracelet, surely. It glowed with an unearthly radiance, almost seeming to give off its own light: a solid gold circle with a small screw clasp, engraved with a series of simple slits — and a tiny little sun with six rays.

Suddenly Sam realized what lay in front of him. Meriweserre's bracelet was the second golden circle! When combined with the seven coins, it was one of only two objects in the world that allowed a person to control his destination in time!

A number of previously random elements suddenly fell into place. Meriweserre, to begin with: the Hyksos pharaoh who had conquered Egypt and looted Imhotep's treasure. Sam remembered the list he had labored over at the end of the black notebook. "Meriweserre = O" must mean that the Hyksos pharaoh was the one who had made the object — a copy of Setni's original — since O could stand for object or the shape of the bracelet itself. After that, the golden circle must have passed through different hands — Xerxes, Caliph Al-Hakim — at different times — 484 B.C., 1010 — and different places — Isfahan, for example — before winding up with Vlad Tepes, its final possessor: "V. = O". From what Allan said a few moments ago, Vlad had stolen it in the city of Izmit. Allan must have set his sights on Bran Castle in the hope of pocketing the million dollars the jewel was certainly worth!

Sam tried to squeeze his fingers between the metal flames, but the cage was designed to thwart anyone reaching inside. "Some have gone mad at the idea of possessing it," said Setni. Had that happened to Allan Faulkner? Sam had to admit there was something fascinating about the bracelet, especially considering its immense powers. How would Vlad Tepes use them, for that matter? And why display this marvel here in the square tower, unguarded?

Sam examined the locking mechanism. The base of the cage was held shut by a four-inch iron jaw operated by the big combination lock his father had warned him about. The lock consisted of four cylinders — each marked with a series of numbers — mounted side by side, with a lever shaped like a wolf's head on the right. You entered the combination, pulled the lever, and got the bracelet — maybe.

He rotated one of the cylinders: 1-2-3-4-5-6-7-8-9-0. That meant there were 10,000 possible solutions. So why didn't the Bran soldiers try their luck? Weren't they gamblers? Or they were afraid of something?

Sam inspected the stand the cage rested on, a column of solidly intertwined crossbars. Inside it, he could see a pulley and the links of a chain that disappeared into the floor. So the lock operated some other mechanism in addition to the one that opened the cage.

Sam walked over to the nearest window, the one that overlooked the castle courtyard, and glanced down. One guard was casually pacing along the parapet; another was sitting on a barrel, jug in hand. Nobody seemed overly concerned about the square tower and its fabulous treasure. But when Sam looked at the top edge of the window frame, he understood why: A portcullis with razor-sharp spikes was hidden in the thickness of the wall. The other windows had them too.

Okay, Sam told himself. *Either the guy who gets here enters the winning combination the first time and bingo! He hits the jackpot. Or the four numbers he enters are wrong, and the grilles all crash down at the same time.* Suddenly the room itself would become a cage, a large-scale replica of the one around Meriweserre's bracelet. Diabolical! And enough to cool the hopes of any Bran soldier, especially considering what would follow: an intimate chat with Dracula!

Sam now knew enough to give his father a convincing picture of the situation. Allan would surely agree that he'd made the only possible decision: not to take a stupid chance. He stood one last time in front of the golden circle, wondering if a million dollars even came close to its real value. The perfection of the jewel's shape, the almost unreal glow it gave off, the striking simplicity of its design — did that actually have a price? To think it would take only four numbers to be able to seize it. Four little numbers — not much at all!

"Some have gone mad at the idea of possessing it," repeated the little voice in Sam's mind, and he shook his head to drive it away. For Allan to have successfully tracked the bracelet to the highest room in Bran Castle, he had to have assembled a colossal amount of information. Ditto to learn about the cage and the lock. Having done that, would he have ventured into Dracula's lair without knowing the right combination? That seemed hard to believe. And Allan had left a fair number of clues for his son. The serpent coin, for example, that he gave to their old neighbor Max. The cry for help scratched onto the wall of his cell. And the black notebook, with all its pages torn out; had Allan forgotten the notebook, or was it an additional clue? Sam was inclined to think it was a clue; otherwise, why leave it in the middle of the history section, where Allan might hope his son would go looking?

Once again, Sam recalled the mysterious list:

MERIWESERRE = 0
CALIPH AL-HAKIM, 1010
$1,000,000!
XERXES, 484 B.C.
LET THE BEGINNING SHOW THE WAY
V. = 0
IZMIT, AROUND 1400?
ISFAHAN, 1386

Could it involve a code? A code that Sam would be able to crack, but a less informed reader would see as only meaningless gibberish?

Yes, a code — that was the approach to take. A code that would have to yield four numbers. But the list consisted of eight lines and a lot of figures, especially in the dates, and they didn't seem to follow in any clear order. From Meriweserre — a couple of thousand years before Christ — the list jumped to Caliph Al-Hakim in 1010, Xerxes in 484 B.C., and then 1400 and 1386. Allan certainly hadn't stuck to the chronology of people and places. Was that confusion deliberate? Probably, assuming he had hidden a message in the text. So would it be enough to put things in the correct order? No, that produced an equally incomprehensible series of words and numbers.

What about the fifth line, the only one that didn't have proper names, dates, or a huge dollar figure? "Let the beginning show the way." Was it the way to the cage? The way of Time? What beginning? The bracelet clearly began with Meriweserre, but what followed that? Because the list had too many names and numbers, maybe he had to just concentrate on the beginning of each of the eight lines. The beginning — meaning the first letter.

Sam looked around for something to write with. A layer of fine dust lay on the floor of the room, so he bent down and wrote in it:

MC$XLVII

That still didn't make a four-digit number, but something told Sam he was on the right track. First, he replaced the $ sign with D for dollar:

MCDXLVII

That was better. Back in the days before Sam went to live with his grandmother, he often used to watch movies with his dad. At the end of the credits, a series of seemingly random letters appeared. Allan explained that the letters — M, C, L, X, I, etc. — were actually Roman numerals, and that early in the twentieth century, producers started using that notation for the dates of their movies. Because people had trouble understanding dates written that way, it might have been a way to fool audiences and distributors, since the studios could release so-called new comedies or Westerns that were already five or ten years old. Whatever the reason, it became a tradition.

Allan had then given Sam a little class in what each letter meant — M = 1000, D = 500, C = 100, etc. — and how to combine them. The general principle was that you added a letter when it was equal to or greater than the following one. For example: MC = M + C = 1000 + 100 = 1100. You subtracted a letter when it was less than the following one. For example: CM = M − C = 1000 − 100 = 900. Sam quickly worked to remember the other letters: L was 50, X stood for 10, V translated to 5, and I equaled one.

Carefully he scratched in the dust:

$$(M = 1000) + (CD = 500 - 100 = 400) +$$
$$(XL = 50 - 10 = 40) + (VII = 5 + 1 + 1 = 7).$$
$$TOTAL = 1447.$$

Four digits, exactly what was needed for the combination lock!

"What if the combination has been changed since your father arrived?" whispered the little voice. *But what if Vlad Tepes figured out how to use Meriweserre's bracelet?* Sam countered. A bloodthirsty madman rampaging through history would mean that all of humanity's safety was at risk! Besides, couldn't Sam trust his father at least as much as his father had trusted him?

He stood in front of the lock and turned the first cylinder to 1, the second to 4, the third also to 4, and the last one to 7. His hands were damp with sweat, and he could feel his pulse pounding at his temples. If he was wrong — or his father was wrong — the portcullis would come crashing down in a deafening clatter of chains and pulleys. The entire castle would be alerted and nothing could ever save him. But if he had guessed right . . .

He had to try.

Sam gently pushed the wolf's-head lever. It caught briefly, then slid smoothly all the way to the bottom. At first nothing happened, but a second later the iron jaw clicked open. A long creaking followed, and majestically the top of the cage unfolded. Meriweserre's bracelet was his!

Sam reached in, carefully took the bracelet, and set it on his palm. Up close, the jewel was even more beautiful. Beyond its own radiance, it gave off the same comforting warmth as the disks of Re. This was better than a dream, yet it was reality: Sam had the second circle of gold in his hand! He had become Setni's equal!

"Congratulations," said a voice behind him.

CHAPTER TWENTY-THREE

Sam the Magician

Sam spun around and reached into his pocket. But when he recognized the figure standing in the doorway, he immediately changed his mind. He would be dead before he could draw his pistol. In doing research on Vlad Tepes, Sam had seen a number of pictures of the voivode, and there was no mistaking him now: somewhat stocky, with long curly hair, a huge mustache, a strong nose and jutting chin, and catlike green eyes that glittered with evil intelligence. Vlad was wearing a red cap sewn with pearls and a black fur coat over a long red tunic. He also had a crossbow pointed right at Sam.

"So the stranger wasn't completely crazy," Vlad muttered. "He said that someone would come."

Sam clutched the golden circle, forcing himself not to move. He knew immediately that this man would never let him leave the castle alive, no matter what he said or did.

"I didn't expect someone so young," Vlad continued, waving the point of his crossbow. "Practically a child. And dressed like a peasant besides. Unless you are just a lucky little thief."

"I'm his son," said Sam soberly.

"His son, eh? How did you get here?"

Sam thought fast. Telling a believable story would do no good because Vlad wouldn't hesitate for a second to execute him. Sam had to impress the Impaler — or better yet, interest him.

"I travel where I please," he said. "Walls can't stop me."

Vlad might easily have burst out laughing, but instead, he examined Sam more sharply. "That is not the case with your father, apparently. He has been rotting in jail for weeks." His lips tightened. "Who gave you the numbers to open the cage?"

"I know things that others don't," said Sam, his mind racing.

"What sorts of things?"

Sam had read a lot about Vlad Tepes, but he had to hit a bull's-eye with his first shot.

"I know you have a mark on your chest, for example — a secret mark put on the boys of your family, so people know you're legitimate the day you ascend the throne. In your case, it's a dragon."

The voivode paused before answering. "Twenty courtiers of my retinue could have seen that dragon at my coronation. Any of them could have told you about it. Not to mention my women!"

Just the same, Sam felt he had scored a point. "I also know that you stole this bracelet in Izmit," he continued. "In 1447."

That was a gamble, but the voivode must have chosen that date for the combination lock because it had special importance, so why not one connected to the jewel?

"Izmit," Vlad repeated thoughtfully. "Only one person could have spoken to you about Izmit. The very person I expected to see this afternoon: Klugg."

Klugg, the Bruges alchemist! The man who had conducted experiments on the stone statue, hoping it would help him make gold! The man Sam had had to confront in his laboratory before he could return to his own time!

"We met once," Sam admitted. "He is an alchemist."

"Yes, an alchemist. And my father should have slit his throat the first time he granted him an audience! He offered to tutor me and my older brother. I was seven or eight at the time."

Sam did a quick calculation. Dracula was born around 1428 and Sam had landed in Bruges in 1430, so the alchemist would have set off for Romania five or six years after their encounter, probably to continue his research on the stone.

"He said he would teach us Western court manners and Latin," the voivode continued bitterly. "But he wanted only one thing: to visit Bran Castle at his leisure. He treated my brother and me badly, and we never learned all that he promised. But I learned something else. One night, when he had drunk too much Wallachian wine, he told me that the Turks possessed a priceless bracelet that allowed one to move around the world at the speed of lightning. And that by using this bracelet in a secret part of Bran Castle, one could find the treasure of treasures: a stone ring that gives its owner eternal life. He said the bracelet was in one of the sultan's palaces in Izmit."

Dracula was now looking at Sam without really seeing him, as if he was unburdening himself of a story he rarely had occasion to tell. Of course, that also meant that once his account was finished, he would have an additional reason to get rid of Sam.

"In the years that followed," the voivode continued, "Klugg advised my father to befriend the Ottomans. He was hoping to obtain the bracelet, of course. And that's when our troubles began. The Hungarians attacked Wallachia and the sultan betrayed us. I was sent to him as a hostage, and the Hungarians killed my father. All this because of that damned Klugg."

With his free hand, Vlad stroked his mustache, which looked like the tail of a large black cat.

"I lived with the Turks for nearly four years. Refined people, who know how to resort to force when necessary. I learned a great deal, and I took the opportunity to ask about Izmit. To my great surprise, I was assured that the bracelet indeed existed, and that it had magic properties. But nobody could remember what they were, because the jewel had been brought there many centuries before. In 1447, my last year of captivity, I was able to steal the bracelet without the sultan suspecting. Which reminds me." His voice deepened into a purr. "Put it back in its cage."

To Sam, this felt like being forced to cut off one of his fingers, but he had no choice: He carefully set the jewel on its silver stand.

"Perfect. During the ten years I spent trying to reconquer Wallachia, I asked all manner of soothsayers and magicians about the bracelet's powers. None was able to help me. I concluded that only Klugg had the necessary knowledge. After all this time, however, the mad dog had disappeared.

"The day I regained my title of voivode, I resolved to draw him here so I could force him to give me his secrets and kill him. It took me many months to reach an understanding with the lord of Bran, to obtain free use of the square tower and to build this high chamber. I was hoping that Klugg would fall into my trap, but your father came instead."

Vlad's mustache framed a predatory smile that revealed his long teeth.

"A poor fool, that one — grotesque and stubborn. Because he refused to talk, I was tempted to impale him at once. But once dead, he would be of no further use to me. I thought a few months in a dank pit would loosen his tongue. But then the affairs of the kingdom caught up with me, as always! One is always making war or preparing for it, isn't that so? One of the sultan's ambassadors is coming to negotiate some 'back taxes,' or so he claims, and I stopped by on my way to see him. And look what a pretty fledgling has flown into my cage!"

He took a step forward, the crossbow aimed straight at Sam's heart.

"I know death well, my boy. I have caused it hundreds of times, and I have seen it take thousands of men and women. It is a curious spectacle. But though I have studied it closely, I always find it disappointing at the end. I do not want it for myself, do you understand? Never! That is why I must have the ring that will make me eternal. That is why I need Klugg. And if you refuse to tell me where he is hiding, I will start in on your father. I will cut off his ears, then his nose and lips, and feed them to the pigs. Then —"

"I've already freed my father," interrupted Sam.

"Then you are not much smarter than he is," Vlad guffawed. "I assume that Dragomir persuaded you to unchain him as well, right?

"Yes . . ." Sam said slowly.

The Impaler now had tears of laughter in his eyes. "Dragomir is my most trusted adviser, you fool! Did you think you got here thanks to your miserable tricks? The bracelet began to glow this morning, so I knew something was afoot! I reduced the sentries' rounds and Dragomir volunteered to keep an eye on your father in case Klugg tried to approach him. I still don't know how you managed to get into the castle, but I'm sure Dragomir will tell me!"

Dragomir, an imposter! And Sam had sent his father with him to the secret stairway — whose existence Vlad hadn't suspected. *Sam had thrown him into the lions' den!*

"Our young wizard seems to have lost some of his arrogance," the voivode jeered. "You have no choice, you little weasel. Either you tell me where Klugg is, or I'll put a bolt through your chest."

"Klugg went back to Bruges," Sam guessed.

"Then that's too bad for you. Unless you can tell me where to put this bracelet in order to get the immortality ring, I will kill you."

Even though the voivode was about to shoot, Sam had no desire to tell him anything about the stone sculpture, especially since the ring of eternal life sounded like something Klugg had made up. Sam was terrified, but there was one last gambit he could try.

Speaking very distinctly, he said, "If I die now, you'll never know the sultan's intentions."

Vlad raised an eyebrow. "What kind of witchcraft is this?"

"I told you that I knew certain things. In my pocket I have an object that allows me to tell the future. If you promise to let my father and me leave the castle, I'll answer your questions about what the future holds."

"And if I don't keep my word?"

"That's a risk I'll have to take. Besides," he continued, emboldened, "what do you have to fear? I'm at your mercy, and the bracelet is in its cage. You just have to give your word."

"All right, I promise," said Vlad, with a sly glint in his eyes that left little doubt about the value of his promise. "So what do you think the sultan's ambitions are?"

"I need my cylinder. If you will allow me . . ." Very slowly, Sam took the tear gas cartridge from his pocket. He didn't dare pull out the pistol; its musket-like shape would likely arouse the Impaler's suspicions.

"What is this new devilry?"

"It's the object I told you about."

"I warn you: if you try to throw it at me or —"

Vlad had his finger on the crossbow trigger again and could fire the bolt at any instant.

"What is that writing?" he asked nervously.

The label on the metal cylinder read, "LACRYMO. Liquid defense gel, 20% CS (orthochlorobenzylidene)" and below that, "Range 5–10 feet." *Just what I need*, thought Sam jubilantly.

"Those are the incantations that must be recited to enter into communication with the cylinder," he answered. "First, I must take off its cap and —"

"I'm warning you: If you lie to me, I swear I will skin you alive."

Cautiously Sam uncovered the nozzle. Now all he had to do was to gain his listener's trust. He stared deeply at the cylinder and began chanting softly. "Ortho-chloro-benzy-lidene, ortho-chloro-benzy-lidene . . ." It was ridiculous, but surely no worse than "Abracadabra!"

"Well?" asked Vlad urgently, sounding both sarcastic and troubled.

"The cylinder says the sultan is laying a trap for you," said Sam, who remembered the episode from Vlad's biography. "It's traditional for the voivode to go back to the border with the ambassador, isn't it? The Turks will be waiting there to capture you."

"The cur!" the Impaler swore. "An ambush! And what will happen next?"

"That will depend on you. If your own men are stationed nearby —"

"Yes, of course," said Vlad heatedly. "We will swoop down on them before they have time to pray to their god! And does your instrument also know how I can finish the sultan once and for all?"

Sam scrutinized the cartridge in search of inspiration, again monotonously repeating "Ortho-chloro-benzy-lidene." The bottom of the label listed user precautions: "Warning! This paralyzing gas attacks the nerve endings, forcing the eyes to shut involuntarily, causing a burning sensation and rendering coordinated movement impossible. Keep away from children!" What about vampires?

"The cylinder says that by disguising yourself as a Turk, you will be able to slip into the Ottoman camp at night. You speak their language, don't you? You will have no trouble finding their leader's tent, and then —"

Again, this was historically accurate, except that in his daring attack, the Impaler picked the wrong tent and assassinated the vizier instead of the sultan!

"A brilliant idea," admitted Vlad. "Disguise myself and surprise them in the night. Of course!" He paused, then snapped: "But how can your cylinder predict all these things? And how do you understand it?"

"It's a magical object. I can't explain how it works. It speaks to me in a kind of murmur."

"Mmm!" grumbled the voivode, not entirely convinced. "If I managed to rid myself of the sultan, that means I would have no more enemies. My rule would be very long then, would it not? Twenty or thirty years? Forever?"

Just six years, buddy, and not a year more, thought Sam. *But I'm not going to clue you in so easily.*

"Ortho-chloro-benzy-lidene," he recited obediently. "Ortho-chloro-benzy-lidene."

The Impaler was getting excited. "Ask it how far beyond Wallachia I will be able to extend my conquests, while we're at it."

Sam paused suddenly, as if the cylinder was telling him something upsetting.

"Well?" asked Vlad impatiently.

"The cylinder believes that someone around you wants to take over the throne."

"What? Someone around me? Who?"

Sam had never been so glad he'd learned a history lesson! In fact it was the voivode's younger brother, Radu, who took the crown from Vlad in 1462.

"I get the impression it's someone in your family," said Sam hesitantly. "But I can't understand the name. You might want to listen yourself."

He held the cartridge out to the Impaler. In his eagerness to learn the traitor's identity, Vlad leaned forward. The crossbow was now pointing at the floor.

Sam pressed the nozzle hard. *Psssssht!* A cloud of colored gas shot out that instantly liquefied and coated the voivode's face with a reddish gel. Vlad jerked backward and the crossbow bolt whizzed through the air, slamming into the floor between Sam's feet. Vlad screamed and clawed at his face. "The devil, the devil! Help me! Soldiers!"

Sam rushed to the cage, snatched the bracelet from its stand, and ran for the door, shielding his eyes against the gas still hanging in the air.

"I'm burning!" screamed Vlad Tepes. He had fallen to the ground and lay writhing. "Soldiers, to the square tower! He has killed me!"

Slamming the heavy door behind him, Sam searched for a way to keep it closed. He snatched one of the lances decorating the doorway and jammed it through the circular handle. That should slow Dracula down a little.

Now to get his father!

CHAPTER TWENTY-FOUR

The Truth About Allan Faulkner

Sam leaped past the bottom step. Where would Dragomir have taken his father? They probably first headed for the armory, as agreed. They would have pushed the cabinet aside, opened the passageway, and . . . What then? The best thing would be if Dragomir had gone ahead to see where the tunnel led, which would give Sam time to warn his father about him. The worst . . .

"He escaped from the square tower!" screamed a guard. "Search everywhere! The dungeons too!"

A patrol was coming, and Sam again ducked behind the column with the Bran coat of arms. He carefully stuffed Meriweserre's bracelet deep in his pocket, followed by the tear gas cartridge, then took out the Browning, his only means of defense. Could he and Allan return to their own time using only the golden circle? There was no other choice. He waited until the patrol headed off toward the kitchens and stepped out from behind the column, pistol in hand.

Suddenly a man armed with a lance stepped through a door hidden by a tapestry. He saw Sam and raised his arm to strike.

Sam automatically lifted his gun in response — aiming for the head, as he usually did in shoot-'em-up video games. But just as his finger tightened around the trigger, he remembered James Faulkner, who had once owned this very gun, and Grandpa's sadness when he spoke about him: "A broken man . . ."

The soldier looked to be about twenty, very blond and a bit baby-faced. At the last moment, Sam moved his wrist slightly and the bullet slammed into a lamp with a crash loud enough to wake the dead. The soldier gave Sam a terrified glance and fled without looking back.

Wiping sweat from his forehead, Sam tucked the gun in his pocket and took the hallway leading to the round tower. Gray stone, waves of dampness, sounds of running feet echoing in every direction . . . Luckily the guardroom was empty. That was hardly surprising; it wasn't the first place you'd look for an escaping prisoner. The fire was still burning in the fireplace, and the meat was still roasting — or being burned to a cinder, in this case.

"Dad?" Sam whispered urgently.

No answer. Had Dragomir taken him back to his cell? Sam silently crept forward. On the armory threshold he suddenly saw something move and jumped aside just as a club slammed into the floor a few inches away.

"Dad?"

Allan stepped out from behind the door. His eyes were wild, and he didn't seem to understand why he was holding the club.

"Dad, it's me, Sam."

"Sa-Sam," he stammered.

"Where's Dragomir?"

With his head, Allan gestured behind him. Dragomir was sprawled full-length in front of the half-open secret passage; Sam was relieved to see he was still breathing. The would-be singing star lay a few yards from him.

"He wasn't a prisoner," his father explained hoarsely. "No, no. He says I'm crazy, but I'm not crazy! I was the prisoner, not him!"

"We have to move the cabinet, Dad. Soldiers will be here any second."

Sam slowly manhandled the cabinet aside, but instead of helping, his father leaned over the guard and talked to him.

"And if you wake up again — *pow!*" he warned with a hysterical cackle.

"Shhh! We've got to get out of here!"

Allan suddenly stopped laughing. "Do you have it?" he asked in a loud voice. "I won't leave without it, you know!"

"Of course I have it! Come on!"

"Show it to me!"

Rather than waste time in talk, Sam took Meriweserre's bracelet out of his pocket and held it under his father's nose. "Here it is! Are you happy now? Come ON!"

The sight of the jewel had a strange, almost hypnotic effect on Allan. He hunched over a little more and fell completely silent. Sam took the opportunity to push him toward the tunnel.

"We need some light," he said. "Wait for me a moment."

He returned to the guardroom and unhooked the first torch he could reach. A detachment of soldiers was climbing up the stairs toward them.

"Maybe Ivan saw something," a voice in the stairway suggested. "He was cooking a haunch of — phew! What's that smoke? Ivan?"

A helmeted head appeared in the doorway, and Sam reacted instantly, grabbing the tear gas cartridge and throwing it into the fireplace. The gas was under pressure; maybe the heat of the fire would work some ortho-chloro-benzy-lidene magic!

"Sound the alarm!" yelled the soldier. "Call the guard!"

Sam jumped into the darkness, hauling his father by the sleeve.

They tumbled into the secret passageway just as the gas cylinder exploded with a loud *Ka-boom!* The walls shook, and Sam slid the heavy door shut in a cloud of foul-smelling dust. Frightened screams could be heard on the other side, but this was no time for pity. Sam hurried down the steps as quickly as he could, half carrying his father. Allan let himself be hustled along, walking mechanically and touching the rock. But half-way down the steps, he seemed to wake from a bad dream.

"Sam? What's — what's going on?"

"We're leaving Bran Castle, Dad. Do you remember Bran Castle?"

"Bran, yes. The secret passageway. Klugg —"

"Klugg? Do you know Klugg?"

"It was Vlad Tepes; he kept repeating that name. But I don't know who Klugg is. You believe me, don't you, Sam?"

"Of course I believe you, Dad."

"'Klugg,' he would say over and over, 'Klugg! Klugg, Klugg, Klugg!' Then he locked me up. I was hungry, I was cold, and they beat me . . . Oh yes, they beat me! I spent a long time there, a very long time! I thought I was going crazy, Sam, I swear. But I'm not crazy, am I?" He started to sob like a little boy.

"It's all over, Dad," Sam said soothingly, even though he felt heartsick. "You'll be able to rest soon." He tried to distract his father. "Tell me, do you know if we can use the bracelet to go home?"

"Meriweserre's bracelet," said Allan, blowing his nose with his fingers. "Ah, yes, the bracelet! We got it, Sam. Did you know that?"

They had just reached the foot of the iron ladder when a noisy horde started down the passageway behind them. From a distance, Sam could hear the clank of weapons, men swearing, and "Kill them! Kill them!" The soldiers had apparently cleared the rubble away from the hidden door, or Dragomir had woken up and told them about the tunnel.

"One foot after the other, Dad, all right? Go at your own pace. I'm right behind you."

They climbed the rungs with great effort and came out inside the abandoned mill. Allan slumped against the wall and groaned with exhaustion, clearly at the end of his strength. Below them, the shouts and sounds of running grew louder. Sam slammed the trapdoor shut and shoved some heavy stones onto it.

"I scratched this sign near the arrow slit for you," gasped his father, pointing to the initials *A. F.* in the rock. "It's all my fault, Sam. I was the one who got you to come here."

"Forget about it, Dad. We're together now."

"No, you don't understand. I deliberately —"

Sam helped him to his feet and Allan gave a yelp of pain.

"My back is a mess," he said with a grimace. "It's my punishment."

"Don't think about that. Come on. Hang in there!"

They left the ruined building with Allan bent almost in two and Sam holding him up by the waist. Rather than follow the river as he had before, they opted for the woods, which offered protection in the gloom.

"I arranged all this," his father continued. "You have to know that, Sam."

"Arranged all what?"

"I wasn't sure, but that was the meaning of the letter. I didn't . . . I didn't want to leave anything to chance, you see. I had to have the bracelet!"

"The letter? What letter?" asked Sam, who was willing to encourage his father's rambling as long as he kept walking.

"The letter from the Turkish ambassador. Kata . . . Kata-something. The one the sultan sent to demand money from Dracula. He wound up impaled too," he added, clearing his throat. "Anyway, Kata-what's-his-name wrote back to the sultan and said that at their first meeting, Tepes was beside himself with rage, because he'd just had something very precious stolen by a boy. A mere boy! He stayed angry for a week. I know, because I saw a copy of the correspondence."

"Do you mean that this boy —"

"I — I couldn't be sure, Sam. I thought I could get into the tower alone and grab the bracelet myself. But in case I failed . . . There was a chance you would be in a better position to succeed than me. Do you understand?"

Sam was stunned.

"You planned the whole thing!" he burst out. "The coin at Max's, the William Faulkner novel — all of it! Not so I could save you if you needed help, but so I would steal the bracelet!"

"I really hoped I would manage it alone," said Allan abashedly. "I really did! It's a very valuable bracelet, Sam."

"I know — a million dollars. You wrote it in the notebook!"

"I was sure if you solved those puzzles, it meant that you could go all the way, you could meet all the challenges! And I was right, wasn't I?"

Sam was speechless with astonishment and rage. His worst fears were all confirmed. His father had *wanted* him to steal Meriweserre's bracelet! He had risked his own life and Sam's for *money*! Was he completely out of his mind?

"Why didn't you tell me before you left? Why did you just take off without letting anyone know, and without even —"

He broke off at a clamor from the direction of the mill. Apparently the stones on the trapdoor hadn't delayed the soldiers for long. And there must be a lot of them, Sam thought, to judge by the glow of torches from the clearing and the shouts he could hear, now joined by an even more dangerous sound: barking.

"Dogs," he groaned. "They're going to send dogs after us."

He started walking faster, practically carrying his father now. The forest was growing darker, but carrying a lighted torch under these conditions was becoming dangerous. He beat it out against a tree and threw it behind them.

How far did they have to go? And where was the stone

exactly? They would have to follow the river or risk missing it. They broke through a tangle of branches and came out at the riverbank. Once out in the open, Sam had the unpleasant fantasy that the dogs were practically on their heels. Then he remembered their next difficulty — no coins!

"Dad, is that bracelet going to get us home?" he asked again.

Allan had been breathing with increasing difficulty since leaving the mill. But he managed to smile as he wheezed, "You still . . . you still need your old dad, don't you? Lesson number one, Sammy: Always bury a coin near the stone statue."

"You're not joking? There really is a coin near the stone?"

"I'm telling you . . . You still have a lot to learn, kiddo!"

The news lent Sam wings. A hundred yards farther on, he recognized the reeds and the tall pine tree with broken branches. "Here's the stone, and it's fine!" he exulted. "Do you remember where you buried the coin?"

Allan gestured vaguely toward the riverbank. Sam made his father sit down, his back against the stone statue, then he started clawing at the ground like a man possessed. The vegetation had clearly grown up in the past six months.

"You're right to be angry at me, Sam," Allan admitted. "I haven't been a very good father to you. Since your mother's death, I know I've been . . . I've been absent. You must have wondered what I was doing instead of taking care of you!"

"Well, I have some idea now," said Sam, trying to keep his tone neutral as he continued to dig. "I heard about the mortgage from the bank and . . . Anyway, all those books and treasures must've been pretty tempting."

"Treasures? What treasures? Do you think I did this for money? You know I don't care about money, don't you?"

Sam poured his anger into his digging. "I went to Delphi, Dad, and I just missed running into you there. The Navel of the World sold for ten million dollars in London! For someone who's not interested in money, that's really not a bad —"

"The Navel of the World?" his father said vehemently. "I've never been to Delphi, Sammy! And I never sold the Navel of the World!"

He sounded sincere, but Sam had no time to think about it. The torches were getting closer and he could now hear the howling of dogs straining to be released to hunt their prey. Then Sam's fingers touched a miraculous metal disk with a hole in it. "I got it!" Quickly wiping the coin on his shirt, he ran over to Allan. "Hang on to me, Dad. We're taking off!"

The stone began to vibrate beneath his hand. Trying to ignore the dogs' ever-closer howls, Sam set the golden circle in the stone's cavity and put the coin on the sun.

"I'm not in very good shape, Sammy," muttered his father, putting an arm around his chest. "I'm not . . . I'm not sure I can survive the trip."

"Don't worry, Dad. It'll be over in a minute."

"No, listen, Sam. If anything happens to me, I want you to know I never stole anything. Not a book, not a treasure, nothing. You have to believe me. That . . . that bracelet isn't like any other, you know. It goes with the stone and . . ."

Sam would have liked to pause then, reassure his father, hug him and tell him everything would be fine; but his

fingers were already tingling and Time was about to carry
them away.

"I'm sure your mother can be saved with that bracelet,"
Allan said almost inaudibly. "Do you understand me, Sam?
You can save your mother with that bracelet!"

How can Sam control his destiny when he can't even control his destination?

The conclusion to the mind-bending time travel trilogy!

Sam's troubles aren't over. Now he has to save his mother—and go back in time to do it. But when the Arkeos man kidnap Alicia, he has to choose whom to rescue first.

ARTHUR A. LEVINE BOOKS

SCHOLASTIC

www.scholastic.com

BKTIME

BEATRICE GOES
TO BRIGHTON

Also published in Large Print
from G.K. Hall by Marion Chesney:

Emily Goes to Exeter
Belinda Goes to Bath
Penelope Goes to Portmouth
Refining Felicity
Perfecting Fiona
Enlightening Delilah
Finessing Clarissa ⋈
Animating Maria
Marrying Harriet
The Miser of Mayfair
Plain Jane
The Wicked Godmother
Rake's Progress
The Adventuress
Rainbird's Revenge
Minerva
The Taming of Annabelle
Deirdre and Desire
Daphne
Diana the Huntress
Frederica in Fashion

BEATRICE GOES TO BRIGHTON

Marion Chesney

Being the Fourth Volume of
The Traveling Matchmaker

G·K·Hall&Co.
Boston, Massachusetts
1993

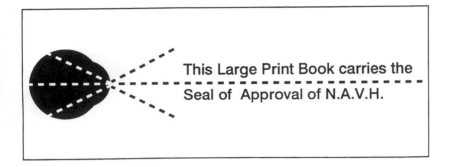

This Large Print Book carries the
Seal of Approval of N.A.V.H.

Published in Large Print by arrangement with
St. Martin's Press.

G.K. Hall Large Print Book Series.

Printed on acid free paper in the United States of
America.

Set in 16 pt. Plantin.

Library of Congress Cataloging-in-Published Data

Chesney, Marion.
  Beatrice goes to Brighton / Marion Chesney.
    p. cm. — (G.K. Hall large print book series)
    (Nightingale series) The Travelling matchmaker ;
    4th v.)
    ISBN 0-8161-5546-1 (acid-free paper)
  1. Large type books. I. Title. II. Series: Chesney,
    Marion. Travelling matchmaker ; 4th v.
  [PR6053.H4535B43   1993]
  823'.914—dc20   92-41194

1

Then dress, then dinner, then awakes the
world!
Then glare the lamps, then whirl the wheels,
then roar
Throughout street and square fast flashing
chariots, hurled
Like harnessed meteors.
                                   —*Lord Byron*

Lady Beatrice Marsham had been a widow for over a year and enjoyed every minute of her now single state.

She well remembered the first day of her freedom, when she had descended the stairs of her husband's town house to see her spouse, Mr. Harry Blackstone, being carried into the hall by his drinking companions.

"Foxed again," they had called cheerfully, dumping the body in a chair. Lady Beatrice had looked at her husband with impatient distaste, called her maid, pulled on her gloves, and gone out to make various calls.

She was surprised on her return to find the blinds down and a hatchment over the door. Her husband, it transpired, was not dead drunk, but simply dead.

As Lady Beatrice—he had never used her married name—settled herself comfortably in a corner seat of the Brighton stagecoach, she remembered her overwhelming feeling of relief when they told her Harry was dead. No more drunken scenes, no more embarrassing fumblings in the bedchamber at night, no more jealous rages. She was free of it all.

Her parents, the Earl and Countess of Debren, had arranged that marriage. Lady Beatrice had assumed that, being a widow of twenty-eight, she would now be left alone. But only two days ago, her father had visited her to say that a marriage had been arranged for her with Sir Geoffrey Handford. In vain had she raged. The earl had pointed out brutally that she had not yet borne any sons. It was her duty to marry again. Then Sir Geoffrey had called, a thickset, brutish man in snuff-stained clothes.

To get rid of both her father and Sir Geoffrey, Lady Beatrice had said she would consider the matter and had then decided to take herself off to Brighton, hoping that by the time she returned, the matter would have been forgotten. She had sent her servants and most of her baggage ahead, having rented a house in Brighton through an agent in London. She had planned to drive down the Brighton road herself, for she was an expert whip, but the weather had turned very wet and so she had decided to take the stage.

It was not unusual for an aristocrat, even a female one, to travel on the Brighton stage. The stage-coaches on that route were becoming very fashionable. Had not the Prince of Wales made Brighton fashionable? And it therefore followed that everything associated with that watering-place should be considered bon ton. Besides, the Brighton road was famous for its inns, and the journey took a mere six hours.

Also, it was amusing to be in such a plebeian carriage and in such low company. Lady Beatrice was an expert at keeping low company at bay. In fact, she had become quite expert at keeping the whole wide

3

world at bay. She had been in love once, when she was eighteen, a tremulous, vulnerable maiden. That was when her parents had betrothed her to Harry. She felt that by that act they had taken everything from her, her hopes, her innocence, and, most of all, her freedom. She grew in beauty and coldness. She despised all men. She occasionally amused herself with flirting with one of the beasts, only to reject him as nastily as she knew how.

She wished the coach would move. It was Sunday, and everything in London was shuttered and closed and sooty and black. All the church bells were ringing, a persistent, irritating cacophony. Not far from the White Bear Inn in Piccadilly was St. James's Church, which, reflected Lady Beatrice sourly, seemed to have a more hellish group of bell-ringers than most as they performed their jangly, insistent triples and majors. What did the workers of the world, after toiling six miserable days a week, think of this day of rest, black and more miserable than all the others, dingy and stale and dull? thought Lady Beatrice. How could one think of spiritual things when no prospect pleased and the air was rent by the clamour of the bells?

She glanced briefly at her fellow passengers. Beside her was a small dumpy man who smelled strongly of ale, and beside him in the other corner was a tired, bedraggled woman with a snivelling child on her lap. Across from her was a soldier, asleep with his mouth open; beside him, a small dwarf of a woman with huge pale eyes like saucers, and opposite Lady Beatrice was a thin lady, elegantly dressed. She had sandy hair under a neat bonnet, a crooked nose, odd eyes which appeared to change colour, and a clever mouth. Lady Beatrice's chilly gaze rested a bit longer on this lady than it had done on the others. To her surprise, the lady smiled and said, "Allow me to introduce myself. I am Miss Hannah Pym of London."

Lady Beatrice allowed her eyelids to droop slightly, her upper lip to raise a fraction, and then she slowly turned her head away and looked out of the window.

Miss Hannah Pym bit her lip in mortification. Although Hannah now had the appearance, clothes, manner, and speech of a lady, inside lurked the servant she all too recently had been, and she thought the cold and beautiful creature opposite had snubbed her because she had recognized in Hannah an inferior person.

She covertly studied the haughty lady. Lady Beatrice had jet-black hair under a Lavinia bonnet, her face shadowed by the wide brim. She had very clear white skin, a straight nose, and large grey eyes fringed with thick lashes. Her mouth was slightly pinched at the corners, as if it had once been a fuller mouth which the years and disappointment had thinned down. Hannah sensed that she was tired and anxious, and yet Hannah was disproportionately worried by that snub, if snub it had been.

Her legacy of five thousand pounds, left her by her late employer, Mr. Clarence, in his will, had initially seemed a vast sum, but now that she had become accustomed to higher society in the shape of Mr. Clarence's brother, Sir George, who had recently taken her out to the opera, and since she had moved her quarters to the fashionable West End, it seemed very little in a world where men and women gambled more than that at the gaming tables of St. James's every night.

And yet, just a little while ago, she had been Hannah Pym of Thornton Hall in Kensington, a housekeeper who had clawed her way up the servants' hierarchy from scullery maid.

Her thoughts drifted back over the years. She should not despise her old life. She had been well-treated, particularly by pretty Mrs. Clarence before she had run off with that footman and left her husband to sink into apathy. The hard times had come when Mr. Clarence had become a semirecluse, locking up half the rooms and dismissing half the servants, and there were no more balls or parties. That was when Hannah had begun to watch the stage-coaches, or Flying Machines as they were called, hurtle along the road at the end of the estate, symbols of freedom and adventure.

This was to be her fourth journey. The past three had been full of adventure. She sighed a little. She was a determined matchmaker and there was no one on this coach she could possibly pair together in her mind. Her footman was on the roof with the outside passengers. Hannah brightened. It surely increased her social standing to have a footman. She had adopted her deaf-and-dumb footman, Benjamin, during her last adventurous journey. He did not seem to want wages. In fact, he had an embarrassing habit of paying her out of his frequent winnings at dice.

The chilly lady opposite turned her gaze

on Hannah again. Hannah immediately said airily, "I do hope my poor footman is not getting a soaking up on the roof."

A slight look of contempt flicked across the fine eyes opposite. Hannah cursed herself and wished she had never spoken. Only parvenus spoke of having footmen. The frigid travelling companion she was trying to impress probably had scores of footmen.

Worse was to come. The small dwarflike woman next to Hannah said in a hoarse whisper, "Ain't no use tryin' to impress the likes o' her. She don't care a fig for any of us."

"I was not trying to impress," said Hannah with a pathetic attempt at hauteur.

The guard on the roof blew a fanfare and the coach rumbled forward.

The coach was to take the new route to Brighton, going by Croydon, Merstham, Reigate, Crawley and Cuckfield, making the distance fifty-three miles exactly.

Hannah looked bleakly out at the driving rain and decided to ignore that cold creature opposite. She should, after all, be looking forward to her first visit to Brighton.

The Prince of Wales had gone to the fishing village, then called Brighthelmstone, as early as 1783 to try a sea-water

8

cure for swollen glands. He rented a small farmhouse on the Steyne, a broad strip of lawn that ran down to the sea. In the summer of 1787, Henry Holland, fresh from planning the reconstruction of Carlton House, built for the prince a bow-fronted house in the classical manner, topped by a shallow dome, which came to be known as the Prince of Wales's Marine Pavilion. The prince, who had a taste for oriental design, was rumoured to want to create an oriental palace for himself. He wanted to enclose the entire pavilion in the style of a Chinese pagoda, but so far had been held in check when it was pointed out that such a design would clash with Holland's classicism.

Hannah had hopes of actually seeing the prince, for he was reported to be in Brighton, and although he longed for privacy and hated the London mob, he was more tolerant of the people who flocked after him to Brighton to stare, some of them armed with opera glasses and even telescopes.

Lady Beatrice was beginning to feel oddly uncomfortable. There had been no reason to be so rude to the lady opposite. Hannah, could she have known, would have been delighted to learn that she was classed in

Lady Beatrice's mind as "lady," rather than "woman."

And yet Lady Beatrice was used to cutting all and sundry. She had no female friends, finding the ladies she met at balls and parties too silly and affected. Although she was dimly aware that she had taken her own misery over her marriage out on everyone else, she had felt more comfortable in her isolation, using her beauty to attract men for the fun of repulsing them.

It must be, reflected Lady Beatrice, because her companion of the stage-coach opposite had such an expressive face. For the first time in years, she would put herself in the way of a snub in order to make amends. Lady Beatrice smiled slightly at Hannah and said, "Dreadful weather, is it not?"

Now, here was Hannah's opportunity, and for the life of her, she could not take it. She started by turning her head away, only to be made aware of the avid stare of those pale, saucer-like eyes next to her. She turned back to face Lady Beatrice. "Yes, quite dreadful," she said calmly.

Then she took a small book out of her reticule and pretended to read.

The coach drew up at The Bear in

Croyden to change horses. The passengers filed into the inn for cakes and tea because it was in that meal-less desert between breakfast, which was usually about nine in the morning, and dinner, normally at four in the afternoon, although some fashionables were already beginning to take their dinner at a later hour.

Hannah was pleased she had her footman, Benjamin, so tall and well-groomed, with his clever East End face, in attendance, well aware of the air of consequence it gave her. Hannah often wondered where Benjamin had come from. She had been instrumental in rescuing Benjamin from the gallows for a crime he had not committed, and he had become her devoted slave. Although he was deaf and dumb, he could write, but he never wrote down for Hannah any of his history. But he had come a long way in appearance from the battered-looking criminal in irons who had touched Hannah's heart on her last stage-coach journey. He wore his plush livery with an air, his hair powdered, his white gloves impeccable.

There was a small altercation when the woman with the pale eyes, who had announced to all in general that she was Mrs.

Hick, pulled a large plate of cakes in front of her and began to demolish them. The woman with the child glared and pointed out that there were others at the table who might like cakes, and her child began to roar and cry as he saw all the treats disappearing down the little woman's large mouth.

Benjamin walked firmly round the table, snatched up the plate of cakes, presented them first to Hannah, then to everyone else, and then set the remainder back down on the table as far away from Mrs. Hick as possible.

"You are fortunate in having such an efficient servant," said Lady Beatrice to Hannah.

"Yes," said Hannah baldly, having not quite forgiven her for that snub.

"Do you travel all the way to Brighton?" pursued Lady Beatrice.

"Yes," said Hannah, and visibly thawing, added, "I am looking forward to seeing the sea again."

"And that is the sole reason for your journey?" Lady Beatrice looked amused.

"Not quite, Miss . . . er . . .".

Lady Beatrice took out a card case and extracted a card and handed it to Hannah.

Hannah coloured. She herself had no cards.

To her surprise, Benjamin leaned over her shoulder and put a small leather case down in front of her. Hannah opened it and saw in amazement that it contained elegantly engraved cards. "Miss Hannah Pym, 16, South Audley Street, London."

She quietly took one out and presented it to Lady Beatrice, determined to ask Benjamin later how he had come by them.

"So, my lady," said Hannah, "what takes you to Brighton?"

"I have rented a house there," said Lady Beatrice. "London fatigues me."

"I do not think I could ever tire of London," said Hannah. Her odd eyes glowed. "But I love to travel. I have had so many adventures."

"Stage-coach travel can be adventurous," said Lady Beatrice drily. "Broken poles, bolting horses, coaches stuck in ruts or snowstorms, not to mention highwaymen."

"Oh, I've had highwaymen," said Hannah proudly, and with the air of a professional invalid saying, "Oh, yes, I have had the smallpox."

Lady Beatrice laughed, and that laugh

13

quite altered her appearance. The eyes shone and that tight mouth relaxed and became fuller. "I see you are an intrepid traveller, Miss Pym."

"And matchmaker," boasted Hannah. "I have been instrumental in making matches between stage-coach passengers . . ."

Her voice faded away. A shutter had come down over Lady Beatrice's eyes.

"I see we are leaving," said Lady Beatrice. She rose quickly and walked out into the inn yard. Hannah followed, sad that her boast of matchmaking had had the effect of freezing this strange Lady Beatrice up again. And then, as Hannah reached the inn door, she saw a strange sight. A handsome travelling carriage was standing in the yard with the coachman on the box and two grooms on the backstrap. There were also two outriders.

A thickset man approached Lady Beatrice and seized her by the arm. She let out a cry. He bent and said something, and Hannah, watching, startled, was sure that he was thrusting something like a pistol or a knife against Lady Beatrice's side.

She ran forward, with Benjamin at her heels. "Lady Beatrice!" called Hannah. "Is aught amiss?"

The thickset man glared at her and said, "Lady Beatrice has decided to continue the journey in the comfort of my carriage. Is that not so, my dear?"

Lady Beatrice was very white. "That is so," she said in a low voice.

The man who held her so tightly called to one of the grooms, "Fetch my lady's baggage from the coach." He then guided Lady Beatrice into his own carriage, climbed in after her and slammed the door.

"Help!" shouted Hannah at the top of her voice. Ostlers, waiters, and the other passengers came running up. "I am sure Lady Beatrice is being abducted," said Hannah wildly.

The groom had found Lady Beatrice's baggage in the coach and was returning with the coachman.

"What's all this, then?" demanded the coachman. There was a babble of voices above which Hannah's sounded loud and clear. "Lady Beatrice is being taken away by force."

"Ho, now." The coachman, like most of his kind, was fat and grog-faced and swathed in shawls. He lumbered towards the carriage. The man inside let down the glass.

"Are you running off wiv thet 'ooman?" demanded the coachman.

"Stow your whids, coachee," growled the man. "I am merely taking Lady Beatrice to Brighton in a more comfortable carriage."

"Let her speak for herself," shouted Mrs. Hick.

Lady Beatrice leaned forward. "I am going of my own free will," she said quietly.

"That's that, then." The coachman rounded truculently on the watchers. "Who started all this 'ere fuss, then? Let's be 'aving ye."

"It was I," said Hannah unrepentantly. "I am sure that man was holding a pistol or a knife to Lady Beatrice's side."

The coachman turned away in disgust and could be heard to mutter something about women with bats in their belfries who read too many romances.

The other passengers surveyed Hannah reproachfully when they were all on board again.

"Trouble is," said Mrs. Hick, who was now eating a large sandwich, "you was so taken up wiff the idea of speakin' to one of the nobs, that you got carried away."

Well, there was one lesson Hannah Pym

had learned from Lady Beatrice. She drooped her eyelids wearily, curled her lip, and turned her head away.

"You learned that offa her," jeered Mrs. Hick with all the dreadful perspicacity of some vulgar women and drunks. "Don't come the 'igh and mighty wiff me. Reckon that so-called footman o' yourn ain't none other than your son."

This was greeted by a roar of laughter from the other passengers and Hannah felt like the uttermost fool. She felt she was standing astride the yawning gulf of servant and lady with a foot on either side and not knowing quite how to behave.

She settled back and closed her eyes firmly. She thought of Mrs. Clarence, her late employer's dainty, pretty wife. Now Mrs. Clarence, mused Hannah, had been a real lady. She had treated everyone just the same. "But she must have had low tastes," jeered an awful Mrs. Hick-like voice in her head, "or she would never have run off with that footman." Hannah turned her thoughts to Sir George Clarence. Now *there* was a gentleman! He had even taken her to Gunter's for ices, introduced her to his bank, taken her to the opera.

"But you can never hope for anything

else," sneered that awful voice again. "I do believe you are getting quite spoony about him, Hannah Pym, and he knew you as a servant."

Hannah opened her eyes and looked out of the window to banish her thoughts. A watery sunlight was struggling through the clouds. There were wild daffodils blowing by the roadside, dipping and swaying in the blustery wind. Soon the leaves would be back on the trees and there would be summer to look forward to.

The journey continued on in blessed silence, blessed for Hannah, who did not think she could bear any more insults.

But when they arrived in Cuckfield and entered the White Hart, somehow the splendour and elegance of the famous inn brought out the worst in Mrs. Hick.

She saw Hannah looking with interest at a tall man who was lounging at his ease in the corner. Hannah was wondering who he was. In an age when most people were not much taller than five feet, he seemed a giant. He had lazy blue, amiable eyes and golden hair, tied back at the nape of his neck with a blue silk ribbon. He had a strong, handsome face, lightly tanned, broad shoulders, and the finest pair of legs

18

Hannah had ever seen. He was wearing a beautifully cut coat of fine blue wool with gold buttons, worn open over a silk waistcoat embroidered with peacocks. His legs were encased in skin-tight leather breeches and Hessian boots with jaunty little gold tassels.

Tiny Mrs. Hick screwed round in her chair and her saucer-like eyes fastened on the focus of Hannah's attention.

"Miss 'Igh and Mighty 'ere is casting her glims at that prime bit o' Fancy," jeered Mrs. Hick. "Next, she'll be over there, chattering about 'er footman."

The waiter, a lofty individual with a sallow face, snickered as he placed another plate of cakes on the table.

"We see 'em all, ma'am," he said to Mrs. Hick. "You've no idea the number o' ladies who come in on the coach pretending to be Quality."

Hannah half-rose from her seat, her face scarlet. But a voice from behind her chair made her sink back down in amazement.

"Shut yer bleeding cake-'ole," said a Cockney voice, "or I'll draw yer cork, you little turd o' a jackanapes."

Hannah twisted round and stared open-mouthed at Benjamin. She was as amazed

19

as if the teapot itself had burst into speech.

"You'll draw *my* cork," sneered the waiter. "I'd like to see you try."

"Outside," roared Benjamin.

"The dumb fellow can speak arter all," cried Mrs. Hick.

Benjamin and the waiter marched outside to the inn yard. "A mill!" cried the soldier, and the whole inn followed them outside, even the aristocratic-looking gentleman, even Hannah, almost as dumb with amazement as Benjamin had pretended to be.

Benjamin carefully removed his coat and placed it on a mounting-block. Bets were rapidly being laid, the betters favouring the waiter. Benjamin then removed his clean shirt and placed that tenderly on top of his coat. Stripped, he revealed a well-muscled chest and strong arms. Some of the bets changed in favour of Benjamin.

Hannah made a move to stop her footman but found her arm taken in a gentle but powerful grasp. She found the aristocrat beside her. "Don't ruin a fight, ma'am," he said plaintively. "I should not really worry about your footman. My money is on him."

"I didn't know he could talk," said Hannah. "All this time and he has pretended to be deaf and dumb."

The waiter and Benjamin squared up. The coachman, who had elected himself as referee, dropped the handkerchief and the pair set to.

Benjamin dodged and feinted, moving like lightning, prancing about on his new leather pumps, which he kept polished like glass.

Then Benjamin's fist seemed to come up from the ground and it smacked the waiter full on the chin with an enormous thwack. There was a silence as the waiter staggered this way and that and then stretched his length on the ground.

In an age when a good fight was expected to last eighteen rounds at least, this was considered a poor sort of match.

Hannah marched up to Benjamin as he carefully donned his shirt.

"What is the meaning of this, Benjamin?" she cried. "Why did you pretend you couldn't speak?"

Benjamin smoothed down the ruffles of his shirt with a fastidious hand and then put on his plush coat. "I couldn't tell you, modom," he said in strangulated accents

21

very different from his Cockney outburst in the inn. "You was that sorry for me. I pretended to be deaf and dumb, 'cos I knew Lady Carsey liked freaks and I needed work. That's how I got started as a footman."

"But when Lady Carsey falsely accused you of taking her brooch, why did you not speak then?"

"I daren't, modom, for the magistrate might have thought that since I was lying about one thing, therefore I might be lying about being innocent of the theft. Not that it did me much good."

"But you had no reason to lie to *me!*"

"Thought you might not be sorry for me no more and turn me off," mumbled Benjamin.

Hannah, aware of the listeners, said, "We shall talk of this further when we get to Brighton."

Lord Alistair Munro watched with amusement as Hannah took her seat with Benjamin standing punctiliously behind her chair.

Mrs. Hick had bet on the waiter and was not feeling charitable. "Fancy not knowing her own footman can speak. That is, if he *is* a footman."

"Stow it, you 'orrid old crow," said Benjamin suddenly. "I'm a proper footman, I am, not that I expects a piece of kennel garbage like yerself to recognize one, not even if you met one in yer soup!" This was said with such blistering venom that not only Mrs. Hick but the whole stage-coach party fell into a deep silence, each one frightened to catch Benjamin's angry eye.

No, thought Hannah, Benjamin had never been a footman before that episode where he had worked for Lady Carsey in Esher, Lady Carsey who had tried to get him hanged for a theft he had not committed, Lady Carsey who liked freaks and wanted Benjamin in her bed. Footmen were indolent creatures and vain. Most would have enjoyed their mistress's discomfiture.

A new waiter bent over Hannah and whispered, "The gentleman over there, Lord Alistair Munro, wishes the honour of entertaining you."

Although she was still bewildered and upset by Benjamin, Hannah was glad to escape from the stage-coach passengers.

She rose and went over to Lord Alistair's table. He got up as she approached and drew out a seat for her. Benjamin, with a last threatening look at the cowed passengers, went to stand behind her chair.

"I hope what I have to say will not offend you," said Lord Alistair. "I have taken a great liking to your footman. I am sorely tempted to steal him away from you."

"Wouldn't go," snapped Benjamin from behind Hannah. "Not foralla tea 'n China. No."

"Benjamin," said Hannah impatiently, "I am touched by your loyalty, but you must not address Lord Alistair in such a manner."

"That's all right," said Lord Alistair amiably. "You were very surprised when he spoke."

Hannah told him the tale of Benjamin's adventures and that led to tales of her other adventures. Lord Alistair appeared fascinated.

"You are a lucky man," he said to Benjamin at last. "Many employers would be furious to find that they had been writing reams of instructions to you when all the time you understood every word."

Benjamin gave a little cough. "The passengers have left, modom."

"I did not even notice," said Hannah, starting up. "Run and tell them I am just coming."

24

Lord Alistair held out his card. "I am bound for Brighton as well. If I can be of service to you, Mrs . . . ?"

"Pym. *Miss* Pym."

"Miss Pym. Do not hesitate to call on me."

Hannah took his card and then hurried out, remembering only when she reached the inn door that she was now the proud possessor of cards of her own, and did not even know yet how Benjamin had come by them.

Benjamin came striding towards her, his face dark with anger. "The bastards 'as gone," he shouted.

"I beg your pardon," said Hannah frostily.

"Sorry, modom, but them passengers must 'ave . . . have . . . told the coachman you was on board and off they've gone, baggage and all."

Lord Alistair emerged from the inn in time to hear this.

"Well, you are fortunate, Miss Pym," he said. "I am just leaving myself and I can take you up. In fact, I can take you all the way to Brighton."

"Please, my lord," said Hannah, "if you could just catch up with the coach so that I may tell them all what I think of them."

"Gladly."

Benjamin's eyes lit up as an ostler led a smart curricle up to the front of the inn. The curricle had only recently become fashionable. It was a two-wheeled carriage with a hood and the only two-wheeled carriage which used two horses abreast. It had been damned as ungraceful; the hinder curve of the sword case had been called positively ugly and the crooked front line and the dashing iron in the worst possible taste. But it was the fastest vehicle on the road, being the lightest.

Lord Alistair's was drawn by two matched bays. He helped Hannah in and then climbed in on the other side and took the reins in his hands. Benjamin jumped on the back just as Lord Alistair called to the ostler, "Stand away."

To Benjamin's disappointment, the carriage moved off at a leisurely pace.

"I fear, Miss Pym," said Lord Alistair, "that being abandoned by the stage-coach is hardly an exciting adventure, merely a tiresome happening."

"But I have had an adventure," said Hannah, "or rather, something terrible has happened."

"And what was that?"

"Lady Beatrice Marsham was one of the passengers." Hannah, so eager to share her worries, did not notice a certain rigidity in Lord Alistair's handsome features. "We stopped at Croyden and we were just about to leave when this ugly-looking individual came up to Lady Beatrice and constrained —I am sure he was holding either a pistol or a knife at her side—constrained her to board his carriage. I cried for help and the coachman and others came running. But when appealed to, Lady Beatrice said she was leaving of her own free will."

"Did she use those words?" asked Lord Alistair.

"Yes."

"I'll admit that's odd. It would be more in character for a cold fish like Lady Beatrice Marsham to say, 'Damn your impertinence' if all was well."

"Do you know her?" asked Hannah eagerly.

"I have had that pleasure." His voice was dry.

"You do not seem to approve of the lady."

"No, I do not. She plays fast and loose with men's affections, and that was when she was married. Harry Blackstone, her husband that was, died drunk about a year ago. He was gambler, rake and swine in general, but that does not give the lady any excuse to flirt shamelessly until the fellows fall in love with her and then turn them down flat."

"Were you . . . were you one of those fellows, my lord?"

"No, Miss Pym. I do not pursue married ladies. Change the subject. Lady Beatrice is well able to protect herself. What do you plan to do in Brighton?"

"Look at the sea," said Hannah with a laugh. "Walk a great deal. Perhaps I might even see the prince."

"Bound to see Prinny," said Lord Alistair. "Southern's giving a ball next week. Prinny's bound to be there, so you'll see him."

What an odd day, thought Hannah. First she was humiliated because she thought Lady Beatrice had considered her too low to speak to, and now she was humiliated because Lord Alistair thought her grand enough to be invited to a ball by the Earl of Southern and she would have to explain she was not. "I am not of the ton," said Hannah in a stifled voice. "In fact, I do not really belong anywhere." In a near whisper, she told him all about her years of service with the Clarences.

He smiled at her. "Miss Pym, you are a citizen of the world and can go anywhere you like. Tell you what, I'll take you there myself—that is, if you promise to tell me more stories."

Tears glistened in Hannah's eyes. "I, my lord? Do you mean that you would take *me?*"

"Yes, Miss Pym. But you'd best tell me where you are staying so that I can call on you."

"I had not thought," said Hannah. "I shall let you know, my lord."

"Don't know if we'll catch any coach at this rate." Benjamin's voice sounded from behind them.

"Really, Benjamin," snapped Hannah, wondering if this new Benjamin complete with voice was going to be a problem.

But Lord Alistair smiled lazily and said, "He has the right of it. Hold tightly. I'm going to spring 'em."

The horses surged forward and soon Hannah was hanging on for dear life as the now sunny countryside became a moving blur. Behind her, Benjamin, exalted by the speed, began to sing loudly and noisily.

At the bottom of a long hill, they at last saw the coach. On and on they sped. Hannah screamed loudly as they swept past the coach with an inch to spare. Lord Alistair drove his team up the next hill and then swung his carriage around to block the road at the top.

"You was in the coach," cried the coachman, leaning down from his high perch, his eyes starting from his head as he brought his heavily laden coach to a halt.

"As you can see, I am not," said Hannah. She climbed down on wobbly legs. "I am going to continue my journey and I expect a refund on my fare, too. Climb aboard, Benjamin." But Benjamin had hauled open the door of the coach and had started to berate the passengers.

Hannah pulled him aside and told him to climb onto the roof and then got in to hear the lying protests of the now thoroughly frightened passengers, each protesting that it hadn't been his or her fault. Actually, it had seemed a prime joke to leave Hannah behind when Mrs. Hick had suggested it, but now all were scared that Hannah might turn that terrible footman of hers loose on them.

Ignoring them all, Hannah sank back in her seat, only grateful to be secure in the stage-coach once more and resolving never to set foot in another curricle. She hoped the velocity had not damaged her brain.

At last, as night fell, they rolled into Brighton. Hannah was glad, when she booked two rooms at the Ship, that she had managed to force the coaching office to refund some of her fare. The rooms at the Ship were terribly expensive.

Benjamin presented himself in her room.

"Now, Benjamin," said Hannah sternly, "out with it. Tell me your story. You may sit down."

Benjamin sat down on a hard chair opposite and regarded her thoughtfully. "All of it, modom?" he asked in the stultifying accent he obviously considered genteel.

"Yes, all of it," said Hannah. "Start with your parents."

"I never knew them," said Benjamin. He told a story of being brought up by a Mrs. Coombes in the East End of London in a broken-down house by the river. He could never find out who his parents had been or why Mrs. Coombes had taken him in. She drank a lot, he said, and often beat him. He had been apprenticed to a sweep who had got rid of him after only six months because he was growing too big to get up the chimneys. Then he had found work as a stable-lad at a livery stable in the West End. He said he had envied the footmen he saw going about their employers' errands. They seemed to have little to do but dress nicely and look tall. He found he was lucky at gambling and he soon became more interested in gambling than work. He did not turn up at the livery stable one morning, because he had been up most of the night gambling and had slept in. He lost that job. He felt the loss of it keenly, too, for a clerk who kept the livery stable's books had taught him to read and write. He decided to give up gambling and try to get into service as a footman. But he did not have any references and no one wanted him and he was too tall for a page. He worked as knife-boy in one establishment and then as odd man in another. Then Mrs. Coombes, the only sort of family he had ever known, had died. Benjamin had decided to leave London and try to find work as a footman in a country household where they might prove to be less particular than city houses. At Esher, he had learned of Lady Carsey from some men he had gambled with. One of them worked for Lady Carsey as a groom and hinted that she had odd tastes and had once made a pet of a housemaid who had a hunched back. Benjamin hit on the idea of appearing to be deaf and dumb, and for a while it had worked, until Lady Carsey had decided to try to amuse the tedium of her country days by taking the footman into her bed. "And so you know the rest," he ended. "I refused, and she tried to get her revenge."

Hannah thought uneasily that Benjamin's story was too simple, and yet it could be true. She assured him that she had no intention of turning him off, but added that the inn was too expensive and that they would need to find cheaper lodgings.

"An apartment," said Benjamin eagerly. "Then you could make calls an' people could call on you."

"All very well, Benjamin," said Hannah, "but it will be difficult to find someone willing to let us a place for a short time."

Benjamin struck his breast in a theatrical manner, which was his old way of showing that he would handle the matter, and then gave a shamefaced laugh and said, "I will find you sumpthin', modom. Leave it to Benjamin."

"While we are on the subject of calls," said Hannah, "where did you manage to get those cards?"

"Printer I used to know," said Benjamin. "Did 'em cheap."

"Then you must tell me what I owe you."

"Later," said Benjamin. "I'll go out now and find us somewhere to live, suitable to our consequences."

"Consequence," corrected Hannah, but Benjamin had gone.

He strolled along the seafront, with his hands in his pockets, listening to the waves crashing on the beach, and looking for his prey.

And then he saw three army officers standing by some steps down to the beach. He judged them to be army officers by their whiskers and pigtails rather than by their dress, for none of them was wearing uniform.

He fished in his pocket for his dice, and as he came abreast of them, he dropped the dice to the ground. He bent down and picked them up and said, "A pair o' sixes."

One of the officers laughed. "You couldn't do that again."

"Try me," said Benjamin with a grin.

Gambling was a democratic sport. Aristocrats would cheerfully gamble with commoners. They would bet on anything—which goose would cross the road first, which fly would reach the top of the window before the other—and so they all crouched down round Benjamin and started to play hazard dice.

At one point in the game, Benjamin was losing so heavily that he began to think he would have to flee the country, but he persevered and, sure enough, the luck began to run his way.

"Enough," cried one. "We have an engagement and we are late already. We will give you our notes of hand."

"Could suggest something easier for you," said Benjamin. "My lady is looking for a snug little apartment for, say, three weeks. Any of you got one? Take that instead of your money."

The men looked at him in surprise and then one turned to the other and said, "What say you, Barnstable? Give him the keys to your place and move in with me."

"Done," said the one called Barnstable cheerfully.

"Has it got a view of the sea?" asked Benjamin, who thought they were getting off very lightly, for they all owed him a great deal of money.

"I'll take you over," said Barnstable, "and give you the keys. Just over there."

Benjamin followed him to one of the new buildings facing the sea. It turned out to be a pleasant apartment on the ground floor, with a large sitting-room with a bay window that overlooked the sea, a small parlour at the back, then two bedrooms, also at the back, and a kitchen which opened onto a weedy garden.

"My lady will want to move in tomorrow morning," said Benjamin, looking around. "Best have your traps moved out tonight. Got a piece o' paper?"

"Why?"

"Want your written agreement."

"You churl. You little toad. My word is my bond."

"I've heard that one afore," said Benjamin. "You give me that there agreement. My mistress is a Hungarian countess and a friend o' the Prince of Wales."

"Oh, really?" sneered Barnstable. "Whoever heard of a countess getting her accommodation this way?"

"Whoever heard o' a countess spending any money she don't have to?"

"Oh, very well." Barnstable signed an agreement that he would allow Miss Hannah Pym to use his apartment for three weeks. He raised his eyebrows at the name.

"Incognito," said Benjamin succinctly. "My lady has a lot of enemies."

"If this is how she goes about her business, you don't surprise me."

Benjamin had decided not to tell Hannah about his gambling. Instead he surprised her with a tale about an army man who was only too happy to let her use his place and did not want any payment.

"I find that hard to believe, Benjamin," commented Hannah suspiciously.

"He was in his cups," said Benjamin. "I got him to sign this here agreement, so that when he sobers up, he can't do nuffin' about it."

Hannah decided to go along with it, and if by chance the mysterious army gentleman had changed his mind, she could always move out again.

2

Mad, bad, and dangerous to know.
            —Lady Caroline Lamb

Hannah was delighted with her new residence. She could now look out at the sea all day long if she pleased. But first, the apartment badly needed cleaning. Hannah donned an apron and covered her hair with a mob-cap and set to work until everything was gleaming and shining. As she worked, she thought ruefully that she must do something with Benjamin.

Benjamin appeared to think that a footman's only duties were to stand behind the mistress's chair and carry her letters. Hannah had sent him out two hours ago to deliver a letter to Lord Alistair Munro. She knew he was probably strolling about the streets with his hands in his pockets.

38

It was evident he had learned nothing while he had been in service to Lady Carsey. Probably, while he was in favour, she had made a pet of him.

Her thoughts turned to what she would wear to the ball. She would need to go out that very day and find Brighton's most modish dressmaker and hope that there was some ball gown already made up which had not been collected by the lady who had ordered it.

She picked up two decanters and studied them. They had not been cleaned, so she took them through to the kitchen, filled them with hot water from a kettle swung over the fire, dropped a few pieces of well-soaped brown paper into each, and left them to stand.

She then went back to the sitting-room and opened the windows and leaned out to smell the fresh salt tang of the sea.

Benjamin came strolling along, whistling, hands in his pockets, and turned in at the gate.

Hannah shook her head in disapproval. A footman should always look as if he were on duty, whether his mistress was with him or not.

So when Benjamin appeared in the sitting-room, Hannah asked him sharply if he would like to learn to be a "real" footman.

"I thought I was, modom," said Benjamin, very stiffly on his stiffs.

Hannah shook her head. "You are a good lad, but you must learn that there is more to being a footman than parading about in livery. What would become of you if I were to die? Now, would you like to be properly trained?"

Benjamin nodded eagerly.

But the look of eagerness left his face as Hannah went on . . . and on . . . and on.

A footman should never hand over anything at all without putting it on a tray first, and always hand it with the left hand and on the left side of the person he serves, and hold it so the guest may take it with ease. In lifting dishes from the table, he should use both hands. This was because, as one foreign visitor to England had noted, "A complete English repast suggested the reason why such large English dishes are to be seen in silver, pewter, china, and crockery shops; to wit, because a quarter of a calf, half a lamb, and monstrous pieces of meat are dished up, and everyone receives almost an entire fish."

After each meal, the footman's place is

at the sink. He should have one wooden bowl of hot water for washing dishes, and one wooden bowl for rinsing. There was less chance of breakages if wood was used. He should rub down the furniture in the sitting-room and parlour before breakfast and then be washed and clean and neat, prepared to go out with his mistress.

He should mind his own business at all times. "There was once a footman at Thornton Hall," said Hannah, "who would stand behind Mrs. Clarence's chair and advise her how to play her cards. You must never do anything like that, Benjamin. I had to speak to that footman very sharply. Also, what your mistress says at the table is none of your business. If a guest is telling a very funny story, you must not even dare to laugh. A good footman should be quiet, almost invisible. You have hitherto been saved all household chores, for I have been in the way of looking after myself. Now, I have put two decanters to soak. This afternoon, empty them out, fill them up with clean water, and add a little muriatic acid, and then leave them to stand. It is very hard to clean dirty decanters.

"I have cleaned here very thoroughly, so you may be excused from proper duties today. But remember, some footmen have a very hard time. Gentlemen often take their footmen with them when they go out of an evening, for the footman's duty is to pick his master up from under the table where said master has fallen after a bout of heavy drinking. If the footman does not remove the master quietly and gracefully from the room, he may lose his job, for if his friends mock him the next day for his drunkenness, he will not blame himself but his footman for not having saved him from ridicule. It is not an easy life."

Benjamin looked crestfallen for a moment, but then brightened. "I will do as well as I can for you, modom," he said, "but, saints preserve us, if you was ever to go to your Maker, I certainly wouldn't work for one of those gents what you was talking about."

"Then decide what you do want to do," retorted Hannah tartly. "For if a life in service don't suit, then you'd better start thinking about apprenticing yourself to some trade. Now, we shall go out. I must find a dressmaker and hope she or he has a made-up gown for sale, for I am determined to go to that ball!"

Hannah, by dint of visiting the circulating

library, found out from the gentleman in charge of it that the main dressmaker of Brighton was Monsieur Blanc. Monsieur Blanc was a voluble man with a strong French accent. He said in answer to Hannah's request that he had not only one, but three ball gowns which had not been collected. One of them, to Hannah's delight, was perfect. It was a heavy white satin slip with a rich overdress of gold satin fastened down the front with gold clasps. It could have been made for her. She tried it on and hardly recognized Hannah Pym in the elegant creature that looked back at her from the glass.

"A mere eight hundred guineas," cooed Monsieur Blanc.

"Cor!" said Benjamin in awe.

Hannah turned a little pale.

"I have not yet made up my mind," she said. "I should like to take a little walk and think about it."

Monsieur Blanc looked disappointed but, ever hopeful, said he was sure that, after a little thought, she would realize the folly of turning down such an exquisite creation.

With Benjamin a few paces behind her, she walked sadly down one of Brighton's twisting, cobbled streets. "Eight hundred guineas," said Hannah over her shoulder. "It's wicked, that's what it is. Wicked! I should be ruined if I paid that."

"Beg parding," said Benjamin. "I left my gloves in that Frog's shop."

"The fact that we are at war with the French does not mean you can go about calling respectable French tradesmen Frogs," snapped Hannah. "Oh, go for your gloves. I shall be in that pastry cook's shop over there."

Benjamin ran off. He opened the door of the dressmaker's and went inside. "Has your mistress decided?" asked Monsieur Blanc.

"Fact is," said Benjamin, "my lady is strapped for the readies. O' course, she could ask 'er friend, the Prince o' Wales, but these foreign royalties is very proud. Very."

Monsieur Blanc looked bewildered. "But she introduced herself as a visitor to Brighton called Miss Pym."

Benjamin grinned and tapped the side of his nose. "Incognito," he said. "Don't want it spread about and I know a man in your position has to be discreet, but you know how it's got around that Mrs. Fitzherbert's had her day."

"Bless me," said the dressmaker in accents almost as Cockney as Benjamin's. "He married her, didn't he?"

"Mrs. Fitzherbert . . . garn," said Benjamin, now more confident because Monsieur Blanc had revealed himself to be not French but very English, and East End of London English at that. "The marriage can't be reckernized. You knows that and I knows that. Our prince is getting tired o' her, like I said. An' why's he tired o' her? 'Cos my mistress has caught his eye."

Everyone knew the prince's penchant for ladies older than himself. Even so, Monsieur Blanc looked bewildered. "But what has it got to do with me?"

"Well, see 'ere. This Miss Pym—we'll call her that, hey?—she's going to Lord Southern's ball. If you were to lend her that gown for a night, then she could tell all it was you she got it from and that she wouldn't dream o' getting her gowns and pretties from anyone else. Of course, the prince himself would get to hear of it."

"My stars and garters." Monsieur Blanc clasped his hands.

"But you're not to tell a soul who she really is. Promise."

"I don't know who she really is!"

45

"But you know now she's a foreign princess what has taken the prince's eye. So promise."

"Promise, as sure as my name's Blanc."

"Which it ain't," said Benjamin with a cheeky grin.

Monsieur Blanc grinned back. "You're a sharp one. It's White, so it's the same thing really, blanc being the French for white. Don't you go letting out I'm not French—the ladies liking to think they got a Frenchie to make their dresses—and I'll let you have the gown. You can take it now. But tell Miss Pym she's got to tell His Highness about me."

"Would I lie?" Benjamin sat down in a little gilt chair and folded his arms. "If you box it up, I'll take it to her."

Hannah wondered what had become of him and whether he might have lost his way. She was just about to leave the pastry cook's and go in search of him when he came running in, carrying a large box.

"The dress, modom," he whispered.

"Oh, heavens!" wailed Hannah. "You've stolen it."

"That's a right fine thing to say to your trusted servant!" exclaimed Benjamin. "I went back to the shop and he ups and says you can borrow it for the evening; only, if anyone compliments you on it, you're to say you gets all your gowns offa him. Right?"

"Well, of course I'll do that," said Hannah. "Are you sure?"

"O' course," said Benjamin loftily. "It's the way he goes about advertising. They all do that. Bless my heart, modom, but you are as innocent as a new-born lamb. Them grand ladies, why, a lot of them haven't paid for a stitch that's on their backs."

This was almost true, as a great number paid their dressmaking bills only when faced with the threat of duns, and some did not pay at all.

"Why, Benjamin, you are amazing. You may sit down with me and take tea."

"Won't do," said Benjamin sternly. "You have to know what's due to your position. I'll get some newspapers and we'll take that box 'ome . . . home . . . and I'll have me tea there."

They bought newspapers and groceries, Hannah disappointed to find the prices were as high as in London. They returned to their temporary home and Hannah said that Benjamin could take the newspapers through to the parlour while she prepared

47

dinner. She went to the kitchen and made up the fire and put a joint of roast lamb on the spit. Benjamin appeared in the kitchen, holding a newspaper. "What was the name of the frosty-faced female what was on the coach?"

"That," said Hannah repressively, "was Lady Beatrice Marsham."

"She's in the newspapers. Her engagement's written right 'ere."

"To whom?"

"Sir Geoffrey Handford."

Hannah shook her head in amazement. "To think of all the fuss I made! She must have thought me quite mad."

"It also says she's here in Brighton, staying with Mrs. Handford, Sir Geoffrey's ma."

"Worse and worse," moaned Hannah, shaking her head at her own folly. "And there I was crying out that she was being taken away by force. I must say, this news does relieve my conscience, for when Lord Alistair told me that Lady Beatrice was well able to take care of herself, I believed him, but last night I found myself worrying about her again."

"You can call on her anyway," said Benjamin. "I mean, she gave you her card. Got to meet a few of the nobs, ha'nt you?"

48

"Well, yes, I could call. Can you find Mrs. Handford's address?"

"Easy," said Benjamin.

He was back in about ten minutes. "Mrs. Handford's just around hard by. One of those big houses on the Steyne."

"How did you find out so quickly?"

"Thought it might be one of them grand houses, so I asked any servant I saw about and got it the third time of asking."

"I wonder if I should go," mused Hannah. "I mean, I would be social climbing, would I not? And what if I were damned as a mushroom?"

"Well, if that's yer attitude, you'd best kiss that Sir George Clarence goodbye."

"Benjamin! I allow you a good deal of licence, but I would not have allowed a footman to address me in such terms even were I still only a housekeeper."

"Sorry, modom," said Benjamin stiffly.

Hannah looked at him for a few moments and then said reluctantly, "Oh, very well."

Late that afternoon, Monsieur Blanc called at the household of a certain Mrs. Cambridge. Mrs. Cambridge was very elegant, a member of the untitled aristocracy and

49

one of Monsieur Blanc's best customers. With a mouthful of pins, he carefully arranged a seam and said, "T' shtrangesht shing 'appened today."

"What?" demanded Mrs. Cambridge, twisting round. "Do take those pins out of your mouth. It is hard to understand you at the best of times."

Monsieur Blanc complied. "Zee strangest thing 'appened this day," he said, his accent stronger than ever, for he regretted bitterly having let it slip in front of Benjamin. "Zis lady, ver' grand, came into my salon. She is amazed at my work. She says she will buy everything from me. She call 'erself Miss Pym. 'Er footman, he return to collect the gown I 'ave fashioned for 'er, and he tells me," went on Monsieur Blanc, dropping most of his accent suddenly in his desire to impart such a stunning piece of gossip, "that this Miss Pym, is, in fact, foreign royalty. Oh, *ma foi!* Why did I tell you? It is so secret."

"Really!" Mrs. Cambridge's eyes glowed. "You silly man. You know I won't tell a soul."

"My lips are sealed."

"Such a pity. I was going to order a whole new summer wardrobe from you."

"But it eez gossip of the most dangerous."

"Pity about that wardrobe. I meant to have at least a dozen ensembles."

Like the shrewd man he was, Monsieur Blanc guessed that the bidding had now gone as high as he could expect it to go. Twelve ensembles was top offer. With affected reluctance, he said, "I must remember that Madame is so discreet."

"Exactly."

"Well," whispered Monsieur Blanc, "her footman told me that our Prince of Wales is madly in love with this Miss Pym, or so she chooses to call herself."

Mrs. Cambridge looked at him with her mouth open. Never since the Prince of Wales had become betrothed to Mrs. Fitzherbert had such a delicious piece of scandal come to Brighton. "I will not breathe a word," she said.

"And so," said Mrs. Cambridge to a rapt audience of ladies over the tea-tray that evening, "what do you think of *that?*"

"Where does she live?" asked a faded little blonde.

"In an apartment on the front promenade. Number two."

"We must leave cards," said another.

"You had best let me go first," said Mrs. Cambridge. "May be all a hum."

Hannah was just dressing to go out the following day when Benjamin announced there was a Mrs. Cambridge to see her.

Puzzled, Hannah told Benjamin to put the visitor in the drawing-room and tell her that she would be with her directly. Hannah finished dressing and then walked through to the drawing-room.

In a rustle of silks and a fluttering of feathers, Mrs. Cambridge swept Hannah a court curtsy. Taken aback, Hannah returned the salute with a startled nod, rather like a shying horse.

"I heard you had honoured our little resort with your presence, Miss . . . er . . . Pym."

"And who told you, ma'am?" asked Hannah, waving a hand to indicate that Mrs. Cambridge should sit down. "Lord Alistair Munro?"

"No, no. Another person. But I am bound to secrecy. How do you like our watering-place?"

"It is very beautiful," said Hannah, looking bewildered.

"And what do you think of our most famous resident, the Prince of Wales?"

Hannah was a royalist to the tip of her fingers. She had never seen the prince but had seen some very flattering prints and engravings of him. "His Highness is a model of what all gentlemen should be," she said firmly. "Such handsome looks, such a regal bearing, such exquisite taste."

"Exactly what we all think of him," breathed Mrs. Cambridge.

She stared at Hannah as if memorizing every detail.

Hannah shifted uncomfortably. "As it happens, Mrs. Cambridge, I was just on the point of going out. I am paying a call on Lady Beatrice Marsham."

Mrs. Cambridge shot to her feet. "I shall not keep you. Shall we have the honour of your presence at Lord Southern's ball?"

"Yes, I shall be there."

"Splendid. May I presume to hope that we may become friends?"

Hannah was more bewildered than ever. "You may," she said. "And now I really must go."

"I shall not detain you any longer," said Mrs. Cambridge and, to Hannah's amazement, she rose and dropped another court curtsy and then *backed* from the room.

"Well!" exclaimed Hannah when she had gone. "Tell me, Benjamin, am I so far out of the world that I do not know how folks go on? I thought one only retreated like that before royalty."

"It's the sea air, modom," said Benjamin, ignoring a stab of guilt, for he was sure the dressmaker had blabbed about Hannah being foreign royalty. "It addles people's brains, or so I have read."

"And," said Mrs. Cambridge a bare quarter of an hour later to her friends, who had been waiting in her drawing-room for her return from the call, "when I curtsied, she only replied with a common nod, just the way royalty goes on, you know. And her voice is so un-English, very clear and every word carefully enounced. And her regal bearing softened when she spoke of the prince. If only you could have seen and heard her."

"What does she look like?" asked one.

Mrs. Cambridge settled down to give a thorough description, and as she talked, Hannah's crooked nose was straightened, her spare housekeeper's figure showed all the signs of royal birth, her sandy hair grew

54

brown, and her sallow skin "white as alabaster." "And," went on Mrs. Cambridge, "she was just leaving to call on Lady Beatrice Marsham. When did Lady Beatrice ever trouble to receive any lady? Mark my words, Lady Beatrice would only stoop to receive royalty. So there!"

"Miss Pym," said Mrs. Handford's butler, "to see Lady Beatrice."

Mrs. Handford sat next to Lady Beatrice on a backless sofa in her drawing-room. She was a squat, powerful, pugnacious woman who looked remarkably like a bulldog guarding a juicy bone.

"Lady Beatrice is not at home," said Mrs. Handford.

Lady Beatrice held up her hand. "You had best allow this lady to come up," she said coldly. "Miss Pym raised a great commotion at the inn when your son abducted me. If she does not find me apparently safe and well, she may make a fuss."

"Geoffrey told me about some spinster yelling and fussing. Very well. Have her up, but remember what will happen to you if you make her suspicious."

"I know what will happen to me. My dear parents have told me that they will cut me

55

off without a shilling if I do not marry
Geoffrey. Geoffrey and you have hinted at
dark things. You need have no fear. If you
all wish to see me wed to another man
whom I detest, that is your affair."

Hannah came in and smiled tentatively
at Lady Beatrice. Lady Beatrice rose gracefully, introduced her to Mrs. Handford,
and asked Hannah to sit down. She then
sank down on the sofa beside Mrs. Handford and said colourlessly, "How kind of
you to call. How did you know my direction? It was not on the card I gave you."

"It was in the newspapers along with your
engagement. May I offer my felicitations?"

Lady Beatrice nodded briefly. There was
a long silence.

"Staying long?" barked Mrs. Handford
suddenly.

"A few weeks," said Hannah, her eyes
still on Lady Beatrice, who was sitting as
still as a statue. "I have found pleasant
lodgings where I can see the sea from my
drawing-room. If your ladyship would care
to call . . . ?"

"Too busy," snapped Mrs. Handford.
"Getting married soon."

Hannah did not like it. She did not like
it at all. There was a thin air of veiled men-

ace emanating from the ugly Mrs. Handford, and Lady Beatrice was so white and still. All her fears for Lady Beatrice came rushing back.

Hannah began to chatter about the weather, about the beneficial effects of sea air, about the fashionable crowd which thronged Brighton's streets.

"You should try sea bathing, Miss Pym," said Lady Beatrice.

"I do not know how to swim," exclaimed Hannah.

"That is not necessary. You get a bathing machine to take you out and the lady in charge will make sure you do not drown."

"Oh, I would like to try that," said Hannah, her eyes shining, and was relieved to see Lady Beatrice smile.

"If you will excuse us," said Mrs. Handford rudely, "we were just about to discuss the wedding arrangements."

Hannah rose and took her leave.

Once outside, she confided her fears to Benjamin. "Rum go," said the footman. "Let's go call on that Lord Alistair. He'll know what to do."

Lord Alistair was at home and pleased to receive Miss Pym. She asked him shyly if he still meant to take her to the ball and flushed with happiness when he said he did.

"I have just been to call on Lady Beatrice," said Hannah. "She does have an odd taste in husbands, that lady," commented Lord Alistair drily. "I see she is engaged to Sir Geoffrey Handford. Handford is a bully and a brute."

"I did not meet him, but I met Mrs. Handford," said Hannah. "She made me feel uneasy. Bless me, but I had this odd impression that she was *guarding* Lady Beatrice."

"I do not think for a moment there is any-thing amiss," said Lord Alistair easily. "Think on the character of Lady Beatrice. She is not a sweet virgin to be easily bullied. She is a widow in her late twenties. She is cold and hard and assured. She can drive better than most men. Her late husband, Blackstone, was, I admit, a degenerate fiend and would have broken the spirit of a meeker woman."

"Why did she marry this Blackstone?"

"Her parents, the Earl and Countess of Debren, arranged it. Medieval couple. Give me the shudders. Live in a great moated castle in Warwickshire. The countess gave birth to Beatrice when she was in her forties and reputed to be long past childbearing.

58

Why Blackstone? That's simple. He was the one prepared to pay the most to marry her. I saw her at her first Season. Different creature entirely, sweet and shy. Anyway, the earl and countess, not content with the marriage settlement, hoped to get their hands on some of the Blackstone fortune. But Harry Blackstone used to gamble thousands and thousands of guineas a night. I believe he left nothing but debts on his death. Now Geoffrey Handford is a rich nabob, made his killing in India. That's the attraction. If Lady Beatrice doesn't like Sir Geoffrey, that would be a pity were she a pleasant female. Friend of mine, Captain Jarret, became obsessed with her. She flirted with him quite shamelessly. Blackstone was never around to stop the flirtation, for he was always in the card-room or dead drunk. The captain asked her to run away with him, and she suddenly turned as cold as ice and told him haughtily that he was overstepping the mark. Broke his heart."

"Hearts do not break, Lord Alistair," said Hannah. "Your friend was at fault for chasing after a married lady."

"You haven't seen Lady Beatrice in action, Miss Pym. Quite dazzling. Gives a fellow a smile that promises him the world and more. Lady Beatrice is not worth your concern. Tell me instead about yourself."

They passed a pleasant half-hour and Hannah finally left, feeling sure that, after all, she had been silly to pity or worry about Lady Beatrice.

When she returned home, she was startled to see a group of people at her gate. As she passed, the men raised their hats and the women curtsied.

"What was that about?" asked Hannah faintly when they were safely indoors.

"Very simple people in these seaside places," said Benjamin quickly. "Like to pay their courtesies to a new face in town."

"How very odd," said Hannah Pym.

"So that's her," said Sir Geoffrey Handford to his friend, Mr. Gully Parks. "Old fright, ain't she? What did you say her name was?"

"Pym. Miss Hannah Pym, or rather, that's what she's calling herself."

"And Prinny is spoony about that crooked-nosed bat?"

"On the best authority, old chap. On the v-e-r-y best authority. You want to be Lord Thingummy, that's your road. Butter her up and get her to pop a word in the royal ear."

3

*Vaulting ambition, which o'erleaps itself
And falls on the other.*
                    —William Shakespeare

Sir Geoffrey made his way home deep in thought. His ambition was to have a title—baron, viscount, earl or marquis. To this end, he had been cultivating friends of the Prince of Wales, and sending the prince handsome presents. So far, all he had received for his pains had been a slight nod from the prince at a ball.

He wandered into his mother's drawing-room, still trying to work out a way to introduce himself to this Miss Pym.

"I am glad you are home, Geoffrey," said his mother. "I've had a tiresome afternoon."

"Beatrice coming over nasty again?"

"No, but cold and insolent as usual. She had a visitor."

Sir Geoffrey's face darkened. "She isn't supposed to have any visitors. Where is she?"

"Gone to sulk in her room."

"And why did you allow this visitor to see her?"

"It was that female you told me about, you know, the one who set up the row at the inn. I handled her. Lady Beatrice knows what she's supposed to do. Not by a flicker did she show that anything was amiss."

"What's the name of this interfering busybody anyway?"

"Miss Hannah Pym."

Sir Geoffrey sat down suddenly. "Is she a middle-aged woman with a bent nose?"

"Yes. You should know. You saw her at the inn."

"I didn't pay her any heed. I was too concerned with getting Beatrice away. Let me tell you, sainted Mother, that this Miss Pym is not what she seems. Travelling by stage-coach must have been an effort on her part to arrive quietly in Brighton. It is said that she is Prinny's latest amour; and not only that—of foreign royalty."

"Tish, and fiddlesticks. Who is spreading such rubbish?"

"Letitia Cambridge."

"Mrs. Cambridge. Good heavens above!"

"Exactly."

Mrs. Cambridge was accounted among the cream of the ton.

"Furthermore, Mrs. Cambridge called on this Miss Pym, not really believing a word of the gossip, but came away perfectly convinced it was true. And you know how that bitch is too easy to damn people as parvenus and upstarts," said Sir Geoffrey with feeling, he and his mother having been at the receiving end of Mrs. Cambridge's high-handedness. "This could be the entrée I need. I've done everything I can to try to get Prinny's ear, and nothing has worked."

"She asked Beatrice to call on her," said Mrs. Handford.

"Then Beatrice had better go. The sooner she forges a friendship with this Miss Pym, or whoever she is, the better."

"And then what? Beatrice will promptly tell her all about the marriage she is being forced into."

"No, I do not think she will. Her parents

have already told her through me that if she does not wed me, they will cut her off without a shilling. There is nothing else she can do but obey me. In fact, I think we should risk turning her loose. She can go to that house she has rented and do what she likes. She cannot escape me—that is, unless she wishes to end up a pauper."

Mrs. Handford shifted her large bulk uneasily. "Do you really think her parents would go ahead and do such a thing?"

"Oh, yes; they said they had brought her to heel over that marriage to Blackstone in the same way."

"But she was, what? Eighteen when she married him. She's a hardened widow of twenty-eight now. Oh, I wish you had not been so dramatic, Geoffrey. There was no need to force her into your carriage at gunpoint. Would it not be better to promise her her freedom if she does all in her power to use her influence with Miss Pym? Surely a title means more to you than a chilly widow who hates you."

"No, Mama. I want her and that's that. I admit I should not have chased her down the Brighton road, but I was mad with fury when I heard she had left London. I did not know then that her parents were going to do all in their power to force the marriage through. I did not get their letter until I arrived here. Let her go. She'll accept this marriage with good grace, you'll see."

"And what if some other man snatches her up in the meantime?"

"No man will. Not now. Not with her reputation. She's broken so many hearts that it's become almost a point of honour *not* to even be seen dancing with her. She was at Derby's ball two weeks ago and spent most of the evening with the wallflowers. A sad come-down for London's beauty, who used to have 'em fighting over her on the ballroom floor. That's why I'm confident she'll end up looking forward to this marriage. I'm a handsome fellow."

"You are that," said his mother, gazing at him with affection. In that moment, both looked remarkably alike with their bulldog faces and long wide mouths that seemed to stretch from ear to ear.

"Right! Fetch her in here and I'll tell her what she's got to do."

A footman was summoned and told to fetch Lady Beatrice. "Make yourself scarce, Mama," said Sir Geoffrey. "May as well kick off with a little wooing."

Lady Beatrice hesitated on the threshold when she saw that he was alone.

"What is it?" she demanded.

He looked at her, at her elegant figure and the beauty of her face, and his senses quickened. She would be magnificent as his wife. He looked forward to getting her in his bed. He was sure there were a few interesting tricks he could show her. That drunk, Blackstone, couldn't have been much of a lover.

"Come sit by me, my sweeting," he said.

Lady Beatrice took a few steps into the room. "I would rather stay here," she said, "in case you decide to hold a gun on me again."

"You must forgive me," he said, putting his hand on his heart. "I would not hurt you for the world."

"Then release me from this engagement."

"Always funning, ain't you? How would you like to move to your own place?"

Lady Beatrice looked startled. "With all my heart."

"Well, and so you may. This very day, in fact. There is something I want you to do for me."

"That being?"

66

"You know that Miss Pym?"

"Of course."

"Did you know she was Prinny's latest flirt?"

Lady Beatrice began to laugh. "Prinny's . . . ? You must be mad. She is a respectable English lady and, I believe, every bit the spinster she claims to be."

"Letitia Cambridge says she is of foreign royalty and Prinny dotes on her, and I want you to call on her and get her to put a word in Prinny's ear about getting me a lordship or an earldom."

Lady Beatrice opened her mouth to say that Mrs. Cambridge was, and always had been, a silly gossip. But then she quickly realized that her freedom, or temporary freedom, from the terrible Handfords somehow depended on her cultivating a friendship with Miss Pym.

She affected surprise. "Well, I never would have believed such a thing. Now, you come to mention it, she did have a certain regal bearing and I was most surprised to find her travelling on the stage."

"Probably hoped to slip quietly into Brighton. Will you do it?"

"Yes, if you will let me leave this evening."

"And you will promise not to tell her about your parents' forcing you to accept me? For, you know, I have only to break off the engagement and tell them it was all your fault for them to turn you out in the street."

"I will do what you wish," said Lady Beatrice. "Tell me, Sir Geoffrey, why on earth do you want to marry me?"

"Come here and I'll show you." He leered at her and she backed away, repulsed.

"I will call on Miss Pym tomorrow," said Lady Beatrice quickly. "But you cannot expect me to ask her any favours right away. I must, you will agree, forge some sort of friendship. The whole of Brighton will be trying to cultivate her society."

"Don't be too long about it," he said.

Lady Beatrice turned and left the room. She almost ran to her bedchamber and then rang for the maid and told her that her bags were to be packed and delivered to her house in Brighton. Then, swinging a cloak about her shoulders, she went downstairs. The butler loomed up just as she was making for the door. "I am afraid the master has not given you permission to leave, my lady," he said.

"That's all right, Foskins," said Sir Geoffrey's voice from the stairs. "Lady Beatrice may go."

Lady Beatrice looked up at him, at his thick gross body and heavy face, and then turned quickly away. The butler held open the door and she walked out, trying hard not to run. After she had gone a little way away, she stood and breathed in great gulps of fresh, salty air.

Hannah was becoming alarmed. The following day, there were so many people clustered outside her flat that she was frightened to go out.

By the afternoon, Benjamin was kept busy turning away visitors, saying that Miss Pym was "not at home."

"There is something badly wrong here," said Hannah. "I cannot look out at the sea, for when I try to, I find myself staring into the eyes of so many watchers. Enough is enough, and you are looking shiftier and guiltier by the minute. There is no reason for so many people to try to call, now is there? Out with it, Benjamin. I shall find out sooner or later, you know."

"You promise not to turn me off?" said Benjamin desperately.

"Oh, very well, for I would do anything now to get at the truth."

"Modom, I did it to get you that ball gown. I told Monsieur Blanc that you was a foreign princess . . ."

"Heavens!"

"There's worse." Benjamin's head sank lower. "I told him that you were the Prince of Wales's latest fancy."

"WHAT? Benjamin, this will reach the ears of the prince and we shall both be in the Tower. Oh, you silly fool. What am I to do? I cannot go to that ball now. And you must take that gown back immediately and tell Monsieur Blanc that you were lying. And tell anyone else who will listen."

"They won't believe me," said Benjamin gloomily. "You're supposed to be incognito, so they'll think you've instructed me to lie to everyone. You see, they would rather believe the lie."

Hannah began to pace up and down the back parlour. "I need help," she said. "This is appalling. Oh, there's the knocker again. Send whoever it is away."

Benjamin opened the door to Lady Beatrice. He recognized her immediately. "I am afraid Miss Pym is not at home, my lady," he said.

70

Lady Beatrice calmly walked past him and then into the drawing-room. Benjamin slammed the door on the watching crowd and followed her.

She was standing by the fireplace, drawing off her gloves. "I will wait," she said.

Benjamin was about to say that Miss Pym was not expected back till midnight when the lady herself walked into the room.

"It is all right, Benjamin," said Hannah quietly. "You may leave us. Pray be seated, Lady Beatrice. Before you begin to speak, I must tell you that I am not of royal blood, nor have I ever met the Prince of Wales."

"I suspected as much," said Lady Beatrice with a little sigh.

"I wish I had never come to Brighton," said Hannah passionately. "First, on the road down, I had a mad idea that you were being abducted, and now, because of my footman, lies about me are circulating all around Brighton and I dare not show my face out of doors."

"Why did your footman start such rumours?" asked Lady Beatrice.

"I do not want to tell you for reasons of pride." Hannah blinked away the tears that had come to her eyes. "Oh, I may as well tell you all. I will never see you again, but it will give me some relief to unburden myself. I am plain common Miss Hannah Pym, formerly housekeeper to the late Mr. Clarence of Thornton Hall, Kensington. He left me a legacy and so I found myself a lady of independent means. After you had left the coach, I met by chance Lord Alistair Munro. The coach went off and left me behind and Lord Alistair took me in his carriage so that I might catch up on the coach. And so we did. But on the journey, Lord Alistair graciously offered to take me to Lord Southern's ball, and Lord Alistair knows exactly who I am. I was elated. I went to Monsieur Blanc, the dressmaker, to see if he had a gown already made up, which he had, and it was a perfect fit.

"Alas, the price was eight hundred guineas, almost a fifth of my small inheritance. I refused. My footman went back, saying he had left his gloves, and spun the dressmaker a parcel of lies about me being of foreign royalty and that I was the Prince of Wales's latest amour."

Lady Beatrice felt like laughing. She realized in the same moment she had not felt like laughing until she had met Hannah Pym.

"But I was under the impression your footman was deaf and dumb?"

"Oh, I wish he were!" cried Hannah. "But that is another story and so very long. You may take your leave now, Lady Beatrice, and if you have a spark of compassion in you, you will tell as many people as possible that I am a fraud."

"I do not think they would believe me," said Lady Beatrice. "You are supposed to be incognito, you know."

"Then I shall leave Brighton this very evening!"

"And not go to the ball? Miss Pym, you have been very frank with me, and so I must be frank with you. You did not imagine I was being abducted."

To the amazed Hannah she told of her forced engagement and her parents' threat and how she had only secured her brief freedom from Sir Geoffrey and his mother by promising to try to get Miss Pym to use her influence on Sir Geoffrey's behalf to get him a title.

It was no use, Hannah reflected, to protest that parents did not force their daughters into marriage, when there was ample proof of it almost every day. Marriages were mostly business deals, and money

was at the root of all such arrangements.

"And you have no money of your own?"
asked Hannah.

"No. My husband gambled away a vast
fortune and left me debts. My parents paid
those debts and settled a generous allowance on me. I naïvely thought my worries
were over."

"But have you no aunts, uncles, other re-
lations to appeal to for help?"

"My parents are elderly now: my aunts
and uncles are dead. I have two nephews,
both in India, that is all."

Hannah twisted her fingers in distress.
"My dear Lady Beatrice, if I thought I
could get away with this masquerade which
has been thrust upon me, I would for your
sake. For when you tell Sir Geoffrey that
it is not true—and *he* is bound to believe
you, knowing that you have every reason
to hope it to be true—then you will be
forced to return to his mother's house."

"Perhaps not," said Lady Beatrice. "He
was not so sure of me until my parents'
letter reached him after we had arrived in
Brighton. In it, they assured him that they
would turn me out into the street if I did
not wed him. But as to your problem, I

do not have the ear of the Prince of Wales, but Lord Alistair Munro does. I do not know him very well, but I know he is much admired. Why not send for him and tell him all?"

Hannah looked at her with hope dawning on her face. "Will he not think me ridiculous?"

"I shall be amazed if he does. Most of society, on the other hand, is ridiculous. He has probably heard the gossip already."

Hannah went to a desk in the corner and pulled forward a sheet of paper. "I shall send Benjamin with a note. Oh, how I wish you could stay, for I dread to think what he will say."

"I will stay," said Lady Beatrice. "No doubt Sir Geoffrey has one of his servants stationed outside this house to report how I am faring. When he hears that I spent a long time with you, he will be in alt. I have no intention of disabusing him. Let him find out for himself."

Benjamin was sent with the note and Hannah went through to the kitchen to make tea, happy that as Lady Beatrice knew her circumstances, she did not have to pretend to have a host of servants tucked away. She clucked angrily when she saw that the twenty-two-pound sugar loaf which Benjamin had brought in that morning was still sitting there, looking as hard as granite. She then reflected that Benjamin had not been trained and therefore did not yet know his duties, and she chipped off the required amount, pounded it into granules, and put it into a sugar-bowl.

When she went back into the parlour, she found that Lady Beatrice had fallen silently and soundlessly asleep in her chair. Hannah set down the tray of tea-things on a table, wondering whether to wake her, wondering why the chilly Lady Beatrice had elected to stay. She did not look hard or cold in sleep, but young and vulnerable.

A log fell on the hearth and Lady Beatrice awoke instantly and blinked and looked around.

"I am sorry, Miss Pym," she said, "but I have not slept well since I arrived in Brighton."

Hannah poured tea. "I must warn you, Lady Beatrice," she said awkwardly, "that although Lord Alistair has been extremely kind to me, he does not appear to approve of you."

"How so? I barely know the man."

Hannah hesitated.

"Out with it. We have both been so frank with each other, 'twere a pity to dissemble now."

"Lord Alistair, I regret to say, damns you as a heartless flirt."

"What ails the man? We all flirt. 'Tis the fashion."

"He had a friend, a captain, and he said you encouraged his advances, only to break his heart."

"Fustian." Lady Beatrice coloured and turned her head slightly away.

Hannah heard a key turning in the front door. "That is Benjamin," she said. "Let us hope he brought Lord Alistair with him."

Lord Alistair strolled into the parlour and put up his quizzing-glass and stared for a few moments at Lady Beatrice. Then he turned to Hannah. "You wished to see me, Miss Pym?"

"Yes, please, my lord. I am in the most dreadful difficulties. But pray be seated and have some tea."

Lord Alistair sat down in an armchair and crossed his booted legs. His golden hair gleamed in the firelight, but his blue eyes were alert and watchful and Hannah knew that he did not like the presence of Lady Beatrice.

But she needed help and so she told the whole story of Benjamin's deception. Lord Alistair carefully placed his cup on the table and leaned back in his chair and laughed and laughed.

"It is no laughing matter," said Hannah distractedly. "What am I to do?"

Lord Alistair wiped his eyes and then grinned at Hannah. "I think your main worry is that the prince himself should get to hear of it and send someone over from the Pavilion to read you a lecture. I shall call on Prinny and hope your story amuses him as much as it has amused me."

"I wanted Lady Beatrice to go around telling everyone that it is all untrue, but she said she would not be believed."

"But I will be," said Lord Alistair, "for everyone knows I am a confidant of the prince. Your worries will soon be over, Miss Pym. By tomorrow, there will be no one at your gate."

"Thank you, my lord," said Hannah, and then turned red.

"There is something else?"

"It all started with that gown. It will need to be taken back. I do not have a ball gown."

"That is no problem," said Lady Beatrice. "We are of the same size in height and both slim. I will send my maid round with something suitable which she can alter to fit you."

Lord Alistair gazed at Lady Beatrice in surprise. "You amaze me, madam," he said. "I thought you cared for neither man, woman, or beast."

"You do not know me," retorted Lady Beatrice haughtily.

"Evidently not." Lord Alistair rose to his feet. "Miss Pym, the ball is on Wednesday. I shall call for you at eight." He bowed and left.

The Prince of Wales was studying plans that would turn his Marine Pavilion into an oriental palace. When he was told that Lord Alistair Munro was demanding an audience, he rolled up the plans and gave his permission for that gentleman to be ushered into the royal presence.

Lord Alistair had managed to remain a friend of the touchy, sensitive prince by always being amiable, and always available to play cards, run races, gamble, or talk lighthearted nonsense.

He was always cautious to be as formal as possible. Other men, regarded as friends of the prince, had overstepped the mark in the past by being too familiar and had fallen from royal favour.

"We heard you were in Brighton," said the prince. "What news?"

He waved a plump beringed hand to indicate that Lord Alistair had his permission to sit down. Lord Alistair was not feeling so easy in his mind as he had led Hannah to believe. The prince, with luck, would be amused. On the other hand, he might be furious.

"I have some gossip that concerns yourself, sire."

"Indeed!" The royal face crumpled in displeasure.

"I trust it will amuse you." Instead of telling the prince simply about Hannah's predicament in Brighton, Lord Alistair began at the beginning, describing the adventures of Miss Pym on the Exeter road, the Bath road, and the Portsmouth road, and the prince listened with delight. Even when he got to the real point of the story, Lord Alistair thought it politic to twist it slightly. He said the gossips had it that Miss Pym was not only a member of some foreign royal family, but besotted with the Prince of Wales.

The prince thought this was a famous joke. Lord Alistair had shrewdly guessed the touchy prince might not have found it so amusing if he had known that it was he who was said to be enamoured of Miss Pym.

"So now," went on Lord Alistair, "our poor Miss Pym cannot even leave her dwelling because of the vulgar crowd at her gate. I shall put the truth about."

"Quite a character, this Miss Pym," remarked the prince, in high good humour. "Shall we see her?"

"I am escorting her to Lord Southern's ball. If it pleases Your Highness, I will point her out to you."

"By all means."

They talked of other things and then Lord Alistair took his leave. He had been just in time. The gossip about Miss Pym was being poured into the royal ears by all his cronies that evening, who were startled when the prince laughed and said he knew all about Miss Pym and was looking forward to meeting her at Lord Southern's ball.

The gossip about Hannah's true identity reached Monsieur Blanc the next morning, and shortly after that, Benjamin arrived, bearing the gown.

"I'm surprised you got the cheek to show your bleeding face in 'ere," said the dressmaker.

"And I'm surprised you've got the cheek to look me in the eye," said Benjamin, unruffled. "You opened that trap o' yourn arter you swore not to. Did I mention you was nothing more but a common Englishman, wiff the emphasis on common? Nah. But I will now. So take this poxy dress and stuff—"

" 'Ere now!" cried Monsieur Blanc, alarmed. "No need to be 'asty."

Benjamin put the dress box down on a chair and made for the door.

"Did I say I wanted it back?" pleaded Monsieur Blanc. "Did I now?"

Benjamin turned round, one eyebrow raised.

"Look, don't go around saying as how I'm plain Mr. White or you'll ruin my trade. You can keep that there dress for the ball and bring it back next day. 'Ave we got a deal?"

Benjamin grinned. "It's a deal."

Mrs. Cambridge's friends clustered around her, all mock sympathy. "Poor Letitia. To be so misled by that charlatan. For Lord Alistair Munro knows the creature. He is even taking her to Lord Southern's ball! She is Miss Pym of nowhere in particular, or so I believe."

Mrs. Cambridge forced a light laugh. "I knew she was common the minute I set eyes on her. But, my dears, you must forgive me. I could not help having a little fun at your expense. Of course, the silly creature is getting quite above herself with all the attention. I shall take pleasure in cutting her at the ball." The friends, disappointed that they had not managed to tease her as they had hoped, vowed that they, too, would cut the dreadful Miss Pym, forgetting in their toadying to their social leader, Mrs. Cambridge, that it is very hard to cut someone who does not know you from Adam.

4

When a woman isn't beautiful, people always say, "You have lovely eyes, you have lovely hair."

—*Anton Chekhov*

Hannah found the very next day that the front of the house was free of sightseers. She went out for a walk, enjoying exploring the little flint-cobbled town with Benjamin behind her. They went for a long stroll along the chain pier, Hannah staring fascinated at the waves surging below. The sun was shining and brown-sailed boats were scudding before a brisk breeze.

"Do you think, Benjamin," she called over her shoulder, "that I should try sea bathing?"

"No, modom," said Benjamin. "I wouldn't go in that nasty stuff, not if you paid me."

"But many ladies go sea bathing. And there is always an attendant. I should be in no danger of drowning."

"You wouldn't get me in there," said Benjamin with a shudder. "Not ever."

They had reached the end of the pier when Hannah saw Lady Beatrice approaching with her maid.

"I called at your home," cried Lady Beatrice as she came up to her, "and saw that the crowd had gone. Lord Alistair appears to have been successful."

"Good for me," said Hannah, "but not for you. Has Sir Geoffrey found out yet that I am of no importance whatsoever?"

"Not yet. He will no doubt call on me as soon as he does."

"When is this wedding to be, my lady?"

"In a month's time."

"So soon?" Hannah was appalled.

"I am afraid so."

They walked together along the pier. Behind Hannah came the sound of Benjamin's voice. He was obviously doing his best to impress Lady Beatrice's lady's maid. She hoped he was not regaling her with horrendous lies.

Lady Beatrice restrained an odd impulse to take Hannah's arm. She wondered why she felt so safe, so at ease with this Miss Pym.

Hannah was reflecting that masters and mistresses would be amazed if they knew how very alike in character they could be to their servants.

There was the case of Fanny, Mrs. Clarence's lady's maid. Hannah vividly remembered her. She had been a haughty, elegant creature, often mistaken for her mistress when she went out shopping. She was generally disliked by the other servant. There was an air of coldness about her which repelled all overtures of friendship. So she was damned as "too hoity-toity" and suffered the consequent punishment handed out to hoity-toity servants. The footmen put spiders in her bed and the chambermaids put dye in her washing-up water.

And then Mrs. Clarence had run away and Fanny's services were no longer required. Hannah had come across Fanny slowly packing her clothes, and had noticed that the lady's maid's fingers were trembling. Something had prompted Hannah to put a comforting arm about those rigid shoulders, and say, "Whatever ails you can be helped, if only you will ask for help." And Fanny had turned her face into Hannah's flat bosom and wept bitterly. It had come out that she would need to return home until she found another post. Her father was a drunken, violent brute and her mother little better, and Fanny was terrified. Hannah had immediately remembered a Mrs. Jessingham, a friend of the absent Mrs. Clarence, who had been complaining that she could not find a suitable lady's maid. So Hannah had taken Fanny to Mrs. Jessingham and Mrs. Jessingham had hired Fanny on the spot. Hannah had caught a glimpse of Fanny one day on one of her rare visits to London. Fanny looked grander and haughtier than ever. But then, Hannah thought, with a little sideways darting glance at Lady Beatrice, perhaps, because of her parents, Fanny had built a brick wall around her to keep humanity at bay, and perhaps Lady Beatrice had done the same.

"I have no plans for the day," said Lady Beatrice. "I have been ordered to cultivate your society. Would it bore you too much to endure my company?"

"I would consider myself honoured," said Hannah. "But will it all not rebound on you when Sir Geoffrey finds out that I am Miss Pym of Nowhere?"

"I shall say I did not know," said Lady

Beatrice. "In this life, it is very important to live in the minute, do you not think? Would you like my maid to bring you one of my ball gowns so that it may be altered?"

Hannah told her that Monsieur Blanc had been unexpectedly generous and had said she might have the gown for the night of the ball. "I do not know how Benjamin managed it," said Hannah uneasily. "But he assured me he had told only the truth."

"He is an unusual fellow," commented Lady Beatrice. "How warm it is today. We must make the most of it, for the English weather is so fickle, it could be snowing tomorrow."

"I would like to go into the water." Hannah stopped short and looked down at the surging sea.

Lady Beatrice laughed. "Then why not?"

"The usual problem. I have nothing to wear."

"Easily remedied. Marianne!" Lady Beatrice called over her shoulder. "Run home and bring two flannel gowns and two caps and a quantity of towels and meet us by the bathing machines. I am sure Miss Pym will allow Benjamin to accompany you."

Hannah was already rehearsing in her mind what she would say to Sir George

Clarence when next they met. "I went sea bathing in Brighton with Lady Beatrice Marsham."

"I do not suppose Princess Caroline will be at the ball," Hannah realized Lady Beatrice was saying. "In Brighton, Mrs. Fitzherbert is the wife, and you would think, to hear the gossips talk, that our prince had never even married Caroline of Brunswick." She gave a bitter little laugh. "At least I have something in common with Prinny; he loathes his wife and I loathed my husband and am well on my way to loathing another. The common people do not have to endure such miseries."

"Oh, yes, they do," said Hannah tartly. "The baker's son may fall in love with a farm labourer's daughter, but he is not allowed to marry her, for she is far beneath him and he will be expected to marry a girl with a good-enough dowry so that his parents may expand their bakery, and so it goes on. It is money that makes the world go round. Romance is a rare luxury." And having said that, Hannah thought of Sir George Clarence, so far above *her,* and felt quite dismal. Even if he were ruined and lost all his money and friends and ended up living in a hovel, there was the tremendous barrier of birth. "But Mrs. Fitzherbert is still the favourite," she said, wrenching her thoughts back to the present. "And surely that is love, for he did marry her, although the marriage is not recognized."

"He has been philandering with Lady Jersey for some time," said Lady Beatrice. "When Princess Caroline arrived on these shores for her wedding, the prince even sent Lady Jersey to meet her. But he keeps the connection with Mrs. Fitzherbert."

Hannah felt uncomfortable. She revered the prince and thought Lady Beatrice's conversation bordered on sedition.

To change the subject, she asked, "Were you so very unhappy with your first husband?"

"To begin with." Lady Beatrice gazed out to sea. "You see, I was so young and so innocent and I found myself married to a drunk, a libertine, and a gamester. He tried his best to degrade me and nigh succeeded. Let us talk of something else." Her face was cold and hard again.

"We are nearly at the bathing machines," said Hannah nervously. "Will the water be very cold, do you think?"

"Yes, very."

"Then perhaps . . ."

"Courage, Miss Pym. It is a fine day and you must at least try. Here comes Marianne and your Benjamin."

Soon Hannah found herself in a dark bathing machine with sand and seaweed on the floor. She undressed and put on the flannel gown and oilskin cap Lady Beatrice had lent her and then rapped on the door as a signal that she was ready. Then she sat down gingerly on the hard little bench at the back of the box as it began to roll forward, pulled by a strong farm horse.

When it stopped, Hannah stayed where she was, cowering at the back of the box. The door of the bathing machine opened.

"Come along, madame," said the bathing attendant, a large, burly woman. Hannah walked out onto the small platform at the front of the box. The horse stood patiently, little waves lapping against its legs. The bathing attendant took Hannah under the arms. "Down you go," she ordered. "Nothing to fear. I'll have you safe."

Hannah cast a wild look around. Lady Beatrice was already in the sea. She waved to Hannah. "You will not drown," she shouted. "You can stand on the bottom. It is not deep here."

Hannah allowed the attendant to lower

her into the water. She gasped with shock as the icy sea flowed around her body. Then she felt ground under her feet. "Are you all right?" asked the attendant.

"Yes," said Hannah faintly. "You may release me."

The attendant removed her arms and Hannah stood still for a moment with her arms spread out to balance herself. Lady Beatrice moved towards her. "Give me your hands," she ordered. "And then jump up and down. You will feel yourself floating."

Hannah obediently did as ordered, feeling exhilarated as a large wave swept her to one side. She experienced a tremendous sense of freedom. Hannah had never followed the extremes of fashion that meant going around without stays. Now that she was used to the chill of the water, all she could feel was a marvellous sense of liberation. She began to laugh and jump up and down and splash the water with her hands. Lady Beatrice began to laugh as well and splashed water into Hannah's face. Hannah splashed water back until they were frolicking and yelling and shouting like schoolchildren.

"My lady is in trouble!" cried Marianne from the stony beach.

"She's laughing, that's all," said Benjamin, sitting on a rock and smoking a cheroot.

"But my lady *never* laughs." The little maid ran up and down on the shore like a worried terrier.

"Miss Pym makes life better for everyone," said Benjamin. "Look! They're both going in. I told you they was all right."

The little maid came back to join him, smoothing down her dress and assuming the air of hauteur she had copied from her mistress. "I must speak to my lady about her behaviour," said Marianne, maintaining that fiction beloved of lady's maids the world over that they were able to remonstrate with their mistresses. "An excess of emotion is vulgar."

"That statue you works for," said Benjamin laconically, "could do with a bit of life."

"I do not understand her behaviour," mourned Marianne. "She would not even let me assist her to undress."

Hannah and Lady Beatrice at last joined them. Hannah's face was glowing. Her clothes were sticking to her salty body, and some sand had worked its way into one of her stockings, but she felt like Sir Francis Drake and every bit as bold.

"We had best return to our lodgings," said Lady Beatrice, "and have warm baths. Salt water is so sticky."

"I shall go tomorrow and tomorrow and tomorrow," said Hannah dreamily, "until I am able to swim like a fish."

"Is that not your friend Lord Alistair?" asked Lady Beatrice. They had reached the promenade. Lady Beatrice pointed with her walking-cane.

Hannah looked and then stared. Lord Alistair Munro, as naked as the day he was born, was strolling nonchalantly towards the sea with a party of friends, all equally naked. He had a beautiful figure, tall and strong and athletic with broad shoulders, slim hips, and a trim waist.

"Come along, Miss Pym," murmured Lady Beatrice, amused. "We are not supposed to stand and stare, you know. When the gentlemen are in their buffs, we are not meant to know they even exist."

"He is a very fine gentleman, a very *kind* gentleman," said Hannah, averting her eyes and walking along beside Lady Beatrice.

Lady Beatrice did not reply. "I mean," pursued Hannah, "it is very reassuring to know that there are kind and noble men in the world."

"I do not believe in the existence of kind and noble men," said Lady Beatrice, suddenly and savagely. "They affect to be in love, but all have gross appetites. I am convinced that when Lord Alistair is not being charming to you, Miss Pym, he is off over the countryside, roistering with his friends, and seducing innocent girls."

"You make all men in general and Lord Alistair in particular sound like villains in Haymarket plays," commented Hannah.

"And fiction is based on fact."

"Indeed! What then of the noble heroes?"

"Miss Pym, let us talk of something else or I shall become cross with you. Ah, here we are at your residence. May I call on you in, say, about an hour's time?"

"Gladly," replied Hannah, suddenly wishing that Lord Alistair could see Lady Beatrice in that moment, as she stood at the gate, the stiff breeze tugging at her muslin skirts, one hand holding her bonnet, her cheeks pink and her large eyes sparkling.

Hannah went indoors to instruct Benjamin on his duties, the first of which was filling a bath. And Hannah took her first bath naked. Like most ladies, she usually wore a shift so that the sight of her own body should not bring a blush to her

95

cheeks. But now it seemed perfectly natural to lie in the water stark naked and not feel ashamed. Sea bathing, mused Hannah dreamily, was almost *pagan*. It changed one's mind about all sorts of things. She wondered if she could find the courage to go about without stays.

She had no sooner dressed again than Lord Alistair Munro called to tell her of his success with the Prince of Wales. He was on the point of telling Hannah also that it might not be a good idea for her to appear at the ball. Brighton society blamed her for tricking it and he knew several ladies who would go out of their way to be nasty to her, but Hannah looked so elated, so happy at the idea of going that he did not have the heart to dim her pleasure.

"Lady Beatrice Marsham," announced Benjamin in the strangulated and refined tones he used for polite company.

Lady Beatrice sailed in. She was wearing a modish bonnet with a high crown and a striped silk gown which flattered her excellent figure. She looked slightly taken aback to see Lord Alistair and Hannah noticed the shutter coming down over her eyes.

"Lord Alistair has been to see the

prince," cried Hannah, "and all is well. His Highness was vastly amused and not cross at all!"

"Then you must have charmed him," said Lady Beatrice to Lord Alistair.

He laughed. "I was diplomacy at its best, I assure you," he said.

"I had my first dip in the sea, my lord," said Hannah proudly, "and would not have dared had not Lady Beatrice elected to join me. It was the most liberating experience. I felt quite *wanton!*"

Lady Beatrice looked at Hannah with affection and Lord Alistair studied her curiously. Why had the haughty Lady Beatrice stopped to be kind to the undistinguished Miss Pym?

Hannah rang the bell and ordered Benjamin to bring in tea and cakes.

"But we haven't got no cakes, modom," said Benjamin in injured tones.

"Then run and get them," snapped Hannah, thinking, not for the first time, that Benjamin had a lot to learn.

"Stay!" said Lord Alistair, holding up his hand. "Allow me to entertain you ladies at a pastry cook's. There is a very good one near the pier, where we may sit and look out of the window at the waves."

Lady Beatrice opened her mouth to refuse. But her eyes fell on Hannah, who looked like a child at Christmas and the refusal died on her lips.

Soon they were seated at a small round table at the bay window of the pastry cook's. Hannah looked out at the fluttering muslins and fringed parasols of the ladies and the military strut of their gallants and beyond them to the magnificence of the restless sea. Her eyes glittered with tears and Lady Beatrice put out an impulsive hand. "What ails you, Miss Pym?"

Hannah took out a small but serviceable handkerchief and dried her eyes. "I was thinking of Sir George Clarence," she said.

"Is he dead?" Lady Beatrice looked anxious.

"Oh, no." Hannah shook her head. "Sir George Clarence took me to tea at Gunter's in Berkeley Square. It was the most wonderful thing that had ever happened to me. I can still hear the chink of china and the smell the confectionery . . ."

"Of course you can," teased Lady Beatrice. "Are you not in a pastry cook's?"

Hannah shook her head. "I was thinking how much my life has changed since that very day. I was thinking how very happy

I am and I was praying that both of you could be as happy."

Lord Alistair looked surprised. "You underrate the charms of your company, Miss Pym. I am having a delightful time."

A shadow fell across Lady Beatrice's face and she studied the table. For she was suddenly and sharply aware that she had been enjoying herself that very day as she had never enjoyed a day since her late husband had led her to the altar. To her horror, tears welled up in her own eyes, and she brushed them angrily away.

Lord Alistair looked at her curiously. He had already damned her as a hard, cold bitch, devoid of feeling. Now all he could see was a beautiful woman in distress. Something tugged at his heart, but his mind told him angrily that Lady Beatrice was an experienced flirt and probably a good actress.

"Getting like a wake," said Benjamin. Hannah sharply reproved him for impertinence, but Lord Alistair laughed and said, "That man of yours must have Scotch blood in him. No one can rival Scotch servants for speaking their minds."

But Benjamin's remark had the effect of lightening the atmosphere. Lord Alistair told them a story of two friends of the prince's who had bet on a couple of geese to see which one would cross the road first. A certain Mr. Rothmere won the bet and was so grateful to his winning bird that he adopted it and took it everywhere with him on a lead, just like a dog.

Lady Beatrice capped that by telling a story of her visit to a ladies' gambling club in London, and how the women turned their pelisses and spencers inside out before playing, imitating the men who wore their coats inside out for luck, and how all had played with the same intensity as their male counterparts, until a Lady James had won a great deal of money and one of her opponents accused her of cheating. Lady James had snatched off that opponent's cap and jumped on it, and so a regular battle had broken out, with women screaming and tearing each other's hair and gowns.

She had just finished her story when she glanced out of the window and saw Sir Geoffrey and his mother walking past. She shrank back in her seat. Lord Alistair twisted his head and looked to see what had frightened her. He recognized Sir Geoffrey.

"That was your fiancé, I think," he said

to Lady Beatrice. "Would you like me to call him?"

"No, that is not necessary," said Lady Beatrice. "I shall no doubt see him this evening. I must go. No, do not rise, Miss Pym. You have not finished your tea."

She hurried out, with her maid scurrying after her.

"Now, what was all that about?" Lord Alistair gave Hannah a quizzical look.

"Oh, my lord," said Hannah earnestly, "I am sore worried about dear Lady Beatrice. She is being constrained to marry a monster."

"Impossible! She is a widow of independent means."

Hannah shook her head. "You see, Blackstone left her nothing but debts. Her parents paid them and settled a comfortable income on her, but she has had only a year to enjoy her freedom. If she does not marry Sir Geoffrey, then her parents say they will cut her off without a shilling."

"How very Gothic," he commented drily. "Are you sure you are not being gulled?"

"No, my lord. I am a good judge of character. Servants must be good judges of character, you know, for they are always being subjected to the whims of their employer or his guests. I got to know which ladies to be wary of. Once one of Mrs. Clarence's guests insisted on giving me two sovereigns. The following day she lost heavily at cards, and instead of just asking me for the money back, she told Mrs. Clarence I had stolen money from her and demanded that my room be searched."

"Which Mrs. Clarence did?"

"Which Mrs. Clarence did not. The guest was told to leave immediately."

"I wish I had met this Mrs. Clarence," said Lord Alistair.

Hannah clasped her hands. "You would have liked her above all things, my lord. So gay and pretty and happy."

"And yet she ran off with a footman?"

"Well, you know, he was a very handsome footman and a happy fellow, not much in the common way of footmen any more than my Benjamin is. I mean he was not vain or lazy. I believe—hope—he truly loved her. And, do you see, Mr. Clarence was so morose and withdrawn and given to criticizing her constantly. Yes, she did a wicked thing, but I cannot find it in my heart to blame her for it."

"Do you know where she is now?"

Hannah shook her head. "I often hope when I am on my travels to meet her."

"Would you recognize her? She may be vastly changed."

Hannah looked stubborn. "I would know her anywhere."

"Your loyalty does you credit, as does your strange loyalty to Lady Beatrice."

"I like her and I wish I could help her," said Hannah. Her odd eyes flashed green as she studied Lord Alistair Munro from his guinea-gold curls to his embroidered waistcoat. "But *you* could surely help her, my lord."

"I? Fan me, ye winds! What on earth could *I* do?"

Hannah gripped the edge of the table and said in a measured voice, "You could marry her yourself, my lord."

His blue eyes were icy and his voice cold as he said, "You forget yourself, Miss Pym. Pray talk of something else."

Hannah blushed and looked so downcast that he felt as if he had just slapped a child. "Forgive me for being so harsh," he said gently, "but your recent successes in match-making may have gone to your head. I am that rarest of creatures, a genuinely happy bachelor. Were I not, I would still not look with any affection on such as Lady Beatrice, a cruel and heartless flirt."

Hannah began to talk of other things and was happy that by the time he had taken his leave of her, he appeared to have forgotten her unfortunate remark.

That evening, Sir Geoffrey strode up and down Lady Beatrice's drawing-room in a fury. "And so I find this Miss Pym is some undistinguished female with no connections whatsoever. You are not to see her again, d'ye hear?"

Lady Beatrice let the piece of embroidery she had been working on fall to her lap. "You may constrain me to marry you, Sir Geoffrey, but I shall choose my own friends until we are married."

"Your parents shall hear of this, madam. Ho, yes. They will hear you are lowering yourself to common company."

Lady Beatrice picked up her embroidery again and set a careful stitch. "I do not think Miss Pym at all common. She is full of surprises and has powerful friends. By all means tell my parents. I shall tell them in turn that you ordered me to befriend her with a view to getting a title. Now, my parents are after your money, as you very well know, but they are high sticklers, and although my ancestors got the title in the first place by ignoble means, they would not look kindly on your machinations."

"They are so anxious to get their hands on my money, they would put up with anything," said Sir Geoffrey brutally. "You'd best pack your traps and come back to Mother's."

"Oh, no." Lady Beatrice looked at him coldly. "You are among my servants now, Sir Geoffrey, and I have only to call for help if you hold a gun to my head. I was a fool to go with you before, for I realize now, I am of no interest to you dead."

He grinned at her. "You forget, sweeting, that if you do not do what I ask, I shall simply break off the engagement and your parents will cast you off just as if you had broken it."

"I thought of that," remarked Lady Beatrice evenly. She selected a thread of purple silk and held it against the cloth, her head a little on one side. "My parents, as you so rightly point out, are anxious to get your money, and believe me, they are even more ruthless than you. Should you terminate this engagement, or try to, they would drag you through the courts. They would sue you for breach of promise. My parents love the courts. My father's lawyers spend most of their time there, suing people over boundaries and tenancies. They would make your life a misery."

"They would not dare!"

"You *have* met my parents, have you not? Ah, that gives you pause. You know I have the right of it. I shall continue to see Miss Pym. She makes me laugh. Good night, Sir Geoffrey!"

Lord Alistair Munro came across a party of acquaintances on the front the following day. They had telescopes trained on the ladies' bathing machines.

Lord Alistair looked to see what the focus of their interest was. He had very good eyesight, and even without a telescope he recognized Lady Beatrice and Miss Pym in the water. They were splashing about like seals and their laughter faintly reached his ears. And then, as he watched, Lady Beatrice, with the help of the attendant, climbed out of the water up the short wooden ladder to the bathing machine. Her gown was moulded to her body. He felt a quickening of his senses, and suddenly impatient with himself, he turned abruptly and began to walk away.

Miss Hannah Pym, without stays, ventured to take a walk, with Benjamin behind her, later that day. Lady Beatrice had had a summons from her parents, who had arrived in Brighton.

The feel of her own unrestricted body seemed somehow sinful, and Hannah felt she had gone too far. In fact, her thin, flat-chested figure looked just the same as it did when held by a long corset, but Hannah, although wearing a smart blue wool gown under a pelisse, for the day had turned chilly, was sure everyone was staring at her and everyone knew she had thrown off her stays.

She chided herself and told herself not to be ridiculous, but she was uneasily aware of hard glances cast in her direction. It came as almost a relief to see Mrs. Cambridge approaching her with a party of ladies. But the welcoming smile died on Hannah's lips as Mrs. Cambridge came straight up to her and said haughtily, "You are an impostor and a charlatan. Do not have the temerity to appear at Southern's ball or it will be the worse for you."

Then she minced on, her friends casting many angry glances back at Hannah.

"Cats!" said Benjamin. But Hannah stood stock-still, a wave of misery flooding her. She had so wanted to go to that ball, but now she could not. The wind was rising and little grey clouds were scudding across the sun and the sea had a restless, angry look. At one corner of the street, a ballad-seller was singing "Death and the Lady Margaret's Ghost," and at the other corner, another ballad-seller was competing by singing "Chevy Chase." Their voices rose and fell on the wind, sometimes a cacophony, sometimes in unexpected harmony as they both hit the same note.

Hannah turned about and went slowly back to her lodgings. She left Benjamin to make tea and went to her bedchamber and put on her stays, feeling obscurely that God had sent Mrs. Cambridge to punish the wanton.

Later, in the parlour, seated in front of a bright fire of sea coal, Hannah said dismally, "You may as well take a letter to Sir Alistair and tell him I cannot go to that ball, Benjamin."

"You got to go, modom," said Benjamin. "The prince will be there. Think o' that?

Ain't that worth putting up wiff a few old cats, mouthing an' staring? Lady Beatrice'll be there and Lord Alistair is a friend o' the prince's, ain't he? Well!"

Hannah leaned her head on her hand and stared into the flames. Although not a very religious woman, she felt that she was flying in the face of Providence by moving out of her class. Once a servant, always a servant. One had to accept one's station in life, however low, for that was where the Good Lord had put one.

"If you don't go," said Benjamin anxiously, "then I can't go and I'll never get to see the prince, not ever!"

Hannah, lost in her own worried thoughts, did not hear him. Was she such a bad woman? Look at the matches she had made on her first three journeys. Had she not brought happiness to others? Was Mrs. Cambridge such a saint, such a fine woman, that Hannah Pym should shrink before her snubs and be terrified at the thought of receiving more? Was she to sit here on the night of the ball, before this very fire, hearing the music in her head, seeing the prince only in her mind's eye? She straightened up. "I shall go," she said quietly.

"Knowed I could talk you out of the megrims," said Benjamin, and went off to make more tea.

Lady Beatrice faced her parents. They were seated opposite her in her drawing-room, side by side on a backless sofa, ramrod-straight. Her father, the earl, was a tall man who still wore his hair powdered. He had pale, cold eyes, set rather closely together, and a large hooked nose. His countess was small and plump with fine eyes in a crumpled, discontented face. They were listening intently to their daughter.

"So you see," Lady Beatrice was saying, "this son-in-law you have picked out held me up at gunpoint on the Brighton road and forced me into his carriage."

The countess flicked open a small gold snuff-box and helped herself to a delicate pinch. "Such passion," she commented in a thin voice. "Very headstrong man, but the strength of his feelings for you does him credit."

"Fiddlesticks," said Lady Beatrice. "Are my feelings not to be taken into consideration? I despise and detest the man."

"From my observation," commented her father, "I have noticed you despise and detest all men."

"Perhaps my feelings for the opposite sex might have been warmer had you not seen fit to marry me off to a lecher and wastrel," snapped Lady Beatrice.

"Oh, Blackstone?" The countess shrugged. "An unfortunate rip. But he's dead now. No, no, do not plague us with more protestations. You are still of an age to breed and we need an heir. Sir Geoffrey will do very well."

Lady Beatrice surveyed her parents, wondering if there was anything she could say that would move them, wondering if there had ever been anything she could have said to spark some parental feeling from them. But they had had little do with her from the day she was born. She had been turned over to a wet-nurse, then a nanny, then a governess, then sent to a seminary. She remembered returning from the seminary to find a houseful of guests and hearing her father ask a footman, "Who is that very pretty young lady? One of our guests?" And the footman's reply, "No, my lord, it is Lady Beatrice."

That evening, for the first time, she had been asked to dine with her parents instead of taking her meal in the schoolroom. They had plied her with questions as to her talents—could she play the pianoforte, were her water-colours passable?—and, flushed and happy under all this sudden attention, Lady Beatrice had chattered away, elated to sense she had done something at last to bring herself to the attention of her parents. She was to learn all too soon that it was her looks that had caused this sudden interest—looks that could be traded profitably on the marriage market.

"So," she said bleakly, "you are still determined to turn me off should I not marry Sir Geoffrey?"

"Oh, yes," said the countess, "but you will not do anything silly. Do we not give you a generous allowance for your clothes and jewels? You are our child and will not do anything to turn yourself into a pauper."

"I might put it to the test," said Lady Beatrice slowly. "Have you both thought of your reputations if I should end in the workhouse?"

"Yes," said her father, "and it is fortunate you have been so thoroughly nasty to so many. No one would care. In fact, society might take a malicious delight in the spectacle of the haughty Lady Beatrice being humbled."

"Leave me," said Lady Beatrice wearily.

Both rose. "We shall go ahead with the arrangements for the wedding," said the countess. "A quiet affair, of course."

When they had gone, Lady Beatrice sat feeling a lump rising in her throat. Her father had said, "No one would care," and that had hurt dreadfully, and then she thought of Hannah Pym. Miss Pym liked her, she was sure of that. Miss Pym would listen to her. Perhaps there was something Miss Pym could do.

She went alone to Hannah's, without her maid, feeling she could not trust her own servants to be loyal to her. If Marianne came with her, Marianne would hear the conversation and might report it to the other servants and one of those servants might report what she said to her parents.

Hannah was surprised but pleased to see Lady Beatrice and led her through to the parlour, where the fire still burned brightly.

"It is an odd time of night to be making a call," said Lady Beatrice, handing her pelisse and walking-cane and gloves to Benjamin.

"You are always welcome," said Hannah. "Benjamin, you may have the evening off."

Benjamin glanced at the clock. Ten in the evening. "No, thank you, modom," he said.

"I am asking you to take yourself off," said Hannah crossly. "If you do not wish to go out, then go to your room."

Hannah wanted rid of Benjamin. She noticed the strain in Lady Beatrice's face and knew she must want to talk privately.

Benjamin decided to go out. His fingers closed over the dice he kept in his pocket. He knew Hannah disapproved of his gambling, but he was determined his mistress should cut a dash in Brighton society and he knew she would need money to do that. He would not gamble much. Just get enough to hire a carriage and pair. Benjamin's eyes gleamed. He felt his mistress should not be seen walking everywhere in Brighton.

Hannah offered Lady Beatrice tea, which she refused, and then asked her gently if there was anything troubling her.

Lady Beatrice, wondering why she had called, feeling no one could help her now, said she merely had come on an impulse and had not realized the hour was so late. She rose to go.

"No, I pray you," said Hannah, "do not leave. I am used to late hours. I am an odd companion for you, am I not? I have an undistinguished background and an undistinguished appearance. I wish my nose were straight and my vowels flawless."

Lady Beatrice surveyed her. "You have very fine eyes, Miss Pym, a wealth of kindness, and a distinguished soul."

"You are kind. Most ladies of your caste would immediately shun me."

Lady Beatrice sat down again and slowly removed her bonnet. "What were your parents like, Miss Pym?"

"Perpetually worried, old before their time," said Hannah ruefully. "I left home very young and saw little of them after that. They died in a smallpox epidemic, as did my brothers and sisters. Mrs. Clarence, my late employer's wife, paid for their funerals."

"Did they give you affection?"

Hannah thought sadly of the damp basement in which she had been brought up. "They did not have much time for affection," she said. "They were very poor, and poverty does not allow much leisure for finer feelings. I gather, somehow, that you have just seen your parents."

"Yes, this very evening."

"And do they show any signs of relenting?"

"No, not a whit."

"Have they considered that, should you not go ahead with this marriage and they carry out their threat, society will consider them monsters?"

Lady Beatrice gave a thin smile. "They pointed out, quite rightly, that I have alienated the affections of all. They have the right of it. I have hit out left and right because of my own misery and now must pay the price of being friendless."

"Except for me," said Hannah quietly. "Except for me."

"Miss Pym, I am deeply indebted to you. There! I declare you have made me cry."

Tears rolled down Lady Beatrice's cheeks and she fumbled in her sleeve for a handkerchief.

Hannah leaned forward and patted her hand. "It will do you good to cry," she said.

"I—I f-feel so weak," sobbed Lady Beatrice. She dried her eyes and blew her nose. "I should be stronger. Surely I could earn some money, find a post as a governess."

"I think the life of a scullery maid is better than that of a governess," said Hannah. "Poor creatures. They are neither fish nor fowl. They are despised by master and servants alike. I have it! You can live with me!"

Lady Beatrice stared at her.

"Why not?" Hannah's eyes were golden. "We should have to live very simply, you know. I plan to retire to some little cottage in the country. I meant to make a few more stage-coach journeys, but there is more to life than travelling. Just think, Lady Beatrice! You would perhaps find it tedious, but you would be free."

"Free," echoed Lady Beatrice, looking at Hannah almost shyly. "Why should you do this for me?"

"Because we are friends, are we not?"

"I could, you know," said Lady Beatrice, her large eyes beginning to sparkle. "How long have you rented this place for?"

"Only three weeks."

"Splendid. You can move in with me, and . . . oh, let me see . . . I will need to give my servants notice . . . and . . . and I have a great quantity of jewels. We could sell those and have enough to keep us comfortably. Why did I never think of that? Oh, Miss Pym. The prison gates are opening at last. And I always thought I was a strong person. I could have done this before, or as soon as I heard about the planned wedding to Sir Geoffrey. It is all so simple. I do not need a carriage or jewels. Yes, I have a carriage of my own in London, although my parents hold the title deeds of my house there. I can sell both carriage and horses. What a vast amount of money we society people do spend. If I do not need to keep up appearances I can be quite comfortable. I do not even need to go to the Southerns' ball."

A shadow crossed Hannah's face. "Oh, do go to this one ball, Lady Beatrice . . . for me. For Mrs. Cambridge met me this day and told me not to go or it would be the worse for me, but I do want to see the prince."

"Then I shall go with you, and in my company, the Mrs. Cambridges of Brighton will steer clear. When can you move in with me?"

"Tomorrow," said Hannah. "But I must get Benjamin to take a letter to Lord Alistair telling him of my new address or he will not know where to fetch me for the ball."

"Ah, Lord Alistair," said Lady Beatrice thoughtfully. "I feel that one does not approve of me."

"I am sure you are mistaken," said Hannah firmly. She looked at the now flushed and radiant Lady Beatrice. Lord Alistair, thought Hannah, disapproved of the old

Lady Beatrice. But perhaps, just perhaps, he could be encouraged to fall in love with the new model . . .

5

I prithee send me back my heart,
Since I cannot have thine:
For if from yours you will not part,
Why then shouldst thou have mine?
          —*Sir John Suckling*

Benjamin, to Hannah's surprise, was not pleased that they were to move into Lady Beatrice's household. She thought he would have been delighted to be part of an aristocrat's staff. But Benjamin said he was her footman and her footman alone and he would not take part in any other work in Lady Beatrice's establishment.

"You are too nice," said Hannah crossly. "Lady Beatrice is giving all her staff their marching orders and so you will soon be the sole servant again. Now as to the matter of the rent. Where is this Mr. Barnstable? He surely wants to be paid something."

"Not he," said Benjamin. "Just you pack your things, modom, and leave Mr. Barnstable to me."

Benjamin went out in search of Mr. Barnstable or Captain Barnstable or Colonel Barnstable, for he was sure he was a military man.

The rank turned out to be that of captain, as Benjamin soon discovered when he finally ran that gentleman to earth in the Ship Tavern. "I'd better count the silver," said the captain, getting to his feet.

"Don't you dare!" said Benjamin shrilly. "If you got any complaints, you will find my lady resident with Lady Beatrice Marsham, and you'll find that hutch of yourn a damned sight cleaner than it was when we moved in."

"You're a mountebank," sneered the captain, "and that mistress of yours is no better. Foreign royalty indeed. I heard all about that trick."

Benjamin removed his white gloves and struck the captain across the cheek with them.

The captain reeled back, horrified. His friends stared at Benjamin, outraged.

121

"Have you run mad?" gasped the captain. "I don't duel with *servants.*" He turned to his friends. "Here, help me drop this hothead off the end of the pier."

Rough hands seized Benjamin and carried him out. He fought and struggled as he was borne remorselessly towards the pier.

Benjamin finally ceased to struggle and lay inert in their hands, but his brain was working furiously. "Hey!" he cried out suddenly. "Ain't that disgraceful? Imagine a lady going into the water without a stitch on."

He was dropped unceremoniously onto the pier while his captors rushed to the edge and stared wildly in the direction of the bathing machines, crying, "Where? Where?"

But the day was cold and there was nothing to be seen and when they turned back the nimble figure of the footman was running hell for leather off the pier.

Lord Alistair Munro was surprised to receive a letter from Miss Pym in which she said she had moved in with Lady Beatrice. He felt Miss Pym was being duped in some way. He was sure Lady Beatrice had some ulterior motive and refused to believe she was being forced into marriage. But there was another surprise in store for him. On the day of the ball, an announcement appeared in the local paper to the effect that the engagement between Lady Beatrice Marsham and Sir Geoffrey Handford was at an end. He studied it for some time and then came to the conclusion that it was merely Lady Beatrice playing her old game but worse than before. She had rejected Sir Geoffrey in a public and humiliating way.

Lady Beatrice's enraged parents called to find she was out walking with Miss Pym. Sir Geoffrey and his mother called, to be told she was "not at home."

By evening, both Hannah and Lady Beatrice were secretly wishing they did not have to go to the ball. Hannah was sure she would be dreadfully insulted by one and all, and Lady Beatrice was sure Sir Geoffrey would make a public scene.

But she was deeply indebted to Hannah Pym and could not bring herself to let that lady go on her own. Admittedly Hannah was being escorted by Lord Alistair, but Lady Beatrice knew Hannah needed the support of another woman. Lord Alistair could dance with Hannah only twice and that left acres of evening in which she could be attacked.

After her maid had dressed her, Lady Beatrice went to Hannah's room and found to her amusement that Benjamin was trying to persuade his mistress to wear pink feathers in her hair. How he had come by the feathers, Hannah did not know, but she could not get him to listen when she protested that pink feathers would look ridiculous with a gold silk gown.

"You must wear jewels, Miss Pym," said Lady Beatrice. "We shall both go armoured in my best jewelry." She herself was wearing a blue silk gown with a fairy-tale tiara of sapphires and diamonds on her black hair. She sent Marianne to fetch a diamond tiara and diamond necklace and then stood back to survey the effect as the necklace was placed around Hannah's neck and the tiara on her sandy hair.

"Very grand," she said at last. "You'll do. Just look at all the jewels I have, Miss Pym. We will be able to live in great comfort. There are some pieces which belong to the Debrens and which must go back to my parents, but the rest are very fine and should fetch a good sum."

Hannah was dazzled as she looked at her

own reflection in the mirror. Who could snub a lady dressed in such magnificence? If only Sir George Clarence could see her now!

Then a shadow crossed her face. Lady Beatrice was now to be her friend and companion, the beautiful, the magnetic Lady Beatrice. Would Sir George be able to look on such a lady and keep heart-whole? A stab of jealousy hit Hannah and in that moment she thought of Lord Alistair Munro, so carefree, so single, so marriageable. Were he to fall in love with Lady Beatrice, all her troubles would be over, and Hannah would be free to see Sir George again without this dangerous beauty in tow.

Lord Alistair arrived promptly at eight o'clock and seemed to take it in good part that he was expected to escort Lady Beatrice as well.

"I saw the announcement of the end of your engagement in the newspaper," he said, "so I assume your parents are reconciled to your single state. Miss Pym told me some Gothic tale that they would cut you off without a penny."

Lady Beatrice went over to an escritoire in the corner of the drawing-room, took out a letter and handed it to him, saying, "This has just arrived."

He raised his quizzing-glass and studied it, his thin eyebrows rising in surprise. It was from her father, the earl.

Dear Beatrice [read Lord Alistair], *I do not call you daughter, for you are no longer a daughter of mine. Your disobedience and folly are beyond words. Perhaps you think I will not carry out my threat? Then I take leave to tell you I have written to my bankers to cancel your allowance and given instructions to my agents to put your London house on the market. If you do not come to your senses, then you will end up on the streets, and may the Lord have mercy on your wicked soul.*

Yrs. Debren.

"And how will you manage?" he asked, putting the letter down.

"I am to be Miss Pym's companion," said Lady Beatrice gaily. "We are to reside in a cottage in the country and be very rustic. Oh, I wish I had thought of this before."

"Life in a cottage for such as you can be a dismal affair." Lord Alistair looked at her cynically. "No more parties or balls or hearts to break."

Lady Beatrice gave a brittle laugh. "I know you have a low opinion of me, my lord, but pray forget it for this one evening —Miss Pym's evening."

Hannah felt very elated as she was helped into Lord Alistair's open carriage, very conscious of the glitter of diamonds at her neck and on her head. The day had been dark and dismal, but now a low sun was sinking into the sea, the air was still and balmy, and the restless sea-gulls of Brighton screamed overhead.

The journey to Lord Southern's house was only a few yards, in fact, they queued from Lady Beatrice's house to the entrance of Lord Southern's mansion rather than drove, but then, one must never arrive on foot.

All Hannah's elation suddenly crumbled. For as they descended from the carriage, helped down by Benjamin, resplendent in gold-and-black livery—where did he get it? wondered Hannah—here was Mrs. Cambridge, and beside her, her friends, just arriving.

They stood and stared at Hannah and then began to titter and giggle maliciously.

"Pay them no heed," urged Lady Beatrice. But Benjamin was suddenly in front of Mrs. Cambridge and her group, a Benjamin white-faced, eyes aglitter, hands clenched. "Wot you staring at, you bleedin' harpies, you rotten scum o' the kennel, you daughters o' whores!"

"BENJAMIN!" shrieked Hannah.

But his outburst had the desired effect. Clucking like a party of outraged hens, Mrs. Cambridge and her friends scuttled quickly into the mansion.

"That footman is disgraceful," said Lady Beatrice to Lord Alistair. "You should be taking him to task, not standing there giggling."

"True," he said with a grin. "How very true. But how refreshing to hear someone say what one would not dare say oneself."

"I shall speak to you later, Benjamin," said Hannah. "I have a good mind to send you away."

Benjamin looked unrepentant as he doggedly followed them up the carpeted stairs. He was determined to wait in the hall with the other footmen so that he might have a good view of the Prince of Wales when he arrived.

Lady Beatrice and Hannah left their

shawls in an anteroom, as if oblivious of the frosty stares from all the ladies present. But as they walked up the stairs, Lady Beatrice said ruefully, "We must be prepared to take the wall this evening, for none will dare dance with us."

But there were young gentlemen there who had never heard of Lady Beatrice's hard-hearted reputation, and soon she was being solicited to dance.

Lord Alistair stood up with Hannah for the first country dance, but was curiously aware of every step that Lady Beatrice took. She looked younger, he thought. Perhaps with parents such as she possessed, there was much to be said in her defence. Mindful of his duties to his partner, he made sure he engaged Hannah for supper, and then, when the dance was over, led her to one of the gilt seats around the ballroom before going off to talk to his friends.

"Of course, it is not Almack's," said a dowager loudly beside Hannah, "so I suppose one must expect to have to rub shoulders with all sorts of peculiar people." Hannah knew this remark was intended for her own ears and was sorry that the reprehensible Benjamin was far away in the hall.

And then, as the cotillion which was being performed finally finished, a rustling and murmuring started up in the room. The Prince of Wales had arrived.

Lord Alistair came up to Hannah and held out his hand and then led her into the line that was being formed to greet the prince. Hannah steeled herself to forget the nastiness of her tormentors. This was a moment to treasure.

The Prince of Wales entered. He was fat and florid, his hair teased and curled all over his head, and his watery blue eyes looking haughtily about. Lord Alistair realized that the prince was in a bad humour and wished suddenly he had not brought Hannah. Although the prince had been amused by Lord Alistair's account of events, he had the fault of believing only the last person who spoke to him. Lord Alistair had a sinking feeling that some malicious gossip had given the prince an unflattering picture of this Miss Pym.

The prince came down the line, stopping here and there to exchange a few words, followed by Lord Southern. He came to a halt in front of Lord Alistair, looked at Hannah and at the sparkle of her diamonds, and said, "That female ain't here, is she?"

In a colourless voice, Lord Alistair said, "May I present Miss Hannah Pym, Your Highness."

Hannah sank into a court curtsy. The prince scowled down at her. Hannah raised her eyes to his. The prince saw they were full of tears. "Why do you cry, hey?" he snapped.

"Oh, sire," said Hannah Pym. "I am overcome with emotion. This night I have met England."

The scowl left the prince's face, for in Hannah's eyes was simple adoration and that was something the touchy, oversensitive prince was not used to seeing in the eyes of his subjects. He forgot that he had recently heard that this Miss Pym was as common as the barber's chair and had been putting about that he was in love with her. His fat cheeks creased in a flattered smile and he slowly held out his arm.

There was a little gasp, someone let out a slow hiss of surprise, and the dazed Hannah took the royal arm and was led forward. At the head of the line, the prince turned and faced Hannah. "Now you can tell everyone you walked with royalty," he said indulgently.

"If I could die now," said Hannah fervently, "1 would die happy. I have long worshipped you from afar, sire."

"Tol-rol!" said the prince dismissively, but highly delighted. "We are pleased to meet a lady of such character and breeding." He signalled to his friends and courtiers, who clustered around him as he was led away. Lady Jenks, a friend of Mrs. Cambridge, whispered in her ear, "Did you hear *that?* Do you not think now the original rumour was true? He called her a lady of character and breeding. And look at the way her footman dared to abuse us!"

Hannah sat down again by the edge of the ballroom in a happy daze. The dowager beside her smiled and said, "I have not had the pleasure of your acquaintance. Miss Pym, is it not?"

But before Hannah could reply, she found she was being asked to dance by Lord Southern himself, Lord Southern who had only given her two fingers to shake on her arrival, and yet who now seemed to wish to mark her out for special attention.

Hannah was still wrapped in rosy clouds of glory. The only thing that marred her pleasure was that she was a childless spinster. What a tale to tell grandchildren before a winter's fire! She did not even notice that Lord Alistair had taken Lady Beatrice onto the floor.

Lord Alistair had noticed that Sir Geoffrey Handford, who had arrived late, was approaching Lady Beatrice in a threatening way, and something had moved him to prevent her from being faced with a nasty scene. The dance was another country one and took quite half an hour to perform, and Lord Alistair had the satisfaction of seeing Sir Geoffrey stride off to the cardroom.

There was not much opportunity for conversation during the figures of the dance, but afterwards, as was the custom, Lord Alistair promenaded with Lady Beatrice round the floor.

"Our Miss Pym is in high alt," said Lady Beatrice. "What did she say to make our sulky Prinny take such a liking to her?"

"She treated him with all the reverence normally accorded to a saint and he reacted favourably. It is now being said that Miss Pym *must* be foreign royalty. That lady attracts adventures, so beware."

"If by adventures you mean distress and danger, I hope her days of adventuring are over. Goodness, this ballroom is hot. They have enough candles to light the Vatican."

"There is a balcony at the end which overlooks the sea, if you would care for a breath of air."

"Gladly."

They walked together to the end of the room and found themselves on a small balcony facing the sea. A small moon was shining on the sea and the susurration of the waves rising and falling on the beach reached their ears.

Lady Beatrice put her hands on the railing of the balcony and looked out. "How very peaceful it is," she said, half to herself. "If only I could leave now. Sir Geoffrey, I feel, is determined to seek me out and make a scene."

"I do not think he can do that with the prince present. It is well known he craves a title higher than that of knight and will do nothing to bring the royal wrath down on his head. How did he come by his knighthood? Stealing money from Indian potentates hardly counts as gallantry."

"I assume he came by it as most men do in these venal days," said Lady Beatrice. "He probably paid vast sums of money to people in the right quarters." She turned and glanced back into the ballroom. "I wonder if I shall miss all this," she said.

"Just at this moment, freedom is so sweet that I doubt it."

"And Miss Pym will be company enough?"

"I am sure of it."

"And will you then cease to flirt? Or will you break hearts in some rural village?"

Lady Beatrice sighed. "How cruel you think me. And yet I do not believe men have hearts to break."

"There speaks a lady who has never been in love."

She turned with her back to the shifting, restless sea and looked up at him. "I have been in love, my lord, or thought I was."

"So what happened?"

She turned back and stood looking out to sea again, so still and quiet that he thought she did not mean to answer him, but at last she said, "I had just returned from the seminary and my parents were delighted to discover they had a marketable daughter and Mr. Blackstone was the highest bidder. But during the period of my engagement, I went to balls and parties during the Season. There I met a young man, handsome and courteous and kind. I was so very much in love with him. I told him I did not want to marry Mr. Blackstone and he said I should have nothing to fear. He would marry me himself. All that was required was his parents' permission, for he was dependent on their fortune. He rode off to York where they lived, promising to be back within a month. How I waited! How I dreamt of his return. He had lent me his handkerchief on one occasion at a ball and I slept with it against my cheek. But the days stretched into weeks and he did not come back. The arrangements for my wedding were going ahead. I could not believe he would forget me. Even when my father was leading me up the aisle of St. George's, I thought he might come bursting into the church to sweep me away. I learned later that he had married."

"His name would not be William Purdey, by any chance?" asked Lord Alistair.

She looked up at him in surprise. "Yes. Do you know him?"

"I met him once when I was visiting friends in Yorkshire. He is about your age and married his bride about the same time as you wed Blackstone. I thought it might be he. Well, I regret to tell you that your lover is a hardened philanderer and causes nothing but grief to his wife and four children."

"How does he look? Is he as handsome as ever?" She put a hand on his arm and looked appealingly up at his face.

He covered her hand with his own and said quietly, "He is fat and vulgar. His looks were ruined a long time ago with drinking and womanizing."

"So," said Lady Beatrice in a low voice, "I have wasted years in worry and wondering what happened."

"He probably was in love with you," said Lord Alistair. "Expert philanderers are usually in love with their victims—that is their charm. So you must not go about breaking hearts any more, Lady Beatrice, if this disappointment is what turned you against men. Or flirt with someone like myself, who has no heart to break."

"And why is that?" she teased. "Am I not then the only one to have been disappointed in love?"

"No, I have not been disappointed in love, for I have never been in love." He raised her hand to his lips and smiled down into her eyes.

She smiled back automatically, in the mocking, caressing way she had perfected.

Why he chose that moment to kiss her, he did not know, but one minute he was smiling down at her, quite at his ease, and the next he had jerked her into his arms and crushed his mouth against hers. Her lips caught fire beneath his own and her body was soft and pliant against his, hip against hip, bosom against bosom. Her scent was in his nostrils and he felt quite dizzy.

He released her abruptly and said in a stifled voice, "You witch!"

"I did not mean . . ." She looked bewildered. She had meant to say that she had never reacted to any man like that before, but his eyes were as cold as ice. She suddenly shivered and with an odd little duck of her head, walked before him into the ballroom.

Lord Alistair remembered he was obliged to take Miss Pym into supper and hurried to that lady's side.

All Hannah wanted to talk about was the Prince of Wales, what he had said and how he had looked. Lord Alistair sat with her throughout supper and appeared to listen to her while all the time every part of his body was aware of Lady Beatrice, a little way away from him down the long table. She had put a poison in his blood, he thought savagely, which had bound him to her so that although he was not near her or touching her, he could feel her body and taste her lips. And he had thought himself immune.

He interrupted Hannah's paean of praise for the prince by saying abruptly, "You should reconsider sharing accommodation with Lady Beatrice."

Hannah looked at him in surprise. "Why, my lord. I think we suit very well."

"She is a dangerous and wicked woman. I would like to strangle her."

"Nonsense, my lord. She is a bitter woman, yes, but surely after the marriage she endured with Blackstone that is understandable. I have found her to have a kind and good heart. Look at her, my lord. All that warmth and beauty to be given away to such an ogre as Sir Geoffrey. Fie! Not if I have anything to say to it!"

Hannah studied him covertly while she ate her food. Something had disturbed him greatly. And then she saw how his eyes kept straying along the table to where Lady Beatrice sat. She was all at once aware of a little glimmer of hope. Lord Alistair's reaction to Lady Beatrice before the ball had been one of calm amusement tinged with disdain. He had not felt powerfully about her at all.

And there was a change in Lady Beatrice. She was partnered at the supper table by an elderly gentleman of staid appearance and yet she was undoubtedly flirting with him, but in a stagy way, as if giving a performance.

Hannah set herself to amuse Lord Alistair by recounting more of her adventures. She wanted to continue to amuse him so that he would continue to call on her and therefore would have ample opportunity of being in Lady Beatrice's company. She succeeded so well in entertaining him that the company, covertly watching her, became even more convinced that this Miss Pym was Someone.

After supper, Lady Beatrice found herself confronted by Sir Geoffrey. Although his eyes sparkled with rage, he appeared to have himself well in check.

"May I suggest," he said, "that you owe me an explanation."

"You are not owed an explanation," said Lady Beatrice. "I have found a way to escape and there is nothing you can do about it."

"You would have come about," he replied, his eyes roving over her body, from the whiteness of her bosom revealed by the low-cut dress down to her feet, as if he could see through her gown. She instinctively shrank back. "It is all the fault of that Pym woman," he said, pasting a smile on his face as he realized they were attracting attention. "Tell her to walk carefully about the streets of Brighton."

"Do not dare harm her! She has done nothing. I have merely decided to escape from both you and my parents."

He moved his face closer to her own. "Hark 'ee," he said thickly, "you will marry me and be glad to by the time I have finished with you."

She turned on her heel and walked away, leaving him staring after her.

Mrs. Cambridge was wondering what to do about Miss Pym. Mrs. Cambridge had openly snubbed her, nay, threatened her! All Brighton would now be courting Miss Pym and she, Letitia Cambridge, would be left out in the cold.

Hannah, mindful of her obligations to the dressmaker, was telling all who complimented her on her gown that she bought all her clothes from Monsieur Blanc.

She looked up in surprise as Mrs. Cambridge came up to her. "My dear Miss

Pym," gushed Mrs. Cambridge, "can you ever forgive me? I was so rude to you, but in faith I thought you were someone else."

"Indeed!" Hannah looked at her frostily.

"Such a terrible, clumsy mistake. Can you forgive me?"

Hannah's odd eyes looked completely colourless as she said, "I do not know who you thought I was, but I take leave to tell you that no lady should have been subjected to such insult." She rose quickly from her chair and walked away. Mrs. Cambridge stood biting her lip with mortification. Then anger took over. How dare this Miss Pym, if that was her name, snub a leading member of Brighton society! Mrs. Cambridge promised herself to get revenge somehow.

Lady Beatrice sought Hannah out. "Is there somewhere we can sit quietly?" she asked.

"I am surprised you have the time," said Hannah. "I would have thought the gentlemen would be queuing up to ask you to dance."

"Well, they were, but the ladies of Brighton have seen fit to broadcast my heartless reputation, and so I am a wallflower again. Look! The prince is taking his leave, and so that means we too can leave whenever we want."

"I think I would like to go." Hannah shook her head ruefully. "What on earth would all these grand people say if they knew they were courting a mere house-keeper?"

"Ex-housekeeper," corrected Lady Beatrice. Then she turned a delicate shade of pink. "Here is Lord Alistair."

Lord Alistair Munro bowed before them. "Would either of you ladies care to honour me with a dance?"

"We were on the point of seeking you out to ask you to escort us home," said Hannah, "but I would dearly like to watch you dance with Lady Beatrice."

To Hannah's surprise there was an awkward silence and then Lady Beatrice said quickly, "No, let us leave. I am fatigued."

It was a silent journey the short distance home. Hannah pressed Lord Alistair to take tea with them, and after a little hesitation, he accepted. Benjamin served them efficiently, Hannah was pleased to notice. She wondered how he was getting on with the other servants. She herself had been relieved to find that the presence of a houseful of servants had not fazed her in the least.

When tea was served and they were sitting by the fire, Hannah decided to pretend to fall asleep in the hope of dissipating the awkward silence between the couple. She closed her eyes and after a few minutes let out a small snore.

"Poor Miss Pym," she heard Lady Beatrice say, "she is quite done up."

"An eventful evening for her," came Lord Alistair's voice. "I must try to dispel this air of embarrassment between us, Lady Beatrice. I should not have kissed you. I crave your forgiveness."

"Granted, my lord. I have forgot it already."

There was a long silence. Hannah was about to give up her pretence and open her eyes when she heard Lady Beatrice say, "I am concerned for Miss Pym."

"How so?"

"Sir Geoffrey blames her for my freedom. He threatened to harm her."

"Then I suggest you and Miss Pym leave Brighton immediately."

"We shall leave soon. I have not told her, for I do not wish to alarm her by what may well turn out to be a choleric and empty threat. More tea?"

"Thank you."

She leaned across the table and he saw the soft roundness of her breasts and shivered. What would it be like to reach out a hand and caress one of those excellent globes? Then he felt himself becoming angry. She probably knew exactly what she was doing.

"I would tell Benjamin to keep a close watch on Sir Geoffrey," said Lord Alistair, "and make sure he does not plan either of you any harm."

"That is a good idea." She handed the teacup to him. As he took it from her, his hand brushed against her own. She gave a little cry, and in snatching her hand away, she knocked the cup of tea all over the splendour of his ruffled white cambric shirt.

"I am so sorry," she said, dabbing furiously at the stain with the edge of the tablecloth.

"It is nothing, nothing at all." He caught her wrist and held it. They stared at each other in a dawning awareness.

"I am sorry I fell asleep." Hannah's voice made them both start. Hannah saw the tableau, Lady Beatrice bending over Lord Alistair and he holding her wrist, and wished she had not pretended to wake so soon.

Lord Alistair released Lady Beatrice and she straightened up. "I am just leaving." Lord Alistair got to his feet. "I will have a word with Benjamin on the road out."

"Why?" asked Hannah, as she was not supposed to have heard their conversation.

"We feel it would be a good idea if your footman kept a close watch on Sir Geoffrey in case . . . in case he plans to make a public scene or something," said Lady Beatrice hurriedly.

"That is something I feel sure Benjamin would enjoy," said Hannah drily. "He is not very domesticated."

When Lord Alistair had left, Hannah looked at Lady Beatrice curiously. She longed to ask about that kiss. Instead she said, "A fine gentleman, Lord Alistair. How amazing he has not been snatched up."

"I would say he is enormously unsnatchable." Lady Beatrice yawned. "I must to bed. I have no doubt you will want to swim in the morning at some unearthly hour."

"Ten o'clock will do," said Hannah.

"That's what I meant," said Lady Beatrice and went off to bed.

Hannah walked about the room snuffing the candles. She heard someone enter and turned around. Benjamin stood there.

"Was you wanting anything else, modom?"

"No, Benjamin, that will be all. But stay. How did you come by that splendid livery, not to mention the feathers?"

Benjamin grinned and rattled the dice in his pocket.

"Benjamin, Benjamin," said Hannah severely. "One of these days you will go too far and your luck will run out. I fear you will ruin us both, for it is I who will have to bail you out."

"Won't happen," said Benjamin confidently. "The trick to gambling is to know when to stop. Anyways, I'll be too busy watching Sir Geoffrey to gamble."

"Yes, Lord Alistair told me he wanted him closely watched." Hannah picked up one remaining candle in its stick to light her way to bed. "Be careful, Benjamin. He may seem a figure of fun, a blustering noisy idiot, but I fear he is also evil and dangerous."

"Pooh!" said Benjamin, and ignoring his mistress's severe remark that good footmen did not pooh, he left the drawing-room and ran lightly down the stairs.

6

A man who is not afraid of the sea will soon be drownded, he said, for he will be going out on a day he shouldn't. But we do be afraid of the sea, and we do only be drownded now and again.

—J.M. Synge

Lady Beatrice's lady's maid left the very next day. The servants had been told to find new posts as soon as possible, but Lady Beatrice had not expected them to be so quick off the mark. But she quickly consoled herself with the thought that she would soon have to live without a retinue of servants.

The news of her rapidly dwindling staff reached the interested ears of Sir Geoffrey Handford and his mother. Although Mrs. Hanford had done much to caution her son against abducting Lady Beatrice and forcing her to marry him, her only reason was that Miss Pym might call on the Prince of Wales to intercede. She had, however, urged her son to bribe one of the housemaids in Lady Beatrice's establishment to report on her comings' and goings. While she was discussing the matter with Sir Geoffrey, a footman entered to tell them both the interesting news that the Prince of Wales had left Brighton that very day for London and most of society was following him to the metropolis.

"Now we have a different scene," said Sir Geoffrey, rubbing his hands.

"But you still must be careful," warned his mother. "You can hardly drag her out of her house or accost her in the street without occasioning a scandal."

"Let's have that housemaid—what's her name—over here to report," said Sir Geoffrey. "I'll send someone to fetch her."

Benjamin, leaning against the railings outside Lady Beatrice's mansion and picking his teeth, saw a footman in Sir Geoffrey's livery scuttling down the area steps. He waited, interested. After ten minutes the footman emerged followed by Josephine, one of the housemaids, and they made their way off together along the street. Benjamin followed them at a discreet distance.

He noticed that Josephine was not taken to the servants' entrance but shown in at the front door.

He decided to wait.

"Well?" demanded Sir Geoffrey when Josephine was ushered in.

Josephine bobbed a curtsy. "Her ladyship has been taking walks with that Miss Pym and she bathes in the sea most mornings."

"Lord Alistair Munro appeared to be paying her particular attention at the ball," said Mrs. Handford. "Has he been calling?"

"Not since the ball, madame," said Josephine. "No gentleman callers, and no ladies neither. Day after the ball, a lot of people called then, but were told that neither Miss Pym nor my lady were receiving company, and so they were both left quiet."

Sir Geoffrey surveyed the housemaid for a long moment. "When they go bathing, do they take a servant with them?"

"Just that footman o' Miss Pym's."

"Can he swim?"

"No, sir. He says that folks who go in

the sea must be mad. He's forever trying to stop his mistress from going in, but she will have none o' it."

"Very well, Josephine. You are a good girl." He took out several coins and passed them over.

Josephine emerged alone from the house and Benjamin let her go a little way and then caught up with her and fell into step beside her. "What are you following me for?" demanded Josephine.

"I'm not following you, you silly wench," said Benjamin. "Where were you anyways?"

"Out looking for a new post, if you must know," said Josephine pertly. "Mistress says as how we could take time off to find new places."

Benjamin regarded her thoughtfully. She was a buxom girl with a turned-up nose and a wide mouth and a quantity of copper curls under a jaunty cap. "You could say as how you was going to see a new employer and take a walk with me," said Benjamin.

"Oh, go on."

"You're a pretty lass and it seems a shame you should spend all your time dusting and cleaning."

Josephine threw him a flirtatious look. "What had you in mind?"

"We could take a walk along the shore, see the nobs."

"Won't that mistress o' yourn be in the sea as usual?"

"She don't really need me," said Benjamin, conscious that his instructions were to take as much free time as he wanted so long as he kept an eye on Sir Geoffrey.

"I'll go," said Josephine. "But only for a little, mind."

Benjamin squeezed her around the waist and she shrieked with laughter and pushed him away in mock horror.

Hannah was therefore told by her footman that the maid Josephine had called at Sir Geoffrey's and was no doubt being paid to keep an eye on *them*.

"I'll turn the hussy off now," said Lady Beatrice, who had been listening.

"No, don't do that," said Benjamin. "I have persuaded her to go out walking with me tomorrow morning. If we challenge her with it now, she will only say as how she was looking for new employ and Sir Geoffrey would no doubt say so as well. As to the rest of the day, ladies, if I'm to follow

Sir Geoffrey, I must ha' some sort o' disguise."

"I have a trunk of my late husband's clothes which were brought down to Brighton by mistake," said Lady Beatrice. "In fact, I thought I had given away all his stuff. Tell the butler to show you where it is, and take what you need, Benjamin. Dressed finely as a gentleman and with your hair unpowdered would be a better disguise that creeping about Brighton under a set of false whiskers."

The peacock that was Benjamin was delighted. He appeared before them later attired in a blue swallow-tail coat, striped waistcoat, canary-yellow pantaloons, and Hessian boots. The coat was padded on the shoulders and chest. Lady Beatrice shuddered. "I had forgot how awful my husband's taste was," she said.

But Benjamin, highly pleased with himself, went off to hunt down Sir Geoffrey. That gentleman emerged late in the afternoon with his mother. They made various calls. In the evening, Sir Geoffrey went out alone. Benjamin followed him to a tavern where Sir Geoffrey sat and drank and bragged with a group of noisy acquaintances, but although Benjamin listened as hard as he could, not once did he hear Lady Beatrice's name mentioned, or see Sir Geoffrey seek out anyone who might do her harm.

Lady Beatrice and Hannah walked out for their usual morning's swim the next day, a footman behind them carrying their bathing dresses and towels. He was instructed to leave them on the beach and return in a half-hour to collect their wet things.

The weather was blustery but not too cold. They were the only ladies on the beach. The other members of their sex did not venture into the water unless the day was sunny and the sea calm.

Benjamin, with Josephine on his arm, came strolling towards the beach where he could keep an eye on Hannah. "Where was you earlier?"demanded Benjamin. "I thought you coming."

"Looking for that job," said Josephine with a toss of her curls.

"With Sir Geoffrey Handford?"

Josephine pulled her arm away. "And what if I was?"

"Nothing against it," said Benjamin with a grin. "But don't it seem odd, you trying to get into a household where the master plans to harm Lady Beatrice?"

Josephine gave a superior titter. "That's what you think. He's mad about her."

Benjamin put an arm about the maid's shoulders. "Come on, now," he said with an indulgent laugh. "You don't know nothing."

"Suit yourself!" said Josephine, looking sulky.

Benjamin drew a guinea from his pocket and held it up so that the gold winked in the pale sunlight. "Tell you what," he said, "you can have this to buy silk ribbons if you tell me what's afoot."

Josephine's eyes gleamed. She reached for the gold but he laughed and held it high above his head. "Come on, now, pretty. Out with it."

"Oh, all right," said Josephine. "But you mustn't tell anyone."

Benjamin solemnly crossed his heart.

"I went there this morning," said Josephine, "for he wanted to know the exact time she was going in the sea. I told him, but I listened at the door when he thought I'd left. He was speaking to that valet of his . . . Jackson. Seems Jackson's hired some men to pluck her out of the sea, put her in a boat, and take her to where Sir Geoffrey can talk to her and tell her how much he loves her. If we stand here, we can watch."

Benjamin's mind raced. He was not even aware of Josephine snatching the gold coin from him. He did not believe Sir Geoffrey wanted a romantic meeting. He wanted to abduct Lady Beatrice again, and this time constrain her by force to marry him. And what of Miss Pym? He would want her out of the way.

Benjamin sprinted down to the water's edge and began to run up and down like a barking terrier, calling to Hannah. But the wind whipped his words away.

He looked this way and that for help. And then he saw, far along the beach, Lord Alistair Munro with his valet, preparing for *his* morning swim.

Hannah Pym was in seventh heaven. She had discovered that if she paddled her arms energetically enough and took her feet off the bottom and thrashed them about, she could keep afloat for a few minutes. When she rested for a moment, she saw with surprise that a rowing-boat with three men in it was lying a little way out, the men resting on the oars.

She frowned and began to make her way towards Lady Beatrice. They had better go in so as to avoid the vulgar gaze of these men, who obviously did not know the etiquette of bathing in Brighton, which was that no man should be seen near the ladies' bathing machines. She then saw to her amazement that her own bathing machine had retreated back up the beach, horse and all. Lady Beatrice's bathing machine was still there, but of her bathing attendant there was no sign.

"Beatrice!" shouted Hannah in sudden terror.

And then someone or something grabbed at her ankles and she felt herself being pulled down under the water.

Benjamin, back on the shore after having alerted Lord Alistair, saw her disappear. All his terror of the ocean fled. Fully clothed, he waded into the sea. A man had surfaced and had caught Lady Beatrice and was swimming out towards the boat with her, but Benjamin's fears were all for his mistress. He ploughed doggedly on until the waves were slapping his face. Hannah suddenly surfaced in front of him and he seized her. She was gasping and spluttering, but very much alive. She clung desperately to

Benjamin crying, "Someone tried to drown me. Lady Beatrice . . ."

Benjamin pulled her towards the shore and with a strong arm around her waist dragged her to the safety of the beach, where he laid her down on the shingle. Hannah turned on her side and was desperately sick.

Lord Alistair was swimming as hard as he could towards Lady Beatrice and her abductor. He knew he had to get to them before they reached the boat. One final powerful stroke brought him up to them. The man let Lady Beatrice go and Lord Alistair raised his fist and struck the man a powerful savage blow on the head, then he dived and caught Lady Beatrice and dragged her to the surface. She began to struggle weakly but she was exhausted, having struggled so long with her captor. "It is I, Munro," he shouted. "Put your arms around my neck and hold tightly and I will get you in."

With a feeling of sheer gladness, Hannah saw Lord Alistair swimming strongly for the shore with Lady Beatrice. The man who had tried to abduct her was being pulled aboard the boat by the other men and then they rowed swiftly away.

Lord Alistair had meant to hand Lady Beatrice into the care of the bathing attendant, but when he reached the machine, there was no one there. He pushed Lady Beatrice forward and up the steps and then followed her up. In the salty darkness of the bathing machine, he picked up a large fleecy towel and wrapped it around her. "You had better get dried as quickly as possible," he said.

Lady Beatrice sat down suddenly on the bench at the back of the box. Her teeth were chattering and her face was white. Stark naked, Lord Alistair stood over her and looked down at her with concern. "Where is your maid?" he demanded.

"Left me," said Lady Beatrice. "Miss Pym? Where is Miss Pym?"

"I shall find out for you."

She held out her hand and said simply, "Thank you, my lord."

He bowed from the waist and courteously kissed her hand. Lady Beatrice began to laugh weakly. "My lord, you are as naked as the day you were born." She stood up. "Leave me and I will dry and change."

He half turned away from her. Her gown was plastered to her body and her hair was like seaweed and her face was as white as milk and yet he suddenly thought he had never seen anything so beautiful in the whole of his life. He wrapped his arms around her and kissed her salty, quivering lips, holding her tightly against his naked body. Then, with a stifled exclamation, he released her, wrenched open the door of the bathing machine, and unhitched the reins of the horse, which were looped over a hook at the side of the door. "Walk forward," he cried.

The obedient horse began to turn in the sea and placidly make its way to its station on the beach. He was relieved to see Hannah standing there, supported by Benjamin. It was only when Hannah blushed and turned her head away that he realized what a spectacle he was making of himself, driving a lady's bathing machine without a stitch on.

His valet came running up and leaped up on the platform and shrouded his master in towels.

The sufferers gathered together in Lady Beatrice's drawing-room two hours later. Hannah reflected that she had never seen either Lady Beatrice or Lord Alistair so grandly dressed or looking so haughty and remote. She wondered just what had happened in that bathing machine.

"The facts as we have them are this," said Hannah. "The maid, Josephine, has disappeared for good. All her belongings are gone, too. The bathing attendants, that is mine and Lady Beatrice's, confess freely that they were heavily bribed to make themselves scarce because they were told a gentleman wanted to keep a romantic assignment in the sea. Both said such a thing had happened before. The authorities are searching for those men but evidently with little hope of finding them. Sir Geoffrey was out walking with his mother, nowhere near the beach. He is complaining bitterly that Lady Beatrice, not content with humiliating him with breaking off the engagement, is hell-bent on humiliating him further by claiming he had paid ruffians to abduct her and that it has nothing to do with him. Asked about his valet, he says his valet is on holiday. What are we to do?"

"I could call him out," said Lord Alistair.

"A duel? No, that would never do," said Lady Beatrice. "I could not bear the scandal."

He looked at her frostily. "There is one fact you may have overlooked, Lady Beatrice. Some interested spectators noticed me entering your bathing box naked. There is already scandal, and to lay such a scandal, I fear you must marry me."

There was a long silence. Hannah looked at the couple hopefully. Lady Beatrice was sitting on a backless sofa. She was wearing a green-and-gold-striped gown which showed her splendid figure to advantage. She was so still that the emerald brooch at the neck of her gown glowed with an unwinking dull green fire.

Then she said in a flat voice, "You have done enough, my lord. There is no need for you to sacrifice yourself on the altar of marriage."

"I think there is every need." He strode to the window and looked out at the sea, his well-tailored back to her.

Hannah signalled to Benjamin and both quietly left the room. Hannah went only as far as the outside of the door. She turned and leaned her ear against the panels. Benjamin, already half-way down the stairs, saw her and darted back to join her and put his ear to the door as well.

"It's awfully quiet in there," he whispered.

"Shhh!" said Hannah fiercely.

"My lord," said Lady Beatrice, "I know you wish to save my reputation, but reputation in my present circumstances no longer concerns me. I shall live quietly in the countryside somewhere with Miss Pym."

"Then have a thought to Miss Pym! Your damaged reputation might taint hers."

"By the end of the week, Brighton will have found something else to talk about. The circumstances were unusual. You saved me, my lord. Everyone knows that. Apart from a few scurrilous tongues, the rest will only admire you. I shall never marry again. And you, my lord, must never feel constrained to marry anyone out of duty."

There was a long silence. Each was obscurely hoping that the other would make some move, show some sign of warmth, but Lady Beatrice was frightened of the effect he had on her senses. She had at long last gained freedom. If she gave in to him, she would never know freedom again. He would possess her mind and feelings and thoughts. Lord Alistair thought she had deliberately bewitched him, as she had bewitched so many. He was damned if he would let her know his proposal was prompted by other than duty.

"As you will," he said indifferently.

Lady Beatrice felt a lump rise in her throat. "Where on earth is Miss Pym?" she demanded.

Hannah opened the door and went in. "I had to fetch something," she said mendaciously.

"I bid you good day," said Lord Alistair. "You will no doubt be much occupied during the remainder of your stay in Brighton. Perhaps we may meet again one day."

"Perhaps," said Lady Beatrice, forcing a smile.

Hannah looked at him miserably. Then she thought of something. As he was making for the door, she said, "I am sad that we can no longer count on your protection."

He stopped and stood frowning. "After today's episode, I doubt if Sir Geoffrey will ever dare to try anything again."

"Oh, I think he will," said Hannah, growing more cheerful. "I should think this setback will make him more than ever determined to succeed."

With something curiously approaching relief, Lord Alistair said slowly, "In that case, perhaps I should call on you. How long do you plan to remain here?"

Hannah looked inquiringly at Lady Beatrice. "Only another week," she said, "if that suits you, Miss Pym. Then I must return to London and sell what effects I can before my parents sell the house."

"That will be quite all right," said Hannah, although the idea of returning to London with the dashing Lady Beatrice did not suit her at all. Always in her mind's eye was the picture of her little apartment in South Audley Street and of Sir George Clarence sitting on the other side of the tea-table listening to her recount her adventures.

"Perhaps," said Hannah firmly, "it might be a good idea if you called on us during the coming week, Lord Alistair. I should feel so uneasy and worried were your protection removed from us."

"I shall be glad to call on you," he said. He swept them a low bow and then he was gone. Lady Beatrice buried her face in her hands and suddenly began to cry. Hannah fussed over her, saying she was overwrought, saying she must rest after her ordeal. But Lady Beatrice was crying over her past behaviour, over all the men she had so cruelly led on and then rejected. She wondered whether any of them had felt so desolate as she did now. She wanted Lord Alistair to admire her, to love her, to cherish her, and she felt he never would. The ice around her heart had melted and all she could feel was pain.

Mrs. Handford's bulldog face was a muddy colour. "Are you mad, Geoffrey?" she demanded, not for the first time. "Let us leave Brighton and leave Lady Beatrice alone. What if just one of those villains that Jackson hired had been caught and decided to talk. Think of the scandal! You could never hope for a title, and that very knighthood you now seem to hold so cheap would be taken from you."

"I covered my tracks," he growled. "Did I not send Jackson off on leave directly he had set the matter up?"

"But that maid, Josephine. What if she were found?"

"She won't be," he said tersely. "I told her what would happen to her if she opened her mouth. Why must the silly wench go blabbing to that footman of Miss Pym's?"

"Because we did not think she would go about listening at doors and that is what she must have done; else why would that footman have been alerted in time to call

Lord Alistair to the rescue? Let the matter drop, my son. Lady Beatrice is not for you."

"I want her," he said passionately. "Cannot you realize that? And I mean to have her. I am rich. Men can be bribed, and yes, even justices, should things go wrong."

"What of Lord Alistair Munro? He has powerful friends, and among those powerful friends is the Prince of Wales. It was said that Lord Alistair was naked in her bathing box!"

Sir Geoffrey's face darkened. "I'll find some discreet way to put him out of commission."

His mother shrank back in her chair. She was beginning to fear for her son's sanity and cursed Lady Beatrice from the bottom of her heart.

With the departure of the Prince of Wales and his entourage from Brighton, gossip about Miss Pym quickly died. She had not been invited to the Marine Pavilion, she had not followed him to London, there was much more exciting gossip about the prince's current mistress, Lady Jersey, and so people no longer turned to stare when she went past. Monsieur Blanc refused to talk about Miss Pym. The ball gown had been returned to him in perfect condition and the terrible footman had not betrayed the secret of the dressmaker's nationality, and so Monsieur Blanc was anxious to distance himself from a lady whose footman had the power to ruin him.

Only Letitia Cambridge was still interested in Miss Pym's comings and goings, although she did not tell her friends this. She did, however, call on Mrs. Handford and warmly pressed that lady's hand and sympathized with her over her "poor" son's broken engagement. "He is not to be blamed," said Mrs. Cambridge. "Neither is Lady Beatrice. The fault, I am convinced, lies with that female, Miss Pym. Mark my words, she has poisoned Lady Beatrice's mind against Sir Geoffrey."

And forgetting that Lady Beatrice had never wanted to marry her beloved son, Mrs. Handford listened eagerly, for surely it was Miss Pym who had persuaded Lady Beatrice to disobey her parents.

"All poor Geoffrey wants," said Mrs. Handford, "is an opportunity to see Lady Beatrice alone. You must admit, Mrs. Cambridge, he is vastly handsome, and I am sure he would succeed in wooing her were he allowed a few moments in private with her. And what of Lord Alistair Munro? Naked in her bathing box!"

"As always," said Mrs. Cambridge sourly, "Lord Alistair has the ear of the influential, and so there is no scandal. Instead he is hailed as a hero for having rescued her. But you have nothing to fear, dear Mrs. Handford. Everyone knows Lord Alistair to be a confirmed bachelor."

"Nonetheless," said Mrs. Hanford uneasily, "why does he remain in Brighton with the prince gone?"

Mrs. Cambridge patted one of Mrs. Handford's fat beringed hands. "He never did follow the prince. I am anxious to help you in any way I can."

Mrs. Handford did not find this behaviour at all strange, although she should have, considering the fact that Mrs. Cambridge had gone out of her way in the past to cut the Handfords socially. "If only you could," she said.

"I could watch them," said Mrs. Cambridge eagerly, "and let you know when Lady Beatrice is alone, and then you could tell Sir Geoffrey to make his call."

"We would be most indebted to you," said Mrs. Handford warmly. She knew her son had already tried to find another servant in Lady Beatrice's household to give him information, but without success.

Mrs. Cambridge threw herself into her new role of spy with enthusiasm. She wore a dark gown and pelisse and a heavy veil for the purpose of following Miss Pym and Lady Beatrice. After one exhausting day, she reflected sourly that the couple seemed to be inseparable. Not only that, but they were followed everywhere by that footman of Miss Pym's.

But on the second day, she had better luck. In the afternoon, Hannah emerged alone. The veiled figure that was Mrs. Cambridge, followed by her veiled maid, set off in pursuit. Hannah stopped for a moment to look out to sea. She had not been bathing since her adventure. She wondered if she would ever have the courage to go into the sea again. She was once more lashed into her stays and a little piece of whalebone had worked itself loose from the cloth and was digging painfully into the soft flesh under her armpit. She glanced back and noticed two heavily veiled women watching her. They looked odd against the background of the green-and-blue sea, two still, mourning figures with noisy sea-gulls wheeling about them.

Hannah turned away and walked on. She was determined to stay away as long as possible. Benjamin had asked for the afternoon off, but Hannah did not mind being on her own. Lady Beatrice was left at home and, with any luck, thought Hannah, Lord Alistair might call, and something might come of that.

Mrs. Cambridge paused and took out a prepared letter and gave it to her maid. "Run with that to Sir Geoffrey Handford," she ordered. The letter told Sir Geoffrey that he might find Lady Beatrice alone if he called immediately. Now, thought Mrs. Cambridge, to try to keep that Pym woman from returning home too soon.

Hannah sat gloomily at the table by the window of the pastry cook's where she had sat before with Lord Alistair and Lady Beatrice. She felt very flat and depressed, but glad for the first time that Lady Beatrice was not with her. Being with Lady Beatrice, reflected Hannah, was rather like becoming invisible. Lady Beatrice was so very beautiful that all stared at *her* and no one seemed to notice plain Miss Pym at her side, particularly now that Miss Pym was no longer a subject of gossip. Hannah thought of entertaining Sir George Clarence to tea. She could see him in her mind's eye, his silver hair, his piercing blue eyes, but those blue eyes, instead of resting on *her*, were resting with admiration on Lady Beatrice's beautiful face.

I must get rid of her, thought Hannah. Why did I ever ask her to live with me? I have not finished my journeys. I have not seen England. She herself, she knew, could learn to become content with a quiet life in some English village. But what of Lady Beatrice? Surely she would soon become restless and bored. Besides, the rent on the flat in South Audley Street had been paid for a year. It was a very fashionable address, but continuing to live there with Lady Beatrice meant putting Lady Beatrice next to Sir George, who lived hard by. Not that Lady Beatrice would surely be interested in a retired diplomat in his fifties. But could he possibly remain uninterested in her?

There must be some way to throw Lady Beatrice and Lord Alistair together.

A shadow fell across her and she looked up. A veiled woman was standing there. She threw back her veil and Hannah immediately recognized Mrs. Cambridge.

"Do not be angry," said Mrs. Cambridge. "I desire to speak to you."

"About what?" demanded Hannah suspiciously.

"You must forgive me for my appalling behaviour, but you see, I was so convinced that you had deliberately set out to make fools of us all."

"Pray be seated." Hannah indicated a chair opposite. She felt somewhat mollified. After all, it was Benjamin's lie to the dressmaker which had started all the fuss.

"I confess," said Hannah, after ordering tea for Mrs. Cambridge, "that I was very angry indeed, but now, on cooler reflection, I can understand why you became so exercised on the matter."

"We shall put it behind us," said Mrs. Cambridge, "and talk of other things. How long do you and Lady Beatrice intend to remain in Brighton?"

"About a week," said Hannah, although her mind was beginning to race. Why should Mrs. Cambridge be interested in the length of their stay? The most normal thing to have asked was all about the attempted abduction of Lady Beatrice.

"Indeed. Brighton will be sorry to lose you. How do you intend to travel? I believe you came on the stage. How original."

Hannah glanced at Mrs. Cambridge's

173

heavy veil, which was now hanging down about her shoulders, pulled back over her hat to reveal her face. She remembered the two heavily veiled women standing a little way away from her. Mrs. Cambridge and her maid?

"Do you know Sir Geoffrey Handford?" asked Hannah, ignoring the last question.

Mrs. Cambridge affected surprise. "Slightly," she said dismissively. "Have you known Lady Beatrice long?"

"Only since I came to Brighton," replied Hannah, thinking suddenly that she had left Lady Beatrice alone apart from the remaining servants. And where was Mrs. Cambridge's maid?

"Where is your maid?" asked Hannah.

"What has that got to do with how long you have known Lady Beatrice?" countered Mrs. Cambridge.

"Nothing," said Hannah, eyeing her. "Again, I ask, where is your maid?"

"I don't know," said Mrs. Cambridge pettishly. "Oh, I remember, I sent her to match silks for me."

"I am curious. I also wonder why you are both so heavily veiled. I saw you and your maid a little way away from me on the promenade," said Hannah.

"It is the rough wind." Mr. Cambridge began to look even more uneasy. "So rough and blustery and so bad for the complexion."

Hannah got to her feet. "I really must go," she said abruptly, and strode out of the pastry cook's, leaving an infuriated Mrs. Cambridge to pay the bill.

She did not trust Mrs. Cambridge. Alert to possible danger on all sides, Hannah felt sure that Mrs. Cambridge had been spying on her. She was now very worried that she had left Lady Beatrice alone.

Lady Beatrice was at that moment confronting Sir Geoffrey Handford. He had pushed his way past her servants, who obviously did not know what to do to restrain him.

"You may think you have had the better of me, madam," raged Sir Geoffrey, "but you shall pay for it."

"With my life?" demanded Lady Beatrice.

He stopped in mid-tirade and looked at her with his mouth open.

"I am not stupid, Sir Geoffrey, and know that you hired those ruffians to abduct me. You cannot do anything to me now with all my servants listening at the door."

He began to pace up and down. He suddenly regretted his impetuousness. The minute he had received that note from Mrs. Cambridge's maid, he had come dashing round. His desire for her had not waned in the least. Rather, it had become an obsession.

He looked at her in baffled fury.

"And now you may take your leave." Lady Beatrice looked at him in contempt. "And do not try to harm me again, Sir Geoffrey, or it will be the worse for you."

"And who will stop me?" he jeered. "The few servants you have left? One faded spinster and her cheeky footman?"

"No, but I will stop you," said a quiet voice from the doorway.

Sir Geoffrey wheeled round. Lord Alistair Munro stood there, tall and elegant as ever.

"So she has caught you in her wiles, like every other poor fool that has had anything to do with her," shouted Sir Geoffrey, beside himself with rage and jealousy. "She plays with us all like a cat plays with a mouse. Well, more fool you, Munro. Take her, and be damned to you!"

He thrust his way past Lord Alistair and past the gaping servants and stormed out of the house.

There was a long silence. The servants retreated to go about their duties, talking in excited whispers.

"Thank you," said Lady Beatrice at last. "Thank you again. Your arrival was most timely."

"I am grateful to be of service." He swept her a low bow.

"Pray be seated, my lord," said Lady Beatrice, "and I will get you some refreshment. Wine? We have a very good claret."

He looked at her thoughtfully. She was wearing a blue muslin gown, cunningly cut and shaped to her handsome figure. Her hair was dressed high on her head but one black curl had been allowed to fall on the whiteness of her shoulder. He felt a surge of desire and was impatient with himself. That churl, Handford, had the right of it. Lady Beatrice was a witch.

"I have calls to make," he said. "I see Miss Pym is not here. I am disappointed. A most entertaining lady."

Lady Beatrice suddenly felt jealous of the absent Hannah. "Then I shall not detain you, my lord."

He bowed again, and backed into Hannah, who had come flying up the stairs.

"My lord!" cried Hannah. "I am so very

glad to see you. I was detained by Mrs. Cambridge and had the maddest idea she was doing it deliberately."

"That might have been the case," said Lord Alistair. "Handford did call, but left in a fury."

"Because you were here?"

"Yes," put in Lady Beatrice, "most certainly because Lord Alistair arrived."

"But you cannot leave now!" said Hannah to Lord Alistair. "You must stay and take a dish of tea with us."

To Lady Beatrice's mortification, Lord Alistair smiled and said he would be delighted.

"I thought you had urgent calls to make," snapped Lady Beatrice.

He smiled at her lazily. "None that take precedence over tea with Miss Pym."

Hannah watched the couple covertly all the while she was telling them about the veiled Mrs. Cambridge who had accosted her at the pastry cook's. Lady Beatrice handed Lord Alistair a plate of cakes. His hand inadvertently brushed against her own and Lady Beatrice's own hand shook.

"There is no doubt," said Lord Alistair when Hannah had finished talking, "that

Handford has people watching you. You must leave Brighton as soon as possible."

"He might pursue us," said Hannah anxiously.

"In that case, may I offer you my escort?"

"Gladly," said Hannah quickly, before Lady Beatrice could speak.

"In that case, I would suggest we leave tomorrow evening, at, say, six o'clock."

"Splendid!" Hannah clapped her hands.

Lady Beatrice said in a voice that sounded pettish to her own ears, "But I have much to arrange. The servants . . ."

"The servants, the few that are left, can be sent to London in the morning," said Hannah eagerly. "I am very good at organizing things, Lady Beatrice. Do, I beg of you, let me arrange all."

Lady Beatrice frowned. She found the very presence of Lord Alistair made her heart ache. He held her in contempt. He had not considered her important enough to put before his other calls and yet he had stayed for Miss Pym. But to protest would mean explaining why, and that she could not possibly do.

And so it was all settled. Lord Alistair would call for them in his travelling carriage at six o'clock the following evening.

After he had left and Hannah had gone off to arrange the servants' affairs, Lady Beatrice rested her head on her hand and for the first time thought bleakly of the future. She would be trapped for life in some quaint English village with the domineering Miss Pym. Miss Pym would no doubt be supremely happy, but what of herself?

7

Love is like the measles, we all have to go through it.

— *Jerome K. Jerome*

Hannah, her arrangements completed, told Benjamin that evening that she wished to take the air and he was to accompany her. Benjamin looked startled, for the rain was rattling against the shutters and a gale howled mournfully in from the sea.

"The almanac says the weather is going to be fine tomorrow, modom," said Benjamin in injured tones. "Why not wait until then?"

"When will you ever learn to obey an order?" shouted Hannah, and Lady Beatrice looked up from the book she was reading in surprise.

Benjamin, injured, stalked off like an offended cat to get his coat and hat. Hannah, already dressed to go out, made for the door. "I have arranged everything for your removal to London," said Hannah, turning on the threshold. "The servants will go ahead first thing in the morning, Lady Beatrice."

"Thank you," said Lady Beatrice in a tired voice. "You are indefatigable, Miss Pym."

"I have great energy," said Hannah. "Do not worry. We shall not be bored in our little village, whichever one we choose. I have great schemes. It has always been my desire to help Fallen Women, and then there are clothes to be made for the poor, and oh, so many things." She walked out and left Lady Beatrice to her gloomy thoughts.

It was all very well to want to atone for a rather selfish and dissolute past, thought Lady Beatrice miserably, but somehow the thought of doing good works under the eagle eye of Hannah Pym was very lowering. She could picture herself stitching away busily by candle-light in some poky cottage, occasionally reviving the tedium of the long winter evenings by reading in the social columns how London's most eligible bachelor,

Lord Alistair Munro, was charming society during the Little Season. She would have been amazed had she but known that Hannah had set out deliberately to give her a dreary picture of their life together. It was not the idea of good works that was so depressing, thought Lady Beatrice, but the idea of being bossed around for the rest of her life by Miss Hannah Pym.

Meanwhile, Hannah strode along the beach, her boots crunching in the shingle, followed by Benjamin. A particularly large wave washed over Benjamin's feet and he cursed and jumped back.

"Tide's coming in," he shouted against the wind.

"We must find somewhere where we can talk," said Hannah, turning to face him. "There is much to be planned."

"I know a nice warm tavern," said Benjamin hopefully. "You'll catch your death being out on a night like this."

The tavern to which Benjamin led Hannah was a modest one. The coffee room served as the dining-room, but dinner had been served long ago and it was empty save for a prim gentleman in the corner smoking a long clay pipe and reading the newspapers.

"You may sit down with me, Benjamin," said Hannah. Benjamin gratefully sank down in a chair next to her. Hannah ordered ratafia for herself and beer for Benjamin and then regarded him thoughtfully.

"I do not want to spend the rest of my life with Lady Beatrice," she said. "I feel she would become bossy and domineering."

Benjamin put a hand up to his mouth to hide a smile.

"I feel that she may be enamoured of Lord Alistair Munro."

"Don't think they care for each other meself," said Benjamin, burying his nose in his tankard.

"I think you are wrong," said Hannah. "Besides, he was naked in her bathing box." Hannah coloured faintly. "It is only fitting they should wed. He is, I believe, immensely rich. 'Twould be all that is suitable, and even her greedy parents would come round."

"Mayhap something will happen on the road to London," said Benjamin comfortably. "I went around to talk to Lord Alistair's coachman. Bang-up rig, he's got. Fifteen-mile-an-hour tits and the best-sprung travelling carriage you ever did see.

184

Better'n a nasty smelly old stage anydays. Brought down from London a few days ago."

"I do not think we shall be travelling with Lord Alistair."

"But you said . . ."

"I didn't say anything, Benjamin. I think we should go quietly ourselves on the stage. There is one that leaves Brighton at six."

"But, modom!" wailed Benjamin in protest.

"Listen! Propinquity is the answer. Without us, they will be forced to travel together, to talk to each other, to get to know each other better."

"Could not they do that in London?" protested Benjamin, who still hoped to be able to journey in Lord Alistair's splendid travelling carriage.

"No, no. They will go their separate ways. Cast off by her parents and living with me will put Lady Beatrice effectively out of society and she will have no chance to see him again. We must hope and pray, Benjamin. Let us go to the booking-office now."

A particularly vicious gust of wind drove rain against the windows of the coffee room. Benjamin shivered. "I'll go first thing in the morning, modom."

"Very well." Hannah looked reluctant. "Have your things packed and ready. Lady Beatrice does not rise until late. We will take our baggage to the Ship and will simply leave the house during the afternoon and then have a letter delivered to Lady Beatrice at ten minutes to six, saying she must go ahead without us."

They finished their drinks and walked back together through the windy rain-swept streets under the swinging oil lamps.

Mrs. Cambridge was on a diet. Although plumpness was in fashion, fat was not, and she had suddenly begun to grow rounder and rounder. Layers of fat had crept up her back, where it hung in ugly creases, and her diamond choker would need to be altered to fit her neck. Mrs. Cambridge sighed. She would never have believed that her very neck could put on weight.

She rose very early, ate a beefsteak and washed it down with a pint of old port and set out to take her morning's constitutional along the beach. She did not take a maid or a footman, for such villains as Brighton possessed were still sleeping off the dissipations of the night and the streets were empty.

Mrs. Cambridge was approaching the Ship Inn and telling herself that a plate of shrimps could hardly be counted as *eating,* when she saw the tall figure of Benjamin going towards the coaching booking-office. She waited around a corner until she saw him emerge and then entered the booking-office herself. She asked about fares to various places and then demanded idly, "I thought I recognized Miss Pym's footman. Is she taking the stage? We are very dear friends and I might be persuaded to go with her."

The clerk said that the footman had booked tickets on the London stage, which was to depart at six o'clock that very evening.

"Perhaps I should consult her first," said Mrs. Cambridge airily and took her leave.

So, thought Mrs. Cambridge, Sir Geoffrey will be most interested in this piece of news. For Mrs. Cambridge assumed that Lady Beatrice would be travelling with Miss Pym. To celebrate her successful bit of spying, she entered the Ship and ordered those shrimps.

It was much later in the morning when she reached Sir Geoffrey's, for an obstacle in the shape of a pastry cook's had loomed in her path and she felt she deserved some cakes after all her exertions. Sir Geoffrey listened to her closely. Mrs. Hanford said, with an air of relief, "She is beyond your reach now, Geoffrey. You cannot descend on her in London and make jealous scenes."

He rounded on his mother furiously— both mother and son having forgotten the very presence of Letitia Cambridge—and said, "She will not reach London."

"You were lucky last time," said Mrs. Handford urgently. "This time, Miss Pym will shout for the constable."

"She won't get a chance," jeered Sir Geoffrey. "High time someone stopped that interfering busybody's mouth."

Mrs. Cambridge shrank back in her chair. Like most ladies of her class, she was only dimly aware of the brutish side of the gentlemen she met in drawing-rooms or balls. Women, although damned as the inferior sex, benefitted in a way by being treated like delicate children. No uncouth words or thoughts were revealed to them, and they were rarely subjected to any shocking lusts, it being tacitly understood that gentlemen who required such diversions took their pleasures outside the home.

She rose to leave. Her stomach felt queasy and her conscience, never much exercised, nonetheless was giving her several painful jabs.

Neither mother nor son appeared aware of her going. Mrs. Cambridge stood outside the house, irresolute. She felt she ought to warn Lady Beatrice. But, on the other hand, perhaps she was reading too much into Sir Geoffrey's remarks about stopping Miss Pym's mouth.

She trailed off home and ate a light luncheon of soup, grilled sole and potatoes and tartlets, all washed down with a bottle of champagne. She felt a little nap would do her good and clear her brain. She was not to wake until late in the evening, long after the London coach had left, and so was able to persuade herself that fate had taken the matter out of her hands.

Hannah climbed inside the coach at six and Benjamin joined the outside passengers on the roof. The day had turned mellow and fine, turning the cobbles of the twisting streets to pure gold. Sea-gulls wheeled and screamed overhead as the coach rumbled off. The other passengers consisted of a clerk, dressed in a showy waistcoat and, over it, a velvet coat which was rather short in the sleeve and showed a large expanse of dirty cuff; a fat and fussy woman who kept peering suspiciously at the other passengers and clutching a large wicker basket on her lap; a large and rubicund farmer in creaking new boots and a shirt so cruelly starched it was a wonder it did not creak as well; a thin, cross-looking woman with finicking genteel mannerisms whom Hannah privately damned as a governess or some other upper servant; and a schoolboy eating sweets from a sticky bag and gazing morosely all around as if hating the whole pernicious race of adults.

New straw had been thrown on the floor on top of the old straw, which had not been cleaned out. Hannah plucked fretfully at bits of straw clinging to her gown and wondered how Lady Beatrice would fare with Lord Alistair.

Usually Hannah's journey home to London was spent in dreaming happily of seeing Sir George Clarence again and rehearsing what she would tell him. But now the shadow of the beautiful Lady Beatrice fell over all. Why had she, Hannah Pym, so recklessly promised to spend the rest of her life with Lady Beatrice? Lady

Beatrice did not need her. By the time she sold her horses, her carriage, and her jewels, there would be enough to keep her in modest comfort for the rest of her life.

And why, thought Hannah, had she herself decided to move next year, when her travels were over, to some poky cottage in some rustic village? Surely only a pastoral poet could find comfort in antique Tudor houses with dry rot in the beams and rising damp in the walls. When Hannah had thought of that cottage before, in her mind it had always been summer, with flowers blooming in the garden, roses tumbling over the door, and pleasant bucolic villagers stopping at the garden gate to pass the time of day. Now she thought of a cottage in the winter: of going to bed at six to spare candles, of being snowed up, of being cold and lonely. Her new odd station in life would mean that she would be above the majority of the villagers socially but below the gentry, rather in the position of a governess who belonged to neither the one class nor the other. She and Lady Beatrice would probably murder each other out of sheer boredom. She could not expect a young man like Benjamin to stay away from the city for long.

Her curiosity in her fellow passengers was dimmed because of worries about her own future. Nor did she look for adventures. The only adventure Hannah Pym wanted now was to sit beside her best tea-service, dispensing tea to Sir George, but without Lady Beatrice. She tried to think hopefully of the possible result of Lady Beatrice and Lord Alistair travelling together, but could not. Lord Alistair would no doubt opt to drive his cattle himself and Lady Beatrice would travel alone inside the coach. I should have stayed with them, thought Hannah. I could perhaps have engineered some accident or some diversion to throw them together.

Before the coach had even left Brighton, Lady Beatrice was pacing agitatedly up and down her drawing-room, the letter Hannah had left for her in her hands. Hannah's message had been brief, almost curt. She liked the Flying Machines and preferred to travel that way. She would call on Lady Beatrice in London and do the best she could to manage that lady's affairs.

Lady Beatrice realized that she had taken Hannah Pym's friendship for granted. She wondered now how she could have been so ungrateful. Without Hannah's strength, she never would have had the courage to defy her parents. Now that Hannah had shown her the road to take, she certainly did not need her. She could live very comfortably in a quiet way from the money she could raise from the sale of her jewels. But the tone of Hannah's short letter seemed to indicate the spinster might be having second thoughts about sharing her life with her, and that came as a rude shock.

The house was empty. The servants had all gone ahead to London. What if Sir Geoffrey had called again to find her unprotected? Had Hannah not considered that possibility?

There was a loud knock at the street door. She automatically waited for some servant to go and answer it before realizing she would need to go down herself.

Lord Alistair stood on the threshold. Behind him stood a magnificent travelling carriage, the one that Benjamin had longed to travel in, with a coachman on the box, two grooms on the backstrap, and two outriders.

"You had better come inside a moment, my lord," said Lady Beatrice.

He followed her into the shadowy hall

and they both stood under the chandelier, which was wrapped up in a bag of holland cloth.

"Miss Pym has decided not to travel with us," said Lady Beatrice. "She has taken the six o'clock coach."

"How strange!" Lord Alistair looked down at her curiously. "Did you offend her in any way?"

"Not that I know of. Do not look so downcast. I can easily catch the coach."

Lady Beatrice looked miserable. "The fact that she left without speaking to me leads me to believe that she regrets our friendship. I must confess I did not realize up until now how much it meant to me. If you can bear my undiluted company, my lord, I think it would be more tactful to leave Miss Pym to her own devices."

He found he was sorry for her. He thought she looked young and defenceless, and yet surely, after the hell of her marriage, she should be hardened to a minor irritation like the possible loss of a friend. And yet, he thought, when had Lady Beatrice had any friends? He had seen her in saloon or ballroom, always beautiful, always icy, always composed.

"Have you eaten?" he asked.

She looked up at him, puzzled, and then her face cleared and she said with a little laugh, "Not since breakfast."

"Then I suggest my servants wait for us until we dine at the Ship, and then we will be on our road. I always get the blue devils when I am hungry."

At the Ship, always the most popular hostelry in Brighton, a table was miraculously found for them at the bay window. About them rose the buzz and chatter of the other diners, mostly fashionable. The unfashionable still dined at two in the afternoon, the medium fashionable at four, and the very fashionable at around seven.

Lady Beatrice was wearing a pretty little hat tilted slightly over her dark curls. Her close-fitting carriage gown of dark-green velvet flattered her figure, and long pearl earrings complemented the whiteness of her skin.

After they had been served, Lord Alistair said, "Are you sure you will be able to settle down with Miss Pym and forgo all the pleasures of a social life?"

She smiled ruefully. "I should be grateful to be free of Sir Geoffrey and my parents, but I confess I am a trifle worried. Miss Pym talks of enlivening our evenings by doing good works, and why not? I have led a shamelessly selfish life."

"Do not be too hard on yourself," he said, signalling to the waiter to refill their wineglasses. "Marriage to Blackstone can hardly have been a bed of roses."

She turned her glass this way and that and said in a low voice, "It was disgusting, although easier in recent years, for he would return home usually drunk and unconscious, and then, as soon as he recovered, he would be off gambling and drinking again." She coloured slightly. Both were aware she had referred obliquely to the fact that Mr. Blackstone had usually been too drunk to demand his marital rights.

"But I shall come about," she said with a slight smile. "Miss Pym will see to that. Let us talk about you for a change. How is it you have escaped marriage for so long?"

His eyes narrowed slightly as he looked at her, wondering if Lady Beatrice was beginning to flirt with him, but her eyes were still sad.

"I enjoy my bachelor life too much," he said lightly. "And I am become very agricultural of late. I own estates in Wiltshire. Good land now, but it was in a shocking state when I got it. At first I hired estate managers to put the land in good heart. The first few were useless and lazy and so I began to study and try to make the changes myself. It became absorbing and interesting. I shall never forget that first good harvest . . . But I must be boring you!"

"Not at all. Do go on."

"It was a bumper harvest. I was so excited, like a schoolboy, I had to help bring it in myself. Then we had a great harvest party. What dancing! What celebration! It made Almack's on assembly night seem a desert of boredom. Each year, I spend longer there, and each year I become more reluctant to leave."

"What is your house called? What is it like?"

"Clarendon Park. It was the Davenants' old place. Colonel Davenant died a while back, if you remember. As a younger son, I found myself with capital from prize money gained during my military service but no property, and so I bought it. It is a fine old house, completely Tudor with great chimneys, dark smoky halls, and mullioned windows. There is a fine park and some good natural vistas, but no mock temples or ornamental lakes; nothing to look at but the deer flitting through the trees of the Holm Wood."

Lady Beatrice leaned slightly back in her chair and half closed her eyes. "Is it peaceful?" she asked.

He laughed. "Nothing to listen to on a wet day but the rain dripping down the chimneys. In fact, I think I shall only spend a few days in London before going there. I adore the place."

"It sounds very pleasant." Lady Beatrice sighed. "That Gothic castle in which I was brought up could hardly be called a home. So huge, so bleak, so menacing. I spent my youth in the east wing with my governess and I hardly ever saw my parents."

He felt an odd desire to protect her. He tried to imagine her at Clarendon Park and could not. But yet, the Lady Beatrice he could not imagine at Clarendon Park was the Lady Beatrice of the ballroom, not the sad and subdued beauty facing him across the table. He began to talk lightly of Brighton society until he had the pleasure of seeing her face relax, and by the time they took their places in his coach, they were on easy, friendly terms. He had meant to travel on the box so as to observe the conventions, but Lady Beatrice was a widow, not a young miss, and so he decided there would be no harm in travelling in her company. He thought briefly of Hannah Pym and wondered what had caused that unpredictable spinster to decide to take the stagecoach.

Hannah was beginning to wonder that very thing herself. The coach was cold and musty. Usually she would have ordered hot bricks for her feet at the first inn they stopped at, but she felt sapped of energy, an unusual state of affairs. She slowly fell asleep, her head jolting with the motion of the coach. She dreamt she was floating in a warm blue sea. She was completely naked. Sir George Clarence was swimming towards her. He was naked as well, and it seemed the most natural thing in the world.

A commotion awoke her. The passengers were screaming. She sat up, blinked, and looked around. The clerk opposite was whey-faced. "Highwaymen," he said through white lips and put his fob-watch in his boot for safety. The thin spinster was praying volubly and the farmer was cursing and the woman holding the basket was weeping copiously. The schoolboy seemed unmoved, as if highwaymen were just another part of the adult world he so detested.

The door of the carriage was jerked open and a masked figure stood there, the light from the carriage lamp shining on the barrel of the long horse-pistol he brandished.

"Out, all of you!" he barked.

Shivering and crying and cursing, the passengers climbed down. "Any interference," shouted the highwayman to the passengers, coachman, and guard on the roof, "and I'll shoot this lot."

Then he glared at the passengers. "Is this the lot of you?" he demanded.

The thin spinster fell to her knees and babbled, "Spare me. I have nothing. Nothing!"

He ignored her. He reached out and caught hold of Hannah's arm and pulled her away from the others. "Get on board," he ordered the rest of the passengers. They did just that, not one seeming to care for Hannah's plight, except Benjamin, who slid quietly down from the roof of the coach on the far side where the highwayman could not see him and crept off into the darkness.

The coachman cracked his whip and the coach rumbled off, leaving Hannah and the highwayman standing on the road together.

"Well, Sir Geoffrey," said Hannah quietly, for she had recognized him despite his mask, "you may stop the charade and release me now."

He shook her arm furiously. "Where is she?"

Hannah looked at him levelly. A small bright moon riding high above silvered the landscape, and the wind from the faraway sea moaned across the downs. "If you mean Lady Beatrice, Sir Geoffrey, she left for London earlier today escorted by Lord Alistair." Hannah had no intention of telling him that Lady Beatrice had probably left at the same time as the coach in case he managed to ride ahead and catch up with them—that is, if they were ahead. Hannah thought they might have passed the coach while she was asleep.

"It's all your fault, you crook-nosed bag," he growled. "You stopped my marriage. You caused my humiliation, and b'Gad, you shall pay for it." He hurled her away from him. Hannah staggered and fell to her knees.

"Say your last prayers, Miss Pym," jeered Sir Geoffrey. He raised the pistol.

Hannah closed her eyes. She thought briefly that she had had a good life. She had not known cold or starvation, and who could ask for more than that?

There was a sickening crack. She felt a great fiery pain in her chest and fell forward.

And then she heard a voice in her ear. "Modom! Are you all right? It is me, Benjamin."

She dazedly opened her eyes. Benjamin was stooped over her, a large tree branch in his hand. Sir Geoffrey was stretched out cold by the edge of the road.

"I am shot, Benjamin," whispered Hannah. "There was a great pain in my chest."

"You ha'n't been," protested Benjamin. "I hit the bleeding shite wiff all me might afore he pulled the poxy trigger. Do get up, modom."

Hannah wonderingly felt her chest and looked at her hand in the moonlight. There was no blood. The crack which she had believed to be a pistol shot must have been caused by Benjamin's hitting Sir Geoffrey on the head and the pain had been caused by her imagination. Helped by Benjamin, she staggered to her feet.

"What shall we do with him, modom?"

Before Hannah could answer, a posse of militia came pounding up the road on horseback, their captain at the head. The captain swung himself down from the saddle while his soldiers surrounded the fallen Sir Geoffrey. The coachman had stopped at the nearest town and had reported the highwayman to the authorities.

To the captain's urgent queries, Hannah gave him her name and address and said shakily that she was unharmed. "The coachman said the felon took you apart from the other passengers," said the captain. "Do you know why?"

Hannah cast a sharp look at Benjamin. "I think he was mad," she said with a shudder. "He would have killed me if my brave footman had not struck him on the head." She had no intention of telling the captain that she had recognized Sir Geoffrey. Let Sir Geoffrey find out what it was like to be treated as a common highwayman.

One of the soldiers had removed Sir Geoffrey's mask. "Ever seen him before?" demanded the captain. "I am very faint and weak," said Hannah feebly. "And my eyes are not strong enough to make out anything in the night. I would like to go to the nearest town and find a bed for the night."

"As you will, madam," said the captain. "We will be taking this felon to the nearest round-house, which is at Castlefort. We'll put you up on a horse and have you there in no time."

But Hannah could not ride, and so Benjamin mounted and held her in front of him as they plodded through the darkness. "Why did you not tell that captain about Sir Geoffrey?" asked Benjamin.

"Sir Geoffrey's name would impress them. He will of course say he did it all as a joke. Give him a little while to suffer."

They reached an inn at Castlefort called the Green Tree. The captain arrived at the same time to explain their luggageless presence to the landlord. Then he saluted smartly and said he would call on them again as soon as the highwayman was safely under lock and key.

He arrived back again just as they were about to begin supper.

"This 'ere highwayman," said the captain, scratching his powdered wig, "says as how he is Sir Geoffrey Handford."

"I know Sir Geoffrey," said Hannah, affecting amazement. "These highwaymen are bold rascals. They would say anything."

"He is demanding to see you, Miss Pym. He says it was all a joke and that he was foxed. He is begging you not to press charges."

"I have suffered too much to face this creature this night," said Hannah, putting a hand to her brow in a gesture worthy of the great tragic actress Mrs. Siddons. "I shall call at the roundhouse at, say, eleven o'clock tomorrow morning."

"Let him rot," said Hannah cheerfully to Benjamin after the captain had gone. "A night in the round-house will do him good. You are a good and brave lad, Benjamin, but if you want to be a good footman, you must realize you are being allowed to sit at table with me because the circumstances are unusual."

"Yes, modom," said Benjamin with a grin and sank his knife into the steaming crust of a large steak-and-kidney pie.

Lord Alistair Munro's travelling coach bowled smoothly along. For a good part of the journey, he and Lady Beatrice had chatted amiably, but as the miles flew past and London approached, both fell silent.

How simple it would be to take her in my arms, thought Lord Alistair. But all that would do would be to hand her another scalp for her belt. He eyed her coldly, and in the light of the carriage lamp Lady Beatrice caught that look and turned her head bleakly away. Why, he despises me still, she thought. Even Miss Pym has taken me in dislike.

How exhilarated she had been when she had first won her freedom! But now life stretched out dull and empty, and lifeless to the grave.

A hard sore lump was rising in her throat. She tried to fight it down. A pathetic little sob was wrung from her, and to her own horror, large tears welled up in her eyes and spilled down her cheeks.

"What is the matter?" cried Lord Alistair. He leaned forward and took her head gently in his long fingers and turned her face towards his, looking with amazement at the large tears rolling unchecked down her cheeks.

"Y-you d-do not like me," whispered Lady Beatrice.

"Beatrice! What can I say? I am terrified of you. I fear one move, one sign of warmth from me would set you laughing at me. You must know you have a bad reputation as a flirt."

She took out a handkerchief and blew her nose and looked blindly at him. "That was when I was so hurt, so furious at what life had done to me. I thought all men like Blackstone, greedy and cruel and lustful."

He wrapped his arms around her and drew her against his chest, holding her gently like a child.

"Do not cry," he said. "All that is over now."

Her lips trembled and he bent his head and kissed her slowly and firmly, then deeper, then with rousing passion as her body was rocked against his own by the motion of the coach.

Never had Lady Beatrice thought to feel passion for any man, or any such burning sweetness as this. Her body now craved the intimacies which had once disgusted her.

He freed his lips and said sadly, "If only you could find it in your heart to love me."

"But I do!" cried Lady Beatrice. "That is the tragedy of it all!"

He gave a laugh of sheer relief and gladness. "That, my sweeting, is the comedy of it all. I love you and you love me and we have been wasting so much time. Kiss me again!"

And so she did and went on returning hot sweet languorous kisses until the carriage began to rattle over the cobbles of London and she had shyly promised to be his bride.

"I now worry about what to say to Miss Pym," she said. "Will she be very angry that I am not to live with her after all?"

"Let me tell you, my love, that that managing spinster has already told me we should both suit, and I have no doubt in my mind now that she deliberately left us to travel alone in the hope that something would happen. We shall call on her tomorrow and tell her our news!"

In the morning, Hannah, accompanied by Benjamin, went to the round-house.

Sir Geoffrey looked a sorry figure. He was unshaven and bits of the straw he had been forced to sleep on clung to his clothes.

"Leave us," said Hannah to the guard. When he had left, she looked sternly at Sir Geoffrey. "If I press charges against you," she said, "you know that you may hang."

"You could not be so cruel," he said, all his former bluster gone.

"My dear sir, why not? You tried to kill me."

He hung his head. "The pistol was not loaded. You can ask the captain. I was only going to take my revenge by giving you a fright."

"You nearly frightened me to death,"

snapped Hannah, "and for that alone, you deserve to hang."

"Please do not do this to me," he whimpered. "I will pay you anything . . . anything."

"Now you're talking sense," said Benjamin cheerfully.

"Be quiet, Benjamin!" cried Hannah. She sat for a few moments and said slowly, "I will let you off on one condition."

"Which is?"

"I want you to write me a full confession of your attempts to abduct Lady Beatrice and give it to me. You must never approach her again. If you do, I shall turn your confession over to the authorities."

"Anything," he gabbled eagerly.

Hannah drew several sheets of paper out of her capacious reticule and then sent Benjamin to fetch ink and a quill. Both sat silently while Sir Geoffrey wrote busily.

At last, when he had finished, Hannah took the confession from him and read it carefully. It was ungrammatical and badly spelt, but she knew it would do. She tucked the papers in her reticule and stood up.

"I shall tell the guard I am not pressing charges," she said severely. "But should I ever see you so much as speak to Lady Beatrice, I shall take these papers to the nearest magistrate."

Humbly Sir Geoffrey thanked her. Hannah went off with Benjamin after her and calmly told the captain that Sir Geoffrey had indeed been foxed and had merely been playing a silly and dangerous prank.

"So that's that, Benjamin," said Hannah. "We will take the next up coach and we will soon be home."

"Had enough of travels?" asked Benjamin.

Hannah laughed. "I have had enough of travels and matchmaking to last me a lifetime. No more stage-coach journeys after this, Benjamin. It's home to London for us!"

8

As false as dicers' oaths.
    —William Shakespeare

Hannah found she was glad to be back in London among the smells and noise. Her little apartment looked pretty and cosy. She felt she should go and call on Lady Beatrice and find when she planned to move in. They would need to share a bed, a prospect Hannah did not relish. But if only Lady Beatrice would stay away until she had a chance to entertain Sir George Clarence in private, then Hannah felt she could cope with whatever was to come.

She was settling down the following afternoon to enjoy a few moments' leisure after cleaning the rooms and lighting the fire. Benjamin had done all the shopping, but she still could not get it through his head that he was supposed to do the housework as well.

He had begged leave to go out and Hannah did hope he was not gambling again. She dreaded the day when a tearful Benjamin would come to her and say he had lost some vast sum.

There was a knock at the door and her thoughts immediately flew to Sir George. But he would not know of her return, she reflected, as she smoothed down her skirt and went to answer the door.

She stepped back a bit, as if dazzled by the glow of happiness on the faces of the couple who stood on the threshold. Hannah looked at Lady Beatrice and Lord Alistair Munro and held out both her hands in welcome. "I told you you were both well suited," she said.

"Well, Matchmaker Pym," said Lord Alistair when they were all seated before the fire, "your plan worked. Did you deliberately leave us to travel together?"

"Yes," said Hannah simply. "I did so hope something would happen."

"And so it has," said Lady Beatrice with a laugh. "We are to be married by special licence in two weeks' time, and you, Miss Pym, are to be my maid of honour."

"I shall be delighted," exclaimed Hannah. "But you have not heard my news."

She told them of Sir Geoffrey's dressing as a highwayman to waylay the coach.

"Enough is enough," said Lord Alistair. "I shall call him out."

"No need for that." Hannah told the amazed couple about Sir Geoffrey's confession.

"You are a miracle worker," said Lady Beatrice and looked so radiant and so beautiful that Hannah heaved a sigh of relief that such a priceless pearl would not be around to dazzle Sir George.

They talked for a long time, reminiscing about their various adventures in Brighton, and then the couple took their leave.

Hannah did a jig on the hearthrug after they had left. Then she brought out a travelling writing-desk and set it on her lap and began to compose an invitation to Sir George Clarence. Would he be free on the morrow for tea at five o'clock?

Then she waited in a frenzy of impatience for Benjamin to return. When he finally did saunter in, she berated him roundly on his laziness before handing him the letter. "Ah, Sir George," said Benjamin with a knowing grin. "Wondered why you was in such a taking." He darted out before Hannah could find something to throw at him.

She paced up and down and up and down, waiting for Benjamin's return, and when he did return at last with a letter which said Sir George was pleased to accept Miss Pym's kind invitation, Hannah felt almost sick with nerves.

She hardly slept that night, imagining how he would look and what he would say while getting up to find a suitable gown to wear and then deciding a moment later it would not do at all.

The next morning dragged its weary length along even though she cleaned everything twice over and tried on several more gowns. The day limped on past two o'clock and then time suddenly began to speed up, moving faster and faster and faster towards the magic hour of five o'clock.

Benjamin was brushed down so many times and so ruthlessly that he said she would wear out his livery.

By ten to five, the cakes and little sandwiches were laid out on a round table before the fire. The silver kettle was steaming on the spirit-stove and a canister of the best tea London could supply was waiting to be opened.

And then there was that knock, and all at once he was there, just as she had imagined him, silver hair brushed and shining, piercing blue eyes resting on her as she told him all about her adventures.

"You are an amazing lady," he said finally. "Where do you plan to visit next?"

"I have had my fill of adventures and travel," said Hannah. "How are the gardens at Thornton Hall? Has the work on them finished? I would dearly like to see them."

"Then you must come with us one day," said Sir George.

Hannah felt suddenly cold. "Us?" she asked.

He smiled. "I am afraid, dear friend, that my bachelor days are over. I cannot wait to introduce the lady to you."

Benjamin stood frozen behind Hannah's chair. Then he put one hand on her shoulder and gripped it hard.

"I should be delighted," said Hannah in a colourless voice. "Who is this lady?"

"A Miss Bearcroft."

"*Miss?*"

He wagged a playful finger at Hannah. "Ah, Miss Pym, you must think I am snatching a maiden out of the schoolroom. Miss Bearcroft is of mature years. In fact,

I took the liberty of asking her to call here to meet you. She should arrive at any moment."

"More tea?" asked Hannah through dry lips.

"No, I thank you."

There was a long and awkward silence. Then Hannah asked, "Are you affianced to this Miss Bearcroft?"

"Not yet. I have still to find the courage. She is so pretty, so gay, and I am afeard she would laugh at an old stick like myself."

"Tish," said Hannah, rallying. "Miss Bearcroft will be the most fortunate of ladies. The door, Benjamin!"

"I didn't hear nothing," said Benjamin flatly and gripping Hannah's shoulder harder.

"Oh yes, you did," said Hannah wearily. "Answer the door."

Benjamin reluctantly did as he was told and Miss Bearcroft bounced in, followed by her maid. Sir George rose and effected the introductions. Miss Bearcroft offered Hannah two fingers to shake. Hannah ignored the fingers and bowed slightly from the waist.

Miss Bearcroft, although in her thirties, was dressed *à la jeune fille* in sprigged muslin with little puffed sleeves worn under a light pelisse of blue silk trimmed with swansdown. Around her tiny waist was a broad blue satin sash. Her brown hair under a frivolous bonnet was a riot of glossy curls and her pansy-brown eyes were very large and slightly protruding. "I am tewwibly pleased to meet you, Miss Pym," she gushed as she sat down. "I adoah meeting old servants."

"Now, now," said Sir George, his face rather pink, "Miss Pym is a lady of private means."

Miss Bearcroft's eyes grew rounder. "But you told me she was your bwother's housekeeper!"

"Those days are gone," said Sir George. "I have just been enjoying hearing about Miss Pym's latest adventures. Do tell Miss Bearcroft about meeting the Prince of Wales, Miss Pym."

Hannah forced a laugh. "In truth, Sir George, I have talked so much this afternoon, I fear I have given myself the headache. Would you be so good as to excuse me?"

"By all means. Come, Miss Bearcroft."

"Yes, you must have your west," lisped Miss. Bearcroft, making Hannah feel at least a hundred. "My old nurse used to get *such* pains in the head. If your son would be so good as to show us out."

Sir George, who had been regarding his beloved up until that moment with a certain amused indulgence in his blue eyes, stiffened. "Your wits are wandering," he said harshly. "How can *Miss* Pym have a son, and why on earth would she have him dressed in livery?"

Miss Bearcroft's eyes filled with tears. "Now you are cwoss with me and I cannot bear it. You know I am just a silly little thing."

Hannah sank down wearily in her chair after they had gone and waved a tired hand to indicate that Benjamin had permission to sit down as well.

"Fool!" said Hannah harshly.

"And no fool like an old fool," agreed Benjamin.

"Meaning me?"

"O' course not. Meaning Sir George. No wonder she ain't been married afore, and I'll tell you something else, mum—that there Miss Bearcroft ain't no better than she should be."

"Come, Benjamin. I am grateful for your attempted moral support, but despite her

218

bitchiness and silliness, she is all that is proper." Hannah lay back and half closed her eyes. "I remember there was a friend of the Clarences', a guest . . . what was his name? Ah, Churchill. Mr. Churchill. A fine upstanding man, very clever, very elegant. Forty-eight if he was a day. He fell in love with a silly vulgar chit. Mrs. Clarence tried all in her power to dissuade him, but he would have none of it. He married the girl."

"And lived unhappily ever after," commented Benjamin gloomily.

"Oh, no, he remained delighted with her and laughed uproariously at all her silliness. She was a constant delight to him. It has always amazed me how gentlemen prefer very silly women. It is what they expect us to be."

"But this Mrs. Churchill was surely just silly, not vicious," asked Benjamin.

"No, she was not vicious," said Hannah slowly.

"There you are. I'm telling you, modom, it's your duty to find out about this Miss Bearcroft and put him wise."

"Sir George is nothing to do with me. He has made his own bed. Let him lie on it."

Benjamin tried to protest, but Hannah reminded him sharply of his duties as a footman and commanded him to take away the tea-things and wash them. She was going to bed.

The footman anxiously watched her go to her bedroom and slam the door. When had the redoubtable Miss Pym ever felt the need to lie down during the day? Benjamin busied himself about his duties while his brain worked furiously. There must be some way Sir George could be made to see the folly of his ways.

Lady Beatrice was surprised next morning to hear that a person called Benjamin Stubbs was demanding an audience with her.

"I do not know any person called Stubbs," said Lady Beatrice. "What sort of fellow is he?"

"Footman, my lady," said the servant. "Tall chap in black livery."

"Ah," said Lady Beatrice, remembering Hannah's servant was called Benjamin, "I think I had better see him. Show him up."

"Is anything wrong with Miss Pym?" asked Lady Beatrice anxiously as Benjamin was ushered in.

"Everythink's wrong, my lady," said Benjamin gloomily.

"Lord Alistair Munro," announced Lady Beatrice's footman from the doorway.

"You are come at the right time," said Lady Beatrice, running to meet him. "Here is Miss Pym's Benjamin and something has happened to her."

Lord Alistair's face darkened. "Not Sir Geoffrey! Don't tell me he has harmed her."

"No, no," protested Benjamin. "Nuffink like that. It's that there Sir George Clarence."

Lady Beatrice frowned in puzzlement and then her face cleared. "Ah, I have it. The brother of her late employer."

"The same," said Benjamin gloomily. "Miss Pym was in high alt because Sir George was coming to tea. Seems he allus visits her after one of her journeys because he likes hearing about her adventures. Well, the mistress was in such a taking, dressing up in one gown and changing it for another and cleaning and cleaning until everything shone like glass. In comes Sir George and it all looks April and May and he can't seem to hear enough of her tales. Then he ups and says he's about to get married or rather pop the question to a Miss Bearcroft, and he has asked this Miss Bearcroft to call round and meet Miss Pym."

"Men!" said Lady Beatrice.

"So in comes this Miss Bearcroft all lisps and giggles and mutton dressed as lamb and *she offers Miss Pym two fingers to shake.* But there's worse. As she was leaving, for Miss Pym said she had the headache, and no wonder if you ask me, this poxy trollop having already referred to Miss Pym as an old servant, she ups and asks Miss Pym to ask her *son* to show them out. Sir George goes all frosty, as if he's just realized the mistake he's about to make, but Miss Pym, and she's very wise, she says gentlemen like fools and more or less says he'll probably be very happy. And then she goes off to bed and it not even bedtime, and her eyes this morning are all red like she's being crying and I can't bear it." Benjamin took out a large grubby handkerchief and blew his nose.

Lady Beatrice spread her hands in a gesture of helplessness. "I do not really see what we can do."

"Well, you see, Miss Pym don't agree with me," said Benjamin earnestly, "but I

222

think this here Miss Bearcroft is Haymarket ware, and if you could find out and if he was put wise, like, the mistress could be happy again."

"You are a very loyal servant, Benjamin," said Lord Alistair. "Are you sure you are not romancing?"

"I can tell a lightskirt a mile off," said Benjamin. "No matter how they's dressed."

"I will see what I can find out," said Lord Alistair slowly, "but I cannot hold out much hope."

When Benjamin had left, he turned to Lady Beatrice and said, "What do you think? Should I waste time I might be spending with you finding out about Benjamin's trollop?"

"Oh, please do something," begged Lady Beatrice. "I always used to think Miss Pym too bossy and dictatorial, but I would rather she stayed that way, for I love her dearly."

"Then I will do it for you, my sweet, but kiss me first!"

Their kisses were so long and so intense that Lord Alistair forgot all about Miss Pym's predicament and would have gladly continued to forget about it had Lady Beatrice not at last freed herself and said in a ragged voice, "I think you should go before we both forget we are not yet married. Do try to do something for Miss Pym."

Lord Alistair first called on the formidable Countess Lieven, one of the patronesses of Almack's. To his inquiries, the countess said she had never heard of Miss Bearcroft and she had certainly never even applied for vouchers to the famous assembly rooms. From there he went to his club and questioned all he met and at last elicited the news that Miss Bearcroft had lately arrived from India and was being sponsored by Lady Beauclerc. Lord Alistair raised his thin eyebrows in surprise. Lady Beauclerc was a grasping harridan who would thrust anyone on society provided she was paid enough money to do so.

"India," mused Lord Alistair.. "Where do I go for gossip now? The military or the East India Company?" He tossed a coin and it came down in favour of the East India Company.

He made his way over to the City and asked to see Sir Miles Burford, one of the directors. It was the only name he could remember. An old clerk asked him to be seated. He came back and said Sir Miles would see Lord Alistair as soon as possible.

Lord Alistair waited and waited. The clerk served him tea. The hands of the yellow-faced clock on the office wall crept slowly round.

"Is he very busy?" Lord Alistair asked the clerk. "Or does he like to keep people waiting?"

"Sir Miles likes to keep people waiting, my lord, no matter what their consequence," said the old clerk with a trace of venom. "He feels it adds to his consequence." A bell rang in the inner office. "Sir Miles will see you now," said the clerk, and shuffled to open the door.

Sir Miles was a portly man, his heavy face hanging down pear-shaped under a small wig perched on top of his head.

"Sit down, Lord Alistair," he said pompously, "and let me know how I may serve you."

"It is a delicate matter," said Lord Alistair. "I am trying to find out about a certain Miss Bearcroft."

Sir Miles placed his podgy hands on the desk and heaved himself up. "I do not wish to insult you, my lord, but I am a busy man and have no time to waste talking about ladies of whom I have never heard. Good day to you!"

"It was a civil question," said Lord Alistair. "I would remind you I own a considerable amount of shares in the East India Company."

Sir Miles forced a smile. "Of course, of course, and if there is anything about the workings of the company you would like to know, we are always at your service."

"But you have never heard of Miss Bearcroft?"

"No. Now, if you will excuse me . . ." He fussily shifted some papers in front of him.

Lord Alistair took his leave. The little old clerk helped him into his greatcoat and peered up into his face in an oddly inquisitive way. Lord Alistair turned in the doorway. "I wonder whether, Mr. . . . ?"

"Chipping."

"I wonder whether you have heard at any time, from anyone arriving back from India, of a Miss Bearcroft."

Mr. Chipping looked quickly at the closed door of Sir Miles Burford's office and then laid a chalky finger alongside his nose. "I go to the chop-house, Brown's, hard by, in five minutes, my lord." He again glanced at that closed door in a warning way.

"Very well," said Lord Alistair in a low voice. "I shall meet you there."

He went to the chop-house and found a dark corner to sit in while he waited for Mr. Chipping. It was much frequented by clerks, all gossiping about stocks and shares and the iniquities of their employers. Mr. Chipping sidled in through the crowd and sat down gingerly next to Lord Alistair and looked at him hopefully, like a robin looking for crumbs.

Lord Alistair smiled. "Shall we say ten guineas?" he asked. Mr. Chipping rubbed his hands gleefully. "We shall indeed, my lord. We shall indeed. Now this Miss Philadelphia Bearcroft came on the London Season back in the late eighties, but she did not take. Father was a colonel, dead this age, mother pushing and ambitious. Decides to take daughter out to India in the hope of catching some homesick prize of an officer for her daughter. Now we comes to Sir Miles's brother, James."

"Do we indeed. You intrigue me."

"Oh, it's a real ten guineas' worth.

"Mr. James Burford is another of the directors of the company, based in Calcutta. I was out there until the climate nigh killed me. Mr. Burford has a marvellous mansion, plenty of money, unlimited power, and a little faded sort of lady of a wife and ten children. He meets Miss Bearcroft at a ball and is smitten. They tried to keep it quiet, but it soon became known that Miss Bearcroft had become the mistress of Mr. James, and she lorded it over the wives of the employees of the East India Company and they had to be nice to her or Mr. James might have sent their husbands packing. Finally the flighty Miss Bearcroft got too much for some of them and a deputation of the ladies went to see Mrs. Burford. No one could have believed that downtrodden lady would have shown such strength of character. Gossip has it that she upped and told her husband that unless he got rid of this Miss Bearcroft, she, Mrs. Burford, would make such a scandal in the courts asking for a divorce that he would never be able to hold up his head again in polite society. So he settled a vast sum on this Miss Bearcroft and then got her a passage home."

"Wonderful!" said Lord Alistair. "You have earned your ten guineas."

Sir George Clarence sat uneasily on a striped satin sofa in Lady Beauclerc's drawing-room, with Miss Bearcroft beside him. Lady Beauclerc had left them alone together and gone out and shut the door behind her. It was too much for the conventional Sir George. No gentleman should be alone in a room with an unmarried lady and with the door closed. He went up and opened it wide and then sat down again.

Miss Bearcroft looked at him coyly over her fan. "I decleah you are cwoss with me still."

"I am a little," said Sir George reluctantly. "Miss Pym is a very dear friend and a most unusual lady. As a friend of mine, you should have offered her your whole hand, nor should you have made that ridiculous remark about her footman being her son."

"But what else was I to think?" pleaded Miss Bearcroft. "I mean, she's only a servant. What is she doing with a servant herself?"

"It's a long story, but do realize this, and then I will say no more on the matter. Whatever status Miss Pym held in the past, she is now a gentlewoman and I would thank you to remember it."

Behind the shelter of her fan, Miss

Bearcroft's face hardened as her mind worked furiously. Yes, she had been jealous of that stupid crooked-nosed creature because Miss Pym and Sir George had looked so comfortable together. And yet, what had she to fear from such as Hannah Pym?

She gave a tinkling little laugh and lowered her fan. "In truth, I was jeawous," she lisped.

"Jealous? Of Miss Pym?"

"Oh, I know it is ridiculous. But you are so careful of the conventions when you are with me but think nothing of being closeted alone with Miss Pym in her apartment. I shall make amends. I would love to hear her tell of her adventures and I shall become her friend, too."

Sir George hesitated. Somewhere at the back of his brain a little alarm bell was beginning to sound. Only that morning, a friend of his had told him that Lady Beauclerc was a thruster of the unfashionable on society. He remembered how he had met both Miss Bearcroft and Lady Beauclerc. He had been leaving his house and Miss Bearcroft had let out a cry and stumbled against him. She said she had twisted her ankle. Lady Beauclerc had eagerly accepted Sir George's offer to escort them both home and had pressed him to stay to tea and then had left them together.

And yet he felt he had somehow to make amends to Hannah Pym.

"I will send a servant to her and suggest we call together tomorrow," he said.

"And you will see how charming I can be!" cried Miss Bearcroft.

Benjamin called on Lord Alistair the following day and learned with great satisfaction of Miss Bearcroft's background. "I did not tell Miss Pym," said Lord Alistair, "for I thought it better to tell you first and leave it to you to break the news to her. She may decide to do nothing. She is a shrewd lady and may know that a gentleman often blames the very person who makes the scales fall from his eyes."

The footman thought about that as he made his way to South Audley Street. He knew that Sir George and Miss Bearcroft were to call that afternoon. Hannah had at first said she would not see them and then had changed her mind. Benjamin said nothing to Hannah but helped to arrange the tea-things. There was no air of excitement and Hannah was wearing a plain gown of green velvet, although it was of good cut and went well with her sandy-coloured hair.

This time Miss Bearcroft startled her by embracing her warmly. Hannah replied by detaching herself as quickly as possible and ushering the couple into chairs.

As tea was dispensed, Miss Bearcroft said with every appearance of eagerness, "I am all agog to hear your adventures, Miss Pym."

Before Hannah could speak, Benjamin gave tongue. "Ain't nothing compared to yourn, Miss Bearcroft."

"I beg your pardon," said Sir George frostily. "Besides, I thought you were deaf and dumb, you jackanapes. I thought there was something wrong when I heard you speak the other day."

"Oh, that is another story," said Hannah with terrible false gaiety. "It all happened—"

"In India," finished Benjamin gleefully.

"Benjamin!" roared Hannah. "Have you taken leave of your senses? I have never been to India."

Benjamin grinned insolently. "But you have, ha'n't you, Miss Bearcroft?"

"Well, really," exclaimed Miss Bearcroft.

"We should leave now, Sir George. Miss Pym has been a servant and that may be why she cannot keep her own in his place."

"And why can't you keep yours?" jeered Benjamin. "Miss Pym is a lady and I don't like to see my mistress making tea for the demi-monde."

Sir George stood up. "Explain yourself now," he demanded.

"Well, sir," said Benjamin, turning all meek and humble, "it's a well-known fact that Miss Bearcroft here was the mistress o' Mr. James Burford o' the East India Company for years."

Sir George's blue gaze fell on Miss Bearcroft. Her face was contorted with fury. "Damn you!" she whispered.

"So," went on Benjamin unrepentantly, "it goes against the grain to see my mistress having to take insults from the likes o' you, the camel o' Calcutta, allus getting humped."

Miss Bearcroft leaped to her feet and threw the contents of her teacupful into Benjamin's face and then ran from the apartment. There was a shocked silence.

Then Sir George collected his hat and stick and said in a strangled voice, "Good day to both of you."

"No," pleaded Hannah, "you must not go. Benjamin has run mad. He will apologize." Her eyes filled with tears.

Sir George sat down again and looked at the floor. "You had better tell me all, young man," he said. And so Benjamin did, in a quiet voice, casting worried looks all the time at Hannah.

"You see," finished Benjamin, "I had to find out. Miss Pym knew none of this, nor would she have let me say a thing if she did, but I could not stand by and see you gulled, sir."

"I am an old fool," said Sir George quietly, "and I should be thankful to you. Indeed, I am thankful to you. I was already coming to the conclusion I had made a sad mistake. I do not go about in the world as often as I used to. That is no doubt why Lady Beauclerc considered me easy prey for her protegée. But if you care so much for the sensitivity of your mistress, Benjamin, then I suggest that in future you do not use the language of the gutter in front of her."

Benjamin hung his head.

"Leave us, Benjamin," said Hannah quietly.

Benjamin shuffled out.

Hannah turned to Sir George. "I am so

very sorry," she said softly. "You must think that association with such as I has made you the butt of that sort of coarseness."

He raised a white hand in protest. "It was strong medicine, I admit. When did he find his voice?"

"Ah, that," said Hannah, carefully pouring him a cup of tea. "Did I not tell you? Well . . ."

Benjamin leaned against the door of his room, anxiously biting his knuckles, listening to the rise and fall of voices until he slowly began to relax.

"And so," said Sir George when he finally rose to leave, "do you go on more travels, Miss Pym?"

Hannah thought quickly. She did not want to stay in London now, waiting and hoping to see him. Better to go away for a little again until he was completely recovered from Miss Bearcroft. She made up her mind.

"I shall go to Dover," she said, "and I shall see the sea again."

"And when do you go?"

"Soon. After the wedding of Lady Beatrice. I am to be maid of honour," said Hannah proudly.

He rose to leave and she looked at him

a little sadly, wondering if they would ever be on their own easy footing again. He paused in the doorway. "I have just remembered. You were anxious to see the gardens at Thornton Hall, were you not? I will drive you there tomorrow if the weather holds fine."

Hannah thanked him shyly. Inside his bedroom, where he had been listening all the while, Benjamin rolled on his bed and kicked his heels in the air and crowed with sheer relief.

The wedding of Lady Beatrice and Lord Alistair Munro was a quiet affair, with only Hannah as maid of honour and a friend of Lord Alistair's as brideman to see them joined in marriage. Hannah cried copiously and loudly all through the wedding service and enjoyed herself immensely. The foursome had a wedding breakfast at an inn near the church. Hannah, unusually for her, became rather tipsy and only Benjamin knew it was caused more by sheer happiness than alcohol. For Hannah had not only visited the gardens at Thornton Hall with Sir George but had taken a drive with him at the fashionable hour in Hyde Park. And he had urged her to call on him again as soon as she reached London after her next adventure and had said that he would take her to Vauxhall Pleasure Gardens.

"So," said Lord Alistair when he was alone with Lady Beatrice in his town house where they were to spend their first night together, "who knows—we may soon be attending Miss Pym's wedding."

"I would like to think so," said Lady Beatrice. "But Miss Pym did let fall that Sir George now regards her in the light of an old friend and Miss Pym thinks gentlemen never fall in love with their lady friends."

"You mean hate is more akin to love than friendship?"

"So Miss Pym would have it."

"And are you happy to be spending the rest of your days with me rather than Miss Pym?"

She looked up at him teasingly. "Instead of asking me about Hannah Pym, why do you not leave me so that my maid can undress me."

He gazed into her eyes and then said in a ragged voice, "Let me be your maid."

She raised her arms above her head and said gently, "By all means."

In a very short time, Hannah Pym, the

matchmaker who had brought them together, was forgotten as they tumbled over each other in a frenzy of love-making.

A few streets away, Hannah closed her Bible and put it beside the bed and composed herself for sleep. Her thoughts turned to Lady Beatrice and Lord Alistair and then jumped away like a scalded cat. Best not to think what they were doing. Better to look forward to that journey to Dover, and then perhaps end her travels for once and for all.

F.